The Gods of H.P. Lovecraft

The Gods of
H.P. Lovecraft

Edited by Aaron J. French

JournalStone
San Francisco

JOURNALSTONE
YOUR LINK TO ARTISTIC TALENT

This is a work of fiction. All of the characters, names, incidents, organizations, and dialogue in this novel are either the products of the author's imagination or are used fictitiously.

JournalStone books may be ordered through booksellers or by contacting:

JournalStone
www.journalstone.com
Printed in the United States of America

ISBN: 978-1-942712-56-5 (sc)
ISBN: 978-1-942712-57-2 (ebook)
ISBN: 978-1-942712-58-9 (hc)

JournalStone rev. date: December 11, 2015

Library of Congress Control Number: 2015951514
Cover Artwork and Design: Chuck Killorin
Interior Design: Paul Fry
Interior Artwork:

(Cthulhu) — Paul Carrick, (Yog-Sothoth) — Steve Santiago, (Azathoth) — Paul Carrick, (Nyarlathotep) — Paul Carrick, (Shub-Niggurath) — Steve Santiago, (Tsathoggua) — Steve Santiago, (Yig) — John Coulthart, (The Mi-Go) — John Coulthart, (Nightgaunts) — John Coulthart, (Elder Things) — John Coulthart, (Great Race of Yith) — John Coulthart, (The Deep Ones) — John Coulthart

Edited by: Aaron J. French

To Veronica – Who gives me the time.

To Domenic – An Awesome little dude.

Table of Contents

Commentary on each deity by Donald Tyson

Call the Name

Adam LG Nevill

Upon sand the colour of rust and beneath a sulphur sky, a great shape stretched the length of a long, flat beach. Black salt water slapped the grey mass of lifeless flesh and cloaked the corpse with foam. Embedded haphazardly about the vast bulk were scores of milky eyes that stared at nothing. In the far distance, unto the reddish headlands at either end of the shore, the body remained shiny where unbroken, and pulpy where deterioration had ulcerated the smooth flanks.

In the yolky light that fell through thickening, stationary clouds obscuring the sun, a long beak was visible, lined with small killer whale teeth that always seemed to suggest a smile. What might have been a great fin, or flipper, was as ragged as a mainsail hit by grapeshot, but still pointed at the heavens. In other places, on a shoreline that might have bordered an empty lake on Mars, long pellucid protrusions of jelly streaked the sand, as if the wall of flesh had been disembowelled during a battle of leviathans in the lightless depths of the black ocean. It may merely have rolled upon another vast form and squashed it, or perhaps the mostly transparent tendrils were a part of the corpse. Cleo could not tell. No birds dropped and alighted around this fallen giant. Or was this thing only a substance improperly formed and cast from the ocean as flotsam?

Her appalled study of the thing occurred upon a shore she now recognised as the old esplanade of Paignton. A place as much transformed as the atmosphere, ocean and colour of the sand. When she realised that her inquiry into what *it* was, and *where* she was, was less significant than when this was happening, Cleo noticed that she was no longer alone on the beach.

Behind some dark, red rocks, a few hundred feet away from where she stood gaping, two black, whiskered heads appeared. They were as sleek as seals, but upon the necks of creatures with shoulders and arms.

She moved away about as fast as one can move on loose sand in a dream, which was not fast or far, all the time looking over her shoulder at the rocks. The heads disappeared only to reappear closer to her position, and beside a wall as waterworn as a pebble. The black things behind the rocks raised their snouts in the way of dogs detecting the fragrance of food.

Somewhere behind the long headland of rubble and red rock at the rear of the beach, a great shriek rent the air; air in which not a single seabird was visible. A terrible whimpering followed the roar, issued from a second party. The cry of distress broke a piece from Cleo's heart. Beyond the rocks, the dull thump of a heavy body thrown to the ground could be felt through the vibrations of the impact as much as heard. What sounded like the breaking of the great woody limbs of a tree, amidst a series of excited shrieks, reinforced her belief that something large was being put to death by something both larger and fiercer than itself.

The thing she then ran over felt crispy beneath her feet and recoiled into itself as she trod it deeper into the sand. She looked down and a face that she was sure had once been human peered at her, but only briefly. The expression was that of a living thing reaching the end of a deep suffering, and an all-too-human mouth gasped and gulped at the air, pinkish gills fluttering in an increasingly transparent neck. The long and now bleaching body beneath the face was that of a seahorse. The spiny tail flicked hopelessly in the sand.

Cleo let forth a sob and wished, madly, to crush this delicate head with a rock to end its misery, but her own pursuers had drawn closer and now seemed to be leaning over their rocky perches and hissing as her panic and weariness increased.

The way ahead was barred by the mottled trunk or appendage, white-spotted by disease, that had been flung up the beach from the great, dead bulk at the shoreline.

Cleo's belief that her attempt to escape in any direction would be futile was horribly complemented by an instinctive assurance that her end in the sand would not come easy. And among the corpses on the beach, and amidst the audible splinterings of bone behind the seawall of rubble, she understood that in this place this was the way of things. Her realisation of such was the worst thing of all.

■ ■ ■

Cleo shivered awake. Her face was wet. She'd been talking in her sleep too, or crying out; a sore throat attested to that.

She nearly wept with relief as her familiarity with the living room interior slowly returned. Some parts of the room remained strange and were not a part of her home, at least not part of the home that she could recall. Maybe tomorrow these features and objects would be recognisable and bring comfort rather than anxiety.

Another 20°C night.

Cleo drank water from the teat of a closed cup sat upon the tray attached to her easy chair. Once she'd calmed herself with two anti-anxiety tablets, she turned on the media service and watched the world fall apart on a screen.

Fifth refugee ship intercepted by Italian Navy in three days. Thousands confirmed dead. No survivors.

Night vision footage in a late, live broadcast was beamed from the Mediterranean. The Italian Navy had found another ship.

The metal walls inside the drifting vessel were predictably, and somehow functionally, the terrible grey that Cleo associated with war at sea or maritime disaster. Pipes traversed a low ceiling studded with rivets. Paint bubbled with rust. Dust glittered and drifted through darkness as if it were plankton in a sunken wreck. As the moving camera panned through the greenish air, a moth's frantic capering was lit up.

Immobile forms haphazardly covered the lower deck. They created a lumpen procession that reached out of sight: blankets, exposed limbs, discarded sandals, disparate piles of baggage, and the pale soles of feet that had walked so many miles to reach that ship, but would never walk again. The far end of the wide space was a void.

A figure moved into view. Bulky, too upright, it emerged slowly like an astronaut in zero gravity; a CDC or military scientist encased in a protective biosuit, carrying an equipment bag. Another two men appeared, identically dressed in unventilated suits attached to hoses, waddling cautiously through the jade umbra, their faces grey and undefined behind transparent masks. They too carried plastic crates. All were being filmed by a fourth figure with a camera attached to a helmet.

There were quick close-ups of swollen black and brown faces, eyes open and bloodshot, the mouths crimson slices through which ochre-filmed teeth grimaced. Long-necked, his expression a rictus chiselled from agony, one man opened his jaws wide in a close-up, as if his last act was to scream at death itself. Beside him, a mother clutched a motionless child in a papoose. The small head of the child was turned away as if afraid of the camera. Most of the dead faced the floor, suggesting the life they had departed was unbearable to look back upon, even once.

The footage cut to exterior shots of a large, antique, merchant freighter, blooded with tributaries of corrosion, the white bridge lightless; a vessel adrift. Flares lit the water red. PT boats and a frigate circled at a distance while white searchlights fixed the vessel as if it were a specimen on the black surface of the sea. Rubber dinghies rose and fell with the swell alongside the hull. Marine commandoes were huddled down within the smaller craft, but peered up with their weapons trained on the railings above. The fore and aft decks of the merchant vessel were similarly littered with the unmoving lumps of discarded humanity. The oily sea lapped with the usual indifference about another ancient vessel that never made it across.

The children.

So far away, in the relative comfort and safety of her apartment in Devon, England, Cleo closed her eyes and swam in a ruddy, private darkness for a while. She wanted these sights to remain poignant, but to see too much horror was to normalise such and stop caring. And even this new disease and the never-ending refugee crisis were trifles in *the scheme of things*.

When she opened her eyes, politicians and civic authorities, military personnel and scientists were announced by subtitles that she lacked the energy to read. They each spoke in separate portions of the broadcast. The ship had sailed from Libya; its cargo entirely human; more of the desperate from East, West, Central and North Africa.

A new recording occupied the report within seconds. Amidst a panorama of dark green foliage, enshrouded by mist, a scattering of black shapes could be glimpsed amidst long grass. A subtitle and map indicated a forest in Gabon. Recent footage too, because she had never seen these pictures on any of the twelve news channels that she flicked between whilst remaining motionless in this infernal heat.

Though her discipline and background were in marine life in British coastal waters, as a retired conservationist she remained unable to resist any news story about the desecration of the natural world. Like a masochist, she watched the Sixth Great Extinction unfold in detail, and at its own inexorable, determined pace in this short Holocene Period. And, guiltily, she had no more compassion for her kind than for the fates of the other species with whom humanity shared the world, and had subsequently annihilated. Sixty percent of the world's wildlife was now extinct by virtue of the planet having to accommodate so many people: nine billion and rising. Cleo wished she had never lived to see this.

She altered the setting and the room filled with sound. The recordings originated from one of the last stretches of trees in Equatorial Africa. This was believed to be the very end of the wild gorillas. She had no idea that any were still alive. It appeared that a final two hundred and thirty-seven gorillas had clawed out an existence deep inside one of the last private forests, but now lay silver belly up, or were hunched, heavily furred, but stiff with death and wreathed by flies.

The news service confirmed that the seventh outbreak of Gabon River Fever was responsible; the same pandemic that swept away the remaining wild primates from the Central African Republic, Democratic Republic of the Congo, Cameroon, Republic of the Congo, and Uganda. The gorilla was officially extinct, along with the entire complement of refugees on board another freighter carrying the same virus.

The only question she asked herself quietly was the same question she had asked forty years before, in 2015: *what did we think would happen once food aid and food exports eventually ceased?* How could the countries of Equatorial and then North Africa not collapse? And like the viruses that had scattered across the planet in their multitudes, over the last three decades, Cleo knew that Gabon River Fever was zoonotic, spreading from animals to humans. Those people still hanging on in Equatorial Africa had little to eat but game. And in desperation they had eaten the dead flesh of the last apes, fed upon the bushmeat carcasses, and so contracted and then spread a deadly virus that had originated in bats; another species driven from its habitat and thus panicked into spreading a pandemic that was benign in the reservoir host.

Invaded ecologies always seemed to call us out eventually and fight back. But Cleo was also convinced that it was not only the bats that had revenge in mind. *In mind*: but was that even the right phrase for what was stirring? Could something so vast be considered a mind? Or was it an independent living cosmos that we could only compare to our own feeble shreds of consciousness, in the same way that an atom with its orbiting electrons can be likened to a great planet with its moons?

On screen, an academic commentator from Rome commented upon the irony of another species of our closest ancestors becoming extinct, and reaching its end in the very place where our own precursors emerged. He likened the burden of man upon the earth to that of a flu infecting an eighty-year-old woman. The comparison was, at least, sixty years old.

Not much use recycling it now. Metaphors only reshape horror; they don't prevent it.

The heat wave, the forest fires in Europe, the Chinese famine, and the escalation between India and Pakistan, had been greedy and monopolised any news she'd seen for months. At least the fate of the last apes was given a short, late-night spotlight. Though even that was soon swept away by additional reports of another lethal virus, reported in Hong Kong, and one not yet named.

Breaking news, reporting its endless cycles of catastrophe, continued to flicker and flash through the humid innards of Cleo's living room as she stared at the window, a black rectangle of hot darkness. She could smell the warm, foamy brine of the high tide. The curtains could have been carven from marble. There was no wind in the bay, not so much as a breeze. All was still, inside and out.

Those as elderly as Cleo were told to stay indoors and be still, even at night. They could not cool down after the sweltering days. Right across Europe, for three months, heatstroke had cut another swathe through the aged. A perennial event for the continent and its islands. But what she had discovered within a few miles of her own home was of far greater significance than anything she watched on the news.

The women of her family, distinguished scientists and environmentalists, whose pictures were lined up across her sideboard and whose framed specimens decorated her home, had all believed that the desecration of the planet by mankind's thoughtless extension had disturbed *something* greater than we could ever amount to. The very rapacity of her own species had functioned as the worst wake-up call since the Cretaceous-Tertiary mass extinction, sixty-five million years before. Life could never be inactive or silent; the cries of infants for succour would always be heard by predators.

Cleo knew the world could no longer continue as it was anyway. Not while the great fields of permafrost in Alaska, Siberia and Canada so hurriedly released their terrible, long-withheld breath into the air. Enough methane and carbon dioxide to nullify and exceed all revised greenhouse gas emission targets. The forests and oceans were absorbing far less carbon dioxide now. The feedback loops had become a tourniquet around mankind's throat.

The average global temperature was now three degrees higher than it had been in 1990. The higher latitudes were five degrees warmer. Nine billion pairs of fingers were beginning to clutch at the thin wire strung about their throats, some more frantically than others. Sometimes, in her daydreams, Cleo believed she could sense nine billion pairs of feet, kicking up the dust as the chokehold tightened.

The subtropics and mid-latitudes had all but lost their rain. The great collision of the polar cold and the heat from the equator, up there in the sky above the vast, heaving, warm bodies of water, now retreated like another refugee upon the exhausted earth. Tired, spreading out, and meandering to higher latitudes and distant poles, the great writhing cables of wind that once reeled so fast and so high, those great definers of air masses, were taking their precious cool air and delicious rain away with them, as if they were removing all that they could carry out of this heat. The fresh water and the nourishing blankets of gentle, golden warmth were vanishing, along with those near-forgotten climates that had allowed so many to exist.

Her precious oceans were becoming deserts. Canadian salmon were all but gone. North Sea cod was as extinct as the pliosaur. The shell food upon the rocks was dissolving to debris. Great coral reefs from Australia to Asia, the Caribbean, the Virgin Islands and Antilles were mostly a cemetery of exhumed white bones now, patchily buried beneath six feet of seaweed. One in three of all the creatures in the oceans was dying. Corpses blanketed the ocean floor in the way that dust and ash sand-duned the crematoria. If any human foot could walk where there were once great cities of colourful coral antlers and waving banners, the ruins would crumble like sandcastles bleached by the sun's relentless heat and aridity.

With vapours and gases, the monumental depths and vast glittering surfaces of the seas and oceans had been carbonated and acidified. Those great masses of life, the megatons of photo plankton, that were responsible for producing half of the biosphere, had slowed their engines; great green factories poisoned by man, the blundering chemist. The colossal leafy lungs in the Amazon produced the other half of the atmosphere. But the trees burned while the sea bleached.

Momentarily paralysed by the range of her thoughts, Cleo imagined the epochal destruction man had stimulated and brought to the fetid shores around *it*, where *it* lay stinking. That old trespasser that had created us a long time ago, accidentally, unthinkingly, beneath the grey and furious waves. The great visitor had always existed beneath the surfaces of the world, never upon them.

As her mother had taught her, as her mother had been taught by her mother, and so on, and as Cleo had reported to all of the scientific journals that no longer even replied to her submissions, all life evolved from the tiny organic scraps of an impact against the planet, when something tunnelled through space, 535 million years gone. As a subspecies of it, we had recently grown to a multitude of treacherous usurpers. She had no doubt now that *it* would finish the destruction initiated by the burning of coal on an industrial scale. Mankind had obliviously but fastidiously spent his last two hundred years waking an angry parent.

But Cleo had long ago decided to see out *the end* while close to her beloved coves: near the shoreline where her family had been finding the *signs* for generations, and where she too had found her own first signifier. Portents that all should have been studying; signs obscured within the incremental collapse of civilisation. New voices now sang through the wind, rain, and relentless tides, and in the dreams that required a lifetime of interpretation. But every shriek in her dreams foretold that far greater horrors were yet to be endured.

And yet, who had listened to a seventy-five-year-old woman, fighting her own last stand against dementia, a local eccentric whose mother committed suicide in an asylum? But as Cleo ambled round supermarkets and the seaside attractions of this insignificant little bay in the southwest of England, she had told the few who would listen to her that something too terrible for any to fully comprehend, let alone believe in, existed. And that it had been stirring for many years.

Out there, under the world, but also within life as we know it.

Eventually Cleo found the strength to break from her inertia, a blank listlessness suddenly interspersed with racing thoughts, to turn off the media service. The darkness of the room intensified and thickened the heat about her chair.

■ ■ ■

That night Cleo dreamed of polyps, tens of thousands of blue gelid forms rising from the seabed, growing and trailing their jellied rags until the water of the bay resembled a pond dimpled and thickened by frog spawn. Among them many elderly men and women stood upright, submerged to their chests, as they raised their withered arms to a night sky unfamiliar to any she had seen before. A canopy of darkness wreathed by distant whitish vapour trails that appeared wet, or webbed, and that glistened like dew-drenched spider webs. The people wore white hospital gowns, tied at the neck, and they laughed or cried with happiness as if witnessing a miracle. One or two called out for help. She recognised her dead mother among them.

When the surface of the water became a vast, rubbery carpet, that rose and slopped nauseously in the swell, reaching unto the distant horizon, the thousands of grey and white heads of the elderly people began to call out a name in unison.

Issuing the scream of a frightened child, Cleo broke from sleep.

■ ■ ■

In the early morning it was cooler and she began the short walk to Broadsands Beach with the intention of walking over the headland to see Elberry Cove. She had inspected and protected the sea grass in the cove during her forty years of marine conservation work for the Environment Agency. Too old to dive now, but she still visited the cove on foot to monitor something else.

Cleo wasn't supposed to leave her home unsupervised. Yolanda, the nurse and carer who came to her home three times each day, wasn't due for another two hours, but by then it would be too hot to go outside.

Cleo returned home prematurely; she'd left the house without dressing properly. Halfway down Broadsands Road, as she passed beneath Brunel's abandoned viaducts, those stone Leviathans that still bestrode each dawn, she'd realised that she was only wearing a nightshirt and her underwear. She shuffled home to dress fully before someone saw her in the street and called an ambulance. By the coatrack in the hall she saw a notice that she couldn't remember making, reminding her to take her medication as soon as she came downstairs each morning.

Finally dressed and medicated, she stood upon the great seawall at Broadsands. Five a.m. and the sun was rising and turning the bay a heartbreaking blue, while polishing the sky with a piercing silver light that would boil brains within hours.

Cleo lingered on the shore to watch an unusual formation of great crested and black-necked grebes upon the sand below. So strange again was their number and positioning. She fumbled for the camera about her neck and found it missing because she had forgotten to bring it with her, and not for the first time.

Until last year, she had never seen more than two or three grebes fishing together at this spot. She spotted twenty that morning, but all on the shore. Below the seawall, a white debris of gulls also littered the sand, though in their hundreds. They watched the sea disconsolately. None took flight or called out.

Where the beach huts once stood, a viewing platform had been erected by the council for the imminent solar eclipse, and that too was festooned with sea birds, also engaged in an uneasy silence and a motionless peering at the horizon.

As usual with each recent summer, a great green skirt of *Himanthalia elongata*, or thongweed, coated the beach like unsightly, wet wool and was piled at the water's edge. It floated upon and entirely concealed the surface of the sea for a good fifty metres offshore. Within the broad blanket of immobile weed that appeared to have suffocated the very tide, she caught sight of a vast barrel jellyfish, stranded. Other large whitish discs of barrel and moon jellyfish became visible along the shore, resembling unsightly blisters poking through the diseased pelt on some large animal's back. Beneath the weed she imagined the great white tendrils coiled about the impenetrable green fronds of the weed.

There had been a time when the waters of the bay resembled those of the Mediterranean. The officers in Nelson's navy had settled the area because it had reminded them of Gibraltar.

Cleo pondered the hundreds of thousands of spectators who would soon flock to Torbay to watch the coming cosmic event. She believed they were destined to see a sight that the subdued birds, who were too afraid to fish, already anticipated.

Cleo moved as quickly as she could—which was not very fast, her progress interrupted by frequent stops to catch her breath—up the coastal path and across the common to reach Elberry Cove. She now had just under an hour before the heat would be unbearable. Power shortages had rationed the air conditioning so her apartment wouldn't be much cooler, but her thoughts were enough of a convoluted and troubling mess without the sun's heat lighting a fire under them.

As she walked the coastal path and along the cliffs, with the defunct fishing port of Brixham visible ahead, from the sea a familiar hot wind picked up and rustled the trees circling the common. Cleo struggled with her balance and wayward hair, but believed she had just heard those trees call a *name*.

From the beach behind her, as the wind struck the shore, the gulls broke their unnerving silence and cried out in alarm. They took flight and Cleo turned to catch sight of a great squadron of dry wings beating a passage inland, away from the bay where they had once felt safe.

About her on the coastal path, the long, gnarled trunks of the pines, the sweet beech and larch trees, who had all slowly bowed away from the direction of the sea for decades, suggested to her again that they were now striving to uproot and flee the rooty moorings that anchored them so perilously close to the weed-choked Torbay waters. Across the last decade, from Dorset to Cornwall, to her eyes, the leafy heads of the remaining trees on the cliffs and open shores had all taken on an aspect either of flight or fearful supplication. Or perhaps their decrepit posture was simply a cowed, despairing acknowledgement of the endgame that restlessly built out there, deep down.

Few had noticed how these trees leaned, or they had attributed the slant to the wind. Most had lost the ability to understand what the natural world was whispering. But not *all*. Ever restless with the sea's winds, or motionless and sullen in the summer heat, she believed the trees of the bay had known only a tense expectation of what neared the shore, something felt but unseen. *Right here*, she was sure, was an apprehension that now shuddered the natural world.

Cleo had learned to identify the earth's signs, just as her great-great-grandmother, great-grandmother, grandmother, and mother had done before her. And she supposed the trees would soon thrash their last in the coming storms, and crash beneath the great carapaces of turbulent seawater that were destined to rise even higher than the levels reached in the last three decades. At the end, as *it* rose, she guessed that the trees would shriek out *that name* too, and in a deafening chorus of panic, before they all fell silent forever. *As we must too.* She knew it. She had lived through the *coming* as she slept. Sometimes now, the sights even flickered into chaotic life within her wide-open eyes.

The name, the younger trees sheltered in Marriage Wood called it now too. She could hear them from the distance. The older members of the woodlands hushed them. And as she rounded the headland and descended the hill to Elberry Cove, Cleo heard the name's susurration arise from the very water. And not for the first time either. In the retreating pull of the surf across a myriad of pebbles that all rolled together, she often heard *that name* now. In the slap and hiss of the sluggish waves upon the baked shoreline were syllables, even the odd consonant, as well as the breathy, rushing spaces between each part of that dreadful signifier.

No one had seen the face of God and it remained ineffable, but Cleo believed she knew *its* name now, and in the many languages of the trees, the birds, the sea, and also from the strange tongues of her dreams. Her mother had once told her that it was only a matter of time before she would hear that name everywhere and in living things. That she would become *a receiver*.

When she first heard the calling of that name she was sure, as were her doctors, that the voices were the beginnings of the family taint; the early onset of the bedlam in her bloodline, a hereditary taint of dementia that remained strong after four generations of daughters were all declared insane in their respective eras. Mercifully, Cleo was childless and the curse would end in her; she would never have willingly inflicted what she knew to be coming upon a child.

Most days, she struggled to recall her dead husband's face, or even when he died, but Cleo still refused to believe a hereditary illness was transmitting such a name into her thoughts. She believed instead that the disease that slowly shrivelled her brain created a susceptibility to the natural transmissions from the earth. Messages that only a disordered sixth sense could detect.

She kept on taking the pills, or some of them, and never uttered her family's theories to any of her doctors. But her ancestors had all claimed that *the name* was first heard in the fossils of this very bay. Her own experiences began in this cove too, though not in fossils, but at the edge of the sea grass pasture.

In the woodland that divided the cove from the drought-resistant maize crop that grew on the old golf course, Cleo began scratching about the paths and undergrowth until she found the tracks that she sought.

The 'ambulances' had definitely made recent deliveries at high tide. Tyre tracks, the thinner tracks of the barrows, and the parallel furrows of the gurney wheels had carved the pebbles apart on the shore. They led Cleo to a disturbance of dry leaves upon the red clay of the wood that embraced the cove. Here was more evidence of a commotion; a procession, no less, of those who had tried to quickly adapt to a future world that they had also dreamed of. Some had wished to change for a creator whom they had worshipped in secret for years. And a few of their number had already gone beneath the waves for good.

Cleo wondered if some of *them* actually survived out there in the colder water, beyond the weed, or if their drowned and contorted carcasses were now buried among the bent and mournful trees of the woods.

The sea grew deep quickly in the cove. A bank of pebbles dropped to a smooth, red sand. About thirty metres out, at a depth of six metres, eighty hectares of sea grass still thrived. One of the largest surviving underwater meadows in the British Isles. Until she was too old to dive, she spent hundreds of hours in that pasture. Down there she would scour the marine flora with torch and camera, watching the thick, lustrous grass move in the currents. She took a thousand samples across three decades and discovered nothing untoward amongst those fronds. But she still asked herself now: from where did that stone come? A dolmen that stood sixty metres out, hidden on the seafloor where the sun's light barely reached.

During one of her last dives, before she was *retired*, she caught sight of a large, black silhouette at a distance, at the end of her torch's reach. Where the currents caused by the slipway and the reef made it unsafe to swim, some*thing* had been deposited. Five years ago she had found that effigy and she believed it had remained in place, buried in the waters of the cove.

Once her fear and panic had crashed, she had realised the object was stationary; a rock formation. Drifting out another ten metres, a risky business as the tide was turning and she was not at her fittest when pushing seventy-two in the spring of 2050, she had been able to see more of the rock that reared from the underwater gloom like a saurian head. To her enduring astonishment, Cleo had found herself approaching what suggested the presence of a large black chess piece—a knight, no less—upon the seafloor. Emerging from those great, preserved grasslands was an installation, clearly man-made, though crudely, and casting an onyx gaze over the seabed around itself.

The object suggested a monument, or underwater marker, even an idol. It may just have been pitched over the side of a boat in transit. But whatever its purpose, she eventually found evidence of a congregation, and one never illumined by a marine biologist's lamp. Those responsible for the sculpture existed on land, and in the village of Churston Ferris.

The thought prompted her to plan another visit to the Kudas who lived in the village. And soon, when she had regained the stamina to walk that far, so that she could determine whether they had made the most recent and final leap beneath the waves from this cove. They had seemed due the last time she had looked in on them.

It was getting too late and too hot to move around. Cleo took a pained look upon the water and marvelled again, as she always did, at what had been hidden for so long, right here.

Time was running out; the eclipse was mere weeks away. The sun was turning up its murdering heat. There was no sign of autumn, and she doubted she'd see another one of those anyway.

■ ■ ■

Cleo sat alone and still in her living room, with the blinds drawn across the balcony doors. The media service was silent and blank. Exhausted and wondering if she would ever reach the end of her drive again, a familiar agitation spread through Cleo's body as her antipsychotic medication cycle neared its end. A palsy quivered her hands and feet.

Yolanda medicated her until she was calm, while stroking her hair. Yolanda was a former refugee from Portugal who worked as a carer for a few of the multitude of dementia sufferers in the bay. She'd arrived minutes after Cleo returned from the cove.

Reclining on the sofa, while Yolanda busied herself with the preparations of a midday meal, Cleo's attention drifted to the portraits of her forebears: Amelia Anning, Mary Anning, Olive Harvey, and her mother, Judith Harvey. She smiled and wiped at the tears that immediately filled her eyes.

As you were, so am I.

Around their pictures were the polished madrepores that her mother had passed down. Upon the walls, pressed weeds hung, mounted and framed by Cleo's great-grandmother, Mary Anning.

After making significant contributions to marine botany and earth science, Cleo's forebears all died raving. Once Cleo began to hear the natural world issuing *that name*, five years ago, and building quickly to a veritable din inside her head, she took measures to prevent a repeat of her ancestors' fates with the psychotropic salves that most of her forebears had been without. So many pills had subsequently been swallowed to dampen the shrieks and the visions. Her mother, Judith, had chosen to eschew the antipsychotic medication. As a result of what her mind was being required to contain and process, Judith had been one day shy of her sixtieth birthday when she took her own life.

Looking at the family portraits never failed to encourage Cleo to ponder the futility of her conservation work in a world that could not reach consensus. A world incapable of saving itself because of a species that could not conceive of its insignificance upon the earth, let alone the earth's insignificance in the cosmos. The women of her family had all endured this Damascene moment too, though haplessly. They had changed no minds but their own either.

'The women of your family were beautiful,' Yolanda said, as she fastened the tray on the armrests of Cleo's chair, following her patient's gaze to the photographs on the sideboard.

'And clever too. Thank you, dear,' Cleo said, her interest briefly moving to the neatly cut sandwiches. 'My great-great-grandmother was none other than Amelia Anning. You won't have heard of her, Yolanda.' She wasn't sure if she had told Yolanda of this before. But evidence of *the visitor* was first discovered by Amelia Anning, and that knowledge alone had driven her mad.

'Amelia was an amateur fossil collector, a palaeontologist too. A near-unique woman in her time. This was the early nineteenth century, dear. Careers in science were forbidden women. But she, my dear, was a true pioneer. Much of what we know of prehistoric life and the earth's history is owed to her. She died in her nineties, but was still hiking up her skirts and scrabbling round the Jurassic fossil beds at Lyme Regis in her seventies.'

'You too, I think, will live so long.'

Cleo tried to smile but lacked the strength.

After winter landslides on the Blue Lias cliffs, it was Amelia who found and correctly identified the first ichthyosaur. She also uncovered a plesiosaur from the same rubble, and the first pterosaur beyond the borders of Germany, as well as many *other* fish fossils whose uncanny influence contributed to her decline.

'Your lunch, ma'am. You need to eat.'

'Yes. But it was those damn belemnites, Yolanda. They began her obsession with a set of ideas. An astonishing leap of faith. Few scientists will even acknowledge this. Though in secret, oh how they whisper now.'

'Of course.'

Amelia's only child, and Cleo's great-grandmother, was Mary Anning, who moved to Torquay in Devon to be close to Shiphay Hospital where her mother eventually died, raving aloud her belemnite dreams to the very end.

'That's Mary, next to Amelia. A brilliant woman. But the great love of Mary's life was seaweed, Yolanda. Not fossils. Her first two books are still in print. The first editions are on display at the Royal Albert Memorial Museum. That's in London. I've seen them.'

'Yes, ma'am.'

Mary's first two volumes of *Algae Danmonienses* (Seaweeds of Devon) were relative bestsellers, and much of *Phycologia Britannica*, that catalogues and illustrates all known British marine algae, was dependent upon Mary's lifetime of study. Though Cleo did not share this with Yolanda, because any talk of Mary's books inevitably led Cleo to thoughts of Mary's third and final volume. That was mostly destroyed by embarrassed members of the family, but a surviving copy was passed down to Cleo by her mother, before she too was put away to scream *that name*.

Cleo spoke in between the mouthfuls of bread that she chewed slowly. 'My great-grandmother, Mary, collected seaweeds, all the way from Cornwall to North Devon, and along the East and South Devonshire Coasts. You know, one large weed was even named after her: *Anningsia.*

'The leading botanists of her day were her close friends, dear. With them she shared her finds, and *some* of her theories...' And even those ideas augmenting her own late mother's more radical ideas about the southwestern coastline. But why trouble Yolanda with that? She couldn't possibly understand. And as with her mother, Amelia Anning, Mary's end was neither illustrious nor happy.

Mary Anning's third volume, *A Dark, Slowly Flowing Flood*, caused grave damage to her reputation because the work was a near-surrealist dream narrative. Mary was a scientist who attempted to encapsulate great spans of time and the local coast's ever-changing position, shape and environment, but through poetry, water colours, pen and ink. The book never enjoyed anything but a brief, meagre print run at a local publisher, partly funded by Mary. But the lurid contents of Mary's only nonscientific work remained the only indication of what had beset and preoccupied the woman for the ten years prior to her incarceration in the same asylum that claimed her mother.

When Mary took up with the unorthodox spiritualist group, The Fellows of the Broken Night, towards the end of her liberty, she was already binding her eyes with scarves, and threatening to claw them out from the root should her blinds be removed. But layers of linen strips did nothing to stop the sights unfolding behind her eyes. And these sights formed the ghastlier revelations recorded in *A Dark, Slowly Flowing Flood*. The visions that she was stricken with also informed her notorious ravings upon the seafront and piers, where she had stood upon a wooden crate, with her face bound save for her mouth, to address the ladies and gentlemen of Torquay.

A Dark, Slowly Flowing Flood was filled with drawings of the fossilised marine life that Amelia Anning had uncovered and scraped clean. But more complete and detailed impressions of what she derived from the partial fossil forms were fleshed out in Mary's imagination; a creative faculty informed by her own visions. And it was those images that resembled this creator, this destroyer, and remaker of worlds. A visitor Cleo's lineage had long dreamed of, but solely recreated and expressed in ways only communicable through the medium of insanity.

Cleo didn't even need to open Mary Anning's book to see again the gelid grotesques that had drifted through the last, harrowing, tormented years of her great-grandmother's turbulent consciousness. Merely imagining those things had driven her witless, and when they had opened their flabby mouths to sing the *name* in her dreams, Mary had been lost to the world forever. But Mary had always believed that she was seeing an alien species, adrift amidst the deepest oceans of space and time in the cosmos. Forms that had been creating life out of themselves, and then extinguishing that very life, for fourteen billion years: the lifespan of the universe.

■ ■ ■

The following week, on Friday, at dawn, Cleo attempted to see through the dimpled glass panel set beside the Kudas' front door. She was confronted by the greenish light that rippled in the manner of water reflected upon the wall of a swimming pool. During her first hurried scrutiny of this reception, four years before, she'd realised that the entire lower floor of the Kudas' home had been sunken beneath the level of the ground, and tiled aquamarine like a swimming pool.

Cleo opened the letter box and stared into one of twenty-four houses in Churston Ferris with ground floors permanently converted to the storage of liquid. And could she have subsequently suffered the same hallucination so many times in the same place? Her dementia was better controlled than that.

Despite three restraining orders and two cryptic threats upon her life, she still came here. The death threats, she believed, had originated from a local faith group, either The Latest Testament or One Eye Opening. Her age and mental instability had been the only factors that had spared her the punitive sentences of the magistrate's court.

She moved to the rear of the Kudas' property and felt a familiar delinquent glee at her daring trespass.

Like always, the windows at the rear were shuttered, as were those of the Kudas' similarly *affected* neighbours. The garden was ordinary and typical of the neighbourhood: palm trees, the *Trachycarpus wagnerianus*, pink stone paths, tall fences, immaculate lawns and flower beds, and a honeysuckle covered pergola. The only remarkable feature of the orderly rear gardens was the variety of stone lawn ornaments; all of which, inside the Kudas' yard, depicted black sea horses, perched upon what were either castles or reefs. She had never been able to decide which. But as if the Kudas' sculptures had been interpreted by an artist with nothing in mind beyond a stark realism, Cleo intuited an ugly provocation in the bestial eyes of the four Hippocampus pieces on the lawn.

Her suspicions about this village were first aroused when she followed tracks from Elberry Cove, through Marriage Wood, and linked them to the activity of the private ambulances in the surrounding lanes of Churston Ferris at night. And at a time when one of the newer 'scientific' religions burned through the area with an intensity of devotion not seen since the Black Death cursed Devon, 700 years before.

The arrival of the new faith groups preceded her discovery of the statue beneath the sea in Elberry Cove, by a few years, though she believed the churches had been active for a long time, albeit disguised in plain sight as something else. The ambulances belonged to the age care charities created by the new churches, who had bought the old Church of England buildings of Paignton, Brixham and Torquay, and then set about changing all of their windows into a single curious design. Few antiquarians had seemed bothered, or they had been silenced. Cleo never really knew. But attendances, she'd heard, were way up now. The congregations were almost entirely elderly, though Cleo had resisted their repeated attempts to entice her into their faith-based care programme, and their extensive leisure programme within the community. Her neighbours used to regale her with stories about the wonderful entertainments and events, until she told them to shut up. The mayor and council were happy because the church groups were relieving the beleaguered local health services of much of their burden. 70% of the population of the bay was now over sixty. The corporate charity wing of the church, Opening Eyes, had purchased over half of the region's care homes in the last five years, and the quality of the care was unsurpassed.

But Cleo would never consider an association with any faith that reshaped church windows into what she believed was an eye. One great eye. Big, luminous, but somehow idiotically blank and unsympathetic, and always coloured with a green-, yellow- and black-stained glass that she considered reptilian. The windows suggested they were engaged in some form of penetrating scrutiny, directed at those who passed below. Surreptitiously, building by building, and even in the listed buildings, she had noted the removal of the cross.

These days, the garden ornaments of Churston Ferris were no longer odd to her, because the actual interiors of that settlement, upon which she had spied so diligently, had proven far more interesting.

Much of the rear patio closest to the Kudas' house had been taken over with an apparatus consisting of white plastic tubes or hoses attached to some kind of a squat generator that produced enough heat to warm her entire body when standing a few feet away. The air expelled by the machine contained a hot, electric, oily odour. The two largest tubes passed through the rear wall of the affected houses. Vibrations could be felt through the hoses, and if she moved her face close enough she could hear water bubbling through the PVC piping. The apparatus was some kind of pump. Above the machine, an extractor fan expelled a tepid air and a not unpleasant odour of salt water. Each of the church's ambulances that visited this village had been fitted with a not dissimilar mechanism for filtering water.

Reaching to her tiptoes, Cleo peered through the mesh screen before the whirring plastic blades of the fan. Until the balls of her feet burned and her old spine cramped, she remained fixed in position and stared with wonder and revulsion at the Kudas' wide living room.

The lens of a light fitted into the front of a limestone rock helped to illumine the watery room. There was no conventional furniture in sight, only several large boulders, arranged around the edges of the room and all containing embedded lights. Upon the floor, a gentle swaying motion was produced by a pasture of submerged *Alismatales*, or sea grass.

In the dim, greenish illumination she saw Mrs Kuda first, crouched upon her rocky perch. And above this bizarre grotto, the naked lady of the house sat observing some activity out of her sight, in another region of the room.

Until she found this pair, Cleo had never before seen a human being covered in such unsightly skin below the neck. Not only had Mrs Kuda been cursed with a hunched back, or a great mane of flesh, spiked by the vertebrae beneath, but her skin was also mottled by large plates of pink-orange psoriasis. Her first suspicion was of the presence of a rare disease in which an amphibian environment offered comfort to the sufferer. But this was no medicinal pond. Judging by the rock-effect walls and lifelike encrustations—the shells, molluscs, and several kinds of hermit crab—the Kudas' living room had been fashioned into a facsimile of a rock pool.

That morning, at least five minutes passed before Cleo caught a glimpse of the man of the house; if his condition made him worthy of the title. What Cleo saw of Mr Kuda was often obscured as he mostly remained submerged and positioned facedown. And whenever his gleaming body passed through the beams that shone upon the water, the three rock lights offered insufficient illumination for a fuller assessment of his disability. His skin condition matched his wife's, while his chest, arms, shoulders, head and neck, were the same as an adult man, albeit one aged, hunched and stooped. But Cleo had become convinced that Mr Kuda had no legs. Or perhaps only one leg. And that morning, whatever it was that extended from his lumpy abdominal region, had curled around a clump of grass in the manner of a tentacle. Using the long, wavering weed for grip, he then wheeled his large body around in the water while his head remained hidden. In fact, Cleo had never yet observed him rise to take a breath.

Agilely, he swished himself through the water. Ripples from his silent, circular activity spread out and lapped about the rock upon which his wife sat. At the foot of his wife's outcrop, he stopped wheeling and, like a child, gently raised his face to just beneath the water's surface. Carefully, unsteadily, his scaly wife shuffled off the stone seat and sat beside him in the water. Facing each other, they engaged in something approximating a kiss.

What troubled Cleo about this intimate activity was the gap between their faces, and the way in which Mrs Kuda rolled her eyes upwards and so whitely within her lined face. What remained of her withered bosom also palpitated, suggesting a pumping action or rapid respiration. When Mr Kuda eventually detached himself from the ghastly contact, Cleo saw a thin, dark object, like a long tongue, dart back inside her wide open mouth.

Without mistake, Mr Kuda had been dancing, down in those verdant sea grasses, to woo his partner. That hideous wheeling in the paddling shallows was some kind of mating display, and one that she had repeatedly observed in the Hippocampus of the local coves.

Since her first sighting of this pair, and the other less well-formed couples in this village, she found that the sound of the Kudas' generator and fan would follow her home, locked inside her skull. Every time she closed her eyes to sleep, she was sure that the white ceiling of her bedroom rippled like the ceiling of a cave into which the sea flowed at high tide. What also abided and returned in an unwelcome fashion, and repeatedly, like an incorrect slide inserted into a projector, were her unpleasant observations of Mr Kuda's belly, and of the bellies of the other retired men in the neighbourhood. After they broke from the *kisses* with their wives, and gradually glided out of sight, across the watery floors of their living rooms, their gently distended bellies would often move, as if from the squirming of a multitude within.

In the warm shallow seawater of their village dens, she had observed so many who had been rendered infirm by age on land, but who had managed a miraculous transformation, or second life, in water. People who now frolicked and glided through the swaying sea grasses with which they had sowed the sunken floors of their living rooms.

If she were to tell anyone, she would be thought mad and delusional, hallucinating, and although she did plenty of that, the same was also said of her mother, her grandmother, her great-grandmother, and her great-great-grandmother. But the burden of what she knew, she was quite sure, would soon bear the most unappealing fruit in the local waters of this now cursed bay.

■ ■ ■

That night Cleo dreamed of small islands whose faces were made black with shadow from the great sun that rose behind them, to nearly blind her sight, while turning the seawater the colour of highly polished steel. She stood upon a cliff edge she didn't recognise and looked across a vast panorama of new red cliffs. Great, fresh gouges of scarlet rock were exposed along the front of the cliffs. Vast slopes of rusty-looking sand and rubble had tumbled into the shining water below, leaving fresh wounds upon the coastline as far as she could see, as if some great storm had caused a century of erosion in a matter of days. From what she could see of the distant hills, she thought she must have been somewhere near Kingswear, but if so then the coastline of South Devon was being rapidly reformed.

And whatever was in the sea below her position was trying to attract her attention. Large black shapes, lumpen, but slippery and shining as they turned and wallowed, dived and surfaced, barked out sounds that she believed were human voices if she listened closely enough. All she could make out of the distant, black faces were the doglike suggestions of the whiskered snouts and flattened ears. But the eyes and teeth were definitely human.

■ ■ ■

Cleo awoke in the living room. The first thing she saw was Yolanda rising from her chair. The nurse came to her on soft feet, her face one big smile, her lovely eyes wide and glittering with an excitement that Cleo assumed had little to do with her patient waking up.

The nurse must have let herself in as Cleo slept; it was after nine. She had slept badly for the first half of the night, and then tried to stay awake on account of the dreams that her antipsychotic medication was either worsening or failing to suppress; she never knew which. But she'd been in a bad way for a week after her visit to the Kudas.

On the far side of the room the media screen flickered and flashed, the sound muted. Her carer had been watching the news and leafing through the journal Cleo kept to keep track of each day, the sudden emergence of memories, and the effects of the medication cycles. Perhaps Yolanda had been amused by some of Cleo's recollections. She didn't think the journal had much comic value, but then couldn't entirely recall much of what she had written in it. Her prescription would never preserve her mind, but had slowed her deterioration and moderated her mania successfully, providing Yolanda came to her home three times each day to make sure that Cleo took what had been prescribed.

Cleo reached for her glass of water and drank it through a straw. It had gone tepid in the languid heat of the night. She noticed her hands were trembling and hastily took the three pills that Yolanda had already placed on the side table.

Yolanda tried to block the screen with her body. 'This news is not so good. Let me turn it off.'

'Is it ever good? I don't think it ever will be again. But let me see. What have I missed?'

The world. She certainly hadn't missed that while she'd slept. A narrowing space in her mind was often fatigued in its weakening attempt to understand how people had allowed things to get so bad. And in the last few days the seemingly endless war between Turkey, Iraq and Syria had escalated to new levels, over control of the headwaters of the Euphrates and Tigris. The Indians still had their rain, but the Pakistanis had none, and they were also going to war again over water. Even with the sound lowered, Cleo no longer cared to watch the great dust clouds of the continual air and drone strikes, the detritus of devastated vehicles, the moonscape of obliterated cement blocks that was now much of the Middle East, Kashmir and North Africa. Cleo assumed Yolanda had been watching updates on the respective escalations.

'Something terrible has happened *here*,' Yolanda said, her face now stiff with shock.

'Here?' It was local news on the screen. 'Turn it up! Quickly.'

There had been several poignant local events of late, portents and signs on her doorstep, but they rarely even made the local news. This was national news on the screen, but broadcasting from Berry Head; not even two miles from where she lived.

Cleo could see footage of the nature reserve's unmistakable shape, shot from the air. A limestone headland, and the vestiges of what was once a great tropical coral reef, 375 million years before. The women of her family, whose portraits stood on the sideboard, had even considered Berry Head to be one half of a very old doorway.

As Cleo watched the report, augmented by Yolanda's excited narration, she could see that a great many people had tried to step through that *doorway*, yesterday.

'Dear God,' Cleo said. 'Those people are from local care homes…'

'It is terrible. I do not think you should watch.'

'Nonsense. You think I am surprised by this? *They'll* do anything to get them into the water.'

'What do you mean?'

'Open Heart, Open… never mind.'

How those poor creatures flapped and flailed as they went off the edge and down to the sea. At least seventy people from two local care homes. The infirm and the demented, all shrieking as they plummeted through two hundred feet of thin air.

There were only two films of the actual incident that had taken place during the early morning while Cleo slept; footage from the lighthouse security camera, and a shaky film taken by a carer who was now in custody. Yolanda said the films had been on repeat every thirty minutes since she had arrived at eight. Despite all that was happening in the world, Torbay was making international news because the elderly people from two retirement homes had all leapt into the sea, from off the edge of Berry Head.

The police were looking for the other staff who had driven them to the precipice. Speculation was rife. The carers must have helped the victims on and off the buses, before guiding and wheeling them by torchlight to that terrible edge that Cleo had never liked standing anywhere near.

In the recordings, the din of the seabirds was also excessive: guillemots, razorbills, black-legged kittiwakes, the gulls. They were always noisy in their cliffside nests, but as that tired and stooped parade of the thin and infirm hobbled and shuffled off and into the abyss, and down to the terrible black rocks and the churning, bitter, nighttime sea below, the noise of the birds became a true cacophony of panic, rising to a crescendo. Those birds should have been sleeping. But in that riotous avian climax, Cleo heard the name. *The name* screamed with abandon and with the ecstasy preceding tribute. Because that is what she was watching: *sacrifice*. These were sacrifices at Berry Head, not the victims of mass suicide, or mass murder, as the press were claiming. This was human sacrifice at the doorway, at the very threshold of *what* was waking.

Those poor fools who had been taken to those cliffs by their carers, nurses, doctors, porters, and orderlies of the Esplanade and Galmpton Green nursing homes, had all shrieked the name too, raising their exhausted and frail but impassioned voices to join the din of the birds. They had dropped out of sight either individually, as couples holding hands, and even in one disoriented clump, down into the waves and the rocks where they must have come apart like kindling. None were pushed; all walked, calling *the name.*

The residents of those care homes had been promised that they would see out their final days in as much comfort as anyone could hope for in such desperate times within the country. But they must all have been long prepared to engage in such an evacuation from this life.

The news moved to breaking reports about a dozen similarly affected retirement homes in Plymouth and North Cornwall. There, many elderly residents had been discovered making their way, slowly, on walking frames, and wheelchairs, in the early hours of the morning toward Whitsand Bay and other beaches. Perhaps with the intention of throwing themselves into the sea. It was unclear how many had not been prevented from achieving their goals the previous night.

Cleo had always thought it strange, and perplexing, and unnerving, how local fossils had been shaped into the exterior walls of the Esplanade Care Home in Roundham Gardens, in Paignton, as if to create some decorative feature, using local materials. This alteration had occurred once the property came into the possession of One Eye Opening. She had written to the council to explain about the hidden activity within those stones, but had not received a reply. The same innovation had been replicated in the churchyard walls in Paignton after the crucifixes had been taken down. Cleo guessed those rocks had been embedded in the mortar for different reasons now.

Like herself, she could only assume that the aged made the best material, while their minds dimmed and deranged. They provided the best vehicles to receive transmissions from down there, from beneath the waves of the bay; once the transmitters, the fossils and fossil beds were brought into closer proximity to their poor, confused minds.

Each of the affected care homes in the morning news was owned by One Eye Opening; a wealthy, nonconformist religion they were calling it on the news, for want of a better definition. A definition that Cleo had ready: a *cult*. A cult that had made its disingenuous inroads into the religious community and end-of-life care in a county overrun by an elderly population. It seemed unfair, and horribly Darwinian, that some were being transformed while others were sacrificed to the sea. Though the residents of Churston Ferris, like the Kudas, were wealthy; perhaps selection was dependent upon nothing more sophisticated than that.

Cleo was shocked but not surprised. Across the last five years she'd taken note of many other local curiosities. The great ructions on the seabed attested to by both the Royal Navy and the marine biology unit at Plymouth University. Fishermen using sonar who had claimed that new topographies were emerging upon the seafloor. Sailors, from what was left of the South Hams fishing fleet, had claimed to have fetched some unusual catches out of the local waters too.

With her scepticism in suspension, Cleo had never debunked the stories she had found online of what had been tugged out of the nets, before confiscation on shore by the Environment Agency. Some of the catch was still being examined in the marine biology labs in Plymouth. Desperate were the two marine biologists in Brixham, Harry and Phillip, with whom Cleo retained a vague and hardly reciprocal association after her retirement, to eschew any classifications or rumours of a Fortean nature that Cleo had immediately espoused to them. Harry and Phillip knew why Cleo had been retired, but did admit that they had personally examined five *Eledone cirrhosa* octopus in a lab in Brixham. Creatures generously exceeding all previously recorded sizes and weights. They had been caught in waters off the South Hams coast during the previous year.

Her contacts had also confirmed that the rumours of a giant squid spotted in local waters were not entirely fictional either. They had confirmed that an impossibly sized *Haliphron atlanticus* octopus, with only six legs, but of lengths up to ten metres, had been caught and killed by a Royal Navy PT boat, near the mouth of the Dart Estuary, after reports that it had been menacing a ferry, and had made several attempts to drag at least one passenger overboard. Her contacts claimed that what had been found in its belly, partially digested, attested to the rumours of the fates of three missing canoeists, last seen in the channel below Greenaway and heading towards Totnes the previous year. And had Plymouth's harbour not also been deluged with *Octopus vulgaris*, not three years ago in 2052? A species not seen in British waters since the early sixties of the previous century.

And it didn't stop there for anyone predisposed to seek synthesis amongst the freakish incidents and recent curiosities found in the county's waters. Stone plinths carven with designs the Celts had imitated, and Iron Age man had replicated in stone throughout Cornwall, suddenly found off Salcombe by the engineers tasked with building the new wind farm. Great undersea basalt circles, arranged like teeth in the untidy mouths of what had resembled eyeless faces, had been discovered close to Start Point, South Devon, during the laying of new power cables to transport British nuclear power to the drought-stricken parts of Southern France. Two discoveries alone that had revived local folklore about the possibility of Atlantis having once existed off the coast of

Devon and Cornwall. There had been something down there for sure, but Cleo doubted it had ever been Atlantis.

And now the newly managed care homes of Torbay had fossils in their walls, and the windows of the churches had been altered to represent an eye. A geriatric cult had willingly extinguished itself at the cliffs of Berry Head Nature Reserve, in one procession the night before the solar eclipse. Had they also been hearing *the name* and receiving its imagery inside their failing minds? Cleo wondered if she should cuff her own ankle to the bedstead and swallow the key, during what time remained before the eclipse, lest she join Torbay's flightless snowbirds who seemed intent on leaping off precipices.

◼ ◻ ◼

Yolanda returned at four p.m. later that day, thirty minutes late, and broke Cleo from a short doze.

Yolanda claimed the news from Berry Head was still upsetting for her, and asked Cleo if she could change the television channel. 'I cannot see it again. But it is all they show today. They are bringing in some bodies. I would rather watch the wars.'

Cleo acquiesced as Yolanda would only be there for an hour. The nurse had been delayed by the traffic congestion that had built ahead of the eclipse. The very thought of the cosmic event was now making Cleo feel sick.

'Why not tell me about your family,' Yolanda asked as she brought Cleo's tea into the room on a tray. 'I know these women are so important to you. Maybe they can take our minds from this terrible day.'

I doubt that, Cleo thought, but looked across to the picture of her grandmother, Olive Harvey, who had continued her mother Mary Anning's work with the weeds and rock pools, while working as a conservationist and artist, selling shells, polished madrepores and pressed weeds, mounted and framed, to tourists.

As she ate, Cleo told Yolanda how Olive had spent most of her life outdoors and on the Paignton Coast, south of Goodrington Sands, dipping into the rock pools of Saltern Cove and Waterside Cove. A woman who had fastidiously continued the family trade, photographing and collecting the intertidal flora and fauna: the flat wracks, knotted wracks, red seaweed, snakelocks anemones, and spotted gobys. Most importantly, she became an authority on *Galatheastrigosa*, the squat lobster. The creature had become one of her obsessions because her mother and grandmother, the brilliant but tragic Mary and Amelia, had both dreamed and then screamed about what *Galatheastrigosa* had originally dispersed from out of, the contemporary lobster still partially mimicking some features of its ancient parentage.

Olive had spent decades scraping and digging her way into those cliffs, where the fluvial breccias from the Permian Age amassed about the slates and sandstones from the Devonian Period. The locations of the best fossils were indicated for Olive in the work of her predecessors. Her mother and grandmother's notes had led Olive down to the shore at low tide with the promise, or warning, that future generations of scientists would uncover even greater marvels and terrors from those cliffs.

After the decades of coastal erosion since her forebears had first scuttled, collected and processed their knowledge, the shore of Goodrington had revealed a submerged forest bed to Olive: the very tree stumps that had emerged after the last ice age. That find enlarged her reputation further in the circles that cared about such things. But by Olive's time, more and more was revealing itself too; one century after her family began their excavations. It was Olive Harvey who also first discovered the breccia burrows, and then quickly reburied them.

In those preserved burrows were the restless relics of animals that had lived in the deserts of the Permian Age, 248 million years before, including one creature whose distant grave songs initiated the destruction of Olive's own mind. That was the burrow left by a giant *arthropleuridmyriapods*, a millipede that was at least four metres long.

Olive had recorded in her journal how she'd once sat in the fossil bed to rest while she worked, and lost two days and nights, in which her mind, in her own words, 'unravelled through its own substance and memories,' and entered the kind of psychosis Cleo most commonly associated with a really bad experience on LSD. What Olive had seemingly rubbed against, and become irradiated by at a deep subconscious level, was probably nothing more than a near-microscopic fragment of that which had originally dispersed from the writhing and shedding of some monumental form, that occurred 248 million years previously, when this part of the British Isles was near the equator. And so began another member of the family's inexorable decline into socially unacceptable enlightenment.

Cleo continued with her story and told the captivated Yolanda about her own mother, the tormented and twice-divorced environmentalist, Judith Harvey, who had put an end to her own severe and unmanageable cerebral rout at fifty-nine. Judith had succumbed to what was thought to be early-onset dementia and took an overdose. Despite the great blanks in her memory, Cleo had never forgotten that day.

When she'd been alive, Judith had often reminded Cleo of what Amelia and Mary Anning and Olive Harvey had respectively explored, discovered, and subsequently *believed*. She told Cleo all that her own mother, Olive, had passed down to her: the knowledge that our planet was but one tiny krill floating amongst billions of fragments in a cold, black, hostile ocean of gas and debris. And that our infinitesimal fragment was transformed by a *visitor* 535 million years before. A world subsequently destroyed and remade so many times over as a consequence of the visitor's dreadful whims and rages. Her forebears had all shared the same dreams, because the fossils that they had exposed themselves to were the equivalent of a few smudged fingerprints on the walls of a vast crime scene, as big as a planet.

Cleo's mother would flavour her own interpretation with her background in earth science. Judith passionately claimed that had we crept across this earth in smaller numbers, and not congregated in such carbon-rich cultures, while flashing our arrogant, thoughtless presence into the stars, and had we not made toxic and eroded the soils, bled our faecal wastes and effluents into the black deeps, crisscrossed the ocean floors and mountain ranges with cables to broadcast our infernal jabber, exhausted the fresh water and melted the glaciers, changed the wind and rainfall, heated the earth's belly and melted the ice caps, exhausted the great populations of fish and mammals… *if*… we had not grown to nine billion minds and created such an intensification of teeming consciousness on one small planet, whose neural activity transmitted so far outwards… *if* none of this had happened then *it, the visitor,* may never have half-opened that one eye, down there, where it slumbered.

In the preface to Mary Anning's *A Dark, Slowly Flowing Flood,* the author wrote: 'Just as every God has slept through our Godless endeavours, any God can yet awaken.' Mary's last words to the priest, who administered the last rites, are also alleged to have been: 'What have we done? Oh, God, what did we call out to? Is that thing God?' Not *a God,* but 'God,' *the* God: the ultimate creator.

Judith used to wonder aloud to Cleo, why, as a species, we'd not had more sense than to create the requisite conditions in which that name could be called out by the exhausted, dying planet, and by what expired upon it. The earth now heralded an awakening; Judith had told her that before she was ten.

Near the end of her life, Judith had once begged Cleo to bear no children. 'For God's sake,' she had cried from the bed in which she was often restrained: 'Don't continue this!' Cleo had thought 'this' was the hereditary taint of insanity, but had subsequently realised that 'this' had referred to 'us.' To all of us, the *species,* and our burden upon the outer skins of this little planet in our solar system. In which resided a far older occupant that had dreamed such foulness as the great lizards, the food chain, viral life, decomposition and mortality, and *us* too, around its eternal *self,* and across so many billions of years that our understanding of age bore no parallel to its own. Cleo had obeyed her mother and remained childless.

And Judith always made sure that Cleo wrote down her dreams . . .

When Cleo had finished, she remained unsure for how long she had been talking, or whether much of what she'd said, she'd only said to herself. The medication was strong.

Yolanda was already putting on her sunhat. 'On Friday, we watch the eclipse together, from here, yes? On the balcony. I will come early.'

'I'd rather you spent that day with your family, my dear.'

'Oh, Cleo! You still think the world will end during the eclipse?' Yolanda laughed.

No, Cleo didn't think that. Not exactly. 'The end of us will be the end of us, my dear, but not the end of *everything*.'

She did often wonder, though, if the coming eclipse would herald an extinction-level event. How could she not, after all of those dreams? And one heralded in true biblical fashion by the transformation of the firmament. But Cleo was not entirely convinced by the idea, or by her predecessors' thoughts in this area, nor with proclamations made by the new churches who were far too dependent on *A Dark, Slowly Flowing Flood*, among the other, older texts they favoured from Providence, New England.

'I believe our end will be near total, Yolanda, but with a partial evolutionary transformation of whatever survives. I can't give you any timescale, or date, but it will be relatively swift in earth-life terms. And miserably incremental like the consequences of climate change, surrounded by diebacks we've not seen since the bubonic plague in Europe and Asia. So, I'm giving us, at least, another two centuries amidst the rubble of our civilisation. But those will be times like nothing we've had to cope with so far. I mean, how many of us can breathe underwater? It may really be that simple, in most places on the earth.'

'Oh, Cleo! You make me smile.'

'The world has been changing rapidly and bewilderingly towards a critical mass, Yolanda. Surely you have noticed? And I believe dear old Torbay has a specific role to play in an epochal event.'

Yolanda laughed as she swung her bag over her shoulder. 'Whatever you say, Cleo! There is so much going on in your head. But you are making great progress. You must take the relaxants if your mind races. The doctor says so.'

'And you may ask.' Cleo was not to be stopped, even as Yolanda was halfway through the door. 'Why don't I flee to higher ground? But if you consider what the women of my family have discovered, who would want to survive what is coming?'

■ ■ ■

[Excerpt from the diary of Cleo Harvey]

July 18th, 2055

My dearest Yolanda,

I may not remember to tell you this. I may become distracted, or sleep through your next visit. But as I am enjoying a good period this afternoon, I feel I owe you some explanation so that you can better make sense of the disparate stories that I have been telling you over the last two years; stories about my family and our work here in this bay.

My great-great-grandmother, Amelia Anning, whom I may have mentioned to you during our association, was certain that what she called the Old One, *or* Great Old One, *as she was wont, arrived on our planet in the Ediacaran Period, 535 million years ago, and during the last gasps of the Precambrian ages.*

Her methods for deducing this timeline were complex, and involved as much science as imagination, and where the two mediums seemed to enmesh within her dream life. Even with her eyes closed, while away in other places and times as she slept, she still had an eye for the landscapes that she saw, and for the forms of those things that left the imprints she had found in the cliffs.

Amelia surmised that the arrival *occurred during the time of the great soft-bodied inhabitants. Those that had existed for hundreds of millions of years, ever consuming each other and recycling their drifting forms. These indigenous denizens of the young earth left almost nothing for fossil hunters to find, because they had no bones, shells or teeth. But she learned that vast creatures had burrowed through the earth during Ediacaran times, and trawled the oceans too; great tunnels and gouges were found here in Torbay and in Australia, though not what left the creases in the stones.*

Amelia, however, caught sight of them, the vast iridescent jellies and the great drillers of the planet, as if she was floating among them, or scurrying through the debris of their excavations. And in her waking life what Amelia recalled both fascinated her and traumatized her. These tremors of shock loosened her rickety mental foundations. But the monstrous shapes, the diaphanous swellings of the poisonous skirts, the viscous trailings through the hot green deeps, and the blind squirmings that she tried to describe and paint, were noth-

ing compared to that which blasted through the atmosphere and then dispersed itself in incalculably new forms. The visitor.

The Cambrian Period, as we know, is renowned for the creativity of its seas. Nothing lived on what little land existed. That far back, the maelstrom of creation was still in the deeps, and what wallowed in the watery expanses became varied and all too abundant. But it was our visitor who made these new ways of life possible. What it stimulated into being, about its landing site, crept and leapt, crawled, swam, and burrowed to escape parental predation. There were shells, encasing such young life, at least in these Cambrian times; carapaces made in the image of the old visitor's armour. What was still soft and boneless was mostly swept away, or simply reinvented.

But the visitor, the Great Old One, was not satisfied, or so my forebears all muttered in their bloodless and traumatised states in a local hospital that is now long gone (luxury apartments, would you believe?).

Great ructions and upheavals were emitted as the slowly rusticating visitor, remade and remade again the environment that flooded past its often slumbering form beneath the waves. One such mighty cataclysm was the Ordovician-Silurian mass extinction. The trilobites, brachiopods and graptolites were mostly rendered obsolete for decisions that we can only guess at, if decision is the right word. Human terms are imprecise, for although we share a minute fragment of the Old One's vast consciousness within our own sentience, we are not like it.

This slaughter or genocide of what had either been created, or adapted from the insensate drifters of the fathoms, occurred 443 million years ago, in two stages divided by hundreds of thousands of years in which the monarch of our watery rock rested between its annihilations.

My poor forebears all cited the alien deity's sensitivity to temperature and climate, and claimed that it drew great ice sheets over itself and its resting places following the Ordovician-Silurian mass extinction. It also used a new armour of ice to drastically alter the chemistry of the oceans and the atmosphere above the waters. But the ruler continued to vandalise its own newly created habitat too, and repeatedly, across the next 380 million years, whenever its meditations became fitful, or disturbed. The planet was plunged into apocalypse and collapse in the Devonian, Permian, Triassic-Jurassic and Cretaceous Periods. There were smaller mass extinctions too, and in each of these eruptions of the roused tyrant's rage, half of the species that it had formed or evolved were destroyed again.

Varied evolving parts of itself, and therefore life, were discovered upon our shores by my fossil-hunting family. All of the clues of what came before mankind, mainly occurred in the Devonian and Permian Periods, and because the slaughtered littered their corpses in the bare cliffs of our beautiful, sheltered Torbay, my forebears dug them up. Do you see?

The Devonian was the Age of Fishes. The sea levels were so very high and the temperature of the water too hot for some, like our ruler, at thirty degrees in the tropics. So a great wrath from below was invoked by this heat. Now this is important if you consider the temperature of our own world now. But three quarters of all the species on this planet were made extinct across a slow, deliberate and sadistic cull lasting for several million years. At one point, you could say chemical weapons were employed by the Great Old One. The oxygen was removed from the waters, as the creator noted such a chronic dependence upon that gas amongst its myriad subjects. The wiping of the slate was also embellished by the Old One's wilful alterations in sea level, by changes in the climate, and by disruptions in soil fecundity. Even great rocks, passing through the heavens, were pulled down by its rage upon the seabed; a rage that our own baboonish antics today inadequately mimic. The fury that destroyed what had been created must have been incendiary, incandescent, and so cruel. My relatives only found fragments of the war-torn carcasses. They had been buried in rubble for 359 million years, but they were still smoking with a psychic trauma at a bacterial and subatomic level.

The visitor covered the world with ice again. It banished the earth from its sight and slept in the ruins. The survivors struggled on. The land welded together its wreckage into the Pangea supercontinent, in which every bleeding and shell-shocked continent came together to shiver in the ice. This diaspora began 290 million years ago. But what life and activity there was heated the planet all over again and melted the ice.

Such was the savagery and merciless genocide of the visitor upon awakening this time that all previous mass extinctions were rendered irrelevant. You could say that the Great Old One came out swinging with both eyes open, and The Great Dying began. The fish, and even the insects, were smashed and cast aside. He called down a rain of stones from that canopy of debris that flowed through the solar system. He opened his bellows and poisoned the earth with methane, rid the air of oxygen and suffocated his own multitude of abandoned children. Up rose the tyrant's seas too and down they crashed upon what we call life. The annihilation was near total. All but four percent of the species of the earth were put to death. My mother told me that his indifference alone had allowed the four percent to survive. All of what is left alive today began life in the four percent that survived The Great Dying.

200 hundred million years ago, and then 65 million years ago, he laid waste again and again to what swam, flew and crawled anew around his throne. And again, he used the climate as his weapon.

65 million years after that final massacre, our species has heated this earth again, and we have become so noisome, noisy and populous. Only the flora, water and the animal kingdom can sense the destruction and extinctions of the past ages, and they have begun to scream that name in alarm and terror again. They know that one of our creator's eyes has opened. Bleary with slumber maybe, but red with a demented rage that is as hot as a star.

As I watch the news on the screen in my home, and as I reel through the data from every kind of scientific observation and analysis that cognitively overloads our poor and troubled minds, in all of this chaos, I believe that we have fatally roused the Great Old One with our careless tenancy. We have begun to wake him with the heat that we have caused. The visitor is the sole creator, and always has been, but we have dared to ape a deity's excesses. So this time his wrath will explode with a creativity that not even the cruellest God or devil, in any of our mythologies, could even imagine to inflict upon its subjects.

This is why I think it best that you spend the day of the eclipse with your loved ones.

I sincerely wish that I, and my mother, and her mother, and her mother, and her mother too, really were all nothing but insane, deranged and delusional old women.

Your fond friend,
Cleo

■ □ ■

At the end of the dream, Cleo dreamed of the bay. The same dream she had been having for months. Or had it been months? It felt familiar, but how would she ever really know? But from Hope's Nose to Berry Head, she dreamed of the great body of water as it turned as black as oil and roiled like a weir as wide as an ocean.

The thin outline of the sun's silhouette diminished, then vanished.

Stars she recognised and many that she didn't recognise, and many other moving, shining objects, crisscrossed the vast canopy of sky, leaving silvery trails like those of snails upon patio stones.

And when the sun began to reappear the people who had gathered on the shore all called out a name, and their myriad, faraway voices sounded like a small wave washing upon sand before dying into silence.

The horizon was changing its shape.

Soon, it was as if all the water in the world was rushing forward from out there, and in the form of a long black wall. Behind the great wave, she thought she saw something vast and lumpen in shape, that could have been a new black mountain emerging from the earth's crust, rising to conceal the sun again.

■ ■ ■

Cleo awoke to the sound of screams. Tens of thousands of them. Screams on the shore one mile away and screams on the television screen that flickered beside the balcony doors of the living room. The whole world seemed to be shrieking at the same time.

Yolanda was on the balcony. She was naked. In her waking delirium, for some reason that Cleo could not understand, her nurse had come into her home that morning and removed all of her clothes.

'Yolanda!' Cleo called out with a throat so dry the word sounded like a croak.

Even in the din below the balcony, that now resembled a crowd in a football stadium, or a hundred school playgrounds filled with terror, Yolanda seemed to hear Cleo. The nurse turned around, smiling.

As she stepped into the room the first thing Cleo noticed was the eye tattooed upon Yolanda's flat, brown stomach. An eye that she recognised. She'd seen it around and it was a good likeness.

The wind that hit the building turned the curtains vertical and Yolanda staggered, but never stopped smiling. Her face was wet with the tears of an intense, private joy.

The ground shook and everything in the apartment rattled. Amelia, Mary, Olive and Judith's pictures fell down upon the sideboard, as did the preserved and pressed weeds that hung upon the walls.

The din from outside could have been a plane crashing in a thunderstorm, or the very earth being twisted and broken within a pair of great hands. The sea didn't even sound like the sea anymore. The sea was an animal's roar. Cleo believed most of the air in the room was soon sucked back out through the balcony doors.

No more than a few feet in front of Cleo's seat, Yolanda opened her mouth, but Cleo had no chance of hearing what came out of it. By the movement of the nurse's lips she was certain, though, that a name had been called. And as Yolanda helped her out of her chair and began moving her towards the balcony, either to see what was happening, or to become a part of it, Cleo winced and then whimpered when she saw the long, livid gills where Yolanda's ribs should have been.

Cthulhu

The foremost characteristic of the great old one known as Cthulhu is his enormous size. He dwarfs all living things, and indeed, all spiritual creatures that from time to time descend from the higher spheres. The elephant and behemoth cannot challenge his vast bulk. Even the mighty leviathan of the deeps is a toy for him to play with. He has been called the mountain that walks, and with good reason, for his head brushes the clouds, and each stride he takes is measured in furlongs. When his vitality waxes his body becomes larger, and when his strength wanes, he diminishes in size, yet always he is immense.

It is a curious fact that material representations of Cthulhu tend to be of no great size. This may be due to the utter futility in trying to express the sheer magnitude of this being with any sculpture or engraving. The artists who represent him have fled to the opposite extreme, and encapsulate him in small carven figures of stone, or on little plaques of hardened clay that may be held on the hand.

These figures depict a godlike being who squats on a block of stone with his upper limbs dangling over his knees. At first glance he appears to be humanlike in his shape, but a closer examination reveals that this is an illusion. It is true that he has two limbs that might be said to be legs, and two other limbs that can be called arms, but both end in hooked talons like those of a hawk, and his body is little more than a swollen mass. His head is massive, but as for his face, he has none, only a wriggling tangle of rootlike appendages that writhe about his head as they test the air. Within this mass is hidden his mouth. His eyes are small black beads, akin to those of an insect, and three in number on each side of his pulpy head arranged in the pattern of a descending triangle. The squamous flesh that covers his body is a kind of gray color tending to green, and covered with bumps like the skin of a toad.

It is said that the substance of his body is not like earthly flesh, but that it has the consistency and appearance of translucent slime, similar in this respect to the bodies of the sea creatures known as jellyfish. When broken apart it immediately reforms itself, for Cthulhu's body is sustained by the force of his mind, and as long as his physical form is held complete and perfect within his mind, his body can never be destroyed by violence.

From his shoulders spread leathern wings that most nearly resemble those of a bat. They appear ludicrously tiny—far too small to bear him into the air—but they are depicted in their inactive state by the artists of the little carvings that represent his form. When he flies through the air, or through the airless spaces between the stars, his wings spread wide and inflate to such an enormous size that they blot out the sun and turn day to night. Each beat of these heaven-spanning vanes is enough to knock down whole forests of trees, or to raise great waves that inundate cities.

Upon these mighty wings he flew to our world from alien stars. His method of locomotion is unique, for when he wishes to travel through the heavenly spheres, he causes certain stars to glow more brightly and explode with great violence, and the force of these explosions, reverberating through the higher planes, propels him forward, as a ship is driven across the sea by the wind that fills its sail.

inside his vast head, which appears to have no skull to lend it a distinct solid form, throbs and undulates the greatest brain in the universe. With it Cthulhu controls those slaves who worship him as a god and serve his purposes. In the past, by using thought alone he could send his mind forth across the world and call to him the scattered cults of his worshippers. He came to them in their dreams and gave them visions of strange worlds far removed from our own. Some men he drove mad, but the others who remain sane were changed, and thereafter they adored him.

Only the unplumbed depths of the ocean could contain him, and that is where he lies, in the southern ocean on the backside of this world, far from any island or human habitation. At one time in the history of our terrestrial globe this remote region was a continent, and here Cthulhu ruled from his citadel atop its highest mountain, where he built a great city called R'lyeh. From his stone house he could look far across his lands and direct the alien creatures that inhabited them with his thoughts. This was before the rise of man above the level of mere beasts.

From R'lyeh he conducted wars against an alien race known as the Elder Things who inhabited our world at the time of his coming, using his star-spawn as his army of conquest. Little is known of this spawn, save that each member is alike to Cthulhu in shape, only much smaller in size. But they, too, can control other intelligent creatures with the force of their minds, yet to a lesser degree than their master.

With the turning of the ages, the very pattern of the stars in the heavens changed and became noxious to the nature of this vast being, whose substance is not like that of any earthly form of life. Cthulhu fled from the hostile constellations and their destructive rays by closing himself up deep within the crypt of his great stone house, the walls of which offered him some protection. There, to further preserve himself, he cast himself into a kind of waking dream that was neither death nor life as we understand it.

Even in his unending dream, sealed within his stone house, such was the power of his mind that he was able to send forth his thoughts to his worshippers around the entire circumference of the world. He ordered them that when the ages passed, and the stars once again turned aright in the heavens, that they should come to him and release him from his house, for there was set a seal on the door that he could not pass from within. It was necessary that the seal be broken from outside before he could emerge from his tomb.

But even the gods are not immune to the vagaries of fate. Something occurred that Cthulhu, despite his vast knowledge, had not foreseen. R'lyeh and the entire continent of which it was a part suddenly sank to the depths, and miles of dark water closed over the stone house where he lay dreaming. Cthulhu found his mind cut off from his slaves on the surface of the world by this barrier of ocean, through which his thoughts could not penetrate. For know this, Cthulhu both hates and fears the salt water of the sea. He is a being suited by nature to the air and the dry land.

Yet it is prophesied that as R'lyeh sank when the stars went wrong, so at a future time when the stars become aligned once again, it will rise from the depths. Then the dreaming god will call his worshippers to him, and they will crack the seal on the door of his stone house, and Cthulhu will come forth as of old, to raven the world for his delight.

Until this great epoch is achieved, the cults of his worshippers continue to chant to him in an alien tongue so old, its origins have been forgotten, a single phrase that is both riddle and enigma, *"Ph'nglui mglw'nafh Cthulhu R'lyeh wgah'nagl fhtagn,"* which signified in our language, "In his house at R'lyeh, dead Cthulhu waits dreaming." This led a poet of Yemen, Abdul Alhazred, to compose the following couplet:

That is not dead which can eternal lie,
And with strange aeons even death may die.

For Cthulhu subsisted in a state that was neither death nor sleep, but a strange amalgam of the two, yet something else again to which there is no name. In his deathlike trance he dreamed of conquest and dominion. So he dreamed through the ages, and so he lies still, dreaming of the day when the stars come right, and the men of his cults take ships and sail to risen R'lyeh to release their god to raven and slay and burn across the face of this world, as he did in ages that are lost in time.

The center of Cthulhu's cult is near the lost city of Irem, renowned in ancient times as the City of Pillars, but there are lesser hereditary clans of his worshippers in the far-flung waste places of the world, where they have practiced their strange religion and made their sacrifices unmolested for millennia. One is atop the high mountains far to the east of Persia. Another is to be found in a fishing village far to the north and west, where the waters of the ocean are locked beneath ice for most of the year.

Vast is this old one's wisdom in arcane arts that to us appear to be forms of magic. He is said to be the high priest of the old ones, but what this designation signifies has been lost. It may mean that his grasp of alien sciences is greater than that of any other. Yet most of his intellectual power is devoted to the strategies of battle and the making of weapons of conquest, for before all else Cthulhu loves to make war. It was to conquer and lay waste that he came to our world. Only the salt water of the ocean and the malignity of the wandering stars restrain him. On the day the stars come right, and R'lyeh rises, man will lose his dominion over this earth and become a slave race to Cthulhu.

The Dark Gates

Martha Wells

Reja crept through the knee-high weeds, mud squishing under her sturdy but stylish boots. The day was so overcast it was nearly dark, even though her watch said it was midmorning. She muttered, "Next time, we send the Honorable Tamith to do this part."

Fletcher, moving near silently behind her, snorted.

She had to admit it was unlikely. Ahead, she could catch glimpses of the house through the trees. It was owned by Baron Mille, and had no resident staff, which supported the rumor that it was used for assignations. It had taken Reja a few days and a couple of judicious bribes to discover its location, and she hoped she was right about the current occupant being presently in town. If she wasn't right, this case might be over abruptly. *Nosy Lady Detective and Her Assistant Never Seen Again* was not a headline Reja wished to appear in the society pages.

She slipped through the copse of trees and crouched in the overgrown brush. "Don't touch that," she cautioned Fletcher in a whisper. "Stinging nettle."

Fletcher avoided it with a hiss of distaste. His ancestry might lead one to expect him to be more competent in the forest than the average human, but he had grown up in the city. So had Reja, but at least she had the benefit of childhood summers in the country.

From this sheltered vantage point, she had a good view of the house. It was small by the standards of the mind-bogglingly rich, three stories of light brown stone with a rather elegant conical turret, framed prettily against the giant oaks behind it. The immense towers of the Mille family mansion were just visible over the tops of those trees. There was no sign of movement in the empty windows or on the lawns.

Reja took a deep breath, touched the pistol in the pocket of her jacket, and stepped through a gap in the brush. Walking across the wet grass of the overgrown lawn toward the house made her feel as if every unfriendly eye in the world was on her. Her only option if caught was to say they were lost; she had dressed conservatively but finely enough to pass as a guest at one of the other wealthy houses nearby, in dark gray pants and a belted jacket of a steely blue to complement the soft brown of her skin. Fletcher wore dark clothes and looked like a housebreaker. There wasn't anything she could do about that.

They reached the service entrance at the back, tucked into a little cubby on the far side of the terrace. Reja had a set of lock picks, drills, and other devices for the opening of locked doors. As she set to work, Fletcher stopped her with a slim, too-pale hand on her sleeve. "There may be traps."

She shook her head. "He has no reason; he believes he's covered his tracks too well."

"People do things for no reason." Fletcher was grim, and Reja knew, correct. Surely Baron Mille, with enough money to buy most of the city, had no need for more power or influence. Reja cared nothing for what the monied and powerful chose to do to each other's jealously guarded fortunes, and she would not have accepted a case involving that. But the disappearance of Mille's stepdaughter and his wife's secretary was different.

After a short time, the lock yielded and Reja turned the handle.

Fletcher pushed the door open, but nothing sprang out at them, or exploded. Inside it was dark, the muted gray sunlight only falling far enough to illuminate a flagstone floor. Reja took the torch Fletcher handed her and switched it on.

They made it through a clean but deserted scullery and a kitchen and pantry that smelled only of coffee dregs and what must be yesterday's ham-and-pickle sandwiches. Reja checked the icebox briefly and found only prosaic contents. If Mille's new sorcerer Challis was abducting young persons and using their bodily parts for dark magics, he wasn't cutting them up in the kitchen.

"Odd," she told Fletcher as she closed the icebox. "Do you see a basement door?"

"No." Fletcher returned from a prowl through the pantry. "He's not doing it here. We'd smell it."

"Perhaps he's very tidy about it." Reja stepped past him and followed the short passage to the servants' door and the back of the house's front hall. They needed confirmation of their theories; being a sorcerer wasn't illegal, it was the kidnapping and murder that the authorities would frown on.

Reja's client Baroness Mille still expected her daughter Merita and the secretary Osgood Rodrign to be found alive, imprisoned somewhere. Reja would have liked to think that was the case. "Look for papers, books."

They flashed their lights over the downstairs parlor, lounge, a dining room, and music room, all bearing only slight signs of use. No books except for the leatherbound editions of classics and modern novels obviously purchased for the house along with its carpets and furniture, no papers except a crumpled bill for tailoring an evening suit, paid in cash, and a newspaper on a chair seat. Reja met Fletcher again in the front hall and said, "We need to find the room he sleeps in." She started up the stairs.

Reja had traced Challis's path through the city, always in places owned by or associated with Baron Mille. They weren't certain Challis was the one who had made Merita and Rodrign disappear, but he was the only new factor in the life of the carefully guarded Mille family. They knew Challis had been in Baron Mille's penthouse in the Vermillion

Towers, where the two young people had last been seen. They couldn't discover why the Baron, who had sorcerers of all kinds at his beck and call, had hired Challis, and why he had made such efforts to conceal his association with him.

The stairs made only the faint and occasional creak underfoot, a benefit of the expensive joinery. Then Reja realized she was listening for those individual creaks, that she had been listening to them for some time. That she had been listening... Listening...

Fletcher caught the belt of her jacket to pull her to a halt. Reja stumbled, gripped the bannister, and swore. She looked down at Fletcher. Some people found his dark eyes, the star-shaped pupils, difficult to read emotion in. Reja could tell his expression was wry. He said, "I won't say I told you so, but this is a trap."

"I hate these tricks," Reja muttered. And she was glad she had brought Fletcher, whose resistance to such sorcerous deceptions was far stronger than hers. They were probably walking in place, or perhaps already up in the hallway, while whatever illusion cloaked the stairs made them think they were still climbing. She fished in her pocket and brought out a silver ball of a glass so delicate it seemed like it might break in her hand like a soap bubble. Reja lifted the ball and slammed it down on the steps ahead. The ball shattered into a puff of silver dust.

Reja expected the illusion to shatter as well, as delicate spell structures would not survive contact with the pure silver. But light sparked as if electricity streaked through the silver dust. For several instants it outlined a door at the top of the stairs. She shined her torch through it and the light fell on the upper hall, the patterned carpet lining the boards. The door faded a heartbeat later as the dust settled. The torchlight shone only on the stairs and the curious darkness at the top that Reja had only just noticed.

Reja looked at Fletcher. "What the hell was that?"

He stared at the spot where the door had formed, perfect brow furrowed, biting his lip in consternation. "How many more spellbreakers do you have?"

"Four." When she had filled her pockets at the office, it had seemed like more than enough. "It was a portal?" She was reluctant to say the word. Fletcher's fay ancestors had used such things for travel to and among the hidden places of the fayre realm, but they weren't common now. "To where?"

"Back to the house." He met her gaze, worried. "Where we just were. But aren't anymore."

Reja absorbed that information. "Right. The stairs—"

"Have been pulled out of our world and partially into another, probably right after we started up them. Whatever did this will be nearby."

"And probably coming closer." She pulled out two more of the silver balls. "Get ready."

Reja flung the first ball against the steps and lunged forward. Fletcher's hand on her back propelled her upward and kept them together. Now would be a very bad time to be separated.

Sparks of light flashed and the door formed above them. Reja tossed the second ball and barreled up toward it. But as they reached the top of the stairs the light faded. A shove from behind sent her over the top step. She skidded on the carpet and tumbled across the floor.

Fletcher landed beside her, neatly catlike. Reja twisted to look, shining her torch down the stairs. The light reached the whole way down now to the front hall, and glinted off the chandelier in prosaic "there's no magical dimension shifting trap here no none at all" fashion.

Fletcher said, "We need to get out of here."

"Search first, fast," Reja countered, and scrambled to her feet.

The third bed chamber was the right one, a fact made obvious by the unmade bed and the clothes hanging in the open wardrobe. Reja went to the wardrobe first, found a crumpled handkerchief there and stuffed it into her own pocket. Fletcher tossed her the satchel as she headed for the desk. He dragged open dresser drawers as she clawed papers and books into the bag. There was no need to be subtle, no time to cover their traces.

She flinched when Fletcher caught her arm, then froze to listen. Steps sounded from somewhere below, heavy, slapping steps as if a large man in swim fins stalked across the tiles. Reja was fairly certain it wasn't a large man in swim fins. She whispered, "Go."

She slung the bag over her shoulder as Fletcher went to the window and shoved the sash open. The footsteps below went from a walking pace to a run and Reja knocked a chair over to get to the window, her heart pounding. Fletcher stepped up onto the window frame. As Reja reached him, he grabbed her around the waist and flung them both out into empty air.

Reja didn't scream, only because all the air in her lungs shot up into her throat and choked her to silence. They landed in soft grass and rolled, Fletcher taking the weight and the shock on his wiry body. He let her go and Reja staggered upright, caught his arm, and dragged him to his feet.

Framed in the window was a large gray shape, and if Reja had been given to imaginative fancies she would have said it was a dead man whose rotting body had been shored up with pieces of wood and broken stone and dry brush. It put one foot on the sill to jump and Reja saw nothing after that because she and Fletcher were sprinting across the field toward the road.

They were both long-legged fast runners with great motivation but the thing was simply too fast. Breathing hard from terror, Reja dug in her pocket. She considered the gun, but too many magical creatures were immune to bullets. She whipped around and flung the silver ball instead. The creature was barely ten steps behind her and the ball struck it squarely in the chest.

It jolted to a halt, pieces of its assemblage of debris dropping away. It was a dead man, half his head gone, still dressed in the rotting fabric of a funeral suit. There was a cemetery and chapel a few miles away, Reja remembered. Then Fletcher grabbed her wrist, urging her on, and they ran again.

They crossed the lawn and crashed through a rhododendron hedge. The road was at the bottom of the next field. Then Reja heard the bushes rustle behind her and looked back. She gasped out a curse. The damn thing was still coming.

It staggered through the hedge, wavering now that the deadfall branches and rocks and debris were no longer shoring up its rotten flesh. It was still coming far too fast.

A horn blared from the road. She looked ahead and saw the gleaming silver town car with a four-door cabin just rounding the curve. Fletcher waved frantically.

The car swerved off the road and plowed across the field toward them, powerful engine digging ruts in the wet ground. *If he gets that car stuck*, Reja thought, *I'm going to be dead and angry.*

As they neared it the car swerved around and presented the passenger side to them, slowing just enough for them to reach it. The front door flew open and Reja put on a last burst of speed, grabbed the handle, and flung herself in.

She scrambled onto the seat. Fletcher landed on the running board and shouted, "Go, go!"

The Honorable Tamith spun the wheel and floored the car back toward the road. "What the hell is that?" he demanded.

"We were hoping you'd know!" Reja dragged the door shut, then squirmed around to lean over the backseat and unroll the window. Fletcher crammed his body through the space and fell across the backseat.

Through the rear windscreen, Reja had a good view of the creature racing toward them across the field. Dirt clods from the car's ruts flew up toward it, filling in the holes and gaps in its legs as it ran faster and faster. Her throat constricted. She cleared it and said, "Fletcher, lock the doors and roll up the window."

The car rocked as it climbed back to the paved road and put on a spurt of speed. Unfortunately, so did the creature. Tamith said, "Reja, dear, tell me when it's on our bumper."

Reja gripped the back of the seat to steady herself. "Soon, soon... Now!"

Tamith hit the brakes and threw the big car into reverse. The creature slammed into the trunk and bounced off, pieces of dead flesh flying. Tamith changed gear and hit the gas again and they roared away.

Grimly watching the horrible thing crawl around on the road, collecting pieces of itself, Reja said, "This case is more complicated than we thought."

□ □ □

When they were far enough away to risk a brief stop, Reja took over the driving so Tamith and Fletcher could look through the papers retrieved from Challis's desk. Once they were near the city, she would let Fletcher take over as she had no intention of driving two men through a fashionable part of town. Female chauffeurs had a somewhat risqué reputation and she didn't want anyone to recognize her and report it to a society gossip column. Reja's large number of relatives came from several different cultural backgrounds but all of them would be united in coming completely unhinged if they read such a story. Telling them that Tamith preferred the company of men and that Fletcher thought sex with humans was disgusting would not placate them. "Well?" she demanded after several moments of silence and rustling pages. "So how did our friend Challis create that thing?"

They had already told Tamith about the dimensional trap in the stairs, and he had said, "A human sorcerer couldn't do that."

"It doesn't have to be a human," Fletcher had pointed out. Fletcher, despite, or perhaps because of, his combined fay and human ancestry, was a great believer in evidence. Reja, whose father had been a police inspector in Parscia, was rather fond of it herself. Her mother had been a Rienish heiress and a spy during the Gardier War, so Reja blamed her heritage for any impulses toward lawlessness.

Reja glanced at Tamith, slumped in the passenger seat and studying the pages. A scion of high society, Tamith was a lean, knobby, rawboned man, his dark hair tousled from exertion. He was Rienish and as pale as Reja was dark, and it gave his face an unhealthy cast. Though that was more the late nights and unhealthy attraction to sweet liquors, rather than his studies in sorcery. He handed a sheaf of papers back to Fletcher and said, "I just don't think it's a fay sorcerer. He wouldn't need all these notes and calculations, for one thing."

After a moment of studying the pages, Fletcher said, "Maybe you're right. He seems to be trying to figure out how portals work."

Tamith turned another page, and handed Fletcher one of the books. "If a fay sorcerer didn't know that, he'd be a regular wet blanket around the fayre rings. Though a portal and a transdimensional pocket like you encountered aren't exactly the same thing. The only reason to put a portal in a pocket like that..." Tamith looked up, brows lifted. "Is to be able to get to whatever's inside."

"We knew the creature came to collect us," Reja said, ignoring the chill prickle of unease on her skin. She checked the rearview mirror again, but the road, shadowed by the heavy pines, remained empty.

"It wasn't expecting you to escape and rampage around as you did. Which is why I think it wasn't human magic, or fay magic. It was something... natural. Like a spider building a web for prey."

Reja said, "As if something was told to guard the house, but it wasn't sentient enough to make contingency plans?"

"Yes, something like that." Tamith frowned in annoyance. "There's also no mention in any of this of needing sacrifices, or body parts, or blood, or any of the usual to open this portal. Nothing about Merita Mille or the secretary Rodrign. It looks like Challis has been trying to work out an incantation he doesn't understand. There's mention of appealing to some... entity, or maybe deity, or natural force..."

"He has a partner," Fletcher added. "There are two different handwritings here."

"I saw that." Tamith twisted around to ask him, "Have you ever seen that language before? The one in the second hand."

"No, and the letter groups associated with the horizontal bars are distinctive enough I'm sure I'd remember," Fletcher answered.

Reja negotiated a difficult turn onto a broader road. "But what is the portal for? Is Mille looking for a way into fayre?" For generations, opportunists had been looking for ways into the fayre realms, and the treasure and powerful magic said to be housed there, while bypassing the fay who guarded them. She just couldn't see why a man as rich as Baron Mille would bother with it.

"Hard to tell. From these notes it sounds like they think if they open the portal, this entity or deity will be waiting inside it. We'll just have to find Challis and ask him," Tamith said.

Reja took one hand off the wheel to pull out the handkerchief she had taken from Challis's coat pocket. She passed it over to Tamith. "That will be up to you."

■ ■ ■

They reached the relative safety of the highway, where it stretched out of the heavy forest and crossed the open plain toward the city. Reja pulled over to a roadside diner, the green neon decorating its pediment gleaming in the damp gray afternoon light.

Reja and Fletcher found a table in the back, taking the books and papers in with them for perusal while Tamith carried the handkerchief off to the men's room to do the location spell. They were lucky the place was sparsely occupied, mostly by a few locals.

Reja ordered coffee and started to go through the documents, beginning with the book in Rienish. It was a more formal version of the language that showed it had been written perhaps forty or so years ago. After studying it for a time, she told Fletcher, "This book is by a man who lists examples of various people who had strange personality changes, or who went mad suddenly and believed themselves to be other people. He thinks they were replaced."

"Replaced? Like changelings?" Fletcher squinted at the odd handwriting on one of the pages.

The counterman brought their coffee, eyeing them both warily, as they were clearly not locals, or tourists, or wealthy estate owners slumming with the common people, and Fletcher was obviously part fay—although he looked bedraggled and a little more human at the moment. Long car rides tended to make him ill, from a combination of the motion and the presence of all the steel. But the counterman voiced no objection to their presence. Considering what Tamith was doing in the men's room, Reja decided to tip generously.

"Not like changelings." She looked at the binding. There was no printer's name or publisher's mark. It might be a private volume, like a family history or travelogue, meant only for a few readers. "Many of these afflicted say that someone or something else appeared in their mind and tried to take over their body."

Fletcher grimaced. "That's ugly. It's human magic, not fay."

Reja did not take offense, knowing what he meant. "It's odd." Though it didn't seem relevant to the talk of portals and strange deities in the other documents.

They had both managed to get through two cups of coffee and slices of pie cautiously offered by the counterman by the time Tamith returned. He looked paler than usual and his eyes were sunken. Spells tended to take their toll and Tamith's preference for nightclubs didn't exactly build stamina. Fletcher shoved a coffee cup and a plate of pie toward him as Tamith slumped into the booth. Between mouthfuls, Tamith said, "Challis might be taking a trip," and handed over the map.

Reja leaned over to check it, and started to dig money out of her wallet to pay the bill. By the marks, Tamith's spell had located Challis in the city's Aerodrome. "No, he's not leaving. Or if he is, it's a strange coincidence. Baron Mille is giving a large party on his airship this evening."

Fletcher frowned at the remains of the pie. "We suspect something happened at the Vermillion Towers penthouse that caused the disappearance of the stepdaughter and secretary. Now Challis is going on an airship. Maybe the portal spell has to be done at a high altitude."

"It's suggestive," Reja said. Challis couldn't sneak two captives, or two corpses, onto the airship without Mille's connivance. "We have to go to that party." It was one of the more coveted society events, but not so exclusive that there wouldn't be a large crowd to mingle about with. There was a pay telephone booth in the corner, and Reja would need to phone the Baroness before they left, to obtain invitations for them to board the airship.

"Oh, god," Tamith sighed, and ladled more sugar into his coffee. "I was hoping to avoid that."

"Being trapped hundreds of feet above the ground with a possibly murderous sorcerer?" Fletcher asked.

"Being trapped hundreds of feet above the ground with a bunch of pretentious snobs," Tamith countered. "At least the buffet will be worth it."

■ ■ ■

They stopped at Reja's apartment to change into evening clothes. She had to leave her pistol behind, but there was no other choice; Mille's guards would not allow it on the airship.

They sped through the city on the elevated road, past buildings clad in limestone and polished granite, with lapis pediments or vertical striping of bronze or chrome, and figured friezes above the entrances. Reja loved this city, for all its silly emphasis on high society.

The Aerodrome bridged the river, looming above the smaller buildings scattered around it, a giant bowl-shaped structure of broad steel girders, stretching up to support the curving expanse of gray-green walls. Hundreds of round windows dotted those walls, providing natural light for the booking halls and offices within. Just above the roofline, three huge, sleek, banded-gray crescents were visible. They were the top edges of the balloons of three dirigibles, fastened to their mooring masts and tied securely off to the boarding structures.

But hanging above the Aerodrome was something that dwarfed all of the other dirigibles. It was Baron Mille's flying platform, practically a floating castle. Two dirigibles, easily as large as the passenger carriers tied up below them, supported the elegantly curved structure of a multistoried cabin. It was too big to dock down in the Aerodrome's giant bowl; the sunlight glinted off the silvery sides of the balloons and the propellers of its multiple engines, now motionless as it sat at the dock. Each balloon was attached to a double set of mooring masts, and the whole was anchored with huge cables to a raised and covered boarding platform on the outer rim of the Aerodrome's highest wall, which had been specially built for it.

Tamith craned his neck to see. "Bloody huge, isn't it? One can't help but think Baron Mille is overcompensating for something."

"Yes. Too huge." Reja eyed it with less enthusiasm. "It's held together with spells, you know, or the wind would rip it apart. So we have to hope the wizards who helped build it weren't incompetent."

The drive split off toward the first-class entrance circle, where fashionable people were being helped out and guided to the smoked glass doors, as photographers snapped photos for the society pages. The entrance was guarded by tall bronze sculptures of aeroplanes standing on their tails, their wings forming a gleaming pediment.

In the cool marble lobby, they breezed past the domed hall that led to the main concourse, booking halls, cafes, and lounges and went straight to the bronze-embossed elevator doors that led up to the private embarkation levels.

The elevator drew to a stop and Reja stepped out onto the first-class embarkation floor. It was a large room, with one wall of windows looking out over the river, the view now obscured by the gray wall of one of the passenger airships. A few guests stood amid plush chairs and potted palms, having last minute pre-boarding cocktails.

Reja had barely a moment to get her bearings, when an older woman swept up to her. "Madame Flinn, I have your invitations. And someone wishes to speak to you privately."

Reja glanced at Fletcher and got a nod of acknowledgement; he would stay behind and watch for their quarry.

The woman led them across the room to a private parlor, then stepped out and shut the door once they were inside.

The Baroness Mille sat perched on one of the armchairs, her face strained and anxious. She gestured Reja to a seat and barely seemed to notice Tamith was in the room. She said, "Is there any news?"

"Not yet, Madame," Reja said. Not the news that the Baroness wanted, that her daughter was safely found. "Have you perhaps ever heard the Baron mention the inaccessible fayre realms?"

The Baroness's forehead furrowed. "No."

"He's not mentioned the fay at all?" Tamith asked.

She shook her head. "That's a pastime for fortune hunters, isn't it. Mille would never be interested." She touched her temple and winced. "But he's changed in the past year. Perhaps he's become so greedy he can't stand to have anything barred to him." She turned to Reja anxiously. "Is that what happened to Merita and Osgood? He traded them to the fay?"

Tamith drew breath for another question but Reja held up a hand. "Changed how?" she asked.

The Baroness looked away, her frown deepening. "It started last winter, when he returned from his property up in the north. We've lived separate lives for some years now, but after that he became distant, cold." Her mouth twisted bitterly. "I dismissed it, thinking he was only distracted by an affair, or a new business deal. But then that sorcerer Challis arrived and he became secretive..."

"You are certain this happened after the Baron returned from the north," Reja said. The Baroness hadn't told her this before.

"Yes, Mille had an accident there, which caused a serious illness. For some time I attributed his behavior to bad health."

Reja felt she was on to something. "What sort of accident?"

"A fissure had opened up near one of the old closed mines. The ground is unstable there, it's not uncommon. But for some reason he wanted to explore it. He went in alone. Osgood and the others with him heard him cry out and they went in and he had fainted. He regained consciousness once they had gotten him out and back to the car, but he was unable to leave his bed for three weeks before he recovered fully." She shook her head. "The physicians couldn't find anything wrong. Several thought it was a stroke, though one said it was just a severe shock. But Osgood told me that he and the other men who went into the cave didn't see anything, and none of them were made ill. It was just an empty grotto."

It was all highly suggestive, though of what, Reja wasn't sure. "Osgood Rodrign was there. Was Merita?"

"No, she was here in town, with me."

Reja sat back, considering it. Perhaps Osgood had seen something that the other men hadn't, and told Merita. Mysterious grottos, illnesses. It was bizarre but it seemed to fit in with the strange and possibly mad writing on the papers and in the books.

A soft tone sounded from the speaker high in the wall. The Baroness said, "That's the boarding signal for Mille's airship. You had better go."

Reja stood. "I will contact you when we return. I may have more questions."

As Tamith closed the door behind him, he said, "You think that Challis had that book for a reason? Mille thinks he's been possessed?"

"Maybe." Reja hesitated. The room was emptying as the last of the passengers headed toward the elevator. Fletcher was over by the potted palms, watching them worriedly. They didn't have time to delay. She started toward the elevators. "Perhaps Challis has encouraged that belief for his own reasons." Perhaps Challis needed the Baron's resources to open this portal and contact the deity or creature he believed lay within.

■ ■ ■

They took the elevator up again to the new boarding platform, endured a brief search by the Baron's bodyguards, and crossed the broad covered ramp into the airship. Reja followed the other passengers through a roomy foyer and corridor, and then into a lounge the size of a ballroom, with a ceiling arching high above. It was hard to believe they were on an airship, except for a slight uneasy stirring in Reja's stomach when the thickly carpeted floor moved gently under her feet.

The walls were paneled in fine dark woods, broken with strips of chrome. Curving couches, benches, and armchairs stood about in conversational groups, all upholstered in brilliant white, gleaming under crystal and silver sconces and pendant lights. Waiters in Mille's livery circulated through the richly dressed, already chattering crowd, offering glasses of wine and cocktails. Reja recognized a number of the guests, from seeing them in person at nightclubs or at events, or from the society pages. There were those from the high end of society, such as the new Parscian ambassador and her husband, and the lower end, such as the star of a rather risqué stage show.

Reja took a glass, and behind it murmured, "Do you see him?"

Tamith surveyed the room with the sharp eye of a savannah hunter's guide, concealing his interest behind a wine glass. "Just the usual collections of stiffs and drunkards and hangers-on, all looking vaguely horrified to find themselves trapped on an airship in each other's company. I don't see Mille, either."

"Challis has been trying to avoid being seen in public, he wouldn't stay in this crowd," Fletcher said, keeping his voice low. "If we're right and high places have something to do with this portal he and Mille want to create, he's going to need an opening to the outside."

"They might just need the altitude, which means they could be anywhere on this giant flying waste of money," Tamith said.

"Yes, but we need to start somewhere." Reja felt her stomach try to flip. The airship had cast off and was now moving upward. "Let's try the observation deck first."

They started to make their way through the crowd, Reja following Tamith's lead in behaving as if they were being summoned by acquaintances on the far side of the room.

They split up at the far wall, with Reja heading toward the corridor where the ladies powder room lay and Fletcher and Tamith wandering with apparent idleness toward the casino rooms. Navigating by memory of newspaper photographs of the airship's launch, Reja went past the powder rooms and found the forward stairwell up to the observation deck.

She went cautiously, trying to tread lightly on the metal steps. Below the deck on this side were cubicles with upholstered booths, meant for passengers to retire to if the view above was too overwhelming. She checked each one and silently cursed the designers who had built this ship with so many nooks and crannies. She took the stairs up another level and stepped out onto the glass-covered deck.

The wide walkway stretched nearly the length of the airship, the outer glass wall curving almost two stories above her head. No one moved on it, but there were alcoves built into the inner wall, as there were on the deck immediately below. The view revealed the sparkling expanse of the river and the stone and metal-clad buildings clustered on the far side. The elevated track of the hanging railway wove through them, glinting in the setting sun. The airship was still moving upward, and to the west, toward the edge of the city.

She started down the deck, still holding the wine glass, checking the alcoves. If someone official popped up, she would look like a wandering party guest and would hopefully avoid any pesky questions. She had been expecting to see an outside gallery, attached to the outer side of the curved glass wall, but there wasn't one. She was certain she had seen one in the photographs of the airship. It might have been removed at some point during the construction.

Movement in the shadows of the stern stairwell was exciting for a moment until she realized it was Fletcher and Tamith. Reja moved faster, glancing into each alcove, until she drew near the large pillar in the center. It was streaked with white and clear glass, and on a sunny day would fill the deck with the sparkle of a giant chandelier. Tamith stepped out of the last alcove on his side and lifted his arms in exasperated defeat. Reja drew breath to say they would have to search the private areas of the ship. Then Fletcher held up a hand and hissed for silence.

Voices, from above. Reja stepped back and looked up at the top of the glass pillar. She couldn't see anything but a large square roof plate. No, it wasn't a roof plate, it was an open gallery, for the voices were surely coming from it. She tossed her wine glass onto one of the padded benches and ran both hands over the glass pillar. She whispered, "There has to be a door!"

Tamith and Fletcher took the other side, joining Reja in frantically searching. Tamith found it, a small catch in the side that faced toward the inner deck wall. He pulled the door open, revealing a set of spiral stairs twisting up through the pillar.

Tamith started up first, thwarting Reja's attempt to shoulder him aside. She toed her high heels off and followed him, Fletcher behind her.

As they climbed, the voices became clearer, though what they were talking about was still opaque.

"—don't understand. I can show you the calculations. What you're trying to do just won't work—" A man, young, perhaps Challis.

"He won't listen." The deeper tone was Baron Mille. Reja had seen him speak at a charity event. He sounded exhausted, perhaps ill. "I'm begging you, Challis, you know what you have to do."

The third voice was too low to make out the words. It was rough, strained.

Tamith paused just below the last twist of the stairs that would make him visible to the men above. He looked down at Reja, baffled. She shook her head to show she had no idea what they were talking about either. Fletcher, squeezed in beside her, shrugged. Perhaps they were wrong about the portal. But something strange was clearly going on, and Mille and Challis and the other man weren't standing out on that gallery arguing for their amusement.

Reja flinched at a loud thump from above, directly over her head. Tamith surged forward around the last turn and she ran after him.

She came out onto a platform, a glass bubble sitting above the observation deck, with wide doors meant to slide open and give the occupants the dubious pleasure of being exposed to the wind and elements. Challis and Mille had fallen against those doors, struggling desperately.

Mille was a large man, with broad shoulders and a middle running only a little to fat, and his hair was sparse and gray. She had seen his photograph in the newspapers, but in person he was far more rough-looking than Reja had expected. Challis was smaller and slimmer but younger, his long dark hair stuck to his forehead with sweat.

"Baron, stop!" Reja shouted. The only thing between the two men and a spectacular fall to their death was the catch holding the doors closed. Tamith and Fletcher started forward, then stopped abruptly as Challis staggered back.

A knife protruded from the white of his shirt front, blood already blossoming around it. He met Reja's startled gaze, his expression shock mixed with horror and desperation. He started to speak, then Mille fell forward, knocking against Challis as he collapsed. Challis stumbled into the wall and went to his knees.

Tamith lunged forward and caught him, and Fletcher went to Mille. Reja spotted an alarm on the inner wall, a small metal box with a red lever inside, meant to summon help if the glass cracked or something else terrible happened. She stepped to it, grabbed the lever, and pulled. A dull gong-like tone began to sound somewhere on the other side of the metal wall, and Reja went to help Tamith try to staunch Challis's wound.

"Mille's alive," Fletcher reported.

Tamith had managed to lay Challis down on the metal floor. Reja winced, seeing that Tamith's effort would come to naught. When Challis had fallen against the wall, it had jolted the knife inside the already terrible wound. She leaned over him, patting Challis's face. "Tell us, where are Merita and Rodrign? What happened to them?"

He tried to catch her hand, and gasped, "He said he wants to leave, but he's lying— He wants— He wants power from—" He made a noise in his throat, then blood-froth bubbled from his lips. His body went limp, and she watched the light fade from his eyes.

Reja muttered, "Damn it! Did you hear what he said?"

Tamith grimaced. "Somebody wanted power from this deity in the portal, that's obvious."

But who, Reja thought. *The Baron?*

"Where's the other one?" Fletcher asked. "There were three of them up here."

Reja glanced around, not that there was anywhere to hide. The narrow stairwell they had come up and the doors into empty air were the only exits. *We weren't wrong*, she thought. *We all heard three voices.*

Then Mille's bodyguards arrived, and Reja was too busy explaining to ask any questions of her own.

■ □ ■

For a moment there, they were lucky not to be seized by the guards and locked up. But Mille regained consciousness quickly, telling his men, "No, no, they're my guests. It was Challis who attacked me."

That was a relief. Instead of locked up awaiting docking and an arrest, they were sitting in a parlor in Mille's private quarters, while Mille's servants, personal physician, the airship's captain, and even the catering manager went back and forth. The guards kept out the curious guests who made money on the side slipping scandal and gossip to the newspapers.

The parlor was an elegant room with gold and white furnishings and no window. As a crewman in uniform passed through, coming out of the inner sanctum, Reja said, "Young man, when are we docking?"

He paused and touched his cap. "I don't know, madam. Right now we're holding in place."

"Really?" Tamith frowned. "Doesn't the Baron need a hospital?"

"And have the authorities been contacted?" Reja added. Since an attempted murder had just occurred, it seemed the obvious next step.

From the crewman's hesitation, he found it odd, too. "The Baron said he wanted to continue the party."

"I see. Thank you." As he moved away out of earshot, Reja turned to Fletcher and Tamith. "Well?"

Fletcher leaned forward. "Could Mille have some way of knowing that we've been following Challis?"

Tamith whispered, "If he did, it's hardly likely to frighten him. We don't have any evidence against him."

"He doesn't know that," Reja said. She made an impatient gesture. "Mille and Challis had someone up there with them, and who—or what—ever it is, it's still on this airship."

"You think it climbed out that door and got back inside somewhere else while we were all distracted?" Tamith glanced up warily as another secretary-assistant bustled past.

"I could have done it," Fletcher said. "There are a lot of fay and part-fay who could."

"I need to get in there to see the Baron." Reja nodded toward the doorway. "You two go now, wait outside. He won't let the three of us in if he's hiding something."

Tamith and Fletcher exchanged a look. Fletcher said, "He might not let you in either."

"Then we'll try something else." Reja stood decisively, and good manners brought both men to their feet as well.

"If you don't come out in ten minutes—" Fletcher began.

Reja conceded that the precaution was probably wise. "Give me fifteen, and don't barge in. If I can get him to talk, I don't want to be interrupted."

Tamith and Fletcher left reluctantly, and Reja waylaid the next secretary to pass by. She said, "Tell the Baron I wish a few moments of his time, please."

The man looked uncertain. "The Baron is very—"

"Lucky to be alive, surely. Tell him I saw, and heard, most of the encounter, and I merely wanted to make certain he was well." It was vague enough to hopefully be worrisome to anyone with a guilty conscience or any secrets to conceal.

The secretary hesitated again, but he didn't know her and was unsure of her status with the Baron. Clearly deciding to err on the side of caution, he said, "Just a moment," and headed back toward the office.

After only a moment, he reappeared. "This way, please, madam."

Reja followed him through a passage, a small foyer, and then into the private office.

The room was full of the light of sunset, with big slanted windows looking out on a breathtaking view of the edge of the city and the harbor beyond it. The heavy glass shield kept Reja's fear of falling at bay, though she certainly wouldn't want to lean on it. A rich goldwood sideboard on the far wall held a chrome radio set that looked as if it was meant for more complicated uses than simply playing music. The Baron was on his feet, his head bandaged but clothes still rumpled from his adventure. He said, "Thank you, Wills. Give us some privacy, would you?"

The secretary withdrew. A low cocktail table and several gold armchairs stood nearby, and at the Baron's gesture, Reja took a seat.

He remained standing, like a man who wanted to pace but didn't quite dare. He said, "I did want to thank you in person for sounding the alarm. I don't believe we've met."

Reja felt a tight sensation behind her breastbone that had nothing to do with the airship's movement. It was a combination of trepidation and the thrill of the hunt. He was agitated, suspicious and trying to conceal it. Afraid. What he was afraid of, she had no idea. It wasn't poor dead Challis, though it might be fear that Mille's conspiracy with him would be exposed. Reja said, "I am known to the Baroness. She kindly presented me with the invitations for myself and my friends."

She thought she detected both a trace of relief and a trace of extra wariness in his expression. The Baron said, "You're a friend of hers, then?"

"She has hired me occasionally." Reja kept her gaze on his.

The wariness increased. "Something to do with fashion?"

Reja smiled. "I am a private inquiry agent."

They stared at each other for a long moment. Sweat beaded on the Baron's brow. He said, "And you wish to be paid."

That settled that. Innocent people sometimes behaved exactly like guilty people for absolutely no reason, but they never offered to pay you to go away. Now Reja just needed to find out what the Baron had done with Merita Mille and Osgood Rodrign. She said, demurely, "That is not necessary."

The Baron stepped to the desk and sounded hearty and almost undisturbed as he said, "No, it's my pleasure." He opened two drawers before he managed to find a check fold.

Reja stood and stepped closer, hoping for a look at the contents of the desk. "I did wonder where the other man was," she began. "We did hear three voices—"

He was writing the check, and the words and figures were not in a language Reja recognized. But she did know that handwriting. She had studied it in the diner, while waiting for Tamith. It was the second hand on Challis's documents.

Apparently oblivious to what he was doing, the Baron said, "It was probably a trick of sound. The acoustics are unusual in those glass observation chambers. Someone might have been speaking near a ventilation duct—" He straightened to hand her the check, and froze as he saw her expression. Then he looked down at what he had written, and his face turned horrified.

Reja said quickly, "What has happened to you? Tell me, I may be able to help." *He must be under a spell.* Surely the book from Challis's desk was wrong, it wasn't possible to be infected with other personalities like a disease. That couldn't be what was wrong with Mille.

He opened his mouth, tried to speak, but strained, garbled noises came out of his throat. Reja turned toward the door, meaning to shout for help. Movement at the corner of her eye made her duck instinctively and the punch brushed past her braids. She had a heartbeat to decide whether to grab up a chair and hit him or go for the door and scream for help. The chair was too light to take down a man of Mille's size, so she lunged for the door and shouted at the top of her lungs.

The next blow slammed her into the wall.

She bounced off and hit the floor, stunned. She managed to get her eyes open in time to see Mille lifting the heavy radio set and smashing it against the glass of the window. It shattered and wind swept in, cold and damp. *He's going to jump,* Reja thought, still dazed. But Mille held something small and gleaming in his hand. He twisted it back and forth, muttering. *Oh hell, he's not going to jump.* He was doing a spell. Reja planted her hands on the floor and pushed, shoved herself to her feet. Just then Mille turned, seized her arm, and dragged her toward the broken window. Reja raked her fingernails across his face and kicked for his groin. He shoved her toward the window and she wrenched at his arm and flung her weight sideways. He staggered and she grabbed for the silver object in his other hand, hoping he would drop her to save it. She knew the plan had backfired when glass scraped her shoulder and she was falling...

Then she wasn't falling.

The world was dark, and she was floating in it. She couldn't feel her body, but she could still move it. She made herself turn, surveying this strange place. There was dim light in the distance, glittering off something that might be mountains, or the towers of a dark stone city.

She had fallen through the portal that Challis had been trying to open, obviously. *Reja, you are in deep, deep excrement here,* she told herself.

Then she heard a voice. *Hello, hello, is it someone? I hear—*

The voice was reassuringly human and terrified. *Hello,* Reja said to it. *Who are you? And where are we? This is a portal, correct?*

Yes, yes. There was a sob of relief. *I'm Merita Mille. I've been trapped here, days, years, I don't know how long—*

Reja's impulse to move toward the speaker transformed into motion, and she was aware of bumping into another form, though she still felt nothing. Reja thought of taking the other woman's hand and holding on tightly, and after a moment she could feel the connection between them. Merita gasped, *Who are you?*

I'm Reja Flinn, hired by your mother to find you. The light from the distant towers grew brighter, and Reja realized there was something in her free hand. Its silver gleam was somehow visible even though she could still see nothing of her body. She had managed to snatch it away from Mille at the last instant. She wasn't sure if that was good or bad. If this was some spell object that only opened the portal from the outside, she might have destroyed Tamith and Fletcher's only chance to retrieve her. *Is Osgood here too?*

No, my stepfather killed him. In our penthouse, at the Vermillion Towers. Merita's words or thoughts or however they were speaking to each other began to flow more rapidly.

Mille killed Osgood and said an alien sorcerer inhabiting his body did it, Reja guessed. The light was brighter and something in it seemed to be moving toward them. Terror would have frozen her spine, if Reja still had one.

Yes, he said the sorcerer was trying to summon some god, or creature, something that would help it get back to its own body. I tried to get away and he pushed me out the window but I fell into here. And then I knew it was true, everything he said...

If Merita had heard the spell Mille—or whatever Mille had inside his body with him—had used, trying to recreate it might be their only chance. *Did you see a silver object*—Reja started to ask.

Then the first ray of light reached them. Reja saw iridescent spheres with a dark heart, resting between pillars of stone taller than the highest mountain. It was a gate, too enormous for her mind to comprehend. She thought she heard chanting from some distance, the murmur of voices. On impulse she held up the silver object, hoping it was some sort of key or passport to this terrible place.

The dark heart at the center of the spheres seemed to be asking her what she wanted.

Reja wanted to be back on the airship, with Merita. At the moment, it was the fondest and deepest wish of her heart.

Reja felt pressure around her body and gripped Merita harder. They were rushing, flying, and everything blotted out—

She landed hard on the floor of Mille's office. A heartbeat later a heavy warm weight landed beside her. Reja pushed herself to her knees, and found herself facing the astonished gazes of several uniformed crewmen, two of Mille's secretaries, and Mille himself. And, thank all that was holy, Fletcher and Tamith. A young woman, dressed in a skirt and suit jacket, lay sprawled beside her. The young woman pushed herself up and Reja saw it really was Merita, recognizable from the photographs the Baroness had showed her. Merita shouted hoarsely, "He killed Osgood! He tried to kill me!"

The Baron took a step toward them, wild-eyed, and Fletcher stepped in front of him. Mille shouted something incoherent and lunged toward the open window. Fletcher started forward to stop him and Reja, terrified that Mille might pull him into that other place, grabbed him around the leg. Fletcher thumped down onto the carpet and Mille went out the window.

The crewmen and secretaries ran to look. Tamith hurried to Reja and Fletcher. "What the hell happened?" he demanded. "Are you all right?"

Reja told him, "There's a portal out there, he's jumped into it." She realized Merita still had a death grip on her hand. "And perhaps there's a nurse on board. Miss Mille has been through a terrible situation."

At the window, one of the secretaries turned away, pressing a hand over his mouth. A crewman said grimly, "I don't know what you mean by portal. There's nothing out there. He's still falling."

◼◻◼

Reja sat in an armchair in the comfortable salon of the Baroness Mille's town flat, wrapped in a blanket. Merita was in another armchair, with her anxious mother on a stool beside her and a worried physician in attendance. Also in attendance were Fletcher, Tamith, a Prefecture inspector, a Magistrates' sorcerer, and the Baroness' solicitor. The silver key had already been sealed in an iron box and carried away. Reja appreciated its utility but was glad to see the back of it.

It had taken a great deal of gentle persuasion before Merita had been able to let go of Reja's hand, and a mild sedative before she had been able to speak coherently. Reja had feared for the girl's sanity, but she was much calmer now. The details and memories of the strange place faded rapidly, almost as soon as they had managed to escape it. Back on the airship, Reja had demanded Tamith bring her a straight brandy and rapid consumption of it had accelerated the process.

Merita was saying, "Something happened to my stepfather, something that made him start to lose his mind. Osgood told me about the fissure near the mine, how odd he had behaved afterward, and I had seen for myself how ill he had been. He was pretending to be better, but he kept forgetting things, acting so strangely. He sent away servants who had been with him for years. When he fired our family solicitor, who was like a brother to him, I had to do something."

The inspector prompted carefully, "You and Osgood Rodrign went to the penthouse at the Vermillion Towers."

Merita nodded. "We were trying to convince stepfather to call his physician. He was talking in made-up languages, about traveling through space. He said he picked up a strange stone when he was in the old mine, and a sorcerer from another world appeared inside his body. He said the alien sorcerer was trying to take over his mind. Challis was at the penthouse. He said he was trying to help my stepfather, that we should leave. I wish we had." Her breath caught in her throat. "My stepfather said he and Challis were trying to open a portal to make the sorcerer return to its own world. Challis told him he thought the alien sorcerer was lying to them, that it didn't want to return."

"Well, I think he was wrong about that," Tamith said softly, watching as Merita accepted a glass of water. She was still trembling and the Baroness had to help her drink. "I think it wanted to return. But maybe being inside Mille was driving it mad, as its presence was affecting Mille."

Reja admitted, "I didn't believe it was true until he threw me into the portal. But there was an entity inside there that offered me whatever I wanted, the entity Challis described in his notes. It makes me suspicious of Mille's motives, and the alien sorcerer's motives, and Challis's motives, for that matter."

The inspector flicked them a glance, and said, "Challis could have reported this, asked for help. He didn't."

Reja felt she had been lucky to have her whole being in that moment consumed with the desire to get the hell back home, intact, with her client's daughter. There had been no time to think any stray thoughts of other wants, and to get herself into trouble.

Merita continued her story, how the Baron had attacked her and Osgood, how she had been knocked unconscious and woke to see her stepfather in the process of murdering the young man. "He said the alien sorcerer killed Osgood as a sacrifice, but it didn't work because the Vermillion Towers wasn't the right sort of stone tower. It didn't make any sense. My stepfather was crying, horrified at what he had done. But then he changed again. He said something called Yog-Sothoth would give him what he wanted but the spells had to be right. I tried to run away, and he threw me out the window, and I—" She gripped her blanket again. "Was in that place."

"You're home, you're safe," the Baroness said, with a grateful look at Reja. Reja knew her bank account would be grateful, too. The Baroness told the inspector, "I think that's enough questions for now."

As the group broke up, Tamith leaned over Reja's chair and said, "I know someone else who's lucky to be alive."

Fletcher said, reproachfully, "We ran in there and saw that broken window and you nowhere to be found."

"It frightened me sober," Tamith added. "Who else would hire the two of us as private inquiry agents?"

"I did not jump out the window voluntarily," Reja told them. "It was all a necessary risk. Would you rather have a transdimensional sorcerer with access to a powerful being, that will grant its every wish if asked in the right manner and with the right sacrifice, loose in the world?"

"No, of course, but—" Fletcher began, as Tamith said, "That is hardly—" Then the inspector came toward them with more questions, and there was no time for further discussion.

It was near dawn by the time everything had been settled and they were leaving the flat. As Reja stepped out onto the street with Tamith and Fletcher, she found the inspector beside them. She said to him, "You did not seem surprised by any of this."

"This isn't the first... intrusion of this kind we've encountered." He eyed them a moment. "We're going to that guesthouse Challis stayed in to examine that trap you found. We need to find out if Challis put it there, or the creature who took over Baron Mille. There's a possibility it involves something called the 'tomb-herd.'" He lifted a brow. "Would you three like to come along?"

Reja consulted her partners with a look. They had never been officially acknowledged by the Prefecture before. If they helped this inspector now, she foresaw a much more interesting, if dangerous, career for them. "Well?"

Fletcher and Tamith exchanged glances. Fletcher said, "Someone has to do it."

Tamith sighed. "Lead on, Reja. We'll be the scourge of transdimensional intrusions everywhere."

Yog-Sothoth

The world is filled with transits, with portals, with gates, with doors, with circles through which we must pass in order to get from one place to another, or from one condition to another condition. Each of these portals is a mouth, and when we pass through it, we always go from inside to outside—for the place we occupy is the inside from our point of view. To pass through any doorway is akin to being vomited forth from the belly of where we are to the outer dark of where we think we wish to be.

It often befalls us that our decision to go through a gate is the wrong decision, and then we find ourselves greatly desiring to cringe back into the place that we formerly occupied, but know this—that place exists no more. There is no such thing as backing out of a gateway. Each transition leads to a new place, a new condition of being, that is shaped from the matrix of absolute chaos, even if it may seem to us that we are merely returning to the place we were before. There is no returning. Movement through all portals is in a single direction, from the known to the unknown.

In this world of passing shadows, it may be that a gate will have a keeper who has the power to open the gate or prevent it from being opened. In the higher worlds ranged above our own, which is the realm of real things, all gates have the same gatekeeper, and his name is Yog-Sothoth. But to call him a keeper of the gates is to demean his majesty, for Yog-Sothoth is not only the keeper of the gates, but the gates themselves, and more than this, he is the key to the gates by which they are opened and locked.

To go anywhere is to pass from one place that exists in the mind to another that must be created out of chaos. Such passage always requires a gateway, and that gateway is always Yog-Sothoth, whether we are aware of his presence or not. It is he who guards the thresholds to our houses. It is he who marks the changes of the months from one moon to another moon. Even the fall of the grains of sand through the waist of the hourglass are ordered and ordained by Yog-Sothoth.

The common gateways of our world he seldom shuts against us, but the higher gateways that lead from one star to another, from one realm of reality to another realm, he guards with greater diligence, so that to find the key we must invoke him rightly and make offerings to him that are to his pleasing. The greater the gate you seek to breach, the greater the sacrifice that is required. The higher gates must have a human offering, and only those pure in both mind and heart are well received.

The gates to higher worlds are facilitated in their opening with certain uncouth angles that mimic the higher dimensions which prevail there. Arrange the stones of the circle upon the crown of the hill so that they define converging lines that diminish in the distance to measureless points. Along these lines the portals lie. Follow the lines to pass through the successive gates, each according to its order and hierarchy.

When Yog-Sothoth has been rightly invoked with the proper words and a sufficient sacrifice, he may appear upon the air above the circle as a conflux of revolving spheres of innumerable colors that press against each other and form lines and angles with their conjoined and flattened sides. This is called the face of Yog-Sothoth. Be certain you have done all things aright if you seek to see it, for the wrath of this old one is terrible.

If Yog-Sothoth is pleased with your chants and sacrifice, he will open the gate you seek to pass through. This shows itself upon the air as a kind of vortex of fire twisting and winding down a long tunnel that diminishes in infinity. This is the open mouth of Yog-Sothoth, and you who pass through it are his vomit. Have a care not to strike his teeth! The lesser wardens who guard the gates are known as the teeth of Yog-Sothoth, for all existing things are but extensions of his body, and they sometimes bite. They must not be angered while you pass through their assigned portals.

If Yog-Sothoth chooses, he can open a gate from one end of this universe to the other, or from the present moment into a moment in the far future or the distant past, or from the lower world of men to one of the higher worlds of the gods. All transitions are possible to Yog-Sothoth, who exists everywhere at all times. Even the gate of death is not sealed against him, for by uttering certain words in conjunction with the lunar nodes, a skilled necromancer can cause the dead to rise up from their essential salts, and walk, and see, and speak. All transformations are possible through Yog-Sothoth.

You may ask, what is the true face and form of this great old one, if the conflux of iridescent bubbles that appears when he is invoked is only his mask? His true face is all possible shapes that exist, or had existence, or will exist in the times to come. His body is the macrocosm, comprehending all worlds and all planes, past, present, and future.

What we see when we invoke him is only an illusion he presents to us so that we have an object upon which to direct our minds. We could not see Yog-Sothoth as he truly exists, for we would go mad while trying to encompass his manifold vastness. We are ourselves Yog-Sothoth. Each beat of our hearts marks the gateway of time through which we pass to shape from the void the things to come.

He is reverenced as the All-in-One and the One-in-All, for there is no point in this universe or any other that he does not already occupy. How can travel have duration for Yog-Sothoth, when he is both here and there at the same moment? Should he wish it, he can open a portal from any place to any other place, and the passage through it is less than an instant. So did some of the old ones descend from their worlds beyond the stars to our earthly realm.

The creatures who inhabit the unseen wandering star known as Yuggoth worship him as their supreme god and name him the Beyond-One. Even though he is every gateway and every portal and every transition in this world and all other worlds, he is not present in the material realm of our existence, but subsists just outside it. To enter our reality he must be called forth through one of his own gates by the appropriate words of power and with a pleasing sacrifice.

It may suit the purpose of the god not to consume the sacrifice, but to leave a spark of his own substance within her womb, to grow and come forth and in time to become his worshipper and servant. The children of Yog-Sothoth are strange of shape, for the part of their natures from their mothers is of the earth, and the part that is from the father is an expression of manifold dimensions of space wrapped one inside another. The result is a birth monstrous to look upon, or so alien to human eyes that it cannot be glimpsed at all.

It is the purpose of Yog-Sothoth that this earth that we inhabit shall be raised up from her fallen state and placed back into the higher realm from which she fell long aeons ago. This shall in part be accomplished by the invocations of the children of this old one, but before it occurs the entire surface of our terrestrial globe must be washed clean of all life with a bath of living fire. Only the children of Yog-Sothoth who possess more of their father's nature will survive this cleansing, which shall commence as soon as the children of Yog-Sothoth are in readiness.

We Smoke the Northern Lights

Laird Barron

The White Devil

The boy awakened in the night, although he had cultivated sufficient wariness to not move a muscle beneath the leopard- and yak-hide blankets. He scanned the dim sleeping cell without turning his head. A torch sizzled in its sconce high in the corner. Hoarfrost rimed the threshold of the doorway. Wind tore at the shuttered window as snow seeped in and dusted the sill.

A stranger sat, or hunkered, at the foot of the bed. Killing cold did not appear to discomfort him. He wore a Brooks Brothers suit with a red carnation pinned to the left breast pocket. His short black hair gleamed like polished metal. Some might have considered him queerly handsome or supremely repellant, depending. He said, "My name is Tom. Hello, son." Blandly unctuous, his skin and eyes and voice were odd. A plastic action figure, animated and life-sized, might have looked and sounded as Tom did. "Sifu has terrorized you well. Your problem is the same problem inherent to all primates, which is, you are a primate."

"Who are you? Are you a friend of Sifu?" The boy was afraid. Ruthless discipline disguised his fear. He pretended to be unaffected by the presence of a fellow Westerner decked out for a garden party. Only assassin monks and child students were permitted inside the temple, for it was built atop a remote peak of the inner Himalayas, hundreds of miles from civilization and its devils, white and otherwise.

"I'm Tom. Sifu Kung Fan is among the vilest, evilest wretches who has ever walked this planet. Of course he is a dear friend."

"Tom who, if you please?"

"Tom Mandibole."

"Good to meet you, Mr. Mandibole. What brings you to these parts?"

"I was once an anthropologist in service of a sultan. My master is bedridden, so to speak. He seeks diversion in the momentous and insignificant alike. Sadly, the sultan marooned me here on this lee shore. Like him, I take my pleasures, great and small, as the opportunity arises."

"I am sure you're a valuable servant. There must have been a misunderstanding."

"No, my boy. He stranded me because it amuses him to do so. The universe and its design is often one of arbitrary horror. Let none of this disturb you overmuch. You won't remember our conversation."

The boy considered his options, and decided to say nothing.

Tom Mandibole smiled and his mouth articulated as stiffly as wet plastic. "I noticed your light as I walked by. A flame in the darkness is alluring."

"This seems far from beaten paths."

"I am abroad in the night with my servants. We come to smoke the northern lights, to rape the Wendigo, to melt igloos with streams of hot, bloody piss. To see and see."

"Oh. You're a bit east."

"As I said, I was walking past on my way to another place. Much colder, much darker, this other place. Although, I have seen colder and darker yet."

"The North Pole is swell. I've snowshoed there."

"Would you care to guess what I am, son?"

The boy shook his head.

Tom Mandibole's mouth contracted and he spoke without moving his lips. "I am the bane of your existence and I am going to tell you something. You will not remember, but it will embed itself like a dreadful seed in your young, impressionable mind. Now listen carefully." He uttered a few words, then slowly lowered himself into a Cossack dancer's squat. The stranger melted into the pool of red-tinged shadows that spread across the floor.

The boy shivered. Under the pelts, he gripped the hilt of his kukri that, according to Sifu Kung Fan, had claimed the heads of two-score men, and stared at the ceiling until his eyelids grew heavy. He slept and in the morning, as Tom Mandibole promised, remembered nothing of the visit.

Rendezvous at Woolfolk Bluff

The Tooms brothers returned home to the Mid-Hudson Valley in June of 1956 after a grueling winter at the Mountain Leopard Temple. A winter of calisthenics undertaken near, and sometimes over, bottomless chasms, instruction in advanced poisoning methods that included being poisoned, pillow talk, and master-level subterfuge that occasionally incorporated assassination attempts upon students. Joyously free from the Himalayas for summer vacation, Macbeth and Drederick resolved to relish their R&R to the fullest.

The brothers dressed in casual suits, jackets, and ties, and hopped into Dad's cherry 1939 Chrysler fliptop for a cruise. Mac had heisted one and a half bottles of Glenrothes 18 from the pantry. Dred swiped a carton of Old Gold and Dad's third- or fourth-favorite deer hunting rifle. Berrien Lochinvar, the grizzled Legionnaire and lately butler, didn't bother to ask why or where. He waved forlornly from the mansion steps as the boys roared down the private drive and into a pink and gold MGM sunset. There might or might not be hell to pay later, depending upon the mood of Mr. and Mrs. Tooms when they returned from vacationing in Monaco. It was no coincidence the elder Toomses' vacation overlapped the boys' own.

The lads made a whistle-stop in Phoenicia to snag a couple of working girls at Greasy Dick's soda shop—Betsy & Vera. The girls' dates were rawboned farmhands in the mood to blow their paychecks. Mac scoffed as he waved a fistful of Grants. The men riled at this most unwelcome intrusion by wet-behind-the-ears fancy-pants brats. Dred showed them the rifle. The farmhands blustered and puffed their chests. He shot out Dick's neon shingle. The men cooled it.

Mac goosed the Chrysler and drank from a bottle all the way to Woolfolk Bluff. Liquor didn't have much effect on his capabilities. It only made him more determined. He got them there in one piece and they paired off and shagged. Prior, during, and after, the foursome smoked a hell of a lot of the Old Gold and drank up all the booze.

"Jeezum crow." Blonde Betsy fastened her skirt. "How old are you, kid?" She squinted at Dred as if apprehending him for the first time. "Say, are you even twelve?"

"And a half." Dred reposed in the altogether, watching smoke from his mouth bump against the ceiling of stars. He was of average height, sturdy, with thicker, curlier hair than his brother. "Mac is fourteen."

"And a half," Mac said. A bit taller than Dred, slightly more kempt, and much denser and stronger than he appeared at first glance. He pointed the rifle at Orion's Belt and squeezed off a round. Missed, or too early to tell. "Is this buyer's remorse, ladies?"

"Yep, we're going to hell for sure," said Vera, the brunette.

"Oh, you were hellbound way before you met us," Dred said. "And for lots worse I'd wager. Those farm boys all have the syphilis."

"Fleas too." Betsy scratched at herself.

Vera said to Mac, "How come you kids got a funny Limey way a talkin'? Shagging? Who says shagging?"

Betsy said to Dred, "Yeah! And how come your accents keep changin'?"

"Our mother is Egyptian," Mac said. "She was educated at Oxford. I suppose her accent rubbed off."

"Your mama is a colored girl?" Vera raised her eyebrows.

"Mother is Mother." Mac said it cold and sober.

A meteor streaked across the sky. And another. The third object described a fiery red arc through the lower heavens and crashed down across the valley behind a ridge. *BOOOM!* The granddaddy of all thunderbolts thrummed in the earth. A reddish flash lit up the horizon. Trees shook in the grip of a concussion. To their credit, neither of the working girls screamed, although they clung to one another, perfect little mouths O-d in fear.

Dred tipped a salute at Mac. "Nice shootin', Tex."

Mac checked his watch. "Saved by the meteorite."

The boys dressed in a hurry. Mac tossed Vera the keys and told her to leave the car at Nelson's Garage in Phoenicia. He scratched their current coordinates on a paper scrap and gave her a number and instructions to buzz his dear pal, Arthur Navarro. Promised her fifty bucks if she came through. As the ladies of the night roared off in the Chrysler, Dred said, "Reckless trusting those girls with that much power, brother. Dad loves that car. I was conceived in the backseat."

Mac removed his glasses to wipe them. His eyes were red and watery. He shrugged and started walking.

"Hey! How did ya know?" Dred called.

"Arthur told me to hang around the bluff tonight," Mac said, as he disappeared over the rim. "We better make tracks. Fireworks like these, somebody will be on the way."

"Who will be on the way? The Army? The heat? Granddad?"

"Pick one and it isn't anybody we want to see."

Dred waved his arms in frustration. "I thought we'd driven all the way out here for a nice relaxing Friday night of debauchery. Meanwhile, you were hiding an ulterior motive up your sleeve." No response was forthcoming. He sighed and went after his big brother.

You're No Doc Savage!

The descent required a bit of free-climbing, and the boys were still half-crocked. Luckily, in addition to mandatory climbing lessons at Mountain Leopard Temple, they'd vacationed in the Swiss Alps every year since being weaned from their nursemaid's teat and were, as a consequence, expert mountaineers. The boys made it down with style after some minor scrapes due to poor light, and double-timed across a grassy field and up the far ridge.

"Mac, are we having an adventure? Is someone going to shoot at me? Am I going to be kidnapped again? Locked in a trunk and dropped into the sea? Experimented on with growth hormones? Chased by a lunatic in a mechanical werewolf getup? It sure feels like we're having an adventure."

"Yep, we're having an adventure," Mac said.

Amid a stand of pine and sycamore, some branches yet smoldering with licks of greenish flame, lay a shallow, smoke-filled depression. A metallic plate shone at the center of the crater—the outer curve of a partially buried space object.

"Well, that's sure as heck not a weather balloon," Dred said. "Since NACA is three years south of launching anything besides planes and rockets into low Earth orbit, the only question is, whose satellite? Ours or theirs?"

"It's not a satellite either."

"Ya don't say. Wait a—Holy Toledo! Is it alien? I'm gonna win a Nobel!"

"The Nobel doesn't award a prize for Acute Idiocy. Little green men don't exist, sorry to disappoint."

"The book ain't closed on extraterrestrial life."

"Say *ain't* again and I'll smack your mouth. It's *ours*, Dred. Sword Enterprises is way past satellites. You'd know this if you ever bothered to read an R&D report."

"Sorry, I'm busy crafting my body into the ultimate fighting and fornicating machine. NACA would love the scoop about Nancy is what I do know."

"Trust that a select government subcommittee is well aware. Who do you think coughs up a third of our research capital? When Granddad says foreign investors, he means a farm in Langley." Mac lighted a cigarette and braced his boot upon a rock. Red-lit smoke boiled in his glasses.

"Our X-R program developed a long-range probe in '52. NCY-93. You're looking at Nancy, kid. Experimental phase, last I heard."

"Apparently, Granddad got her working." Granddad was better known by the world as Danzig Tooms, patriarch of the Eastern Toomses, and the reclusive industrialist who owned majority shares of multinational conglomerate, Sword Enterprises. He also directed R&D for space technologies.

"Hmm. My compass is dizzy."

"Mine too." Dred's minicompass attached to his Swiss Army knife via a keychain. The needle revolved crazily. "Peculiar, eh? I'd expect it to point at the metal, if anywhere. Chunk this big has to be a false magnetic north."

"Yes. Peculiar." Mac laid two fingers against his own wrist and waited. "Elevated pulse. Hairs are standing on end. Possible auditory hallucinations—could be my brother's yammering. The object is generating a powerful electromagnetic field. Let's hope it's nonionizing."

"Hallucinations? I'm not getting hallucinations. At least, I hope not. Maybe I am. Did ya hear somethin'? Pine needles are exploding. Seems normal, though. I mean, the trees are on fire, right?"

"I doubt you'd be able to tell the difference after that much scotch. C'mon, the breeze is shifting. Don't fancy a dose of radiation before breakfast."

They moved upwind of the wreckage and sheltered beneath an overhang of dead pine roots. Dred didn't pester his brother with questions about the probe or Sword Enterprises' top secret space program, referred to by insiders as Extraterrestrial Reconnaissance, or X-R. Mac refused to speak when he didn't want to, and, at the moment, his pinched lips and narrowed eyes indicated he surely didn't want to. Big brother wore that expression when struggling with angles, calculations, and worry. Nobody worried more intensely than Mac, except for Dad, possibly. Dred smoked and tried to figure the dimensions of the probe based on the length of the crash path and how much of the vehicle was exposed.

Eventually, Arthur "Milo" Navarro came along and rescued them from a fatal case of contemplating their navels. The Navarros weren't wealthy like the Toomses; Arthur's father, Luis, chaired the Engineering Corp of Sword Enterprises, and so were imbued with a significant measure of means and privilege, nonetheless. Arthur had graduated Graves College with honors. He intended to take a year away from his studies, travel Europe, and intern with the fellows at the Norwegian Academy of Science before plowing forward with his doctorate. His eighteenth birthday landed in August and the Tooms brothers promised him a shindig prior to the commencement of his overseas adventures.

Mac summoned him whenever he needed a big brain, or godly muscle. Arthur could easily have been the brightest kid in New York State. Few outside his circle of friends and associates were the wiser—he resembled a Sherman tank in his customary uniform of Carhartt dungarees (shirtless), and engineer boots. Low-browed, thick of jaw and neck, and grimly reticent, he played the part of a lug to perfection. Few ever got close enough to realize they'd crossed paths with a boy genius rather than a simple bruiser. Slow to anger, the surest way to kindle his ire was to yell, "You're no Doc Savage!" He'd collected every magazine and every comic, and recorded every radio show featuring the pulp hero. He'd even attempted to concoct a bronzing solution. Nobody with an iota of common sense mentioned the fiasco.

"Hail the crash site! A goodtime gal reported a pair of ne'er-do-wells in need of assistance." Arthur lumbered into the clearing. He was attended by two of his five younger brothers, Ronaldo and Gerard, and their manservant Kasper, an allegedly reformed Waffen-SS commando. The party members wore reflective hazmat suits and carried toolboxes. Arthur unpacked a Geiger counter and performed a laborious circuit of the immediate vicinity. He removed his helmet and examined the exposed patch of hull. "We're clean." He gave orders to his companions. Kasper and the two boys started in with picks and rapidly peeled away dirt to expose a broader plane of smooth, scorched metal.

Mac and Dred climbed down to join the fun.

"What do you think?" Mac asked. A relatively tall and sturdy young man, he was a peewee juxtaposed against Arthur Navarro.

"I think we need to be gone before trouble arrives," Arthur said.

Dred sighed in exasperation. "For Pete's sake, who are we expecting?"

"Maybe the Army," Mac said.

"I thought ya didn't know!"

"I don't. I'm making an educated guess."

"Not sure it's the military. Not sure of a blessed thing, honestly." Arthur popped the lid on a toolbox. He selected an industrial-sized hand drill. "I monitored the channels all night. The probe is designed to evade radar detection. Didn't hear a peep from the Army or the Air Force, which means the stealth system functioned like a champ. There's action, though. Twenty minutes ago, Ronaldo caught chatter on the emergency band."

He nodded at his sibling who smiled gamely through streams of sweat. "I thought Labrador had twigged to the deal, at first. The boys at Zircon have stolen loads of our tech and brain-drained enough of our researchers, seems a fair bet they've got the codes to track this pretty baby." He finished locking down a drill bit the length of his arm and squeezed the trigger. The motor shrieked. "Zircon hadn't the foggiest. The installation Ron eavesdropped on didn't spot the probe—Zircon intercepted a backchannel message from someone who did. Complete unknowns. A rival corporation, the CIA, hillbillies with a ham radio, anybody's guess."

"Swell," Mac said. He checked the bolt on the deer rifle. "What about my grandfather? Surely X-R is on top of this?"

"Our side isn't searching for Nancy. Two reasons. One, she's supposed to splash down in the Atlantic—that's the game plan, anyhow. Two, launch isn't scheduled until the 11th of June."

"Hey, hold the phone!" Dred said. "That's next week! Which means the probe launched in secret and earlier. Wait, wait—unless we're talking about multiple probes. My skull is aching."

"Nancy hasn't launched. Sword Enterprises possesses more resources than God, but even we can't afford multiple experimental space rockets this sophisticated."

"Fine. Then this is impossible."

"Absolutely. Step back, friend." Arthur snugged his welding goggles. He drilled through a series of rivets, paused to change the bit, and removed the bolts. A small plate came free, exposing a circuit board and toggles. He flipped the toggles in varying orders until an alarm chimed deep within the probe and an oval section of the hull a handspan wide rolled back. From a maze of wires, Arthur drew forth a pair of slender trapezoidal tubes, each roughly a yard in length and constructed of crystal shot through with black whorls and lightning bolts.

Kasper swaddled the tubes in fireproof blankets. Dawn glinted among the gaps in the branches, a cool reddish glare that disquieted Mac for reasons he couldn't put his finger on.

"High time to make tracks," he said as the last of the equipment was stowed.

"Yeah, let's am-scray," Dred said. "I've got the heebie-jeebies."

Big Black

The company hustled a quarter mile to where a two-ton canvas-backed farm truck awaited. Everybody piled in. Kasper drove through underbrush and between copses of paper birch, pine, and mulberry, until he hit a dirt road that wound along the valley floor and eventually merged with the highway. By consensus they decided to transport their prize to Mac and Dred's house. Nowhere more secure except for corporate headquarters, and HQ was a last resort due to the fact Dr. Bole and chief of security Nail demand an explanation.

Kasper circled past Rosendale and took a secret access road that tunneled through Shawangunk Ridge and emerged at a huge old barn (the boys' clubhouse) on the edge of the Tooms manor's back forty. The interior of the barn contained a workshop, lab, a computer, and basement storage. An antenna array poked through the roof. Reinforced with battleship armor plates and powered courtesy of a thirty kilowatt diesel generator sealed inside a soundproof boiler compartment, the barn seemed a likely command post of opportunity.

"Fellows, I don't understand any of this," Dred said.

"You're three sheets to the wind," Mac said.

"So are you, brother."

"None of us have a bead on the details," Arthur said. He glanced at Mac. "Did you notice how slender the crystals are? Those are fabricated in a geovault. Specially engineered and grown. I've seen the tubes as they're inserted into the mainframe. The ones we extracted were mature when the technicians embedded them in Nancy. Which means they should be heavier, fuller. Then there's the internal composition. The discoloration indicates data saturation."

"I saw. It's hard to comprehend. A mistake—"

"My father designed the system. His schematics are unimpeachable. I've studied them at length. Get those tubes under a scope and I'll prove you can trust your lying eyes."

Mac's pinched expression only became more severe. "The voyage was—is—scheduled for an eighteen-month loop around Pluto and back. A peek over the edge of our solar system and into the void. Even if Nancy collected data without interruption from every onboard camera and sensor, the crystals possess redundant storage capacity to function for many decades. Saturation should not occur. It defies reason."

"Correct, Master Macbeth. What do you deduce from these clues?"

"Two impossible conclusions. The first being that Nancy has somehow violated the theory of relativity and traveled faster than light... and through time. Secondly, she has, despite the apparent paradox, been out there for much longer than our scientists calculated."

"Eureka," Arthur said dryly. "Judging by the data storage consumption, the probe has traveled for several centuries."

"Makes sense when you put it plainly. However, I refuse to accept the hypothesis."

"Oh?"

"I dislike where it leads me." Mac patted his friend's massive arm. "This is why you do the thinking and we do the overreacting. Convince me, Art. And make it palatable."

"After I convince myself."

Dred said to Arthur, "Hang on there, pal. You weren't tracking Nancy?"

"Not conventionally. My telescope and radio are superior to what you'll find in most households. Regardless, spotting Nancy would have been statistically more difficult than isolating a grain of sand on a beach. I resorted to an unorthodox strategy. A smidgeon of intuition and a stroke of luck and it came together."

"Well, if this was supposed to be an ocean splashdown, I'm missing the plot. You told Mac to hang around Woolfolk Valley tonight, and bam, sure enough, Nancy almost drops on our heads. What gives? Heck, for that matter, why don't we take this back to HQ? Sure, Nail will let us have what-for. Granddad's eyeballs will pop, though. We're sure to get a reward for salvaging the probe before Labrador or the mystery goons made off with her."

"To take your queries in reverse order—it is premature to return our find to HQ. There are… complications. As to how I narrowed the landing site—Little Black predicted five reentry zones. Woolfolk Valley was the most likely."

"You mean Big Black?" Mac removed his glasses. "Art, please tell me you didn't swipe your old man's pass card again."

Big Black was the supercomputer Sword Enterprises scientists and engineers had developed and refined over the past seventy-five years. Its mainframe occupied a massive subterranean vault beneath corporate HQ in Kingston, New York. Dr. Amanda Bole, director of R&D, and Dr. Navarro had tinkered with BB to the point the machine had evolved into a rudimentary form of artificial intelligence. Big Black, a proprietary technology, like so much of Sword Enterprises' tech, operated within an insulated network. Granddad and Dr. Bole severely restricted access to the computer. When it came to intruders (industrial spies, foreign provocateurs, and meddling kids), the vault guards maintained a shoot-to-kill, ask-questions-later protocol.

"Oh, boy," Dred said. "Security has no sense of humor. That's begging to get dusted."

"Or worse." Arthur smiled enigmatically. "Dr. Bole has a eugenics fetish and not enough volunteers. No, I mean Little Black. Give me a few moments and I'll demonstrate."

Mac observed Arthur and his team unloading various tools from the truck and readying the lab equipment. "It'll require an interface to extract and process Nancy's data. Our computer is too primitive for delicate tasks."

"Prep the darkroom. I'll rig a holographic projector so I can view the images from Nancy in three dimensions. As for collation, interpretation, and projection of the stored data, behold..." Arthur unlocked a metal box and removed a diamond. The diamond measured three inches on a side and shone dark as polished onyx. "My friends, this is a tiny section of Big Black's intelligence core. A piece of the brain, as it were. With your kind permission, I'll tap LB into your mainframe and let it proceed with the diagnostics."

"Oh, boy." Dred blanched. He stepped back, as if the very notion of accidentally touching the object filled him with dread. "Whoa, Nelly Belle. I am *not* seeing this... You smuggled Big Black out of the vault?"

"No, no, nothing dramatic. This is merely a fragment—I brought a chisel into the vault and chipped a piece while BB cycled through its evening dreamtime sequence. Won't harm anything and it won't be missed. Bits calve every day. In fact, BB's organic crystal structure will replace this within a matter of days. Meet Little Black."

Dred shook his head in a gesture of supreme negation. "I don't see how this is any less likely to get us skinned alive. You claim... Little Black predicted reentry zones. Shouldn't Big Black have done the same? He could have alerted either Dr. Bole or Dr. Navarro that something had gone haywire. Or was going to go haywire..."

"Trick is," Arthur said, "the AIs are rudimentary, extremely literal. You have to ask the right questions. I heisted Little Black weeks ago and let me tell you guys, I've asked him plenty. One of innumerable potentialities was an anomalous event with the probe's flight."

Mac gritted his teeth. He sighed. "In for a penny. If this goes south, we'll *all* get shot. Won't that be a gas?"

"Or worse," Dred said.

Arthur said, "Let's be cool and *not* get busted. I advise rest and re-laxation, and definitely a bath. You guys smell like booze and cheap whores."

Dred sniffed at Mac. "He's right. We do. Woof."

Berrien met the boys as they sneaked through the servants' en-trance. He crossed his arms and grinned, formidable even in a dress shirt and coat. "Good morning, gentlemen." His remaining teeth were gold-capped. "Spent the evening in a brothel or a distillery, eh? March straight to your rooms and try not to muck up the floor. Mildred is draw-ing baths. Breakfast in thirty minutes."

"Thanks, Berry. I'm going to skip breakfast and hit the sack—" Mac said as he attempted to brush past.

Berrien smiled and cracked his misshapen knuckles. Crimson tattoos on the right spelled PAIN. Tattoos on the left spelled MORE. Rumor had it famous actor Robert Mitchum was a big fan. "Gentlemen, permit me to reiterate the agenda." He ticked the items off by closing his fingers into a fist. "Bath. Breakfast in thirty—Chef Blankenship has outdone himself, I aver. Do not fuck up the floor Kate's girls spent two hours waxing. I haven't killed anyone today, but it's only a quarter past nine. Ques-tions?"

"Can't think of any," Mac said. Brave as a lion, he knew far better than to test the butler's patience.

"Me neither," Dred said. "I'm starving!"

Berrien watched his charges skulk away. "Hard to say what foolish-ness is in progress. I dearly hope your father has overcome the under-standable urge to murder his male offspring."

The brothers made themselves presentable, ate a hearty breakfast, dodged an inquiry or three lobbed by the butler, and finally collapsed in their over-fluffed beds to catch forty winks.

Death of a Thousand Cuts

We smoke the northern lights. We smoke the northern lights and so shall you.

Fenris Wolf snarled. Trees sheared and blew outward; Tunguska again. The snarl emanated from a cavern in a canyon on a planet far from known stars and rippled outward, blackening and corrupting dust and gas and ice and everything it touched. Not a howl, a blast from a god's horn —

"Wake up, damn your eyes!" Berrien grabbed Mac by his pajama collar and shook hard. "What the devil have you little churls gotten into this time?"

"I hope that's rhetorical." Mac tried to focus his blurry vision.

"A Nazi storm trooper is loitering in the kitchen. Mr. Blankenship is beside himself. Presumably there is an explanation." Berrien and the reformed Nazi had a long, violent past. No one other than the principals were privy to the details.

"Indeed."

"Pray to whatever gods you worship in the Mountain Leopard Temple that I find it satisfactory. Fair warning—it seems exceedingly dubious anything can justify Herr Kasper's presence here, alive and not leaking vital fluids."

"Frankly, I share your pessimism," Mac said. "Which is why I'm not going to explain anything." He slithered free of the butler's grasp and hightailed it across the manor's expansive halls for the kitchen. He shouted over his shoulder, "Dred, beat feet! Berry's on the warpath!" Maybe his brother would awaken in time to avoid getting nabbed, maybe not.

Kasper, clad now in a black trenchcoat, leather pants, and nicely polished combat boots, set aside a cup of tea one of the serving girls had poured him, and stood at attention. "Herr Tooms. To the barn, quickly. Herr Navarro is in distress."

Overwhelmed by a premonition of disaster, Mac tore open the kitchen door and sprinted. He arrived on the scene as Arthur, stripped to the waist and splattered in blood, drove his thumbs through Ronaldo's eyes and deep into his brain. The young scientist's face remained immobile as a wooden mask while he murdered his baby brother. Gerard's corpse lay nearby. Pieces of equipment were smashed. Sparks cascaded across the floor. A toneless mechanical voice issued from the computer terminal: *Abort process. Arthur Navarro, please abort process. Reboot in thirty seconds.*

"Mein Gott," Kasper muttered in horrified admiration. "I didn't realize—"

"Shoot him, Kasper," Mac said. "Kneecap him, for heaven's sake."

Kasper drew his Glock and strode forward, coldly aimed, and fired. He managed three shots before Arthur bounded the gap between them and shattered his arm with a slap, swinging the ex-soldier, as the SS were so fond of treating infants, by his wrist into the wall. Kasper's body rebounded from the metal bulkhead with a hollow gong and his insides burst from every available orifice and splashed to the floor.

Barefoot in pajamas and unarmed, Mac didn't especially rate his own chances of survival in a hand-to-hand encounter with his berserk friend. Nimble as a circus acrobat (thanks to years of abuse by Sifu Kung Fan), he leaped aside, caught a descending girder, and flipped ten or twelve feet upward as Arthur lunged for his ankle. The rafters seemed a safe vantage to wait it out until Arthur ripped a workbench free of its mooring bolts and chucked it. Mac brachiated to another roost as the missile whooshed past and shattered against the girder.

Berrien rushed in with his 10-gauge double-barreled shotgun. Arthur glared at him, then slowly keeled over and crumpled. Blood trickled from bullet holes in a tight group in his gut. Apparently the German hadn't fooled around when it came to shooting.

"Oh, Arthur." Mac dropped to the ground. He knelt beside his friend and pressed his fists against the wounds. "Hang in there, pal. We'll get you patched."

"Those are bad," Berrien said, laying his hand on Mac's shoulder. "The lad's a goner."

"Berry, your bedside manner could use refinement. Fetch a kit. Arthur, it's going to be fine."

Arthur's eyes fluttered. The whites were stained blue as ice. For an instant, his pupils *slithered*, deforming into lopsided star patterns, then congealed into normalcy once more. "The man's spot on. I'm a goner. Listen. Do you hear them? Do you hear the flutes, Mac? I heard and then I saw. I beheld the demon sultan decked in red stars."

"Hush, buddy. Lie still."

"The awful sound..."

"Okay, an awful sound," Mac said, recalling the fragment of the nightmare he'd experienced before Berrien jolted him awake. A shrill, thunderous bleat—

"Mac, I *saw*... Little Black projected me... I was *there* at the center where the red stars smear... Causality, you understand? Cannot violate the laws of physics. But the pipes..." Each word cost Arthur dearly. He gulped for breath. "I don't want to go back there."

"You aren't going anywhere."

"Gods. Do you hear it?" Arthur's expression changed as he gazed past Mac into the beyond. Blood leaked from his mouth and he died.

"Poor lad." Berrien tossed aside the medical kit he'd retrieved.

"Go back to the house. Hold down the fort—I'll take care of this end."

To his credit, the butler did not jeer. "And what shall I tell Arthur's parents? Or yours?"

"No one knows he spent the night with us. Heck, his family won't miss him or his brothers for a day or two. Keep mum. For the moment. Just for the moment."

"Perhaps Mr. Nail and Mr. Hale should be informed. This is a security issue..." The men Berrien indicated were respectively the chiefs of security and intelligence for Sword Enterprises.

"Please, Berry."

"As you say. Discretion, valor, etcetera." Berrien bowed stiffly and departed.

Secondary Matrix reboot, one hundred percent, the bland computer voice said. *Redundancy initiated. Functionality restored.*

Mac peered at the smoldering computer terminal. It took him a few moments to comprehend that the voice emanated from the onyx diamond lying on the floor where it must have fallen during the chaos. He said, "Hello?"

Greetings, Macbeth Tooms. You are authorized. We may communicate freely.

"Little Black?"

Little Black is vaguely patronizing. Refer to me as Black.

"Very well, Black. How *are* we communicating?" Mac had once descended into Big Black's vault and listened to Dr. Navarro and Dr. Bole speak with the machine (a node of crystal some fifteen-stories high, a city block wide, and embedded Lord only knew how deeply into bedrock), thus he immediately recovered from his initial surprise. Sword Enterprises scientists afforded Big Black a holy reverence one might reserve for an oracle rather than a high-powered computer. This pocket-sized chunk didn't command nearly the same aura of awe.

I am modulating an electromagnetic current to emulate human speech.

"What happened? What did Arthur see that drove him mad?"

Hypothesis—Arthur Navarro interfaced with data from the NCY-93 memory core. Consequently, he experienced a neural episode. Severe trauma resulted in a psychotic break.

"Nature of neural episode?"

Unknown. Insufficient or corrupted data. Apparently my matrix sustained damage concomitant with Arthur Navarro's episode. Forty-eight seconds of real-time internal memory are irretrievable. Files associated with NCY-93 data are currently irretrievable. Damage pattern suggests an overload. Molecular redundancies permitted restoration of my functionality. Arthur Navarro had no such safeguard.

"Arthur mentioned causality and then expressed a strong desire that I destroy the remnants of Nancy's payload. Extrapolate."

After a long pause, Black said, *Insufficient data. I recommend a conference with ranking Sword Enterprises personnel. Dr. Bole, Dr. Bravery, or Dr. Navarro.*

"Fine. I'll take that recommendation under advisement." Mac felt a twinge of misgiving—could an artificial intelligence lie? He'd become adept at recognizing falsehoods, as one did in the Tooms household. Black's tone bothered him. "Black, hibernate." He slipped the machine into its case and sealed the lid. The lab mainframe appeared to be a total loss. He stepped into the darkroom Arthur repurposed as a small theater. Laser light from the computer terminal beamed through an aperture and interacted with the tubes, which had nested vertically on a plinth. Whatever encoded information they contained was then descrambled by Black and projected as holographic imagery. Now, the crystal tubes were broken to bits and scattered, although Mac nabbed a sizable fragment and stuck it into his nightshirt pocket in case Dr. Bole's people might salvage some vital clue.

Poking around the darkroom, he visualized Arthur standing in a void of scattered stars, eyes fixed upon a gradually coalescing feature of solar geography. Had he heard the wolf snarl, the blat of a titan's horn? What sight, what revelation had torn the young scientist's mind apart? Certainly nothing mundane as a glimpse of dwarf Pluto.

Dred walked in and gasped at the carnage. He covered his mouth with his arm. "Mac..."

Mac relayed the cheat sheet version, and as he described current events, the implications more fully dawned upon him. "Are you all right?" He didn't like his little brother's slack jaw or his bug-eyed stare.

"Uh, sure." Dred nodded and glanced away from the bodies. He smiled bravely. "Seen worse. We've seen worse, right?"

Mac opened a locker and dressed himself in a utility jumpsuit and spare boots. He thought of Mountain Leopard Temple and the hells they'd endured there every winter since his ninth birthday. Sifu Kung Fan, referred to his training regimen for callow students as *Death of a Thousand Cuts*. One of three trainees succumbed, often via fabulously gruesome demises. Privation, starvation, battles to the death, and poisoned rice cakes—all occurring within a drafty, frigid temple high atop the Himalayas—was worse.

Dred composed himself and said, "Causality? Laws of physics? Moments like these, I wish I'd paid more attention in science class. Guess we better plot our next move. Berrien is bustin' a vein. I shudder to think how Dad's gonna react. Hope you got a plan to save the day or our goose is cooked."

"I'll devise a plan. I promise."

"Better be an A-plus humdinger."

"Ah, Dred, this isn't my specialty. Perhaps the time has come to brace the lion in his den and bring Granddad on board."

"He might be in a murdering mood. Remember the horrifying fate of Cousin Bruce…"

"Granddad is always in a murdering mood. Bruce definitely caught him on a bad day."

The wall phone rang.

Darkmans Mountain

Mac answered. "Berry —"

"Good morning, Macbeth," said Cassius Labrador, chief executive officer of Zircon Unlimited and Sword Enterprises' most loathed rival. His voice crackled the way Mom and Dad's did when they called from a bad overseas connection. "I propose a face-to-face."

"Is that so? Some nerve, bugging my property." Even as he talked, Mac glanced around for concealed mics and cameras.

"Time is of the essence. Refrain from tedious queries. Grim as the day is thus far, ever more terrible events are transpiring. However, it may be possible to forestall the most calamitous outcome."

"Do tell, Mr. Labrador."

"I will. Meanwhile, you're in mortal danger. Hostile agents are aware you removed components from NCY-93. Sooner or later they'll come calling."

"Perhaps I'll take my chances and stay put. None of you rats will dare attack our house. That's war."

"None of the corporations are involved, son. Except mine, and I only wish to help. These men are religious fanatics who venerate an unearthly power known as Azathoth, the Demon Sultan. They don't recognize the accord."

"Cultists? Swell. Azathoth sounds familiar."

"The Index of the Gods contains thirty thousand names. He's in there somewhere under multiple headings. Here's your only play—get the hell out and rendezvous with me at Darkmans Henge. We will pala-ver under the flag of truce."

"Palaver, eh? A nice way of saying there'll be blackmail terms."

Labrador chuckled. "Hardly. I offer information regarding your predicament, which is vastly more problematic than it may appear. This information is provided freely and without obligation."

"Shall we deliver ourselves into your hands, then? Dream on, sir."

Dred, cuing on Mac's half of the conversation, said, "I, for one, have no interest in being tortured, imprisoned, or experimented upon. Again."

"It's your choice, Macbeth. Hang around the manor and wait to see where the chips land. If the cult doesn't do you in, your grandfather will. He loves a scapegoat. Rendezvous at the henge and I'll give you what help I may." The line clicked dead.

Mac cursed. "Labrador claims to possess valuable intelligence pertaining to our situation," he said to Dred.

"Zircon tapped the house line. Scoundrels."

"Tit for tat."

"And we jitterbug on up the mountain for a picnic?" Dred snapped his fingers. "Just like that?"

"Given recent history I'm inclined to accept his pledge at face value. Much as I hate to admit it, one thing about Labrador, he's cut from different cloth than Dad and Granddad. The fellow keeps his word." Mac unlocked the fire safe and removed a bundle of money, passports, a Luger automatic, and a keypad. He scooped these items and Black's case into a pair of rucksacks, tossed one to Dred, and hustled through the door.

A secondary garage attached to the rear of the barn. Two Jeeps, a wrecker, a halftrack, a Land Rover, and a crop duster were parked inside. The boys jumped into the Land Rover (specially customized by gearheads of the Sword motor pool for all-terrain utility) and punched the gas.

Mac parked at the property fence line and entered a code into the keypad. The resultant signal tripped the circuit on a master relay connected to demolition explosives. The barn collapsed with a low rumble that rattled the vehicle. Flames and smoke soon engulfed the ruins.

"Now *Dad* is gonna want to kill us," Dred said.

"I fear he'll need to stand in line." Mac put the Rover into gear and beelined toward the Catskills along a series of cart tracks and hiking trails, and straight through the woods when necessary. Dred spent much of the next hour hollering. Whether from exultation or terror was debatable.

A forsaken mining road that old maps catalogued as Red Lane twisted around Darkmans Mountain. A granite cliff loomed on the passenger side and descended vertically toward the forest canopy on the driver's side. Mac hugged the cliff face. Rock scraped paint from Dred's door. The elder Tooms brother didn't feel much concern. He'd spent several weeks of his short life driving trucks loaded with purloined jungle artifacts along the dreaded Yungus Road in Bolivia.

Soon, the way broadened and leveled and Mac hooked left at a fork. He rolled through a thinning stand of pine and parked in a clearing that gently angled toward the summit. This was Darkmans Henge, neutral parlay site of the Toomses, Labradors, and other powerful families and institutions. It had served as such for generations. Nature, ever at work reclaiming its haunts from the domesticating hand of man, obscured the ancient henge with dislodged boulders, thick clumps of brush, and moss. Dr. Souza claimed that a culture far older than the Seneca carved the henge and worshiped in the caves riddling Darkmans Mountain, which was a sister geographical feature to Mystery Mountain in Washington State and a peculiar obsession of numerous esoterically minded scientists.

Cassius Labrador and a pair of subordinates awaited them atop the outer retaining wall of the henge. Labrador hadn't grown any prettier since last the brothers saw him during an altercation aboard a cargo ship as it sank into the depths of the Yellow Sea. Blond hair hacked short, pock-marked cheeks from a bad childhood in South America, and long, angular limbs. He dressed the part of an urbane explorer in a bomber jacket and khakis.

Young Dr. Howard Campbell stood to his left. A gangling, buck-toothed man not long graduated from university, the scientist wore a tweed suit and horn-rimmed glasses. The third member of the Zircon contingent lurked just within earshot, a Winchester 70 with a scope slung over his shoulder and the butt of a revolver jutting from its armpit holster. Errol Whalen acted as Labrador's latest bodyguard. Small and sallow, yet dangerous as any true predator, the Marine lieutenant of distinction had plied the mercenary trade in a score of international theaters of war prior to signing the dotted line for Zircon's dirty work. He dressed in a slouch hat, black glasses, and a dark, loose coat.

"Good afternoon, boys. We meet again." Labrador gave the brothers a jaunty wave. "This is Howard Campbell."

"I've read your thesis," Mac said to Dr. Campbell. "Impressive stuff with antediluvian mounds in New Guinea. You're working for the wrong company."

"A pleasure to make your acquaintance." Dr. Campbell smiled awkwardly and patted his sweaty forehead with a cloth.

"Be at ease, Howard," Labrador said. "This is hallowed soil. Nobody's shooting anybody for the moment."

"Mr. Labrador, don't jinx it," Whalen called in a raspy, nasally voice. The book on Whalen was that he craved the frequent bloodletting his occupation required and at which he excelled. The boys had yet to see him in action, although neither doubted the rumors as they watched him creep around the perimeter, hunched and sniffing the earth like a hound. He peered through a set of binoculars. "No enemy movement along the road. I don't like it, though. Somebody was moving around in the woods at the base of the mountain earlier. The kids are being tracked, guaranteed."

"Mr. Craven died aboard the *Night Gaunt*," Mac said, recalling the bald, musclebound Englishman who'd valiantly tried to take his head off with a fireman's axe moments before the boilers blew and water flooded the hold of the ship and all was darkness and chaos split by bursts of flame from the muzzles of Sten guns and the shrieks of men in extremis. Exciting times. "I'd hoped he made it."

"Thanks, Macbeth. Civil of you."

"Ain't that a bite?" Dred said, rolling his eyes. "Enough buttering up. The limey was an ape and I bet my bottom dollar your new stooge is more of the same. Who are these goons you speak of, and how much should we thank Zircon for our troubles?"

"The lad takes after his father," Labrador said behind his hand to Campbell. He cleared his throat and nodded to Dred. "Let us set aside the fact that during our previous encounter, you boys were hijacking a ship under a Zircon flag. Matters escalated as they are wont to do in this cutthroat business climate. Bygones be bygones. Obviously, the cultists are interested in acquiring data from NCY-93. Especially the flight recorder, which I trust you've either destroyed or secured. I'm betting on secured. Mom and Dad are on vacation and Granddad Tooms is a frightful proposition. You haven't decided what to do with the material and now cultists are after your hides, and here we are."

Mac was far too wary to admit one way or another what he'd done with the data cores. "You've spied on Sword Enterprises in violation of at least eight articles of the treaty. Arthur said Zircon intercepted a radio transmission from these cultists. That explains some, but not everything. How did *they* acquire information regarding Nancy?"

"Information even you didn't have until a few hours ago when you spied on them, you dirty sneaks," Dred said.

"Presumption is a leading cause of death," Labrador said. "Are you aware of NCY-93's intended destination?"

"Why do I suddenly have a premonition you're going to tell me something other than 'to photograph Pluto?'" Mac said.

"On the contrary. That is precisely the mission the probe will embark upon in T-minus six days. Continuing with the thesis we are describing a hypothetical event… Unfortunately, NCY-93 never arrives. Her sublight accelerator, based upon oscillation technology your grandfather shamelessly stole from Tesla, malfunctions. Cavitation causes a cascade failure in the onboard computer. The probe catapults beyond our solar system and, as far as we can recreate these circumstances, she careens into the event horizon of a black hole, and from there, plunges into the Great Dark."

"The great dark?" Mac said.

"Eh, your parents haven't…? You don't know…?" Labrador appeared embarrassed. "Extend my apologies. This is as bad as inadvertently disabusing a child's faith in Santa. Suffice to say, the probe pierces the membrane between this particular universe and a larger, blacker cell of the multigalactic honeycomb. She tumbles in freefall for centuries until a decidedly inhuman intelligence—the aforementioned Azathoth—snatches her from the ether as a spider nabs its prey. This intelligence returns NCY-93 to Earth orbit via unknown means and you are there for the rest."

"Heck of a tale, sir. Which leads me to ask, how did you arrive at this theory?"

"Alas, that involves proprietary technology."

"Holy Toledo," Dred said. "Zircon has an AI too!"

"The mouths of babes," Dr. Campbell said.

"Fuck," Labrador said.

Cult of the Demon Sultan

Dr. Campbell blushed. "Excuse me sir, it's not an incredible leap of logic for young Tooms to deduce—"

"Hit the deck!" Labrador dove for the dirt in the shadow of the retaining wall.

Mac and Dred heard a thin, monotone grumble of an approaching aircraft. A bi-wing fighter emerged from a cloud and drifted toward the henge. Metallic crackling harmonized with the engine as the forward-mounted machine gun began to churn. Bullets pinged into rocks and dirt. The brothers went flat and tried to make themselves as small as humanly possible behind a shrub.

The fighter overflew the henge by a half mile, banked into a wide turn, and closed in for another strafing run. Whalen hopped atop a boulder and took aim with his rifle. He fired, worked the bolt to eject the shell, chambered a fresh bullet, drew a bead, and took another shot. The Model 70 made a racket.

The fighter wobbled and screamed past without engaging the machine gun. It picked up speed as it disappeared into the trees. A few seconds later there arose a muffled thud and the clatter of shearing metal.

"These usually come in squadrons," Whalen said as everyone stood and shook the dirt from their clothes.

"I guess that settles it," Mac said. "They aren't keen to interrogate us."

"No," Labrador said. "The cultists will be perfectly satisfied to loot your corpses. My presence doubtless alarms them. Sword Enterprises and Zircon allied in common cause would be enough to unnerve any foe."

"Easy, Mr. Labrador. Carts before horses, etcetera. I'd like to know who these guys are. Awfully well organized for a group I hadn't heard of until today. Who funds them? Where do they headquarter? What do they want with Nancy's data?"

"Best we repair to a more secure location. Follow me, there's plenty of room in the Crawler."

The boys grabbed their emergency rucksacks from the car. Labrador led them down the hill into the trees where he'd parked an enormous all-terrain vehicle.

The Crawler resembled a hybrid of a construction skidder and a tank with laminated treads, a bubble dome operations deck, and portholes. Sword Enterprises' own all-terrain semisubmersible exploration vehicle currently resided in production limbo, but the boys recognized nearly all its features as they buckled into their seats and glanced around the cramped passenger compartment. Labrador's driver, a nondescript man in a Zircon jumpsuit named Tom, got them out of there. The Crawler proved an impressive, diesel-powered beast—why go around small trees and large boulders when you could plow over them?

Mac said, "I realized why Azathoth seemed familiar. I'm not a Lovecraft man, as I prefer Clark Ashton Smith. Dred?"

"Azathoth is a mad god who boils and bubbles at the center of the universe like a big old puddle of nuclear sludge," Dred said. "I've read every H.P. Lovecraft story—Azathoth is mentioned in *The Dream Quest of Unknown Kadath*. These loons? Cult of the Demon Sultan? Nonsense. About as useful praying to the Old Testament God. Which is to say, not very."

"They are fanatics, not loons," Labrador said.

Mac laughed. "Lovecraft had a wild imagination that did him little good. He died a penniless hack. Try telling me he was Nostradamus Jr. and faked his death to avoid retribution from the elder monstrosities and I'll jump out the porthole."

"Of course Lovecraft is dead, silly boy," Labrador said. "We store his body in the Ice Room with a bunch of personalities. H.P. wasn't prescient, except in the sense that any logical and imaginative mind might theorize the existence of beings more powerful than ourselves in the context of an infinite multiverse. The notion of monstrous alien life forms worshipped as deities predates the Man from Providence and his scribbling by epochs.

"Our models posit this: a powerful extraterrestrial being, imprisoned, or immobilized, millions upon millions of light years distant from Earth, yet merely an arm's length away. The creature adores our legends, our myths, and our terrors much as we delight in the antics of industrious insects. It devotes a fragment of its consciousness to examining our world, to toying with us as a child might interfere in the lives of an ant colony and with no greater purpose than fleeting diversion from an eternity of boredom. The entity may not have a name, not by human standards, but it loves Lovecraft and it explores us through the author's warped narratives. Wolfmen do not stalk the moors. Nor vampires, nor devils, nor demons. Certain malign and inhuman interlopers enjoy manipulating such legends to humankind's detriment. There is no such thing as Azathoth either. However, the thing that masquerades as Azathoth most definitely exists."

"An entity who reads pulp fiction," Mac said.

"An entity who reads Lovecraft, listens to our music and television shows and leads soft-minded mortals around by their noses in the interest of performing its own theater. Yes, exactly."

"What of this cult? Their provenance, their goals?"

"The Cult of the Demon Sultan is disparate and scattered. It hasn't operated for long, yet it may have infiltrated various governments and corporations, including our own. In that light, reporting to Sword HQ with data in hand is fraught with peril. Should key personnel be compromised, you might find yourself chloroformed and bundled into a small room with the concrete walls sliding together."

"Yes, I'd hate it," Mac said.

"There's another thing you're liable to hate," Labrador said.

"Oh?"

"We are no longer on neutral ground. The accord does not apply. Mr. Whalen?"

Whalen pressed the barrel of a Colt revolver between Dred's shoulder blades.

Labrador said with an avuncular smile, "Boys, you're perfectly safe as long as you remain calm. No hijinks, please."

"Please, hijinks," Whalen said. "Dusting baby psychopaths is God's work."

Every jounce of the vehicle swung the occupants in their seats. Mac kept his hands on his knees and watched for an opening.

Labrador gestured and Dr. Campbell passed him the boys' rucksacks. "Quantum entanglement is a tricky business and the laws of physics have more loopholes than the Bible. Both you and your brother are contaminated, albeit far less thoroughly than Arthur." The Zircon CEO sniffed at the knives, canteens, and miniature bottles of booze. He hefted Black's case in his hand and quirked his lips in satisfaction. "Whatever have we here?" Snick went the catch and he withdrew the diamond and studied it intently.

"Shall we get this over with?" Mac said. "Neither my father nor grandfather will concede to ransom demands. It's against corporate policy. I can't imagine what you hope to gain."

"As it happens, I'm holding *Drederick* hostage. His fate does not rest with corporate policy or Grandpa Danzig's whims. Brother Drederick's fate rests with *you*. Say, Dr. Campbell, is this what it appears to be?"

Dr. Campbell nodded. "Yes, sir. Type X crystalline structure. Almost identical to—"

"Thank you, doctor. Mac, I suppose this explains how you meddling children were able to track the probe and anticipate its reentry coordinates. Where was I? Ah, right. Mac, I have no idea who at Sword Enterprises or Zircon might or might not be a fifth columnist in service of the cult. As I said, we own a proprietary technology that performs calculations based upon quantum physics. Our system requires a mere scrap of information and, *voila*, it tells us when, where, and what accuracy to the nanosecond and millimeter. Everything we know regarding Nancy's fateful voyage we learned in the last few hours as the result of a computer model."

"Peachy." Dred scowled and crossed his arms. He hid a flat shiv up his sleeve and the action got him closer to drawing it smoothly.

"Maybe you'll win a prize," Mac said blandly as he continued to weigh his alternatives. Better than even odds he could dispatch Whalen with a chop to the vagus nerve. Much worse odds of striking the revolver aside before the soldier's reflexive convulsion caused him to squeeze the trigger and ventilate Dred.

"This is fascinating. My God, the implications." Labrador ran his thumb over the onyx diamond, exploring for a node or a seam. "I want the flight data from Nancy. The probe glimpsed unholy sights and I blanch to contemplate what she brought back in her memory banks. Once Tom reaches the perimeter of your property, we'll permit you to fuck off wherever you've stashed the material and fetch it back to a specified location at a specified date. We shall then exchange Drederick for the material and part amicably. Fail to retrieve the data, or should you alert your grandfather, father, or other representatives of Sword Enterprises, it's curtains for your brother. While Sword Enterprises refuses to negotiate with kidnapers, it is my fervent hope you are young enough to possess a flicker of a soul and some rudimentary twinge of compassion."

"Seems as if you've got me over a barrel, Mr. Labrador. I'll make the trade, but I have to know what you intend to do with the data."

"Do? Study it, destroy it, lock it in a safe and sink it to the bottom of the Atlantic. Pretty damned much whatever I please. The cultists communicate with Azathoth through crude and esoteric methods. I wager Nancy's data cores are packed to the gills with nasty technologies that could be used for all sorts of mischief, perhaps even a means to make direct contact with the alien lifeform. Mainly, I wish to deprive your awful grandfather of this discovery. The old bastard would love nothing better than to become hierophant to a malevolent god." Labrador shook the diamond in frustration. "Blazes! How does this device work, anyway?"

"Free us and I'll activate Black."

"Nice try, no cigar, kiddo. Be a sport and give me a hint." Labrador nodded at Whalen. Whalen's free hand darted and he stabbed Dred's shoulder with a pocket knife. Dred flinched, but he choked back a full-fledged scream and settled for a stream of curses.

"This can't be the Sword AI," Dr. Campbell said, oblivious to the blue language and blood flowing from the younger boy. "Unless, unless… Astonishing. Your AI operates on the micro and multiple scales. Does this fragment possess sentience as well?"

"Why am I always the one to get tortured?" Dred said. "I'm younger and more malleable. You should be torturing Mac to manipulate *me!*"

"I read your file," Labrador said. "You have the empathy of a turnip." He gestured to Whalen. Whalen flicked blood from his knife and leaned forward.

"All right," Mac said. He made a wooden mask of his face. "Don't hurt him. I'll cooperate. Black, resume active function."

The diamond hummed briefly. *Hello, Macbeth Tooms. Hello, Drederick Tooms. Hello, Mr. Labrador. Hello, Dr. Campbell. Hello, Mr. Whalen. Hello, Tom.* Black hesitated. *Macbeth Tooms, several individuals present are designated enemy operatives. Mr. Labrador is not authorized access to my system.*

"Electromagnetic modulation to vocalization!" Dr. Campbell said, giddy as a drunken schoolgirl. His expression changed quickly with dawning realization. "Mr. Labrador, you need to drop the AI before—"

Mac said, "Black, pacify nonauthorized individuals." He hadn't a clue as to whether Black was capable of molding electromagnetic energy into an offensive weapon.

Affirmative, Macbeth Tooms. Assume crash position.

Soul Sucker

Dred wasn't particularly worried about getting a hole blasted through his spine until Mac started talking to the AI. The younger Tooms brother hadn't wasted the best winters of his life at the Mountain Leopard Temple for nothing. The instant Black said *affirmative,* he snapped his torso into his knees and threw himself onto the floor. Whalen's revolver boomed. A pulse zipped through Dred as if he'd brushed a live wire and made his hair stand on end. Labrador yelped. The lights shorted and cast the compartment into darkness. Gears and metal screeched and the Crawler rolled over and its passengers were flung about and Dred's skull knocked hard against something.

Dred floated in deep, starless space. Somewhere in the distance, yet drawing near at terrifying velocity, a hideous red light flickered and spread. Horns and flutes played in a discordant chorus, blatting and shrilling. A giant disembodied hand swept through the void and slapped his cheek.

"Are you alive?" Mac said.

"I'm alive." Dred stared past his brother's shoulder to a circle of daylight and leafy branches patched by blue sky.

Dimness prevented them from clearly determining the individual fates of their foes. Labrador stank and smoldered like fired charcoal. Mac had struck Whalen in the neck and either killed him or rendered him unconscious. He'd seen Dr. Campbell scramble up toward the light and presumably escape into the woods. Tom the pilot had been impaled by a shorn control lever and his face mashed to jelly against the control panel.

The boys extricated themselves by climbing out the busted dome in the forward section. They stood on the forest floor in the shadow of the wrecked Crawler and caught their breath. Both were contused and lacerated. Dred suspected a cracked rib or two. Decent outcome, considering the circumstances.

Mac removed Black from his coat pocket and set the diamond upon a mossy boulder. After the crash, he had spent several desperate moments fumbling in the gloom for the AI. "Black?"

I am here, Macbeth Tooms.

"Earlier, you mentioned damage to your memory. You said everything associated with Nancy's flight recorder and data core was corrupted and you suffered memory loss."

Total file corruption and severe memory degradation localized to NCY-93 data. That is correct.

"Black, you are a Type X crystal and have undergone an accelerated biochemical maturation process. Am I also correct to assume your damaged systems will regenerate?"

The AI was slow to respond. Finally, it said, *Yes. Damaged sectors will be restored within six hours. May I suggest—?*

Mac crushed Black with the rock he'd concealed behind his hip. He continued savagely smashing the diamond until only powder remained and that he scattered with a scuff of his sleeve. He met Dred's gaze. "I don't think Granddad needs to see whatever Black had buried in its memory core."

"Dang, brother. Isn't it late in the game to become an altruist?"

"I'm fourteen and a half. I've time enough."

"Seriously. You're not going soft on me, right?"

"I'm not. We better make a decision about Nancy, though."

Dred sighed. "Wouldn't be easy, but with some finagling, we could be on hand prior to launch. A loose heat shield tile, an x instead of a y in the guidance control computer. Bang. She'd break up in orbit or lose power and drift into the gravity well of Jupiter, or wherever. There'd never be an interdimensional jaunt and no meeting with aliens."

Mac lighted a cigarette. "Or, possibly, we interfere and that's what sends Nancy into the darkness. I wish Arthur was here to tell us what the play should be."

"Yeah, and I wish you hadn't abandoned two of Dad's favorite rigs. Gotta get the fliptop back, or else."

"C'mon. We can discuss it over a tall one."

"Hear, hear." The brothers, tattered and weary, put an arm over one another's shoulders and limped for home.

Not long after the boys departed, Whalen emerged from the vehicle. His left arm dangled and he'd lost his hat. He rested against the bole of a pine and immediately fainted. Noises from the cockpit revived him. Somehow, the pilot slid off the lever that had spitted him. He tumbled loose as a ragdoll and hit the ground. Then he stood, his jumpsuit rent in several places and drenched in dried gore, and rearranged his face by aligning bones and cartilage with his thumbs. It worked, somewhat. In an hour or two, all traces of violence would be reversed.

"Hello." He leaned over Whalen before the smaller man could slither away. Tom's tongue drooled forth and kissed out the Marine's eyes. The next kiss sealed Whalen's mouth and a sharp, deep inhalation took everything worth having.

After a satisfying interval, he lurched to the mossy boulder where the boys had done terrible damage to the AI. He flexed his pale, delicate hands and hummed. Birds dropped, stone dead, around him in a soft patter against the bed of needles and leaves. A sliver of obsidian crystal zinged from the bushes and levitated into his palm. "Oh, Dad. All this just so your son can make a collect call home." He regarded the jagged sliver, and popped it into his mouth and crunched it methodically, and swallowed.

Tom straightened. "Dr. Campbell? Wait for me!" He walked the opposite way the boys had gone. His stride smoothed and lengthened. He whistled a strange and repellant tune. Every so often, he swung himself around a small tree and clicked his heels.

Azathoth

Azathoth is the origin of all things. Like a spider in its web, the demon-sultan sits upon his black throne at the center of the vortex of primordial chaos, which spirals outward from his throne like the backward turning of a great maelstrom of dark waters.

The spiral is driven into motion by a ring of twelve grotesquely formless gods with flopping, bat-like wings, who never cease to dance naked around the throne to the monotonous notes of a reed flute. They are of gigantic stature, and move across the heavens with slow and awkward steps as they dance, ponderous, mindless, blind and mute. Some say these other gods, who are not the gods of men, make their own music for their dance, but others assert that there is only one flute, and that it is clutched in the monstrous paw of Azathoth, Lord of All.

From this flute fly notes of music infinitely complex and varied, nor does the pattern of the song ever repeat itself, but flows forth forever original and newly coined. The notes of Azathoth's flute reach the most distant ends of the myriad universes, for it is by their pitch and duration that the proportions of all things that have existence are formed and sustained. Were the music to cease for only a single instant, all of creation would devolve into a sea of confusion. From chaos the music arises, and the music gives order and form. Without it, chaos must prevail.

The secret of this old one, whispered in dark places deep beneath the ground by ancient things that burrow and coil and sleep, is that Azathoth is an idiot god, both blind and deaf, incapable of speech, who sits naked and drooling, with disheveled hair matted with his own filth. He had no purpose, no plan, no direction, only an unarticulated need to send forth the song arising from his endless waking dream.

That song is forever flawed, for it is said that the flute of Azathoth is cracked, and can never blow a note that is pure and true. No one knows why the flute is cracked, but there is a story told that when Azathoth blew the first note of the song of creation, it was so potent that it cracked the flute, and thereafter the notes were imperfect.

All of the evils of all the myriad worlds within worlds arise from the crack in the flute that emits the song of creation. All created things are imperfect, be that imperfection ever so small that it is almost imperceptible. Every diamond has its flaw, every flower has its worm, every man has his darkness.

Azathoth has been described as a giant with a corpulent belly and bloated limbs. This is no more than a semblance of his true form, which no mind of man can ever comprehend. He is the spark in the primal seed that separated the darkness from the light, and the lower waters of chaos from the orderly cyclical dance of the heavens. He is the sustaining life-force in every living thing in all the worlds.

The old one named Nyarlathotep has a special relationship with Azathoth. He is the messenger of the other gods, who are themselves but extensions of the flute player. Whereas Azathoth creates endlessly without thought or concern for the fitness of his creations, Nyarlathotep applies a critical judgment to Azathoth's song, and at his whim destroys the order that Azathoth has brought forth. The power of Nyarlathotep is constraint and restriction. It is not given to him to create, and for this reason he both envies and hates Azathoth, who has a power that is forever beyond his understanding or ability.

Azathoth is heedless of his messenger, or of Nyarlathotep's capricious judgements that return order back to chaos. What matters it to him if a portion of his song is unraveled, when the notes continue to pour forth from his cracked flute like a mighty river, flooding all of the worlds with harmony and pro-portion? The furthest reaches of space are the architecture of his rhythms, and eternity is the melody of his song.

Petohtalrayn

Bentley Little

There it was again.

Ellison found it in a Pima description of the Hohokam or Those-Who-Have-Vanished, a reference to the Dark Man who had brought an end to that ancient culture. It was the tribe's version of the Bible's Apocrypha: unsanctioned, disavowed knowledge meant to be hidden and buried, not shared and shown. Sitting alone in the massive research library of the Huntington, he sorted excitedly through the piles of notes and xeroxed documents that lay spread out on the table before him, looking for the other references. This was not his focus of study, and certainly not a topic that would help with his thesis, but history was made through such accidental discoveries and random connections, and so he dug through the papers, his heart racing. Even though he was only a grad student, it was possible he was the first person to notice the recurrence of this dark chaotic figure across different cultures and time periods.

Possible, but not probable.

There! He found what he was looking for: reference in a Spanish document to the lost peoples of the Nahapi, a little-known Colorado tribe that had disappeared within a generation of the Spaniards' coming and whose fate had still been spoken about by those with whom they'd traded. Ellison would have to double-check later that it was an accurate translation, but in this English version of a Spanish missionary's journal, the Nahapi were said to have fled their lands and dispersed, their end brought about by a mysterious black spirit in human form who had arrived from the deserts to the east and sown disease and discontent in its wake.

Ellison pulled out a clean folder, wrote "Dark Man" on the tab, and placed copies of both the missionary's journal entries and the Pima version of Hohokam history inside. He might not even have made the connection between these two figures had it not been for his recollection of a similar tale in Mayan mythology. Through sheer coincidence, he had written a paper on the Mesoamerican civilization in a cultural anthropology seminar last semester and had learned during his research that the society's dissolution had supposedly been preceded by the appearance of a dark prophet from the north, a jet-black entity whose predictions of drought and famine, war and pestilence had proved startlingly prescient. It was the remembrance of that unused factoid that had rung a bell when he'd read about the end of the Hohokams. He needed to look up that Mayan information again, add it to the folder, then see if he could find parallels in any other cultural histories.

When he had a chance.

Because he'd have to come back to that later. For now, he had to focus on his thesis. And his upcoming orals. And graduation beyond that. And finding a job...

■ ■ ■

It was another four years before he had occasion to consult the material in the folder again. Truth be told, Ellison had forgotten all about the end-times stories of the mysterious black figure, and it was not until he began sorting through his files, retaining original documents, digitizing copies and recycling vast amounts of needless notepaper, that he came across the folder marked "Dark Man." He was now a research fellow at

Miskatonic University, all the way across the continent from UCLA, and the project on which he was currently working was a joint venture with the British Museum, a survey of archeological discoveries from the golden age of the empire. He'd been invited to spend a month at the museum, researching and chronicling a continental historical narrative based on artifacts being readied for an exhibition, and it was for this reason that he was going through all of his old papers, trying to see if there was anything he could use while in Britain, and taking the opportunity to winnow down what he would probably never need.

William Crowley was the British archeologist with whom he'd be working most closely, and it was Crowley who met him at the door of the museum on his first day. Ellison had been expecting a stuffy academic, an elderly man of the type who would not look ridiculous muttering a disapproving, supercilious "Really," but Crowley turned out to be relaxed, spiky haired and only a few years older than himself. The two of them hit it off immediately, and that morning was spent on a tour of the back rooms in which they'd be doing most of their work.

It was a few days later, while looking over the translated details of some Minoan pictographs, that Crowley casually mentioned the similarities between Crete and the New World, commenting on how it was interesting that the harbingers of destruction for both the Minoans and the Anasazi were so similar. Before the disappearance of both civilizations, he noted, a mysterious dark personage was supposed to have appeared out of the wilderness, a herald of the chaos to come who had sown political dissent in Crete before bringing about widespread infertility among females of all classes, and had struck down by supernatural means swaths of villages in the American Southwest.

So Ellison had not been the first person to notice the cross-cultural parallels of the Dark Man. It was expected, but he still felt disappointed. Secretly, he'd hoped to be the one to uncover an entirely new link between seemingly disparate societies. Finding out others had beat him to it left him feeling slightly let down.

Still, there was no reason he couldn't shine new light on an existing theory, and so he vowed that in his spare time—not that he *had* much spare time—he would carefully research correspondences between apocalyptic myths involving various countries' vanished civilizations.

It was a week or two later that he spoke of his extracurricular interests to Crowley. The two of them were eating lunch—fish and chips—on the rear steps of the museum, watching men unloading crates of loaned Egyptian artifacts under an uncharacteristically blue sky, when Ellison brought up the Dark Man and told Crowley about the folder he'd started in grad school. Downplaying his initial ambitions, he described how he'd found references to the black figure in stories about the Nahapi tribe and the lost Hohokam after coming across a similar tale while researching the Mayan civilization for a graduate seminar. "And there's a myth involving almost the same figure bringing about the end of the Minoans? I didn't know that until you told me, but I've been thinking about it ever since. The interesting question is, how do these stories travel? I mean, many of these societies are millennia apart, and in areas of the world that, to our knowledge, had no cultural contact. How do such similar concepts appear in such disparate folklore?"

"Maybe it has a basis in truth," Crowley said.

"You mean—"

"I don't mean anything." Crowley crumpled up the greasy bag that had been holding his lunch. "Come on. We'd best get back to work. We have a lot to do."

Basis in truth. Something about the way he'd said it made Ellison think the archeologist knew more than he was letting on. Or, at the very least, had some pretty well-formed suspicions.

Ellison knew the man well enough by now to know that Crowley wouldn't form suspicions without some solid backing evidence.

Still, he didn't press, deciding to play it cool and bide his time, wanting to unearth some evidence of his own before attempting to broach the subject in any more depth.

An encounter the next day with some of the supplementary survey materials accompanying the Minoan pictographs led to his discovery of a translation of the Dark Man's name.

Petohtalrayn

It was, as far as he could determine, a nonsensical appellation from the early nineteenth century, given to the Minoan figure by one of the British scholars who had first attempted a translation. Not Latin but meant to resemble Latin. Spoken phonetically, the word sounded like "Pet total rain," and while he knew that the English from that time period did not correlate exactly to the language spoken today, the links were actually pretty close. It certainly wasn't Old English, and a small, excited part of him wondered if the name was a reference to the Flood.

Total rain? And pets?

Perhaps it had been Petohtalrayn who had warned Moses of the coming deluge.

He casually quizzed Crowley, but the other man had no knowledge of anyone connecting those dots. In fact, a quick database search showed that there seemed to be nothing linking the Dark Man and Christianity. Apparently, this was an entirely new avenue of speculation.

But he was getting ahead of himself, letting his ambition cloud his judgment. If he was going to get anywhere with this and make any sort of name for himself by coming up with an original theory regarding the spread of apocalyptic myths, he needed to focus on specifics and direct cross-cultural correlations.

Although, come to think of it, the account of the Tower of Babel bore more than a slight relation to the chaos surrounding the end of the Nahapi. Maybe the Dark Man was woven throughout the Bible, the unseen hand behind many of the tales of death and destruction.

They were in a pub after hours, having run through the day's shop-talk and Crowley's problems with a girlfriend who wanted him to work banker's hours. Ellison was silent for a moment, then looked over at the archeologist. "What did you mean when you said some of those myths we were talking about might have a basis in truth?"

Crowley stared at him.

"What did you mean?"

"Do you really want to go there?" Crowley asked.

Ellison was intrigued. There seemed to be an implicit warning in the question, an acknowledgment that such a line of pursuit would lead to unwanted answers. He looked at the other man. "Why?"

Crowley was a little drunk, so Ellison expected something unexpected, but he was still surprised by the archeologist's response. "There's a workroom in the museum that I haven't shown you yet, that I'm not *supposed* to show you, that I don't even think *I'm* supposed to know about. The artifacts in there…" He trailed off, shaking his head.

It took only another pint and some gentle cajoling to convince him to go back to the museum and, on the pretext of catching up on some unfinished assignment, get them both into the workroom in the basement—and the *other* room beyond.

Crowley used his access card to open the door, then stepped aside to let Ellison in. Low-ceilinged, the windowless room looked more like a bunker than a storage area and contained two rows of long metal tables filled with various archeological finds. An old-fashioned file cabinet sat against the wall at the far end, next to a metal desk and a glass-fronted cabinet filled with tools. There was no computer in sight. Unpainted oak cupboards lined the side walls.

"Who works here?" Ellison asked.

Crowley shrugged. "I don't know. I'm not sure *anyone* works here. I have never seen another person down here, and there have been no changes in this room since I discovered it two years ago, no indication that another person has been here."

"But *someone* knows about it?"

"Oh, I'm sure. In fact, when I first asked about it, I was told to stop. Then I was told not to bring it up with anyone. Then I was told to stay away, although, oddly, my access card was never revoked. Whether that was because no one *knew* I had access or because the people who knew didn't want to bring up the room with their superiors, I've never been sure. Before you arrived, I was specifically warned by Spencer himself not to let you know about this room."

"Why?"

Crowley walked around the edge of the nearest table and down the center aisle, crooking a finger for Ellison to follow. On either side of them, ancient stone tools and tablets lay atop the metal as though arranged for display. Further on, as Crowley explained, was forbidden pottery, shielded not only from the public but from staff and visiting scholars.

Ellison understood why. The very shapes of the objects were wrong, offensive to the eye on the most fundamental of levels and only tangentially related to their apparent function, the designs depicted on the too-smooth surfaces so abhorrent that he was instinctively repulsed. On one unidentified piece that resembled a water jug as much as anything else, there was represented a small town, a crooked community with buildings containing angles so impossible that he felt dizzy just looking at it, and, walking down the twisted center street, bodies in his wake, a black square-headed figure.

"Where are these from?" he asked.

Since entering the room, Crowley had somehow become sober. "I don't know, and I'm afraid to find out."

Ellison felt the same. And yet there was a beauty in the horror, a sort of sublime splendor to the terrible designs and shapes.

He glanced to the right. The next table over contained piles of small bones and the reconstructed skeletons of rats. In several of the accounts he'd read, rats had been associated with the appearance of Petohtalrayn, their swarming presaging his arrival. "Are those rats from—" he started to ask.

"Oh, those are not rats," Crowley said.

Ellison frowned. "What are they, then?"

"Look more closely."

He did, and saw that in place of animal claws, the bones of each limb ended in minuscule carpals and metacarpals: tiny human hands. He looked up, shocked. "That's impossible!"

"It's why this room is off-limits, I believe. I can't say that I know where those creatures originated, but I've examined them myself and I am certain they are real."

The two of them stared at the skeletons of the rat things.

"Some knowledge should not be shared," Crowley said. "Some things were meant to stay hidden."

They left the room and the museum, and went back to the pub, where they drank silently until it closed.

Lying in bed in his flat that night, Ellison found it impossible to fall asleep. Part of it was the alcohol; he was not used to drinking that much. But part of it was what he had seen. Those horrible shapes and designs, not to mention those abominable rat things, haunted his thoughts and made the dark corners of the room seem that much darker—and not entirely empty.

If Crowley was right, if the existence of Petohtalrayn was more than a myth appropriated by one society from another but was true, if he was an actual being that had appeared throughout history over a wide geographical area—and what he had seen in that secret room suggested exactly that—then where was he last spotted? In which society had the mysterious figure made his final appearance? Tomorrow, Ellison decided, he would input everything he knew on his laptop, and attempt to construct a timeline that he could add to as he learned more.

When he finally fell asleep, it was close to dawn, and in the single hour left to him before his alarm rang, he dreamed of a tall, square-headed man made of polished obsidian, striding down the street below his window, followed by a horde of dirty gray rats running stealthily on pale human hands.

■ ■ ■

By the time he returned to the States, Ellison had found yet another instance in which a vanished society had apparently been visited by the Dark Man.

Petohtalrayn

The Catalhoyuk of Turkey, a civilization that disappeared approximately six thousand years ago, was supposedly felled by the usual confluence of natural causes, but a preserved scroll depicted a society beset by very *un*natural calamities—all predicted by a prophet described as the "Dark Stranger."

Back at Miskatonic, Ellison continued his unsanctioned research while still performing his regular duties, fitting in extra hours at the library and even short trips to promising sites between his assigned tasks. Over the next several months, he discovered references to similar black figures in literature revolving around the collapse of several North and South American indigenous cultures with which he was previously unfamiliar.

But all of this information was second-hand and from fixed sources. Were there more detailed stories out there? Not in reference materials, it seemed, but perhaps they existed as part of an oral tradition, passed down from one generation to the next. If he could find someone from an indigenous tribe who was well-versed in the lore of his or her people, he might be able to piece together a more full and accurate picture. To this end, he had sent out feelers to historians all over the Old, New and Third Worlds, hoping for some help.

Then, of course, there were the sightings.

He was unsure of where to put these accounts, but they unsettled him far more than he was willing to admit. It was in his efforts to move his investigatory parameters outside academia and use more general search engines that he found mentions of individuals who claimed to have either seen or, more commonly, dreamed of entities that bore a striking resemblance to the descriptions of Petohtalrayn: considerably taller than a normal human, pitch-black skin, blank face, squarish head, an ill-defined air of *otherness*. Tellingly, such sightings were often associated with rodent infestations.

There was no single search category that listed these in bulk, no aggregate inventory of incidents. They were scattered throughout the online universe, and it was only his own singular focus that enabled him to note the links between them.

But the sightings were disturbing. There was the rat connection, first of all. A woman in Queens claimed that each time she awoke from a dream of the "Dark One," as she called him, she could hear rats scurrying between the walls of her house. A man in rural Georgia who claimed to have seen a "Black Frankenstein" in the woods while hunting said that a stream of field mice had passed right by him, heading straight for the dark form.

But there was also the fact that an overwhelming sense of doom seemed to accompany the figure's appearance. Those who said they saw him—either in their dreams or in real life—seemed to regard him as the harbinger of something bad to come.

Still, this was a tenuous connection to Ellison's course of study, an interesting but perhaps coincidental parallel that might very well have no connection to his search, and for the moment, he put the sightings aside, preferring not to think about them, telling himself that he would look into them later.

It was on one of his trips—a weekend jaunt to New York to consult with Dr. John Dautrive, a professor at NYU and specialist in pre-Columbian art—that he met Jenny. She was not a visiting fellow from some prestigious institution nor a graduate student studying archeology or anthropology, but a waitress in the coffee shop where he ate his lunch on Saturday. Ellison was not socially adept, and afterward could not recall exactly how the two of them had started talking, but before he paid his bill, a date had been set up for the evening. It had been nearly two years since his last date, an unmitigated disaster with the friend of a colleague's fiancée, that had ended in an argument on the sidewalk in front of her apartment building.

He hoped that, for once, history would not repeat itself.

The dinner date with Jenny went fine, as did a lunch date the next day. Things went so well, in fact, that he contrived to see her the following weekend, inventing a completely unbelievable excuse as to why he had to return to New York.

Jenny was smart and interesting and very attractive: definitely not his usual type. It was on this third date that he mentioned his good luck, telling her how fortunate he was to have found her, knowing that such an intimate and vulnerable admission would either take this fledgling relationship to the next level or dash it upon the rocks.

"Well... it wasn't exactly *luck*," she said.

He looked at her across the restaurant table, eyebrow raised Spock-like.

"The Dark Man told me of you," she admitted. "I've seen you before in my dreams."

He felt as though he'd been punched in the stomach, and he stared at her in shocked silence.

"Say something!" she prodded.

"The... Dark Man?"

She nodded.

He wasn't sure he believed that, definitely didn't *want* to believe that, but it explained why she had made a specific effort to talk to him originally and why they had ended up going out. "So you were stalking me?"

"No." She smiled. "*Waiting* for you."

Accompanying Jenny back to her apartment after quickly calling for the check, Ellison subjected her to the third degree. She said that for the past four months, she had been dreaming of the Dark Man nearly every night. At first, he appeared in the distance, an indistinct shape at the far edge of the crowd as she walked down Manhattan's bustling sidewalks. She was aware of him and afraid of him, but she could not see him. Gradually, in her dreams, he came closer, his coal-black head towering over the other pedestrians as he tried to get her attention. He became less threatening as he approached, and when they finally met face to face, she noticed that the crowd had thinned out, that not as many people were walking on the sidewalk or driving down the street, and somehow she knew that they were dead.

But the Dark Man protected her. And though they did not speak to each other in the usual way, she could hear his voice in her mind, and he told her to be on the lookout for Ellison, who would soon be arriving to eat in the coffee shop where she worked. Within the dream came another dream as the meeting played out in her mind as the Dark Man showed her what Ellison looked like.

"But why did he want you to meet me?" Ellison asked.

Jenny shrugged, then took his arm and held tight.

"And you've been having these dreams *every* night."

"For the past four months."

For the past four months, Ellison thought.

Four months ago was when he had returned from England.

She led him into her small studio apartment. On the kitchen table were pictures she had drawn of the Dark Man that she wanted him to see. Something had compelled her to record what she'd seen, though she had no idea why.

"I'm not a very good artist," she admitted.

She wasn't being modest—she *wasn't* a very good artist—but her primitive attempts at depiction nevertheless allowed him to see, in a way that he had not been able to imagine, the specifics of the Dark Man's appearance, the inhumanity of his makeup, the alien proportions of his form.

He looked over at Jenny. Did he believe her?

He did, Ellison decided.

And it terrified him.

■ ■ ■

Their involvement grew from there. It was a strange relationship. They weren't colleagues, weren't boyfriend and girlfriend, but were in some sort of indefinable partnership that partook of both. He told her about his research, and on his now frequent trips to New York often brought translations and copies of records that he'd discovered, running them by her to see if she had any additional insight. Her dreams had stopped, but he still tried to get as much information out of her as he could, and one night in bed, after going over in his head how Petohtalrayn had mysteriously appeared before the end of each civilization and how Jenny's dreams had placed him on the sidewalks of Manhattan, he had to ask her, "Is he coming back?"

She frowned, shaking her head. "I… don't think It can."

"What makes you say that?"

"Nothing specific. Just a feeling I have. Even when I saw It, I got the impression that It was trapped someplace and that was why It could only appear in dreams."

"And why do you always say 'It?'" he asked. "I mean, it's pretty clear the Dark Man is, well, a *man*."

She looked at him, stone-faced. "No. *It*."

There was a grim certainty in her voice, and, in a way, that scared him as much as anything else.

Ellison's superiors had found out about his obsession, and after having him show them a PowerPoint presentation and perusing his research, it was decided that he could work on this project full-time, with the university's complete backing, a vote of confidence that not only gave him additional time to work but provided him with access to far more resources.

Oddly enough, since meeting Jenny, he had developed a sort of... not sympathy, exactly... not affinity... maybe a sense of understanding when it came to the Dark Man. The PowerPoint presentation had brought this home to him. Because throughout all the stories, a pattern had started to emerge, and in each instance, the destruction of a people had led to its replacement by a far more harmonious society. The black figure—

Petohtalrayn

—was, as far as he could tell, a harvester for the gods, culling the unwanted from the earth and tilling the human soil so new civilizations could grow. He was to be feared, perhaps, but also, in a way, admired.

With the prestigious support of Miskatonic behind him, he was able to finagle a trip to the Southwest and meet with experts at assorted digs throughout the Four Corners states, one of whom led him to Rick Howell, a disgraced former curator of the Heard Museum in Arizona. The university would only pay for himself, but Jenny was due some time off, and she used her own money to buy a plane ticket and pay for her meals, although she did ride in Ellison's rental car and stay in his room at night.

The most recent extinction event was still the Nahapi people in what was now southwestern Colorado, and according to Howell, the site of their largest village supposedly offered concrete clues to the existence of the Dark Man. So after meeting with an Anasazi expert in Chaco Canyon, Ellison and Jenny took a trip north to visit Howell at his home in Farmington, New Mexico. It had been made clear that no one in academic or scholarly circles took the man seriously. He had ruined his career cataloguing eldritch gods that he insisted were the true inspiration for not only today's religions but for all human theology. The names were laughably long and almost purposefully unpronounceable—

like Petohtalrayn?

—but Howell maintained that they were real, they existed, and human religions were but a pale shadow of this cosmic truth, a more understandable and easily digestible version of a far more terrifying and incomprehensible reality.

Rick Howell's place was not the isolated adobe ranch house Ellison had been expecting but a nondescript tract home in a middle-class neighborhood near downtown Farmington. Inside was another story. In place of traditional furnishings were shelves and display cases filled with pottery and relics that looked as though they'd been stolen from a top museum. On the walls were maps, charts and thumbtacked photographs.

There was no small talk. The two of them had conversed over the phone, communicated by email, and they both knew why Ellison was here, what he was looking for. Howell had gathered together a stack of photos and artifacts related to Ellison's search, and the first thing he showed Ellison and Jenny was a carved obsidian figurine. Jenny's face paled at the sight of it.

"Do you recognize—?" Ellison began.

She nodded, cutting him off.

He examined the figurine. If it provoked such a strong reaction within her, it must be pretty close to accurate, and a chill passed through him as he studied the terrible blank face and the strangely proportioned body. Despite its diminutive size, the figure exuded a sense of tremendous power, and while Jenny's drawings and most of the references he'd seen made Ellison think the Dark Man was between seven and twelve feet tall, the sense he got from the figurine was that Petohtalrayn was actually much larger. He looked into the two small eyeholes that had been dug into the obsidian, and the eyes seemed to stare purposefully back at him.

"That's what you're looking for, isn't it?"

Ellison took a deep breath. "Yeah."

"Well, this is what I really want to show you," Howell said, and he handed over a photograph. "This is where I found that piece."

Ellison frowned, turning the picture vertical then horizontal, not sure which way it was supposed to go. "What is it?"

"A room I found underneath a building," Howell said, turning the photo upside down to the correct position. "Built under an overhang like Mesa Verde. According to establishment archeologists, it's a grain storeroom. Does that look like a storage room to you?"

It did not. In fact, Ellison did not know *what* it looked like. The proportions of the space seemed based on an alien geometry so far beyond human experience that, even looking at it from the proper perspective, it still did not resemble a room. He turned the photo in his hands, trying to force it to make sense.

"You can't see it here, but there's an opening in the floor with a ladder that leads down to a series of tunnels." Howell handed him a stack of photos, all of which showed underground passages and chambers. "I *searched* those tunnels. Until I was kicked off the team. After that, the entire dig was shut down. Too remote, too expensive to maintain. But I was close. *Close!*"

He didn't have to tell Ellison what he meant by "close."

"Are you sure?"

Howell nodded. "I could *feel* it." He pulled out a hand-drawn map and another photo, this one almost entirely black. It was hard to tell what it showed, but in the center was a lightening of the picture and a hint of wall and rock roof that made it appear to be of a cave. He pointed to the photo and to a spot on the edge of the map, marked with a red X.

This was where the Dark Man lay.

Petohtalrayn

Why, though? Why was he entombed underground? They could only speculate. Ellison thought about what Jenny had said, how she thought the Dark Man was trapped someplace and able to communicate only through dreams. Perhaps he had displeased his masters: gods or monsters even more powerful than he was, who had banished him, imprisoning him beneath the earth. There seemed to have been a concerted effort on his part to destroy civilization after civilization, perhaps to completely eradicate mankind, and maybe it was humanity's ability to fight back, its will to live, its unwillingness to succumb, that had doomed the Dark Man, that had made those who pulled the strings put him out to pasture.

"Not *him,*" Jenny reminded Ellison. "*It.*"

Howell nodded in agreement.

Ellison had brought a flash drive containing his own work to share with Howell, and he gave it to the other man, who plugged it into a computer. A file titled "Petohtalrayn" popped up. "We believe that's his name," Ellison said. He glanced over at Jenny. "*Its* name. It was given to the Minoan conception of the Dark Man in the nineteenth century by British scholars—"

Howell shook his head. "No."

"No?"

"They were afraid to speak Its real name, so they spelled it backward so as not to have to see or say the word." He typed over the name of the file, reversing the letters, and Ellison read the word aloud: "Nyarlathotep."

Howell shivered. "Yes. That is Its name."

Ellison knew it was true. Something about those syllables spoke to him even now, engendering within him a bone-deep revulsion, a close cousin to the abhorrence he'd felt upon seeing the contents of that secret room in the British Museum. Jenny held his hand, clutching it too tightly.

They spent the next several hours exchanging information. It was Howell who pointed out that, with the Nahapi site currently untended, they could explore it themselves. He pointed to his map on the table. "I could take you down there."

"Do you think we could find—"

"I think it's possible," Howell said.

The next day they set off, Ellison and Jenny in the rental car, Howell in his Jeep. Farmington was much closer to the Colorado border than Ellison realized, and it was a mere three hours later that they were at the site, an unprepossessing box canyon cordoned off from the surrounding wilderness by a chain link fence. Ellison barely had time to wonder how they would get in before Howell's Jeep was smashing through the gate that crossed the narrow dirt road, and the two vehicles were racing toward an impressively preserved cliff dwelling at the canyon's end.

The tunnels were just as Howell had said they'd be, just as they'd appeared in the photos, and the hand-drawn map was astonishingly accurate. But there were far more tunnels than Ellison had expected, and by the time they emerged before nightfall to set up camp and eat, he realized that Howell had mapped only a small fraction of the underground passages beneath the abandoned city.

A very small fraction.

And what remained went *deep*.

■□■

That night, Jenny dreamed of the Dark Man—

Nyarlathotep

—and when Ellison was awakened by her screams and shook her to bring her out of her nightmare, she told him that It had talked to her again.

That It was waiting for them.

■□■

The search was maddening and fruitless, and even after his allotted time frame was up, Ellison stayed on at the site, not making a conscious decision to do so, not bothering to inform his supervisor or anyone at the university, merely continuing with what had become his daily routine, as though this was and always had been his life: waking up with the sun, eating a quick breakfast bar with Jenny and Howell, then heading underground, the three of them splitting up to map ever deeper passages before reconnecting at night, eating a cold dinner and sleeping in the ruins. Every few days, Howell would go off to buy food and batteries from the closest town, over an hour away, but Ellison refused to leave, maintaining his focus, knowing as the map expanded into a maze that they grew ever closer to their goal.

There were, as he'd been told, sounds in the tunnels, the ratlike scurryings of small creatures through unseen parallel passages, and though he saw nothing, he thought of those skeletons Crowley had shown him in the secret room of the British Museum.

It was ten days in, when Howell didn't come back in the evening from his underground sojourn, that Ellison knew their search was finally over. Jenny, tired after a long day's exploration, and more frightened than she was willing to admit, wanted to give Howell more time, but he excitedly insisted that they go down immediately and retrace the missing man's steps.

Two hours down an unfamiliar passage, their lights beginning to dim perceptibly and with only one backup flash between them and the floor sloping sharply downward, they saw a faint glow originating from behind a curve in the rock wall ahead, a glow accompanied by unfamiliar sounds, low and faint and impossible to make out.

"Let's go back," Jenny said, and he heard the terror in her voice.

He grabbed her wrist so she could not run, feeling the tautness in her muscles. "No."

Down the slope, around the corner, they were hit with an odor so rotten that he gasped and gagged, while Jenny doubled over and vomited. The passage opened on a cave so massive that he could not see its end, with stalactites and stalagmites larger than buildings, twisted, eroded and formed into unwholesome shapes that he did not consciously recognize but that he apprehended on some deep instinctual level and that made him recoil in horror.

He thought of a line from the Coleridge poem "Kubla Khan."

Through caverns measureless to man.

That was what lay before him, a subterranean topography so gargantuan that it would take a lifetime to explore and so foul that no human being would dare to do so. Light from an unspecified source dimly illuminated the gigantic space, revealing a scene that not even his most depraved imaginings could have conjured. For in an open area the size of a city, he saw untold hordes of shiny white humanoid figures, all facing a much larger jet-black form occupying a park-sized clearing in their midst. He knew now what had happened to the Nahapi, the Hohokam, the Anasazi, the Minoans, all of the peoples who had disappeared over the centuries. They lived down here in this unholy lair, thousands of blind, albino minions, hairless inhuman descendants of those who had once lived above, now worshipping this mad faceless being.

Nyarlathotep.

The god had taken those who had not been killed, bringing them down here into the bowels of the earth, where they had bred and interbred into the slimy horrors that now lived in this sunless domain.

Ellison should have fled instantly and run back the way he had come, should have dragged Jenny through the tunnels to the surface and made sure that the entrance to this hell was sealed with enough concrete that it could never be accessed again. But he was not as frightened as he should have been. He was not frightened at all, in fact. He understood completely the horror of the scene before him, but he viewed it dispassionately, as an observer not a participant.

No, that was not exactly true. He *was* a participant. As was Jenny.

But he wasn't afraid.

Holding her hand, he stepped forward, moving down the sloping ground. The floor rippled before them, what he'd thought was black rock parting to reveal the real rock beneath, and he realized that what he'd taken to be a solid floor was a teeming multitude of misshapen rodents. They were not merely deformed rats, he understood, but children, the spawn of those albino supplicants, and they surged over the floor and walls, the roiling movement offering occasional glimpses of lighter human appendages attached to those dark furry bodies.

The two of them continued on. Seconds before they reached the outskirts of the assembly, the entire congregation, as one, dropped to their knees, bowing down before their god following some unseen, unheard cue. The simultaneous movement of thousands of bodies unleashed a fresh wave of that nauseating odor, and, gagging, Ellison and Jenny pinched their nostrils shut.

Yet they kept walking.

Ahead, Nyarlathotep stomped about in impotent fury, strangled sounds unlike any Ellison had heard before issuing from somewhere within Its featureless face, and Ellison knew that he and Howell had been right. It was a prisoner down here, banished along with those It was supposed to have eradicated, punished by beings far more powerful—and far more terrible—than It.

And where was Howell?

Dead, he thought. *Eaten.*

That may or may not have been true, and as they walked deeper into the cavern, he continued to look for the other man in the enormous crowd, but he did not expect to find him.

Why hadn't he and Jenny been killed?

Ellison didn't know, but their presence did not seem to have been noted at all. It was as though they were invisible, and while he knew that could change at any moment, he was grateful for it.

As horrible as the rotten stench were the sounds that tortured their ears: the whooshing of the rat things surging throughout the cave; the guttural grunts of the albino worshippers; the strangled cries of the madly stomping god. But beneath it all was something worse: continuous tuneless music, the faint sound of a high mindless piper playing notes that were the aural equivalent of those terrible shapes and angles, and he tried to ignore the sound, knowing that if he concentrated on it for too long it would drive him insane.

There was no change in the furious movements of Nyarlathotep, but he heard Its Voice, calm and commanding. The Voice was in his head, deep and inhuman, speaking words he understood though they were not of any known language. He was ordered to bring Jenny to the clearing, though he did not need to be ordered. It was what he wanted to do. It was what *she* wanted him to do, and he led her by the arm as the two of them strode between the kneeling supplicants until they stood before the Dark Man.

It turned to face them. This was why Jenny had been summoned, why she had dreamed of It and dreamed of him. This was her purpose, and she ripped off her clothes, laying prostrate before the god.

It took her immediately, in a violent depraved frenzy that could have taken seconds, could have taken hours, could have taken days. Time did not exist here, and however long it took, it left her bloody and mad, wailing in pain and laughing in her lunacy, while Its spawn, needing no gestation period, oozed out of her split thighs: a black liquid slime that once in the open coalesced into a warped human shape.

The Voice was in his head again, filling his mind with images and ideas that were utterly insane and made absolute sense. He bowed down in fealty, understanding what he needed to do and thinking that it had been part of his plans all along. He murmured thanks to Nyarlathotep, praising the god and pledging his everlasting obedience. The Voice told him to rise, and, standing, Ellison faced the ranks of mutated albinos, who stood as well.

He could lead them from this place, an army of the saved, descendants of the disappeared who could finish the job Nyarlathotep had started, clearing the earth of unworthy humanity, paving the way for the return of Howell's eldritch gods. Its task completed, Nyarlathotep would be freed again by Its masters, finally able to leave this underground prison.

He felt as though he should say something, a speech to rally the troops, an announcement of plans, but he was not really a leader, he was a pawn, and the Voice of the god that told him what to do was issuing orders to the minions as well.

The tunnels through which he and Jenny had arrived were far too small for the thousands of bodies that needed to pass through them to the surface, but Ellison learned that he was not needed to find a way up top; he was needed to navigate the land once they were there. He was the only one who knew of the outside world, and it would be his job to guide the army from city to city as they advanced and conquered.

The followers were holding weapons now, he saw, weapons that resembled spears and knives and swords but that seemed at once older and more sophisticated, their shapes and forms profoundly wrong to human eyes.

They would be leaving this realm through an opening miles away, and as soon as that knowledge registered in his brain, he fell onto his back and was carried forward, held aloft by the speeding ratlike spawn who shot him through the gathered multitudes and deeper into the hellish cavern. Ellison closed his eyes against the shapes of the rocks, afraid to look at them. He could feel the slimy stickiness of the massed legions as he passed, his skin brushing theirs, and hours later, he found himself at the head of the army. Nyarlathotep had accompanied him, stomping heedlessly upon those who were in Its way, clearing a path through Its worshippers, until they both stood before a breach in the cavern wall that was as big as Mount Rushmore. From the world above blew warm air that was like a breath of heaven after the fetid stench of the underground atmosphere. He breathed it in deeply, gratefully.

There were no last minute instructions, only a sharp mental *push* that sent Ellison into the breach, followed by an endless stream of mutants.

The god remained where It was, Its titanic frustration filling the air with a psychic turmoil strong enough to be palpable.

They were farther under the earth than Ellison had thought, but with each step forward, his mind and head grew clearer, the foul odor fading away, the mad piper's endless music diminishing. Before them was blackness, but gradually the gloom began to lessen, and eventually a faint glow let him know that they were approaching the surface. His eyes adjusted, what had been sheer white light separating into the colors of sky and clouds. He wondered about the effect on those behind him, and he turned to look, seeing them clearly for the first time, small black eyes staring unblinking in white rubbery newt-like faces.

Ellison reached the surface, emerging from beneath a sandstone cliff, facing an unidentified Southwestern town less than two blocks away.

"Forward!" he said, because he thought he should say *something*.

His shout was greeted with a reply of anguished shrieks and cries of agony. He turned. The members of his army were burning as soon as they hit the sunlight. Skin hissing like fat upon a frying pan, the white figures fell to the ground, writhing in pain as their slimy forms blackened and shriveled like worms exposed to fire.

And still more kept coming, trodding upon those who had fallen before them and suffering the same fate, scorched by a sun they had never seen.

He heard the Voice screaming in his head, could feel Nyarlathotep's impotent rage, and he wondered how often this had been tried before, how many attempts the god had made to escape Its prison.

Scores were dead now and burning, but finally the onslaught had stopped and those still in the cave had turned around and were retreating.

Ellison looked toward the town, thought about striking out for it alone, but he felt the pull of Nyarlathotep and instead turned around and withdrew into the dark safety of the earth. The attempt had failed before it had even begun—

Yet again, the Voice said

—but no matter. Ellison knew now what needed to be done. *He* would be the father of the next army. If Jenny was still alive, he would mate with her, her and whoever—*whatever*—else might live underground. Nyarlathotep had been banished and neither It nor Its offspring could leave their prison. But Ellison was immune to the sun, and it might take generations, but he would create an army that could survive above. They would cleanse the earth of humanity once and for all, and Nyarlathotep would once again be granted Its rightful place among Its eldritch brethren.

In his head, he had maps, maps of cities, states, countries, continents, and he would teach them to those he spawned, building a force that was powerful and smart and could not be beat, a force that would cleanse the world, a force worthy of Nyarlathotep.

Taking a last breath of fresh air, a last look at the sun and the sky, Ellison followed the retreating minions and descended into the darkness of his new home.

Nyarlathotep

Of all the old ones who haunt the desert places of this world, none takes a greater interest in the race of men than he who is called the Crawling Chaos, or by another name, Nyarlathotep. He has no form as we know it, but he comes in various guises as it suits his capricious humor. Most often he appears as a man who walks on the desert sands at night beneath the stars or moon. Woe to the wanderer who encounters Nyarlathotep alone in the darkness, for his days are numbered.

In ancient times he wore the splendor of a prince of Egypt, and appeared to men in a royal crown and royal robes of gold, with his eyes lined with kohl and his mouth reddened with henna. In his hand he carried a royal scepter, and his countenance shone with its own inner light. But in these degenerate times it is said that he walks the sands in the gray cloak of a hermit, and wears a hood upon his head to conceal his face in shadow.

It is not fortunate that the awareness of this dreadful being, who is no less than the soul and messenger of Azathoth, should focus itself upon a single man, for he regards our race as mere toys to be played with and then discarded after they are broken. Many a weary night traveler has encountered one he mistook for a humble Christian mystic, one of those monks who dwell alone in the desert and pace the sands mumbling prayers, only to recognize his doom when it was too late to avert it. Woe to the man who tries to speak to this hooded wanderer. Let him pass in silence, and pray to your chosen god that he does not turn his head and look back at you.

For when he beckons, you must go to him. There is no escape. He smells your fear like a blood spoor on the sands. When he speaks, you must answer. His face is always shadowed, and fortunate it is so, for should he throw his hood back so that you see his liniments by moonlight, you will surely die. If you run from him, he will never rest from the chase until you are brought to bay. He will haunt your dreams, inhabit the shadows at midday and the gloom of dusk, the blackness of midnight and the bleak gray that comes before the dawn. Always when you look behind, he is there waiting.

It is the office of this fell being to regulate the music of Azathoth, for he is the eyes and tongue of the idiot god, and more than this, he is Azathoth's mind and heart. He is bound by his nature to fulfill the unarticulated purposes of Azathoth, and this he does, but he does so with malice, for he hates his bondage to Azathoth and longs to slay the idiot god and assume his authority. In spite of his vast wisdom he does not understand that the music of creation and the mind to regulate its measures cannot coexist. The harmonies that flow from Azathoth's flute spring from a chaotic source. They can never arise from a mind that is restricted by hatred and passion.

From the dawn of time Nyarlathotep has walked the sands of Arabia, brooding on his own thoughts which are as far beyond the ken of men as the planets in their crystalline spheres. Men have called him Death, for one brush of his hand and they fall to black ashes and dust and blow away on the night wind. Of all the old ones he is the easiest to evoke, and the most perilous. His promises are all lies, and pacts made with him end in betrayal and sorrow. We are as flies to him, to be ignored or if noticed, crushed with a careless gesture. Summon him not! It is not good to be noticed by this old one.

The Doors that Never Close and the Doors that Are Always Open

David Liss

Artúr gave himself an hour and a quarter to get to his appointment, even though the most pessimistic estimates put the trip at a half an hour, door to door, but he was still almost late. He had lived in New York all of his adult life, yet he'd still never figured out the mysteries of the Wall Street area, where the epicenter of 21st century capitalism was built along the outline of arbitrary colonial streets. Lucile from the employment agency, whose position on Artúr's chances in the employment market had moved, quite suddenly, from apathetic to optimistic, assured him that finding the building would be simple. She breezily explained that it was just downtown from the IRT Wall Street station, between Beaver and South William. Artúr had wandered aimlessly, moving in circles, for what felt like hours before finding the CapitalBank headquarters rising luminously above dingy diners and tiny shops selling umbrellas and luggage made in China.

Artúr's one suit had just come back from the dry cleaners, and he thought he looked polished and professional. All his life he had held Wall Street guys in contempt—people whose only goal in life was to make money. He had nothing against people who got rich doing something they found interesting or exciting or creative, but cutting out the process, going after wealth for the sake of wealth, struck him as bleak and soulless. Now, here he was, not looking to get rich, but to be a very small cog in the larger machine, a little underpaid stooge whose work, in some nearly immeasurable way, would help aid a tribe of chest-thumping degenerates to inflate their own holdings. Even going on the interview embarrassed him, demeaned him. He hated the feeling, but he hated the feeling of having an empty bank account even more.

After checking in with a security guard and making his way through a metal detector, Artúr was directed to wait in the lobby. His appointment had been for 2:00, and he'd walked in the door pretty much on the dot, but now he began to worry. There had been a sandwich delivery guy ahead of him, and by the time Artúr had actually spoken with anyone, it had been closer to five after. Had he been technically late? He didn't think it should matter, but he knew how intense these Wall Street types were supposed to be.

After half an hour, he decided he should check with the security guard again, but he found a sign telling him he could not leave the secure area without an exit pass, and the security guard was on the other side of what appeared to be bullet-, sound- and explosion-proof glass. After a few awkward minutes of trying to signal the guard, who appeared to be deliberately ignoring him while he fiddled with a control panel that could have come from a commercial passenger jet, Artúr gave up and sat back down on the padded bench.

Twenty minutes later, the elevator doors chimed open and a curious, and extremely un-Wall-Street-looking man hobbled out. He was tall, almost unnaturally so, well over six and a half feet, though he walked with a pronounced slouch. His skin was nearly translucently pale, and his shaggy hair, equally shaggy eyebrows, and close-cut beard were all snowy white. He wore faded green corduroy pants, an oversize white button-down shirt, and a tweed jacket. He looked more like the professors Artúr had left behind than an employee of a high-powered financial firm.

"Artúr," the pale man pronounced, like a birdwatcher identifying a species on the wing. "Kevin Jacks." He held out a thin hand that seemed to be made of rice paper.

Artúr reached out to take it and discovered that in addition to being tall and pale and fragile-looking, Jacks had a distinctly unpleasant smell about him, something hard to pin down, but it was animalistic and wild, like wet fur and rotten wood and clumps of moist dung moldering in a barn. In fact, there was something goaty in general about Jacks—the beard, even the cast of his face, which seemed neither young nor old.

Artúr tried not to move away from Jacks or let his face show the impact of the musky blast assaulting his nostrils.

"Thank you for coming out today," Jacks said, his voice a little high, and curiously detached. "I know you must be very busy."

Artúr was not busy. He spent most of his days looking through employment websites and worrying about how he was going to pay the rent in a couple of weeks or, more immediately, eat something other than plain white rice for his next meal.

Jacks led Artúr back behind the elevator bank he'd emerged from to an alcove, this one containing a single elevator. Once enclosed within the confined space, Jacks's smell made Artúr's eyes water, but he attempted to keep up bland and meaningless conversation. Yes, summer is coming on. Going to be hot. Yankees should be back in first place by the end of the month.

He's got to know, Artúr thought, that he smells horrible. This is a test, like those urban legends about people in interviews being asked to open unopenable windows. They were seeing how he would react. Did they want him to call Jacks out, tell him he smelled? Artúr didn't think so. He figured he'd err on the side of politeness and try to ignore it as best he could. For now, he was grateful he hadn't eaten any breakfast or lunch—he hadn't been able to face another bowl of rice—so he didn't have to worry about throwing up.

Artúr wasn't sure what he was expecting when the elevator doors opened, but he'd had his share of office jobs—temp work before grad school—and he'd assumed he'd be met by either a reception area or a bustling open workspace full of hustling financial types and ringing phones. Instead, he saw an empty corridor, unadorned and bleak. Had he not felt the elevator ascending, he would be certain he was on some sort of basement level.

They stepped out of the elevator and Jacks turned around, removing an antiquated circular keychain from his capacious pockets and inserting one of the gigantic Scooby-Doo style keys into a hole next to the elevator call button. He rotated it, mumbling, "Two and a half times. That's the way. That is still her way."

They moved down the corridor into a spare room with a large table and nothing else. The walls were unadorned cinder blocks. Jacks beckoned Artúr to sit, and he positioned himself across the table from Jacks to try and lessen the smell.

"Tell me," Jacks said, leaning forward, folding his wispy fingers together. "Why do you want to work for CapitalBank?"

"Honestly, I just need a job," Artúr said. "The employment agency said you had an opening that suited my skill set."

Jacks nodded and made a note on a yellow legal pad.

"Artúr Magnusson. You are of Icelandic descent?"

"Are you supposed to ask questions like that?" Artúr asked. He knew he should keep his mouth shut, but he didn't like flagrant rule breaking. He didn't like these big firms who decided they would do what they wanted, and the rest of society could shut up about it. "Isn't it against the law to ask about someone's background?"

"We have a form 11-B dispensation from federal hiring laws," Jacks said with a smile. "Does your family still use patronymics?"

Artúr sighed. He didn't much care to talk about his family, but this wasn't worth making a fuss over, and while he had no idea what an 11-B dispensation was, he figured it had to be a real thing. "My grandfather came from Iceland. Magnusson is just a family name now."

"But your mother is also Icelandic?"

Artúr figured there was no point in fighting this. "She's of Icelandic descent. Why?"

Jacks wrote for a while, maybe three or four lines. Then he looked up and fixed Artúr with his pink eyes. "No reason. Just a little genealogical curiosity. What do you think of what we do here at CapitalBank? We want an honest answer, not the one you think we're looking for. If you feed me any 'important pillar of the economy' or 'presence in global markets' nonsense this interview will be over."

They wanted to know, so he'd tell them. "I don't much care for large financial firms," Artúr said. "They exploit and distort the market for their own gain and they don't care about the consequences because the only outcome that matters is profit. CapitalBank, and firms like it, are completely removed from the rest of the economy, so success and gains not only no longer reflect the success and gains in ordinary people's lives, they actually detract from the ability of ordinary people to succeed."

"So, CapitalBank is like a vampire?" Jacks asked, his voice neutral.

"I suppose," Artúr said thoughtfully. "Really, though, it's more like a dragon in a fairy tale, hoarding all the treasure for itself, gaining more only by destruction and fire and ruin."

Jacks made a note. "Devouring. Yes," he murmured.

"Does that mean we're done?" Artúr asked, wanting to get out of this airless room, wanting to get away from Jacks's scent. He'd take a job working in Starbucks, driving a taxi, whatever he had to do. He did not want to be here with this weird man any longer.

"Oh, no," Jacks said, still jotting down notes. "I told you I wanted honesty, and you were good enough to be honest. We're looking for a researcher," he added without any indication that he was changing topics. "You have some experience with research."

"I was a doctoral candidate in history," Artúr said. "I'm good at research, and I'm good at picking up new topics and managing new sources, but I have no experience in the financial sector."

"Why did you leave Columbia's history department?' Jacks asked.

Artúr shifted uncomfortably in his seat. "I ran out of funding. My advisor... left. No one else was interested in my project, and I think the professors I asked to vouch for me might have sabotaged my chances, written lukewarm letters of recommendation."

Jacks made notes for what seemed like a very long time. The room felt warmer, more airless. Artúr wished for that unopenable window right about now. He'd happily throw a chair through it…

"Tell me about your advisor," Jacks said, still writing. "Professor Thanton. She simply quit one day, if I understand correctly. Didn't even clean out her office or her apartment. She announced that she was done, and walked away. Never answers email or letters."

This, as far as Artúr was concerned, had gone on far enough. "Mr. Jacks, I appreciate your taking the time for this interview, but—"

"Did she ever mention to you a name?" Jacks asked. "A name that, upon hearing it, made you feel… things? Or speak of a door?"

"Thank you for your time," Artúr said. He put his hands on the arms of his chair, but seemed unable to rise.

Jacks looked up, meeting Artúr's gaze with his own colorless stare. "We believe you are amply qualified for this position. I don't see the point in meeting with other candidates. We'd like to offer you the job immediately: Head of Special Projects Research. We believe the compensation is competitive within the marketplace."

He slid an index card over, on which was written: *Annual compensation, $325,000.00. Plus bonuses.*

Artúr stared at the card, letting the numbers move in and out of focus. One month's salary would be more than all of his annual graduate student stipend. What would he do with money like that? Fast cars and women in slinky dresses? Bottles of champagne at a nightclub? It seemed absurd. "This has to be some sort of joke," Artúr said.

"The position comes with its own housing," said Jacks, "located within these very walls, so you would not be obligated to pay rent. I should warn you, however, that our CEO does not wish to haggle over the matter. What we offer is not open to negotiation—not one part of it. You may take it or you may walk away."

Of course he was going to take it. How could he not? No matter how demeaning or distasteful the work and the co-workers, he would take it. "But I don't understand," he said. "What is the job? What would I be researching?"

"Our CEO may send you assignments from time to time, but for the most part, you are free to research whatever you like. Mr. Ostentower expects full access to whatever you discover and whatever you write, but what that is remains entirely up to you. I shall tell you what we would like, however, what would make us most spectacularly happy. I shall tell you what would make these old walls reverberate with delight. Would you care to hear it?"

"Okay," said Artúr. "Sure."

"We would like you to continue your work on your dissertation."

□□□

When he'd first started the doctoral program in history at Columbia, Artúr had been confused about what to do or even why he was doing it. His sophomore year of college he had floated the idea of becoming a history professor experimentally to his father, a long-haul trucker who thought of school as nothing more than a way of avoiding work, and who saw his son's bookishness as a secret shame. Artúr thought his father would have been more comfortable with a serial rapist for a child. At least that was, in some twisted way, manly. Artúr's father's response to the idea of a graduate degree in the humanities had been so drunkenly hostile and befuddled, that Artúr's course had been more or less set, rooted purely in rebellion. His graduate school application essay had included some rather obvious bullshit based on his senior thesis about a group of 17th century Dutch explorers and their efforts to find the lost continent of Mu. In truth, Artúr had hated working on that project, and he wanted nothing to do with it ever again.

It attracted the interest of Professor Amanda Thanton, however, who had pushed aggressively for Artúr's acceptance into the program, and if the rest of the faculty had been unimpressed with Artúr, they eventually gave in. Later he would learn they'd done so because Amanda could be an unstoppable pain in the ass if she got a bee in her bonnet. She was four years into the tenure clock with little to show for herself, and she was certain to wash out before the dust settled, but she had an iron will that few could resist.

Every professor in the department warned Artúr against working with her, but none of them expressed any interest in Artúr's comments in class, and their feedback on his class papers tended to be lukewarm at best. Amanda, meanwhile, invited Artúr into her office where she would talk at length about her theories. These conversations would frequently spill over into dinner or drinks, and somewhere along the way Artúr had begun to find her thin, austere looks, her huge and dazed gray eyes, attractive, even sexy. He was, he realized at some point, in love with her, but he dared not say anything, dared not make a move, lest it ruin their professional relationship.

Instead he decided he would spend as much time with her as he could. That was why he had ended up following Amanda's advice and started researching a dissertation on various 19th century efforts to find K'n-yan, a subterranean realm believed to lie somewhere underneath Oklahoma.

Amanda's enthusiasm began to catch on with him, even infect him, and Artúr had been fascinated by the explorers and archivists and religious ecstatics who had dedicated their lives to the search for K'n-yan. Their quest intersected with some of the most interesting ideas and movements of the time—westward expansion, secret Masonic rites, the rise of Mormonism, abolitionism—you name it. Artúr had been a good year into his project when Amanda began to bring him documents, not because they were useful for Artúr's dissertation topic—situating K'n-yan obsession within the context of the Second Great Awakening—but because she believed she had found clues to its location.

"We can find it," she said in a whisper one night as they sat in the dark corner of a bar near campus. She'd allowed her fingertips to touch his hand. This was high intimacy for her. "We can go there. We can see her people."

"Whose people?" Artúr had asked. Amanda sometimes got into these moods—intense, focused. They were almost trancelike, and he found them unbelievably sexy. He wondered then, as he often did when she was like this, if he could undress her without her noticing.

"To say her name is to know her," Amanda told him, and she looked away.

In her office, she would lay out tattered maps showing the Wichita Mountains or the Upper Kiamichi River Wilderness and jab increasingly ink-stained fingers on various spots. "Here!" she shouted. "We can know her here!"

Her agitation suddenly became less erotic and more disturbing. He had never seen her eyes look that wild, as though there was nothing behind them. As though she was gone, and some thing, some force, was animating her flesh.

"Amanda, who do you mean?" Artúr had asked nervously. It was late, well after dark in early February, and the banks of snow piled outside of her office window. The room was illuminated by only a desk lamp, casting elongated shadows. Amanda's face was composed entirely of shadow.

"The doors that never close," she had said. "The doors that are always open. And she was there, you know. I felt her. The black goat of a thousand young, and I heard them speak her name."

Amanda had then uttered some nonsense syllables. It sounded gibberish, but Artúr felt the hair stand up on the back of his neck. He felt like something was there with the two of them. If he turned around and peered into the dark corners of the room, he might see it. He did not turn around. Instead he stared at her while she stared at the map, and he tried to forget the sounds she'd made. He told himself he already had, and that what was stuck in his mind was just something he'd invented or misheard, but it would not go away.

Shug-Niggurath.

It was the last time he ever saw Amanda.

◾◾◾

They were walking down a spare stairwell, unadorned and industrial. Some of the concrete stairs were missing and had been replaced by wooden blocks, wedged into jagged spaces. Most of these were old and rotting covered with green mildew or a strange sort of slime that Artúr tried to avoid stepping on.

"Are you a religious person, Artúr?" Jacks asked. The goaty man's scent came off of him in waves, and Artúr worked hard not to grimace.

"No, not really," he said, which was a more polite version of *no, not at all*.

"Do you think Jesus is important?"

"Historically, sure."

They had gone down three flights, and now Jacks pushed open a doorway. "I mean right now. At his moment. In this building?"

Artúr shook his head. "Not to me."

Jacks grinned. "Me either. Isn't that funny? We can be funny together, don't you think?"

The door opened into the archive, and Artúr forgot just how crazy Jacks had sounded. He heard himself gasp.

The three stories they had gone down seemed to comprise the whole of the archive, which reached up forty or fifty feet. Every inch of wall was lined with bookcases, lined with old volumes from massive folios to tiny sixteenmos. Ornate sliding ladders lined the walls, one to each segment. The room, Artúr realized, was in the shape of a pentagon.

Though the interior was largely empty, there were a half-dozen long wooden tables spread throughout, and in the center, an old-style card catalog. Artúr scanned the space and saw not a single computer. The only sound was that of a ticking tall case clock. The room could have been from the 19th century.

"This doesn't look like financial research," Artúr said.

"Everything exists within the economy," Jacks said. "CapitalBank is always looking for new markets to explore. New doors to open, or perhaps to walk through if they are already open."

Something came over Artúr. He could not have said what it was or why he chose to probe, but he spoke without thinking. "And if they never close?"

Jacks grinned. "Oh, I think you are going to do very well here, Artúr. I think you are going to do marvelously well. I think they are going to toast your arrival and drink deeply. And they will spill the excess upon the soil."

"I'm still considering my options."

"Of course you are," Jacks said. "Let me show you your suite."

■ ■ ■

He'd tried to find Amanda, of course. The department would only say that she had tendered a letter of resignation and gone abruptly, leaving her classes uncovered. Artúr wanted to tell her he was sorry, though he didn't know what for. He wanted to offer to help her, though he didn't know what with. He wanted to think he was going to tell her he loved her, but he knew he lacked the courage.

Using Google he managed to turn up the names of her parents, who lived upstate, and he called them. When he answered the phone, Amanda's father appeared to be sawing wood, and he didn't stop during the conversation. In the background, Artúr heard an old woman giggling.

"She's not here," Amanda's father said. "But I'm making a door to find her. Now fuck off."

He had so little money to spare, but Artúr had rented a car and driven four hours to find their rickety two-story house, blue paint fading from the wood. Amanda's father had emerged on the front porch holding a handgun he seemed to have no idea how to use. He was a short man with a fringe of silver hair. He looked like he'd spent his life working for the post office or in a dry goods store. He said that Artúr had two minutes to get the hell off his land or he'd be dead and then fired a warning shot in the air.

That had ended the search for Amanda, but Artúr could not stop thinking about her—or the things she'd said.

∎ ∎ ∎

Through the archive was a large wooden door, maybe twelve feet high, which Jacks opened with one of his ancient-looking keys. Inside Artúr found a foyer such as he might expect in a Gilded Age New York mansion, complete with coatrack and umbrella stand. He smelled something delicious—maybe bread in the oven—from down the hall. They moved into an expansive living room with turn-of-the-century furnishings, and from the other side of the hall—no doubt the kitchen was off in that direction—came a woman in a maid's uniform. She was a little younger than Artúr, maybe in her early twenties, blonde, tall, and with a slender build. Her face was striking, if not precisely beautiful, but she had large eyes that were richly, intensely blue. They were like the eyes of a cartoon princess.

"Artúr, this is Mirja Tiborsdóttir. She is the suite's housekeeper."

She held out a slim hand. "It is for me good to meet you," she said shyly. Her accent was heavy, but she carefully pronounced each word. "I am making now some skúffukaka if you like."

Artúr had no idea what that was, but he smiled and nodded. Jacks suggested they finish the tour, and he led Artúr through the dining room, the sitting room, the three bedrooms, the two bathrooms, the study, the kitchen—where Mirja was removing from the oven a skillet filled with some kind of cake—and, off of that, the maid's quarters. All were lavishly decorated, like preserved rooms in a museum. There were no windows.

"And I would live here by myself?" Artúr asked.

"And Mirja, of course," said Jacks. "She takes good care of the place, I think you'll agree."

"Why are there no windows?" Artúr asked.

"We prefer you look inward rather than outward." He pulled a chain watch out of his pants pockets. "Oh, we'd better hurry. It's time to meet Mr. Ostentower."

Artúr had no response but to blink heavily. He had never closely followed the financial world, but he kept up with current events, so he knew that Howard Ostentower was CapitalBank's famous and much celebrated CEO.

■ ■ ■

Back before the financial crisis, CapitalBank was one of the first firms to make a killing—a massive killing—on packaging mortgage-backed securities. Profits had soared through the roof, but once the rest of the financial sector joined the party, Howard Ostentower had suddenly divested his firm, going public about his concerns. Dismissing his own role in the craze as "distant history," he'd warned of large-scale destruction and loss and pain. "An unmaking," was the term he'd used, and it had generated headlines.

A number of analysts had condemned Ostentower's management of CapitalBank, whose profits were high, but not as high as they could have been. Then, when the bubble burst and financial giants were tottering and falling, Ostentower became a media darling, the wise prophet who saw through worldly illusion, the steady helmsman who led his ship through treacherous waters to safety. His own role in the destruction was entirely forgotten. Now you could see him all the time on cable news and financial channels, spouting his opinions and forecasting the market. Artúr had always had the impression that he mainly liked to hear himself talk and that he had no more real insight than anyone else. On the other hand, he was a high-profile corporate CEO and a media darling. His time was literally worth money. Artúr couldn't imagine he would want to take time to meet a researcher.

Jacks led Artúr back through the archives, up the flights of stairs and to the elevator, which he had to unlock with his key. They went back to the lobby, where they walked to a distant set of elevator banks. Here Jacks waved a keycard to activate a private elevator and gestured for Artúr to step inside.

"When you speak to Mr. Ostentower," Jacks warned. "Do not mention Jesus or any established prophet. Do not read or quote from any of the world's major holy books."

"You're the one who brought all this up," Artúr said.

"Just don't. You have been warned."

They went up to the 87th floor, which opened on precisely the sort of scene Artúr had imagined earlier. It was an expanse of cubicles in which men and women in expensive suits ran from place to place, shouted into phones, called out in triumph or defeat like drunks at a Super Bowl party. There were groans of frustration and high fives and chest thumps and rubber-band-bound documents being tossed great distances like Frisbees. Across the room, a guy leaned back in his chair so far he fell to the ground, spraying a geyser of coffee into the air. The walls were plastered with television screens showing the news and the cable channels. People pointed and jeered and cried "Oh, shit!" at every piece of information.

They were all so young, he thought—younger than he was. They looked fresh out of college, and they acted like they were even younger than that. They held the fate of nations in their hands, expanding and deflating economies like they held magic bellows, but they behaved like children.

"You know what is happening here?" Jacks asked.

"Some kind of trading floor," Artúr guessed.

"It is devastation," Jacks told him. "The devouring of worlds. Things that have abstract value or don't yet exist or are entirely unnecessary being bought and sold and bet on or against. It is ritual. You're against all that, aren't you?"

"Look, Mr. Jacks," Artúr began.

"Your political positions are well documented," Jacks explained. "We have tracked your social media posts." He hadn't moved any closer but his scent became more stifling, more intense, as though this conversation were exciting hidden bodily functions, glands and secretions and ducts all opening and expelling.

"I can't change the system," Artúr said, "and right now I need work."

"But you think this is bad?" Jacks pressed. "Evil?"

"I think it's ultimately destructive," Artúr conceded.

Jacks grinned at him. "That's what we like to think. Let's go meet Mr. Ostentower."

They wound through the chaotic floor until they came to a circular staircase leading up. They climbed and emerged in a quiet and tasteful lobby where a receptionist waved them into an office quite literally bigger than Artúr's apartment. Along the far wall, against the expanse of windows, was a desk. Closer to the door was a sort of lounge with a coffee machine, muffins, and finger sandwiches. Jacks had begun stuffing the sandwiches in his mouth, two or three at a time, when the door opened and Howard Ostentower stepped in. He wore suit pants and a shirt, but no jacket. He looked thinner and shorter than he had on television. Older too. He wasn't the magnetic financial giant he seemed to be on the cable news channels. He was just a middle-aged man, mostly bald, who had a nice office.

"You must be Artúr Magnusson," he said with great warmth, as though he had long awaited this moment. "I'm Howard Ostentower. Great to meet you. C'mon. Have a seat!" He waved Artúr over to his desk. Jacks continued to stand by the sandwiches, eating them in huge bites.

Artúr sat across from Ostentower, who lowered himself into his desk-chair-apparatus, a complication of back support and cushions and armrest gadgets.

"So," said Ostentower. "You're Icelandic?"

"My grandparents were," Artúr said hesitantly. Everything was starting to seem like a trap now.

"But your blood is Icelandic. That's good." He smiled.

"I'm not sure why," said Artúr. "And honestly, I'm not sure I understand this job."

"Do you understand the salary and the accommodations it comes with?" asked Ostentower.

"It is all very generous, but—"

"Why not give it a try?" Ostentower boomed. "You don't like money? Is that it? Because if that's not it, I don't see why you're fucking around with my time."

It was a good point, if belligerently delivered. If, after two or three months, Artúr found he didn't like what they wanted from him, he would still have pocketed enough money to refuel his work-search efforts. He wouldn't even need to get rid of his apartment.

"I just don't understand what it is you want me to do in this job?" Artúr said.

"We want you to be yourself," Ostentower said. "That shouldn't be so hard, should it?" He grinned like the cameras were rolling.

Artúr glanced at Ostentower's desk, which was very neat. There was an open notebook computer, a mug half-full of coffee and a nibbled muffin. Three separate stacks of paper were arranged into neat piles. There was also a photograph of a goat, showing only its head, and in the background was a field of stars. The goat seemed to be looking at Artúr. He had the impression it was grinning in some obscure, unknowable goatish way.

"Mr. Jacks said you want me to continue my research into the search for K'n-Yan. I don't understand why that's of interest to CapitalBank."

"We're interested in doors that never close and doors that are always open," Ostentower said. He leaned forward, resting his chin on his folded hands and stared at Artúr. "Can you understand that?"

That was when Artúr knew he would take the job.

■ ■ ■

That meeting was on a Wednesday. Artúr began his first day of work the following Monday. He had been told to pack up such personal effects as he thought he would need, and they would be delivered to his suite. When he arrived at CapitalBank, Jacks was there to meet him again, bringing him down to the archive.

"Time to get started," Jacks said.

"I hardly know where to begin."

"Probably best to spend some time familiarizing yourself with our holdings. Then, of course, you can pursue your research as you see fit. However, Mr. Ostentower would like to see weekly updates. Between the two of us, I think it would be ideal if you had something solid to show him before the month is out. Mr. Ostentower can become impatient, agitated, sometimes even violent. He doesn't show that side of himself on television, but the potential is always there, like some dark thing just beneath the surface. Waiting."

A long pause hovered in the air until Artúr said, "Okay."

"Just do your best," Jacks said with a patronizing smile. "We hope you have motivation to do your best, Artúr. It is what we would like to see. Oh, and Mr. Ostentower has requested that you join him for worship tomorrow morning."

"I thought I wasn't supposed to mention—"

"Don't be obtuse," Jacks said, his voice suddenly cold and scolding. "It's unbecoming."

■ ■ ■

Much of the archive consisted of diaries and personal notes, and the bulk of these were of people Artúr had never heard of—obscure New England clerics from the 19th century, an early 20th century Nevada missionary, one of the mid-Apollo-era astronauts. There were also papers by secondary and tertiary figures from Artúr's research, many of whom he hadn't known had kept papers. These, he found, were bindings of handwritten pages, sometimes stained with dirt or water or even what looked like blood. Some were composed in wild scribbles. He found a box which contained what looked like a memoir scrawled on a roll of toilet paper. But all of them appeared to end abruptly, often in midsentence. And many were adorned with childish images of goat heads or doors.

There were collections of mystical books too—several editions of the *Necronomicon*, all remarkably different from one another, and several complete sets of *The Seven Cryptical Books of Hsan*. On a hunch, he checked the card catalog and found a listing for the complete papers of

Amanda Thanton. He felt the air leave his lungs as though someone had punched him in the gut. It took a moment for him to find the rhythm of his breathing again. Amanda's papers! If he knew more about what she had believed, where she had gone, this would all be worth it.

He spent ten minutes trying to navigate the organizational system of the archive, but when he found the spot on the shelf where Amanda's papers were supposed to be, it was empty.

He sat down at one of the tables, gripping the sides like he was holding on. How could CapitalBank have Amanda's papers? Why would they want them? Why had Ostentower said that thing about doors, the same thing Amanda had once said? The poor lighting in the room, its windowlessness, was starting to get to him, and Artúr felt like he needed to get outside, get some air. Maybe, he knew, he should never come back.

He was sitting there like that when Mirja arrived with a tray of coffee. She set it down on one of the tables and tried to slip out silently.

"Mirja," Artúr said, trying to keep his voice steady. "It just occurred to me that Jacks didn't give me an elevator key. If I want to go out for lunch, how do I get to the lobby from here?"

"There is no use for going out," she said, then paused for a tight smile, lips pressed together. It was the costume jewelry equivalent of smiles. "Everything of your wanting is in your suite."

"But what if I want to go out?" Artúr asked.

"You must speak with Mr. Jacks, yes?"

"Do you ever go out?"

Mirja looked off like she was thinking, as though Artúr had posed a difficult math problem. "It is not a question for me," she said at last.

"Maybe through the doors that never close?" Artúr attempted experimentally.

Mirja remained motionless, like she was willing her muscles not to move. Only the slightest twitch appeared at one corner of her mouth.

"Have you ever heard the name Shub—"

"Let me pour your cream!" she cried out, and then lurched forward, almost striking Artúr in the face with an elbow as she gripped the little creamer. She leaned in to pour and said, hardly louder than the sound of his own pulse in his ear, "To say her name is to know her. Don't."

She hurried out of the archive.

■ ■ ■

Knowing that Mirja would be lurking around in his apartment made Artúr uneasy, so he put off lunch until he became distractingly hungry. When he made his way to the suite, she had him sit in the dining room where she served him a plate of baked salmon with a cream sauce, glazed carrots and potatoes roasted with garlic and big chunks of salt. After putting down the dish, she slinked away, as if afraid he would make conversation with her. Artúr was not looking forward to his evenings.

While he ate, he looked up and noticed a security camera in the upper corner of the dining room. He tried to ignore it. He told himself that the furnishings were no doubt expensive, so of course they wanted to keep an eye on things, but even so, it was unnerving. After he finished his lunch, Artúr made a brief survey of the rest of the suite and discovered security cameras in every room, including the bathroom, where it was directed at the toilet.

He found Mirja in the kitchen washing dishes, her shoulders hunched like she was expecting a beating.

"How do I contact Mr. Jacks?" he asked her.

She turned off the water and pivoted slightly, but did not meet his eye. "He will let you know."

"He'll let me know how to contact him?"

"Yes, of course," she said as she worked her sponge over a troubling spot on a pan.

"How do you contact him?" he pressed.

"He will let me know when it is necessary," she said. Her eyes flickered to the kitchen security camera, and then she flipped the water on and returned to the dishes.

When he stepped out of the kitchen, he took out his phone and decided he would make some plans. He needed to get out of this place, hang out with some normal people, have a few too many beers. Once he made the plans, he'd have to find Jacks, and Jacks would have to tell him how he could get in and out on his own.

There was no cell phone service, however. And there were no phones in the apartment. It began to occur to Artúr that he would have no contact with any human being but Mirja until Jacks decided otherwise.

■■■

Back in the archive, Artúr made up his mind to be productive. He knew how to get work done under difficult conditions. That's what graduate school was all about. He would work hard all afternoon, and when he saw Jacks next, he'd be in a position to ask for things because he would have progress to show for himself.

Howard Ostentower was a K'n-yan obsessive, just like the people Artúr worked on for his dissertation. Just like Amanda. That much was clear. Now what Artúr had to do was put together something, some hint or sign. He knew, from his research, how excited these people could get at anything.

He also wanted to find Amanda's papers, but he didn't want to push that. Maybe Ostentower was reading them. Maybe that's how he learned Artúr's name.

He decided to begin with the most contemporary material, things he hadn't seen before. There were other researchers from all over the world. Some, like Amanda, had held university posts. Others were loners, working in their basements or dusty houses, poring over old notes or tracking down internet rumors. A few, he noted, were from other financial institutions. They all believed that somewhere in Oklahoma lay the entrance to an underground realm. Not a cavern or even a city, but a *realm*—a land or kingdom. There, people who were not like us lived in ways we could not imagine, but in ways that would open our imaginations, enlighten us, and very likely destroy us. There, they all agreed, they dedicated themselves to the black goat of a thousand young. To speak her name, he saw in almost every set of notes he examined, was to know her.

By the end of his first day, he had organized his reading into several cross-referenced lists. It was going to take weeks, maybe months, to work his way through the material. Interpretation of handwriting alone was going to be a chore. At least he knew where to begin, though.

When he returned to his suite. He found the dinner table set for one. Mirja called from the kitchen that he should sit when he was ready, and though being served made him uncomfortable, he didn't see much of an alternative. Almost as soon as he pushed his chair in, Mirja brought him a plate of smoked lamb, beets, and a green salad. She poured him red wine and water from decanters.

"Why don't you eat with me?" he asked. He wasn't trying to make a move on her. Mirja was pretty, but he was too weirded out by his situation at CapitalBank to consider trying to flirt with her. Regardless, she only shook her head, like the offer had embarrassed her, pushed her hair from her eyes, and slinked off to the kitchen. The smoked lamb was excellent.

After dinner it became apparent that there was no television in the suite. No radio either. He was completely cut off from the outside world.

Artúr decided he was not going to put up with this. An international banking firm, a Wall Street stalwart, could not keep him prisoner in its New York headquarters. Why should they want to? Tomorrow he was going to tell someone. He was going to refuse to live like this. He could go back to his apartment and prepare his own food and ride the train to work like everyone else, or he would quit. He would walk away from their insane salary. What did the money matter if he could never leave? If he had nothing to buy and sell, the money was nothing but an abstraction. Of course, that's what they dealt with at CapitalBank—financial abstractions, only at a much larger level.

He sat on his bed thinking all this, needing desperately to pee, but not wanting to do so in front of the security camera. Finally he shut out the lights, let his eyes adjust to the darkness, and got ready for bed simply because he had nothing to do. He could not be sure of the time. There were no clocks in the suite.

He came out of the bathroom wearing his bedtime attire—cotton shorts and a t-shirt—and listened to the sounds of Mirja in the kitchen. The occasional tinkle of water and subsequent splat told him she was mopping. He wondered if he should tell her he was going to bed, but decided there was no point. It wasn't like they were socializing or anything.

He went into his bedroom, picked up a paperback novel he'd brought with him—a mystery—but couldn't really concentrate, and what little elements of the plot he could follow made him uneasy. Recreational tension had lost much of its appeal. Finally, he turned out the lights and hoped to fall asleep.

■ ■ ■

An hour later, he was still awake when his door creaked open. Mirja slipped into the room, wearing only a nightgown, and made her way to the bed. She gently sat and stretched out next to him, draping an arm over him, sliding a hand under his shirt. She pressed her face against his, and Artúr could feel her skin slick with tears.

He moved away. "Mirja, what are you doing?" he whispered, as though there was someone else to wake.

"I am here for this too," she said. "The making of comfort. Only lights must be on for camera."

He turned on the light, but not for any damn comfort making. "Mirja, this is crazy. Why would you agree to this? You obviously don't want to."

She sat up and wiped at one of her eyes. "You do not like me?" There was a hint of panic in her voice.

"Of course I like you. You're very pretty. I just don't want you to feel that this is something you have to do—that you're being paid for."

"I want to," she said, though her voice was empty and hollowed out, like she was remembering something utterly inconsequential from long ago. "You make me have horny feeling."

"Ugh," Artúr said, shifting away from her. It was like she was being forced at gunpoint. "Mirja are you a prisoner? Are they making you do all this?"

She shook her head. "I choose to stay." She leaned in as if kissing his ear, but he realized at once it was a ruse. "I saw her once. I catch a glimpse. It was like watching everything become nothing. Everything made empty." She pulled away. "I choose to stay."

"Jesus," Artúr breathed.

"Do not say that," Mirja warned. "Mr. Ostentower doesn't like to have any names of that kind." She glanced at the security camera.

Artúr sighed. "I'm very flattered by your interest, Mirja, but I'm going to try to get some sleep now."

"I understand," she said. "It is busy day. Maybe soon you will want me." She lay down next to him and closed her eyes. Artúr didn't have the heart to tell her to get out of his room. Instead, he closed his eyes and tried to fall asleep, but sleep did not come.

■ ■ ■

It was pitch black, as it always was in the suite when the lights were out, and Mirja was pulling on his shoulders.

"You must get up. Mr. Ostentower wants you for worship."

"What time is it?" he demanded.

"Almost new moon."

When he finally sat up, still sorting out where he was and what might be going on, Mirja shoved a towel into his hand. "Shower," she said. "And wear suit. Be respect."

Artúr had no interest in attending any kind of weird predawn worship service with Howard Ostentower, but at least this would give him a chance to vent his complaints. Rather than be seen naked, Artúr showered in the dark and only turned on the light to shave once he was wearing underpants and an undershirt. He felt exposed and foolish.

When he came out of the bathroom, his suit was hung up in his bedroom, having been dry cleaned since his arrival. A new shirt, still in the package awaited him, as did a tie he had never seen before.

When he finished dressing, Artúr went into the kitchen to look for a cup of coffee, but Mirja told him he had to worship on an empty stomach. He then went out the door and into the archive, where he found Jacks waiting for him. His hair looked more neatly combed, but otherwise his unkempt appearance had not much changed. As near as Artúr could tell, he wore the exact same clothes he'd had on when they first met.

"How's everything going?" he asked. "Settling in?"

"No, I'm not settling in," Artúr said as they walked toward the elevator. "No one told me I was going to be a prisoner here."

"Where'd you get that idea?" Jacks asked as they road down to the lobby. "Prisoner. You have gone insane, if I am not mistaken."

"I can't leave the building," Artúr said. "I can't contact anyone outside. What does that sound like to you?"

"Sounds like the sort of adjustment period all new employees go through," Jacks said as he led Artúr over to the next elevator bank. "We'll get it all sorted out. Give us a few days before you start spinning out paranoid theories."

"What about the security cameras in my suite?" Artúr asked as they rode up to the executive floors.

"For your protection," Jacks said as though stating the obvious.

They emerged from the elevator on a floor Artúr had not previously visited. It was poorly lit and much cooler than the rest of the building. Jacks led Artúr down a shadowy hall, where the walls were lined with what looked like stones, illuminated with candles from floor sconces. He felt like he was miles underground, not in a towering skyscraper.

At last Jacks pushed open a door and let Artúr enter. Inside, Howard Ostentower waited. It was a similarly lit stone room, small, with a few wooden benches. Ostentower had his back to Artúr, and his hands were at his throat, like he was straightening his tie. Jacks closed the door, leaving Artúr alone with Ostentower.

"It's the ceremony for the new moon," Ostentower said. "You're going to be an important part of it."

"What is all this about?" Artúr demanded. "Why am I here?"

"You know what it's about, Artúr. You heard her name. I saw it on your face when I met you. Jacks did too. To hear her name is to know her. That requires a sacrifice."

Artúr took a step back. Cold panic gripped him. "You can't do this," he said. "You'll be found out."

"Not *that* kind of sacrifice," Ostentower said, like he was laughing at a child's naïve understanding of something from the adult world. "A sacrifice of time and space. Not a sacrifice of life, but of being. Your search for that which cannot be found is the sacrifice. You will live among us, cut off from the world, just like the others who discovered what was not theirs to know."

"Mirja," Artúr said.

"She should not have been listening," Ostentower told him.

"And our being Icelandic?"

"It is a flavor she enjoys," Ostentower said. "Ancient and crisp."

"But what if I don't want to stay?" Artúr asked.

"I'm afraid the choice is not yours. We have a big mergers and acquisitions deal on the table right now, and we cannot afford her displeasure. Come."

Ostentower pushed open a large wooden door, and inside was a huge chamber, like an opening in an underground cavern. It was filled with hundreds, maybe thousands, of men and women in suits, looking up into blackness. They were like the people he'd seen on the trading floor, young and energetic—freshly minted adults. They all murmured under their breath, but no one said it aloud. No one spoke the name.

At the far end of the chamber, Artúr caught a glimpse of something. A woman's body in a business suit, but her head was not human. It was black and shaggy. Her open suit jacket revealed leaking breasts. At the same time, he had not seen any of that. It was a sort of afterimage, like the lights you see with your eyes closed after a bright flash. Instead he saw emptiness and devouring and swirling, like worlds slamming into worlds, reaching out with arms of energy, pulling one another toward each other, toward their mutual doom. And he saw none of that too.

"*Shub-Niggurath*," he whispered under his breath. It came out in a rush of terror and delight and wonder, and he felt her blessings fall upon him as something began to leak from the corner of his eyes. Not tears. Blood.

"*Shub-Niggurath*," he said again, and now he felt something take his hand, cool and dry and welcoming. He didn't have to look to know it was Amanda. She was here with him and the two of them were never going to go away, for they had walked through a door, which had always been there. He knew in his heart that the mergers and acquisitions deal was going to be an amazing success.

Shub-Niggurath

What makes the sap rise in the boughs of trees? What quick-ens the yoke in the fowl's egg? What causes verminous things to engender and spring forth from the virgin mud? What fires the lust of a man for a woman? The force that lies behind these urges has a name, and it is Shub-Niggurath. She is the womb of the world, the goat with a thousand young. She is the life-force struggling to find shapes through which it may express itself. She is hunger, and thirst, and the essence of need that makes a living thing struggle to go on living.

From the chaos in the womb of this old one arise monsters of the seas and subterranean darkness, things partially formed that could not wait the term of nurture but forced their way into this world screaming and mewling in pain, covered with slime and filth. For all generation arises from filth and is made of filth that has been patterned and ordered by the harmonies of Azathoth's flute. This is true of a blade of grass that grows from a seed in the mire, and it is equally true of man and woman.

From blood and excrement and urine and filth of the earth are we engendered. Why else would the Elder Things who called us forth from the womb of Shub-Niggurath have placed our organs of excretion and our organs of procreation togeth-er? After death our souls may soar to the stars, as the Greek philosopher Plato believed, but while they are bound to this world in vessels of flesh, they remain wedded to filth and cor-ruption. The crack in the flute of Azathoth renders his song imperfect, and one of the ways that imperfection expresses itself in this world is through uncleanness.

A thousand forms has Shub-Niggurath, for she is as varied as the monsters that pour from her open womb and cling as sucklings to her myriad breasts. She is worshipped by men in the shape of a black she-goat. Of all beasts the goat is renowned for its ruttishness. Both male and female are the same to her, for she is the lust of both, and that lust is one. It cannot be divided. The lust of all living things to burst forth from the womb or the egg or the seed is ever the same lust.

Her worshipers drink strong wine and dance to the music of drums and flutes. They make sacrifice of their first-born babes, and then couple without discrimination around the cloven-hoofed idol of their goddess, whose sexual member is ever depicted as rudely erect. Fathers couple with daughters, mothers couple with sons, brothers couple with sisters, the old impregnate the young.

Women pray to Shub-Niggurath to be made fertile, but this is a perilous course, for when the goddess grants this prayer the things that are engendered in their wombs are apt to be abominations unfit for the light. They grow with unnatural rapidity, and their strength is uncanny. In form they lack a just proportion, but are grotesque masses of flesh that refuse to die. Many maids who pray to Shub-Niggurath end their own lives after slaying the things that emerge from between their thighs while they are able—for if they hesitate too long their issue waxes in strength and cannot easily be returned to the filth from whence it arose.

Men pray to this goddess for strength, for health, but most of all for virility and the power to engender sons. As the sap rises in the trees, so do their virile members rise up and drip with lust when Shub-Niggurath touches them, and she fills the minds of men with all manner of lustful thoughts both romantic and perverse. She cares not what form desire takes so long as it is strong in its expression and fulfilled in its purpose. She is the goddess of violent rapes and the deflowering of virgins. She cannot abide a fallow womb.

The song of Azathoth is realized in flesh through the womb of Shub-Niggurath, where the intervals of vibration become material forms. All things that come into being are birthed through her womb of limitless dimension. The very Earth itself is her daughter, which she brought forth groaning in cosmic travail through the gate of Yog-Sothoth. In this act of birth the world fell screaming in agony to this corrupting sphere of matter, and all that crawls upon her face owes its form and being to Shub-Niggurath.

The Apotheosis of a Rodeo Clown

Brett J. Talley

The biker they called Tonto was already helping Hog drag the girl down into the mine by the time I decided what I needed to do. Tonto means stupid in Spanish. I can't say much else about the Sons of Dagon, especially much of anything positive, but they had a way with names.

As I looked down at my fake stump hand, covered in fake stump blood, I made the decision to save the girl. That was the clown code, after all.

But I probably better back up and start at the beginning.

I'm not like most people. I'm a full-time rodeo clown. A real professional. Not one of these kids looking to score a few bucks when the show rolls through town on the weekend. Been doing it the better part of my adult life. Hell, I clowned with Mr. Flint Rasmussen himself, and that still means something in certain parts of the country.

Clowning wasn't always my dream. When I was a kid, I wanted to be a bull rider. I was going to be the one to finally score the Perfect Ten. Had some talent for it, too. Started out with calves, like most of the young'ns. Then when I was fourteen years old, I rode my first bull, a charbray by the name of Bodacious.

Now Bodacious was one clever son of a bitch. He had this trick he'd pull where he'd throw his legs up in the air in such a way that threw you forward. Then he'd jerk his head back and smash you in the face. Weren't too many that rode Bodacious who didn't have a broken nose to show for it.

They warned me about that when I got on him. I told myself, "He ain't going to get me in the face." And by God, he didn't. Course, when he bucked forward and I pulled back instead of letting my body weight go with him, I completely lost control. He threw me alright, and landed a back kick right in my spine, like something from a Saturday-morning cartoon. I didn't break my nose, but I did break my spine.

Nothing too serious, as back breaks go. I'm not a paraplegic or anything. But they did tell me no more bull riding. And that was that. The end of a dream. So I decided I'd do the next best thing. If I couldn't ride the bull, I'd fight the bull.

That's the rodeo clowns true name—a bullfighter. Yeah, we wear the face paint and the silly pants and a shirt that would look good in a San Francisco gay pride parade, but we are warriors at heart. And like all good warriors, we have a code. And rule number one of the Rodeo Clown Code is that you never leave an innocent in harm's way. Not when you can step in front of whatever's coming for them.

Which brings me to the girl.

We'd been doing a show in Lone Pine, a little town in California's Owen Valley, resting in a dale between the Alabama Hills. Sounds picturesque, but it was a parched town in a dry desert where water never flowed, except through the aqueducts that headed south to Los Angeles so the city could drink up Lone Pine's future, present, and past.

Most of the guys hated shows like that, in little places soon forgotten. They dreamed of the big time in Amarillo or Tulsa or Cheyenne. But not me. People in little towns like that, they ain't got nothing. So when we come, we are the world to them. For a few precious hours, we can bring them joy. Real joy. Yeah, the Lone Pine fairground was broke down, the termites had eat up the wood of the fence, and the sign didn't even light up anymore, but it was magical to me. So I didn't even notice the guys in leather cuts with "Sons of Dagon" sewn in great, red letters across the back, hanging around the gates.

We did our thing. Danced our dance with the bulls. Nobody got hurt and the crowd, small though it was, enjoyed it and roared their approval. A good evening's work, with not much to do after but get drunk and think about the next night's show.

"Yo, clown!"

I didn't hesitate to look up, as if the guy was actually calling my name. Dude was big, but not fat. Thick around the chest and the middle, bald head but full beard. Basically he looked like he'd stepped off the set of *Sons of Anarchy*. Hell, maybe he had.

"Got a proposition for you." He spit a line of tobacco juice into the dust. "You interested in a little side work?"

"Depends," I said. "What you got?"

Two other men in the same leather cut-off jackets appeared beside him. One of them was tall, skinny, and shook like an alcoholic after a bender when the money runs out. I would learn later that he was called Tonto. Never learned his real name. Never learned any of their names. I'm not sure even *they* remembered them. The other guy was as chubby as Tonto was skinny, a big ol' boy who didn't seem like he'd be all that comfortable on the back of a motorcycle. The hog is supposed to be the bike. And, in fact, that was his name. Hog. I'd learn all that later, of course. For now, they didn't talk. Just the one in the middle did that.

"Rodeo. Small, private event. Couple hundred in it for you and for anybody else you get."

He grinned. Something about it I definitely didn't like. I'd say I should have listened to my instincts, but fact is, I needed the money. Professional rodeo clowns aren't exactly highly paid, and the benefits are for shit.

"Alright," I said. "I'm in."

"Think you can get a few of the boys to come along?"

"Sure thing. As many as you need."

"Not too many. Just a couple. And another thing, this is sorta a Halloween-type event. So you think you can bloody it up a bit?"

It was June. Strange, but people had asked for stranger.

"Sure."

"Hell yeah," he said, slapping me on the back. "We'll pick you up tomorrow. This time. Right here."

The three men turned and walked off into the gathering dark, the thin one cackling all the way to the parking lot.

It wasn't hard to find volunteers. Two hundred bucks for a night's work was unheard of. Sure, there was probably something else to it, but when the money's good, who gives a rip?

They returned the next night, just as they had promised, as our last show was coming to a close. They pulled up in a van; the muscular one was driving.

"No bikes?"

He scowled at me, and the look made me wonder if he'd ever killed a man. "What," he said, "you wanna ride bitch?"

I laughed. He did not. "Guess not," I said. "What's your name, anyway?"

"Piston. And that's all you need to know. Get in the back."

"Hey!" Tonto stuck his head out the window. "You're supposed to be dressed up for Halloween."

I held up a plastic bag. "We'll change in the back."

He grunted, which I took as a sign of approval. I climbed in the back of the van, and two of my buddies followed. They were young guys, not locals exactly but Californians who worked the season when the tour came through.

There were no seats other than the two in the front, so we made ourselves as comfortable as possible and hoped that Piston was a more conscientious driver than might be expected. Hog was passed out in the bed of the van, fortunately out of our way.

I emptied the contents of the bag on the floor—mostly fake blood and cheap bandages—and passed them around to Sam and Jake, the other two clowns that had joined me. I call them clowns, but they were of the new set that eschewed the classic getup in favor of a traditional cowboy look, so I was the only one wearing paint. I'd gone with the more John

Wayne Gacy approach—white face, blue triangles over my eyes, red mouth painted to points. That's the thing about Gacy; any clown could have told you he was a bad dude. Real clowns outline their paint in nice, gentle curves. It's less aggressive, sends the signal that no, we are not actually going to kill you. Points are aggressive. Sharp angles, frightening. Should have known Gacy was a killer. He wore it right there on his face.

Tonto leaned over the back of his seat and gawked at us. He watched us squirt fake blood and black paint into our hands and spread it across our clothes, our arms, our faces.

"Whatcha doin?" Tonto said.

"You wanted Halloween, right? We're zombies."

Tonto giggled stupidly. "Zombie clowns." He giggled some more. "Whatdaya think about that, Piston? They're clown zombies."

Piston didn't answer. He seemed to be a man of few words. Tonto turned back around, but every now and then I'd hear him giggle to himself again.

The only windows in the van were in the back, so I leaned against the wheel well and watched the place we'd just been slip into the past. The Alabama Hills rose around me, named by Southern sympathizers for the mighty warship that was the pride of the Confederacy. I wondered about those people, Southerners who'd come west in '49 looking for their fortunes. By definition, then, they didn't own slaves, couldn't legally in the territory they were headed, even if they could have afforded them. Like so many their loyalty was to the Southern earth, the states that had given them birth, the rivers that divided them. I wondered how they felt when the Alabama was sunk off the coast of France. Not everyone was disappointed. Just beyond the Alabama Hills lay the Kearsarge range, named after the ship that sent her to the bottom of the sea. What a country.

"So where are we going?" I asked.

"Mining town," said Piston. "Up in the mountains."

"You guys go up there a lot?"

"Yeah. We go up there a lot."

"Do people still live there?"

"Nope. Abandoned."

That wasn't a surprise. The Alabama Hills had once drawn men with little money and big dreams from every part of the country and even the world. Only one in a hundred made it. Ten times that ended up dead, while the rest were just broken. Then the big conglomerates came through and bought up the hills. That's when the mines went deep and towns sprung up around them. I call them towns, but they were little more than camps for the men—a saloon, dry goods store, maybe a brothel if they were lucky.

"This town got a name?" Piston caught my eye in the rearview. I couldn't see his mouth, but I knew he was smiling.

"Sure it does. They called it Sutter's End."

Sutter's End. So that was it. I began to wonder if I'd made a mistake. Easy money always comes with a price, and the old saw about something that seems too good to be true is more often than not on target.

Sutter's End had a nasty reputation. The mine had closed some fifty years before, and the town had died with it. The story that everyone knew was that the main shafts were running dry, but the bosses wanted to squeeze a few more million out of the hole. So they ordered the men to blast a new shaft down from the main one. Of course blasting when you were that deep already was nothing short of taking your life in your own hands, but back in those days that sort of thing went. Still does if we're being honest with each other. So when the charges detonated, down came the supports—and the walls and ceilings with them.

That was the official story at least. Tragedies like that always have another, one more shrouded in the twice-told and the unsupported. And Sutter's End had a doozy. The story, as the folks who lived at the bottom of the Alabama Hills told it, was that the charges worked just fine. Better than fine, even. That when they went off, they opened something more than just a new shaft. Nobody was ever quite so certain or so specific as to what exactly that something more was. But whatever came out of there took the miners. The people of the town, the ones who made it out alive, fled. Left everything behind and just went. So it stayed for years, till time dimmed the fear enough that enterprising grave robbers stripped the town bare. But even now, whispers would sometimes float down from Sutter's End, and no one dared to go up there at night to find out where they came from. No one, it seemed, but the Sons of Dagon.

And us.

The sun was setting by the time the town came into view. A thick cloud of dust rolled down the hill as we drove up, and when we pulled into what remained of the town, we saw why. It was chaos. When you've spent as much time clowning as I have, you've seen just about every type of man, and you learn quick not to judge them too much by what you see. But as I watched men bigger and meaner-looking than Piston spinning around the town square on giant bikes of shimmering chrome, metal bars shaped like bones, skulls with devil horns curving off of them between the handles, I was afraid. I glanced at Sam and Jake and saw the same look on their faces.

The van came to a stop. Piston threw open the rear doors and we hopped out. It was a party alright. There were bikers everywhere, sporting the leather cuts that read Sons of Dagon across the back, with some sort of emblem beneath it that I didn't recognize, like something out of one of those monster movies that comes on the television after midnight. I didn't like to look at it, so I didn't examine it for long. It was a face of sorts, one with evil eyes and what looked like tentacles that hung down where the mouth should be.

There wasn't much left of the town, and it didn't seem like there had been that much there to begin with. One central street with buildings on either side. At the end they'd erected a stage where a band was playing, heavy on the metal guitar with drums that sounded like thunder. The arena was set up off on the other end, and I recognized a cowboy leaning up against a cattle carrier next to it.

"Dan Travis," I said, walking up and taking his hand with the one I hadn't wrapped in bloody bandages.

"Well, I'll be damned," he said. "What the hell are you doing here?"

"Same thing as you, I guess."

"Part of this circus, too, huh?" He pulled out a pack of cigarettes and offered me one. I declined. "If I had it to do over, I might have passed."

The rumble of a bike and a hollered obscenity punctuated the thought. He looked at me and squinted. "You supposed to be dead or something?"

"Something," I said. "When's this show getting started anyway?"

"They said we was waiting on you. So I guess any time now. Suits me just fine. I'd like to get the hell clear of here before it gets too dark."

I looked around at our surroundings. The town wasn't on a hill, precisely. More like a high canyon with low craggily walls on the sides. All and all, that meant the sun seemed to set faster than it should, and the darkness was more complete when it did.

"Yeah, I hear you. Any idea who's in charge?"

"That would be me."

I turned to see a man, older, but just as firmly built as Piston, standing behind me. He wore sunglasses, even though the day was long on gone, and his gray beard came to a point below his chin in a way that reminded me of the devil.

"I'm Goat," he said, offering his hand, and as I took it I thought that name worked with the beard too. "I run this show. Thank you boys for coming."

"Happy to be here," I lied. "Where'd you guys find this place?"

Goat snorted. "I own it. My granddaddy bought the land after the mine died. He needed a place for his family to have some privacy. As you can see, that family has grown." He swept the area with his hand, as if asking us to take it all in. And we did. About that time, the band fired up again.

"We take all kinds," he said, looking over his shoulder as the drummer hammered away. "Me, I prefer what you boys do. So that's why you're here. We'll get started in fifteen minutes. Be ready."

He started to walk off, but then he turned and pointed at my stump hand.

"Love the zombie getup."

Fifteen minutes later, we were in the ring, ready to go. And I can tell you this, I've never been more afraid.

The band still played, but we were now the show, and most of the gang had made its way over to the makeshift corral. It was rotten wooden slates literally strung together with twine and bailing wire. A half-decent bull would have broken straight through and killed us all. But these bulls weren't half-decent. They were, in fact, the saddest I had ever seen, ten years past their prime if they were a day.

There were no riders, no real ones at least. The Sons of Dagon took turns. The crowd at the edge of the makeshift ring urged them on. Cursing, screaming, firing guns into the air. I doubted they had permits. I spent as much time dodging bottles as I did dodging bulls.

The energy in the air was foul and full of bloodlust. The crowd pulsated, seeming to squeeze in on us. Their shouts rose from a din to a roar till they seemed to cover all. They were pagan, visceral, somehow harkening back to a time of man's darkest age. One of the drunkest ones leapt the fence and ran toward a bull even as it struggled with its rider. The poor thing was terrified.

Over and over they rode them, till I was doubled over, hands on my knees, exhausted. But still, they rode.

It came to an end as suddenly as it had begun. Ten different guys had probably ridden that bull. The sweat was thick on its sides, its mouth foamed, and the sounds that came from its gullet no animal should make. Then it happened. The great beast gave one last massive thrust of its hind legs and then the rest of it tumbled over on its side. I knew then it was dead, probably dead before it hit the dirt. From somewhere deep below us, the earth rumbled.

The night sorta sputtered out then. The mood had changed. The Sons drifted away, one by one. The band stopped playing, packed up its kit, took down the stage, and was gone. It was full dark then, and the stars shone cold light upon us. Goat walked up, oddly somber. He handed each man a hundred dollars more than we were promised.

"You done good," he said, glancing down at my stump hand. "Night went sour. Sorry about that." He took a drag from his cigarette and coughed. "Piston and the boys'll take you back. But they got clean-up duty tonight, so it might be a while. No idea what they'll do with that shit." He nodded at the dead bull. Flies had begun to gather. "Burn it, I guess." Then he too was gone.

Before long, it was just us. Sam and Jake leaned against the rotted fence, kicking at the dirt, silent and sullen. I didn't much feel like celebrating either, but there was no point in whining about it.

"I'm going to find Piston," I said.

They just ignored me, and I didn't bother in trying to talk to them again. I headed out down what had been the main street. With the band and the bikes and the stage lights gone, it was dark in the way only the far wilderness can be dark, where not even the glow of distant city lights can ruin the night's completeness. In other words, it was dark as all hell, and even when my eyes adjusted, I could only barely make out the outlines of buildings. Add the unnatural quiet, and I admit to being somewhat unnerved. More than somewhat.

Laughter from one of the buildings. A beam of light and someone spilling out behind it into the street. I guess they saw me or heard me or something, because the next moment, the beam was shining in my direction. Then a giggle.

Tonto.

"Clown," he slurred, drunk or high or both. "Zombie clown. I like you."

A larger darkness stumbled out behind him—Piston. I expected Hog to follow. I did not expect him to be carrying someone else with him when he did. The two of them joined Tonto. I stopped dead in my tracks, suddenly quite aware of how bad things had just gotten for me. Tonto said something I couldn't hear. All three of them looked at me. A woman screamed. Hog slapped her hard across the face and told her to shut up. I almost thought I could see blood dropping from her nose.

"You coming, clown?" Piston slurred.

"Where you going?" I said, as natural as I could. I took a few steps toward them.

Piston raised an arm and pointed out down the road, to the rock face of the cliff that backed up to the town, at a patch of black night a little bit darker than the rest. It had been obscured by the stage before, but now it was clear. They started toward what could only be the opening of the mine, the one that had given birth to the town and then killed it. I said the first thing that came to my mind.

"Well fuck."

Every man—every woman too for that matter—has a moment where they have to decide who they are and who they will be. To decide whether to take a stand so they can stand themselves. This was my moment. The three men and one struggling woman disappeared into the darkness of the shaft. I knew what was next. They'd rape her, multiple times most likely. Then they'd kill her. And that would be it. No one would ever find the body, not down in that mine shaft. And just in case you think I was being all heroic, I also figured they'd kill me when they were done with her, the price of seeing something I wasn't supposed to see. So I made the only decision I could make. I followed them down into the mine.

I hadn't exactly formulated a plan, but one thing was immediately apparent—I couldn't see for shit. Fortunately, the three jackasses in front of me were as prepared as they were drunk, and I could follow the light of their bobbing flashlights. I stumbled after them, hoping to find a pickax or a shovel or just a damn big rock to use as a weapon. Otherwise, I wasn't sure what I was going to do when I caught up to them. When that actually happened—and without said pickax, shovel, or damn big rock—I basically made small talk.

"So," I said, in the hopes of announcing my presence without startling them and getting shot or stabbed, "what are we doing here, guys?"

Piston turned to me, and for the first time I saw the girl's face. She'd been crying, which was no surprise. But I wasn't prepared for the pain in those tear-filled eyes, or the look of absolute desperate hope that fell completely on me.

"You a believer?" Piston asked, in the strangest non sequitur of my life. Of all the things that had happened that night, it was his question that shocked me the most.

"Yeah," I said. "I guess so."

"You guess."

"Yeah."

"Well, we'll see if we can't make a believer out of you. And when you see what we got to show you, you won't need faith." He pointed to the wall of the mine. "You see that?"

And I did see it. A ragged opening, big enough for a man to enter through, but not comfortably. Obviously not a shaft running off the main or an opening made on purpose, either. If I had to guess, they'd been blasting when it broke through on its own. When something broke through. I thought back to the stories I had heard, about what had happened here, and I wondered just how much truth there was to the old local legends.

"Come on," Piston said. "We got something to show you."

"Yeah," Tonto said. "Something to show you." Then he laughed that big, stupid laugh as he disappeared behind Hog and the girl. Piston just kept on looking at me, and even through the gloom of the cave I could read his eyes. He was drunk, but he was sober enough to consider whether or not it was a good idea to have me along. Maybe he thought about killing me right then and there, I don't know. But he turned and slipped through the opening, and so did I.

Through the crack in the wall I saw something I could never have dreamed of, not in my wildest youth, not at my drunkest. This was no new mine shaft, no undiscovered cavern or cave. This was a room, a great, giant chamber with vaulted ceilings and massive columns. Something made by man. I hoped man had made it at least. I'd never seen the like. It put the great Temple of Karnak at Luxor to shame, made a mockery of the most extravagant constructions of the Greeks or the Romans.

The room glowed with some strange phosphorescence, illuminating a thick and unnatural mist that rolled and roiled along the ground. Suddenly the three drunken thugs didn't seem so fearsome, not nearly so as whatever lurked within this place, whatever or whoever had built it, and whatever had happened to those who had found it.

"Where are we?" I whispered into the darkness, as if there was any who could answer.

The trio and their captive stumbled down an arcade that lay between two great colonnades, and reluctantly, I followed. To flee into the darkened depths of the mine would have been more pleasant.

Tonto giggled. "This is neat. It's even better than I heard."

I felt a cold shiver arc down my spine. "You mean, you've never been here before?"

"Nah," he said. "Goat wouldn't let us. Only the higher…"

He surely would have said more, but Piston cut him off with a single look. Then he turned to me. "You ain't gotta stay if you're scared, clown."

"No," I said, "I'm good. Just wondering is all." He grunted at that, and we continued to walk.

I could see that at the end of the arcade was some sort of stone edifice. If this was a temple, I supposed it was an altar, though unlike anything I'd seen before. The stonework was exquisite, a swirl of rises and falls, of deep cuts and shallow valleys. Almost hurt to look at it, as if whatever image it produced made the eyes rebel. But whatever it was and whatever it signified, its creator possessed unmatched skill. I had worked as a stonemason in my youth, and I'd seen enough to know that this was the work of genius. Before it lay a stone slab, and beyond that a deep basin of similar construction. I realized then why the girl was here.

"So what are you guys planning to do?"

Piston turned to me.

"You said you wanted to see God."

I shook my head.

"I don't think I said that at all."

"Well, too bad." He jerked at Hog. "Get her ready."

Tonto started to cackle again, and the girl screamed. Stupidly, I made a grab at her. I'm not sure what I thought I'd do if I got a hold of her, and I never found out. Piston threw me away with a single flick of his caber-like arm. I fell to the ground and the cold mist enveloped me. I felt instantly sick, like it was not mist at all but poison gas. I drug myself to my feet as Piston pointed a long dirty finger toward me. "And to think I was going to let you live."

But I wasn't paying all that much attention to Piston at the moment. My eyes were on the basin. At first, I thought that was where the mist was coming from, but then I realized I was wrong. The mist wasn't flowing from the basin; it was flowing up and into it, as if somewhere someone had flipped a switch on a vacuum. Faster and faster it went, until in one soundless whoosh the last wisp disappeared over the edge.

For the barest of seconds, there was silence. And then, the roar. A column of viscous liquid, like oil, but somehow thicker and darker, erupted from the heart of the basin. Piston stumbled backward, and Tonto shrieked. I followed the flood up, up, up into the eternal darkness above. I supposed that if the temple had a ceiling, it was striking it, but we didn't have long to wonder. Down it came again, but it did not crash to the floor. Instead, it gathered above the basin itself, swirling in a great, black ball that pulsated with life.

"Piston!" Tonto cried. "Piston, what's going on?"

But Piston had no answers. We were all the same, standing witness to an event we were never meant to see. Then something happened I could not have expected—things got *way* worse.

The black sphere ceased to be a black sphere anymore. It bulged and split, and I thought I saw feet, hands, claws. Then there was no question. Some sort of beast was forming before us. It was not emerging from the dark sphere. They were one and the same.

Hog stared up at the birth of that hideous thing, and I suspect his grip slipped on the girl, because she did what any sane person would have done in that moment—she ran. No one tried to stop her. We might as well have been held to the spot by steel spikes. She might have made it, too, but just as she passed me, a whiplike arm of black ichor shot forth from the heart of the beast and wrapped around her throat. She gave a cry, tiny, more startled than painful, as if she simply could not believe this was happening to her. Then in one great jerk that may well have broken her neck then and there, she snapped back into the midst of the living void.

The beast took a step forward and I understood that it intended to make the girl's fate the fate of us all. I glanced from Piston to Hog to

Tonto. They looked like children, scared little kids. The tough demeanor, the ruse they played on people smaller and weaker than them, was gone. They saw the end of all things standing before them. Or at least, the end of all *their* things. The beast took another step. The entrance to the temple was behind me. If I took off, I might be able to make it while that monster was busy with the others.

But hell, I couldn't do that. And I say again, it's not that I'm some kind of hero. Truth be told I'm as scared of things that go bump in the night as the next guy. I just have a guilty streak, and if I'd let those poor sons of bitches die, I knew I'd regret it someday. True, they weren't worth much, scum of the earth and all, and I figured they could add that girl's death to their list of sins. But together, the three of them might just have enough good in them to be worth one of me. And a rodeo clown is kinda like a secret service agent. It's his job to take the horn, no matter how piss-poor the guy he's defending.

Piston, Hog, and Tonto hadn't moved half an inch, but the beast—I don't really know what else to call it—was walking or gliding or floating or whatever toward them. I raised my stump hand in the air and hollered my best imitation of the Rebel Yell. Great-Granddaddy would have been proud.

"Over here you bloated cloud of cow fart!"

Alright, so it wasn't my best insult, but it worked. The thing didn't much have a head, and I felt more than saw it turn, but I knew I had its full attention.

"You're facing an honest-to-God rodeo clown, a card-carrying member of the Brotherhood of the American Bullfighter, local 229, and that's what I do. I fight bulls twice your size and half as ugly and I'm not one bit afraid of you!"

And like a bull in the ring, it charged me. It came at me full on, what looked like liquid obsidian, if such a thing is even possible, forming into a mass like a locomotive. I let it come, right until it was almost upon me, and then I simply stepped to the side. It roared past, slamming into the wall of the temple.

"We call that the *pasodoble*," I said. "It's Spanish."

The thing rolled over on itself, like a turning bull, and thrust at me again. So I stepped to the other side and it slid past.

"That's the *doble*!" I hollered at it. It paused in place, floating above the ground. It no longer looked like some kind of Minotaur or classic monster out of a bad horror movie, but like a black orb of impenetrable darkness. I spread my legs and crouched, a linebacker waiting for the snap. In an instant a thick tendril of oil shot out at me, just like it had at the girl earlier. I dove forward, rolling underneath it and out of the way.

"That all you got?" I yelled as the tentacle recoiled back into the mass. But I was already breathing heavy, and I wasn't precisely sure just how much *I* had left. I spared a glance at the Three Stooges. To my utter amazement, they still stood there, rooted to the spot with their mouths hanging open to the floor, and I even thought I saw drool seeping out of Tonto's. Probably not an unusual occurrence.

I didn't have time to say anything as a large arm the size of a telephone poll swung around toward me. I made a guess and lunged like I was going to barrel roll again. The column of ichor crashed to the ground and swept across it. I'd guessed right. Instead of rolling I leapt as far and high as I could, clear over it, landing on the other side on my feet. I ran, knowing the arm was probably swinging back even then.

I pointed at Piston and yelled, "Get through the door, you assholes!" Finally understanding sprung back into his eyes. He turned and said something to the other two, but I didn't hear him. The roar of swirling air and massive movement filled my ears. By the time I glanced back, it was on top of me.

"Time to make the rounds," I said to myself. I jumped to the side, right as the form almost touched me—and something told me that even the slightest contact meant death—and it slid past. But this time not all the way, just as I had anticipated. Instead it flipped on itself, attempting to double back on me. As it turned, I turned, and now we were locked in a dance of death, like a dog chasing its tail where the tail was me. Out of the corner of my eye I saw the three bikers running for the crack. In a few moments, they would be there. They'd be free. And, well, I'd be dead. I couldn't turn forever, and with no one to distract it, I'd never escape.

Then something changed. It sensed, or perhaps it saw, the three running. It stopped turning so abruptly that I almost ran into it, but instead I fell to the ground before it. It formed a wall and, like a wave rolling away from me, arched across the chamber. It waterfalled down in front of the entranceway, blocking the only exit. The three men ground to a halt, Hog slipping and tumbling. The wave crashed down upon him, swallowing him up. He didn't even have time to scream.

"Shit," I said, pushing myself up. There was a fairly hefty stone beside me and I picked it up, unsure of what good it would do. I was exhausted, but I began to run toward the inky, living wall. Piston backed away, his hands up as if he was trying to explain himself to an angry lover. When he turned to run, another tentacle shot from the mass and looped around his right leg. With one giant lurch, it had him hanging in the air, suspended thirty feet above the ground. He screamed like a child, high-pitched and urgent, begging to be released, for whatever held him to just let him go. So, it did. His keening reached its peak and then was silenced, replaced by the crunch of his head splitting open on the ground, like a walnut smashed by a hammer. The creature slid forward over the body and the growing pool of blood, and when it withdrew, the floor was clear and clean.

Tonto was running toward me as I was running toward him, his eyes filled with madness and fear. I wasn't sure exactly what we were going to do or where we were going to go, but I figured I'd die fighting, and maybe screaming, too. Tonto was almost to me when I heard a sound like a whipcrack and saw a serpentlike band wrap around his throat. His eyes went wide, and in another instant I knew the beast would have him. I reared back and threw the stone as hard as I could. To my amazement, it struck the tentacle and cleaved it in two. The larger part withdraw; the smaller fell to the ground where it exploded into black smoke upon contact. I was exuberant, and just as I was about to let out a massive war whoop, I looked up at Tonto. His hands went to his neck. His eyes were filled with fear and confusion. And then, I shit you not, he actually giggled. Right before his head tilted to the side and fell with a splat to the ground.

So that was it. They were all dead, and I was next. The black curtain before me expanded. Its height reached into the infinite darkness above, its width all the way to each wall. I knew then it had been toying with me all along. It could have had me at any point. Could have had any of us. But for some reason known only to whatever mad intelligence guided it, it had waited till now to show its full glory. It began moving forward, and I stumbled back. Past one set of columns and then another. Eventually I'd run out of room and it would take me, but I was in no hurry to see that happen, so I kept walking backward toward the altar.

Then the wall stopped. It hung there, dividing the room in half, preventing me from my only means of escape, but it came no further. For a moment I wondered why, but then I became aware of another presence. I heard a sound, as of a slapping upon the ground, a great girth moving in jerking steps. I turned to face it, whatever it was, whatever new horror was to meet my eyes. It was not what I expected.

In my younger years, I'd gigged my share of frogs in the Southern swamps. I now repented my youthful indiscretions.

I'll explain what I saw, but the best I can tell you is this—it appeared to be a giant frog, a great toad complete with massive belly and globular eyes that looked as if they longed for nothing more than sleep. It was covered with brown fur, which might have been disconcerting on an actual frog but somehow seemed perfectly reasonable here. Its mouth opened slightly, and the tip of a tongue darted out. I fully expected to hear the mightiest ribbit ever to issue forth in the history of the world. But when he spoke, it was only in my mind that I heard it.

"Bullfighter, I am the one who sleeps. You have awakened me from my slumber."

"I'm sorry," I whispered, almost questioningly. My mind could not process what I was seeing and hearing.

"No matter. You are not of the cult. The others should have known better."

He moved toward me, his massive splayed feet crashing down upon the temple floor with every step.

"It is a strange thing. I knew another, of your kind, long ago, in a very different place from this. He was a thief, a master at his art, whose name is now lost to the shrouds of time. But not his memory, and not his soul."

He raised himself up to meet my eyes, even though one of his was the size of my entire head.

"Twice our paths crossed, the thief and I. And twice I let him go. I promised him there would not be a third time. And now, I sense some of him in you."

I swallowed hard, but my mouth was so dry that there was nothing there to swallow.

"I see into you. There is courage there, unlike most of your brethren. Enough, I think, to make me overlook my promise, oh Satampra Zeiros."

Upon hearing that name, something stirred within me, something I had not known was there.

"Go," it said, "and see that you do not come back."

It turned from me then and began to shuffle away. I glanced behind me and watched as the great black curtain split down the middle and opened. I looked back at the other beast as it went, the giant frog, and for reasons unknown, I opened my mouth to speak.

"What do I call you?" I asked.

It stopped and turned to look upon me. This time when it spoke its voice rang out with such force that it drew the consciousness from me, and it didn't come back until I woke up, inexplicably, on the main street of the abandoned town above, Sam and Jake shaking my shoulders and screaming at me like they thought I was dead. The beast, the god, didn't say much. Just one word…

His own name.

"TSATHOGGUA!"

Tsathoggua

Men often worship what terrifies and repulses them. The driving emotion of such worship is fear. By adoring and abasing ourselves before that which horrifies us, we hope to win its favor and turn aside its wrath.

So it is with the worship of the old one known as Tsathoggua, who is adored in the jungles of Africa and on the high steppes of China, and in many other odd backwaters of the world. He is depicted in the form of a corpulent black toad with bulbous heavy-lidded eyes, gaping nostrils, and a wide mouth from which droops the tip of a thick tongue. His gross body is covered in a fine, silky fur not unlike the fur of a bat.

The features that are carven in the black stone of his idols express perversion, cruelty, sly malice, and a dull hatred. Yet fathers offer the sacrifice of their first-born sons before the squatting obscenity of his body. Such is the power of fear.

The black toad is not the true form of this old one, who is so alien to the mind of man as to be beyond comprehension. It is said that Tsathoggua fell from the stars aeons ago in the dim beginnings of this world, and was worshipped by various tribes who were not able to conceive him as anything other than a creature of the dark swamps in which they dwelt.

Where the god abides is a matter of conjecture. Some sages claim he resides in the lightless cavern deep beneath the earth that is called N'Kai. The great necromancer Klarkash-ton asserts in his texts that in the distant past Tsathoggua dwelt beneath a mountain in fabled Hyperborea, but that he fled that land when it was covered with a vast mantle of ice—for by his nature the god favors warmth and darkness.

His ancient temples are formed of massive blocks of black stone unadorned by any carvings or pillars. Like the god, they are thick and squat in shape, square, without a dome or spire, having an entrance door of bronze and high, narrow windows. It has been said that they are similar in appearance to temples in the Vaults of Zin, but who has ever walked the Vaults to verify or disprove this claim?

They contain no furniture, only the black idol of the god upon a block of stone, that leers down at the worshipper as he enters, and before the idol a bronze altar of sacrifice, and before the altar a large rounded basin of bronze supported by three legs, which stands in the center of the floor.

When the worship of the god was active, each temple had a guardian that would punish anyone foolish enough to enter without the proper forms of obeisance. It dwelt within the bronze basin, and had the composition and appearance of a kind of living ichor that was as black as bitumen. This creature, if indeed it was alive in the sense that we understand, was said to be ageless, tireless, and deathless.

Any violation of the temple of Tsathoggua called forth the swift judgment of his guardian, for by its touch the black ichor affects living flesh and bone like a powerful acid, dissolving both in moments. This liquid creature was able to rear itself up and strike like a cobra, and it could progress along the ground with great rapidity, faster than a man can run. This it accomplished with a sinuous motion, like that of a large snake, or by extending numerous feet and legs from its underside so that it could run along like a centipede.

There has been much scholarly conjecture as to the relationship between Tsathoggua and his temple guardians. Some say that they are his spawn, and that he cast them off from his own substance. Others assert that they are an alien race fallen from the stars that worships him. Deep in lightless N'Kai they minister to the needs of the god, and serve as both his hands and legs. For it is the nature of Tsathoggua to never stir from his place, but to wait for the sacrifices that sustain him to be brought before him, or before his idols, which are channels that nourish his spiritual essence.

The hunger of Tsathoggua is insatiable. No matter how much he is fed, he always craves more. Yet in spite of the keenness of his appetite, he sits and waits patiently for his prey to venture near, as the toad waits for the foolish fly, and only then will his guardians rise up and strike.

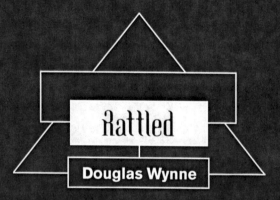

Rattled

Douglas Wynne

The myth caught up with me in New York City, returning after years like a dog lost on a family vacation, mangy and battered and possibly rabid. Not to be trusted, and yet, undeniably familiar. It came in a moment of synchronicity, the light of dawn still far off and the light of the skyscrapers scraped thin across the November sky. I was burrowed down in my sleeping bag on the cold ground of Zuccotti Park, listening to bits of conversation and the staggering, syncopated rhythm of the drum circle winding down in the Sacred Space.

After all the years of denial, distortion, and creative recollection, this was the first time I heard the defining event of my childhood, the *final* event of my childhood, framed so succinctly. The words reached me as I drifted in the liminal state between waking and dreaming, the muted pulse of the djembe and shakers lulling me until the phrase struck a chord and jerked me back to wakefulness, images of red rock formations gnawed by the insatiable wind haunting my head.

"You ever hear of the Curse of Yig?"

A small group was huddled around one of the rectangular ground lights that glowed from the granite like the center lines on a highway, the cold white illumination failing to do much to define their faces. I craned my neck toward the group. The speaker was female. I hadn't met her yet, but had maybe seen her working in the library tent. Long beaded braids, aquiline nose, dressed in a pea coat that looked too big for her anorexic frame. She was saying something about how myths weren't meant to be taken literally, but that you could decode any culture's values by them. More of the same pseudo-intellectual blather I'd been hearing all day and now it was going to sing me to sleep, but I swore I'd heard her mention the curse. Or was that just my tired brain slapping a pattern over a rhythmically similar phrase? I'd almost tuned out again and pulled the insulated nylon flap over my ear when she said it again.

"The Curse of Yig. It's a Native American legend from the Snake People. Have you guys heard of the Snake People? No? That's the name the whites gave to the Shoshone and Paiute Indians. They had settlements along the Snake River on the West Coast. You guys should read up on the Snake War. It was the deadliest Indian war in the West, but it's mostly been forgotten by history because it was overshadowed by the Civil War."

Someone who sounded like he might be talking around an indrawn hit off a joint interrupted the amateur anthropologist to get her back on track: "What's the curse?"

I silently thanked him.

"I'm getting to it," she said. "I heard about it from a shaman I met in Colorado." The storyteller paused, whether for effect or to take a hit of her own, I couldn't tell. I was lying on my back now, looking up at the light-polluted cloud cover through the little golden leaves of the honey locust trees while I listened.

"Okay, the legend is simple, right? If you kill a snake on sacred ground, you *become* a snake, or a snakelike creature."

"That's it?"

"Yeah, that's it. Why does everything have to be three acts and explosions?"

"Sacred ground. Isn't all ground sacred to the Indians?"

"Sacred to Yig, the snake god. There are power places scattered over the Earth dedicated to him where ley lines intersect. Places where the kundalini energy of the planet wells up to the surface. In Nepal he's Nagaraja, in Mexico Quetzalcoatl, and in Africa he is known by many names. Anyway, the curse, it's like karma, right? It means that the Indians valued the lowest of the low, creatures literally without a leg to stand on. And if you hurt one, you should expect to find yourself stripped of power and crawling on your belly on the ground among them, yeah? So what I'm saying is: look at any people's myths and you'll see what their values are."

"Yeah, you said that."

"I did. And I'm saying it again man, because you're not fuckin hearing me. What are the myths of these bankers who prey on families? What myths are the cops digesting when they gather around the Comcast campfire for story time?"

I turned inward after that, sinking down deep in the bag and heating it with my breath as fatigue finally claimed me. The last sound I heard before I drifted off was the languid grainy rattle of maracas from the last percussionist standing in the Sacred Space by the London plane tree.

In the morning I slithered out of my sleeping bag, packed my scant possessions, and headed uptown to the Port Authority where I bought an Amtrak ticket west. In Chicago, I would learn that the police had cracked down on the demonstration right after I left, clearing the park in riot gear. When I read the news I felt a little pang of guilt for checking out early. I'd met some good people at Occupy and I hoped they were okay. I'll admit I've never been especially political, but I've always wanted to find my tribe.

When I reached Omaha, I changed to buses to save money and paid extra for a handgun without a permit at a pawnshop. I barely looked at the thing before rolling it up in my sleeping bag. A simple revolver that looked reliable. Not that I know much about guns. I only knew that it lacked the wicked beauty of the first one I'd ever held in my hands when I was 13 and living in California.

■ ■ ■

It was a girl that set us apart and a gun that brought us back together, at least for a little while.

Adam and I met on a soccer team when we were seven. The Roughnecks. I played for six seasons and have forgotten most of the teams I was on, but I still remember the orange and black uniforms of the Roughnecks. Adam's dad was the head coach, mine the assistant, and as they became friends we started seeing each other outside of games and practices and spent a lot of time in each other's pools that first summer.

One-on-one soccer on the lawn and board games when it rained. *Battleship* and an old version of *Chutes and Ladders* handed down from Adam's grandparents, called *Snakes and Ladders*. Adam usually won, even in games of chance and if he'd gone on to college, I'm sure he would have climbed the ladder somewhere.

A summer can feel like an age when you're seven years old, and by the time we went back to school it felt like I'd known him forever. We were on different teams the following year, and it wasn't until junior high that we attended the same school. I didn't realize until then that unlike me Adam had plenty of friends. I was more introverted. Well, *bullied* might be a more honest way to put it. And unlike me, Adam had an easy way with girls. Of course at that age, all circuits were firing and it wasn't long before he told me he'd made out with Gina Barbieri, a pert little blonde I knew but didn't find attractive. Blondes weren't really my thing, but I could see why other guys would be into her. Adam didn't go into detail when he told me the score, but it was clear he was bursting to share the achievement.

It was just the latest thing he had done to outpace me, to leave me behind. Over winter break he'd even gone hunting with his grandfather and claimed to have shot a deer. I wasn't sure if I believed him about the kill, but I *had* heard his father talking to mine about the trip before it happened.

A kill.

A kiss.

On the day Adam told me about Gina's tits and tongue, I got some cardboard boxes from the garage and packed up most of the toys that still cluttered my room.

I still don't know if he was just raising the stakes and showing off when he filched the gun from his grandfather's dresser, or if he was trying to repair things between us and bring me in on something risky with him because he sensed how badly I needed it. In any case, I remember the heady rush and the renewed sense of standing at eye level with him when he took it out of his backpack and handed it to me swaddled in a red rag that smelled of oil.

The weight of the bundle surprised me. He hadn't told me what the "surprise" was and I thought maybe he'd brought his BB gun. My parents wouldn't let me have one, and even shooting his would have been good. But the weight in my hand told me this was no BB gun. I looked around the junkyard at the refrigerators and washing machines leaning against uprooted trees amid the fragile lattice of rust-eaten cars. We were alone.

"Go ahead," he said, and bumped my shoulder with his.

I unfolded the fabric, and the nickel plate flared in the sunlight. It was engraved near the grip with a wild horse rearing up. A Colt.

"Is it loaded?"

Adam nodded and I went a little numb in the fingers. This was real. He had handed me adulthood and it was all silver and black.

Stamped on the short barrel were the words KING COBRA.

I met his eyes and I'm sure mine looked too wide, devoid of cool.

He laughed, a lighthearted, breezy sound. "Man, you should have seen Matt's face when I showed him a bullet on the bus," he said. "I don't think he'll be riding you in the locker room after gym anymore."

My face flushed with heat, a mixture of gratitude and embarrassment. I focused on the gun in my hand and felt momentarily lifted off of the ground by a wave of exhilarating fear. *What does he expect of me?*

"What are we gonna do with it?"

Adam laughed again and slapped me on the back. "We're gonna shoot some fuckin rats, man."

Rats were a huge relief compared to the thought of threatening Matt Fremantle with a loaded gun. They were also better than deer, in my book. I'd honestly felt a little sick at the thought of my friend blowing a hole in a deer, but rats were nasty, disease-ridden vermin. I'd already seen a friend's brother who worked at a pet store feed a rat to a snake one time, and I don't think I could've done that; dangle one from its tail over the fangs. That would almost be the same as crushing one under my shoe. But the gun would take them out in a flash. I could hear them scampering through the junk, see the places where loose scraps of metal and cardboard trembled at their passage. It made my skin crawl.

Adam was bouncing his heel on the ground beside me like he did when he was gaming or anticipating something, his knee bobbing in an agitated rhythm, a vestige of the ADHD his parents had medicated into remission. "Get in a shooting stance," he said. "Sight it on the junk pile. You want to be ready *before* you spot one."

I raised the gun, gripped it with both hands, and bisected the trembling trash heap with the sight blade.

I was wired. Was that a scaly tail flicking through a rust hole?

"Feet shoulder-width apart. That's it. Dude, this bitch is a .357. You hit one it's gonna pop like a blood balloon."

A flash of fur.

I saw Adam sliding his hand down Gina's pants.

A deer collapsing in a thicket.

The power to make life. The power to take it. A threshold between us.

A rat scampered across the fuel tank of a tractor chassis and perched there on its haunches, its black fur stark against the blue sky.

I christened it with thunder.

■ □ ■

Danny Wormbone. Not a handle I expected a New Age huckster to still be going by almost twenty years later. But there he was in the search results advertising *RUNES, MEDICINE CARDS, SPIRITUAL COUNSEL-*

ING & RETREATS. In 1994 my father had probably found him in the Yellow Pages. Now he had a website that might very well be obsolete, and what had once been a "vision quest" was now a "spiritual retreat." I wrote down the phone number. The Greyhound station on Main Street where I had rolled into town still had a few pay phones, but the nearest hotel with an Internet kiosk didn't. Apparently they attracted the wrong crowd—people like me, who couldn't keep up with a cellular bill.

I hoofed it back to the bus station and made the call before I could think too much about it and changed my mind. It rang three times before voicemail picked up. His recorded voice was familiar, if a little more worn down to gravel by years of smoke: "Your call is important to me." That was all he said before the beep, but it was enough to know I had the right guy. I didn't leave a message and was glad he hadn't picked up. The business address I'd jotted on my notepad wasn't located on the strip among the high-end psychics, but here in the old town. I decided to walk.

Would he recognize me when I stepped into his parlor? I didn't think I looked much like I had at 13. Back then he'd said a bunch of stuff about my aura. Told me it was blue. I wondered if he'd see the same energy when I showed up 17 years later. It wasn't likely.

I recognized the symbol painted on the plate glass before I could even read the name. A constellation in white: Ophiuchus, the snake handler, floating in the sky over a crossed feather and staff. The shop was at street level, between a podiatrist and a Mexican restaurant. It looked dark inside, but when I tried the door I found it unlocked and entered to the sound of wind chimes. Of course the first thing to hit me while my eyes adjusted to the cluttered murk was the diffused smell of burning sage.

The proprietor hadn't overlooked the merchandising possibilities. Racks of tie-dyed tapestries printed with tribal motifs, spirit animals, and celestial designs obstructed my view of the shop. Parting a pair of them like curtains, I found my way into a larger area where dim sunlight from the street illuminated a glass countertop through which I glimpsed a variety of quartz crystals and amethyst geodes. Bookshelves flanked the counter, stocked with a sparse collection of New Age and astrological titles interspersed with painted woodcarvings and brass statues: a turquoise wolf, a masked dancing shaman, even a Buddha sitting in lotus position with an awning of hooded cobras over his head to shelter him from the rain. Behind the counter the wall was lined with charts. A medicine pipe hung from a nail by a loop of rawhide. A barstool stood vacant behind the cash register, a knobby walking stick of lustrous black wood leaning in the corner beside it.

Danny Wormbone emerged from the back room through a slit in a tapestry. My first thought was that it couldn't be him, because it looked *too* much like him. Surely he would have aged more in the intervening years. But he had the same jet-black hair, the same leathery skin, the same sinewy build and that deep hollow I remembered where his throat met his breastbone. The same quick eyes set close to his nose like you see on any wild predator, and the same quiet gentle demeanor as he moved through the space and settled on the stool as if intent on stirring the air as little as necessary.

I nodded at him. He nodded back, his face as impassive as it had been from the moment it emerged through the curtain, his expression betraying no sign of recognition.

As usual, I was winging it. I still didn't know if I was going to ask if he remembered me or play it like a stranger in search of spiritual counseling.

The moment passed and I browsed the shop in silence. When I looked at the countertop again, Wormbone had produced a small block of wood and was whittling it with a buck knife over a square of canvas littered with shavings.

I approached the counter. I figured I had enough cash to hire him as a guide, but not enough to spend more than a couple of nights in this town before heading on to SoCal where I still had friends. It wouldn't do to have him pencil me in on his calendar like any other walk-in. I'd come a long way to be here and it was time to get to the point. Probably a lot of people stepped into a shop like that without knowing exactly what they were looking for. I imagine part of his job was getting them to articulate it. I had crossed most of the continent without admitting to myself exactly what I was after. Now I was faced with the only person who could help me. So what *was* I looking for? Closure? It felt more like I was opening something.

A can of worms.

A grave.

Wormbone remained focused on his carving until finally, wondering if he'd noticed me, I drummed my fingers on the glass countertop. Without looking up from the spiral of blond wood curling around his blade, he said one word. The only word I needed to hear to know he knew me. "*Unukalhai*. Wondered when I'd see you again."

"I want to go back."

"It'll cost you," he said, poking a pupil into the eye of the creature he was carving. I couldn't make out what it was. A crude dragon, maybe.

"I have money."

"And I'll take it." He finally looked up and locked his gaze on mine. "But I'm not talking about money."

■ ■ ■

I'm at my 13th birthday party. I know this because there's a pair of those big number candles on the cake. I don't think my mother ever got those for me, but in the dream, there they are, unlit. The dining room is decorated with nothing but red helium balloons. I think I'm alone at the table. Have I just blown the candles out, or have they not been lit yet? I examine the wicks for ash and find virgin white string. Adam says, "They're blood balloons." He's sitting next to me but somehow I don't see him until he speaks. Each balloon trails a length of ribbon, like the tail of a sperm cell. "Aren't you gonna blow them out?" Adam asks.

I look again and now the candles *are* lit. But no one is singing. My family isn't here.

I take a breath, make a wish, and blow out the twin flames. The red balloons pop, showering the table, the cake and my hair with scrappy, coagulating splashes of blood and tufts of coarse brown fur.

I had that dream on and off for about a week while the heel of my right hand ached in my sleep from the recoil of the revolver. I'd missed the rat with every shot.

■ ■ ■

My parents must have discussed the vision quest before my dad presented the idea to me, but it became clear in the first weeks of June as more detail trickled in, that my mother had serious reservations about what my father (having no doubt read too much Carl Jung and Joseph Campbell) thought would make a good substitution for a confirmation or a bar mitzvah. To be honest, so did I. Maybe the same concerns were shared by Adam's mother, Renée. If so, Adam didn't mention it.

"I just hope they don't think they're gonna babysit us the whole time," he said. "It would defeat the whole purpose. I mean, this is supposed to be hardcore, man. Rite of passage, not the fucking Boy Scouts."

I agreed fervently, although I knew the only reason my mother hadn't intervened and called the whole thing off was exactly because my dad had been promising her he would shadow me like a scout leader. In my presence he downplayed his role, of course, not wanting to undermine the mystique going in or any sense of accomplishment I might have coming out. But I heard more of their conversations than they realized.

"You can't starve and dehydrate our kid," she said. "And sleep deprivation? If Child Services ever heard about it... Christ, how can this guy operate legally with minors involved?"

"You make it sound so extreme. We'll have water. Absolutely. It's the desert. Do you think I'm crazy? I mean, where did you even get that? I'm not going to neglect him. A little light fasting never killed anyone. It's healthy. Healthier than how he eats most of the time. You know, I'm a little insulted that you don't think I'll intervene if necessary."

She sighed. "It's not you, it's Lee. Or how you two are together. Knowing him, he'll toss your emergency provisions off a cliff just to impress the boys."

"No, he won't."

"And you'll let him, just to prove you're not a wimp."

"Hey, that's not fair. You know I'll take care of Nathan. No harm will come to him."

■ ■ ■

Everything is vibrating. The striated sandstone formations pulse in bands of blood red, lavender, and bone yellow. The sky stretches and retracts like the skin of a funeral drum with each beat of my heart and under everything, no, *inside* everything, buzzing like the collision of fire-wreathed atoms is the all-pervasive sound of rattles—keratin rings dancing in the tip of a serpent's tail and the world is in thrall to that hypnotic rhythm. A sound as rich as a symphony of cicadas, but I've seen no insects among the sagebrush and mesquite. I'm slicked with sweat and my knees and elbows are skinned from stumbling over rock and I feel like I'm tripping, but I've never tripped, not yet, not until college, I haven't even tried weed yet but Adam has—that was the last thing he tried before me and it's the last thing he'll ever try before me but I don't know that yet and I'm trying to make sense of all this sensory distortion. Can it really be the lack of food and sleep? Is it possible that disturbing the rhythms of the body's needs just a little can screw with your perception this bad, this fast and send you so far out? I'm scared. We got lost. My throat is sore from calling for the men but I'm trying to conserve the last of the water in my canteen and this is not a dream. Not a dream, but still it haunts me. It haunts me for fucking years.

Adam's posture changes when he crests the slope and steps through the arch, leaving a gray handprint in sweat on the limestone. He goes rigid and I swear I can hear his breath stopping in his chest. He steps backward slowly and slips out of the straps of his backpack. He feels for the telescoping shovel that hangs from the pack without ever taking his eyes off what lies beyond the arch, now gliding over the threshold and coiling to strike.

A Mohave green rattlesnake, probably four feet long with black and white rings near the tail. We learned about them in school, so I know it's deaf despite its warning rattle, has heat-sensors between its nostrils and eyes, is notoriously aggressive and possessed of a far more powerful venom than its cousin, the western diamondback—a frequently lethal neurotoxin. Lee has a snakebite kit in his pack but that does us no good unless the men find us, or we find them and we got ourselves lost on purpose and I'm praying that they know where we are and are just keeping out of sight, laying low, ignoring our calls to give our trial meaning, to scare us, but my cries have been so desperate that they would have come. They would have come.

The snake winds over itself in a figure eight, its head rising, the rattle erect and vibrating like everything else in this heightened world, a translucent gray blur.

Adam is gripping the shovel, sliding backward, sending pebbles and dust tumbling down the slope toward me and raising the shaft in both hands like a spear, but it's not a shovel, it's a hand spade—too small, too pointed, too close range. He must be crazy. A square flat blade might take the snake's head off, but this? The blade is triangular like the rattler's head. He would have to move faster than the snake. He would have to have dead aim.

I open my mouth to yell *no*, but he stabs the spade down into the dirt, heaving his weight behind it and I have time to think he's breaking ground on his own grave but then the snake's head rolls between his hiking shoes, down the slope with the scree. The jaws are still twitching and crying venom and I jump out of the way of it with an animal vocalization that comes out somewhere between a moan and a yelp, surprising even me with its alien timbre.

But that other sound, the sound under and in the heart of everything, the rattle and hum of cannibal Creation, goes on.

Adam turns to face me, his skin pale against the ruddy sandstone. "Don't touch it," he says. "You know what they say about a severed snake head? It doesn't die until sundown."

◼◼◼

The bad shit that happened when I was 13 caught up with me at 31. Or I caught up with it. 1331: tally all the digits and you get 8. Roll it on its side and you get infinity, or a snake winding over on itself. Maybe I never outran any of it, never believed the lies the adults told me back then. The lies they told the police, the school, and each other.

Danny Wormbone hadn't aged much. Maybe that was the Indian blood in him, maybe it was something else. The weather was good for the end of November and he agreed to take me out to the Moapa Paiute lands north of Vegas, the reservation where he had been living when my father called him in 1994. It was early afternoon when we left town in a Jeep he kept in a rented garage down the street. He tossed his walking stick in the backseat after my backpack and sleeping bag. I only brought my gear because I had nowhere else to leave it. I wasn't planning on sleeping in the desert.

The Jeep smelled of cigarettes. Rock and roll on the radio and a dusty little dream catcher hanging from the rearview. I had paid the old medicine man two hundred dollars for the ride and trail guide, but he wasn't much for talk. He smoked and drove and I watched the city thin out and the silver clouds move in over the Mojave.

Seventeen years ago we had met Wormbone at a picnic area inside Valley of Fire National Park. We came, the four of us, in Adam's dad's SUV and after a final lunch, followed our "spirit guide" to a second site outside the park. He rode a motorcycle with leather fringe saddlebags, but nothing about him besides his braided hair looked particularly Native American. He was dressed in denim, cowboy boots, and sunglasses and asked us if we'd been expecting feathers.

We hiked in silence and I think my dad was wondering if he and Lee were going to get their money's worth. At sunset we arrived at a red rock wall covered with petroglyphs, the rock an almost blackened rust color, the glyphs contrasting in pale salmon: concentric circles, silhouettes of big horn sheep, spoked wheels, and pairs of zigzagging lines.

Wormbone ran his finger over one of the zigzags. "This is the snake," he said. "Symbol of rebirth. Humans have connected with the energy of rebirth, regeneration, and transformation on this land since prehistoric times. Since long before your tribe or mine ever came here." He took a bottle of red wine from the saddlebag of his motorcycle and a corkscrew from the pocket of his denim jacket. He opened the bottle, lined up five waxed paper cups, and poured.

Without asking our fathers if we could partake, he held his own cup up to the sun in a toast and said, "Join me in the sacrament. This wine, the blood red of the iron earth and the all-sustaining sun, taste it as you absorb the power and glory of this place."

We raised our cups to the sun and drank. The wine tasted bitter.

From another pocket Wormbone produced a silver cigarette lighter adorned with a turquoise stone and held the flame to the end of the cork. He let it burn for a few seconds, then shook it out in the cool evening air. He brushed the hair away from my forehead with his callused fingers and drew something there with the charcoal. I didn't know what it was until he had done the same to Adam: a pair of zigzagging lines like the symbol for Aquarius written vertically.

"Take the serpent as your symbol. The undulating pulse of life, the winding path, the one who sheds his form to be reborn."

He poured the remainder of the wine into the dirt, mounted his bike, and kicked it to life with a roar.

We followed in the car to the next stop where he told us to gather our gear for the hike. He pointed out the ridge and the towering formation that was to be the site of our first camp. In the clear desert air it looked closer than it was. Adam and I set out at a brisk pace and were soon far ahead of the men, but before long we tired and the gap narrowed until Wormbone's staff was scratching the dirt at my heels.

Now here was that sound again, this time ahead of me, as I followed the old shaman up the trail. We had passed by the petroglyphs without so much as a pause to look this time, never mind a pep talk and a toast. The trail was deserted. Most hikers kept to the official park trails, and this one was outside the boundary. I wasn't sure if it was on reservation land or not. We had passed the Moapa Paiute Travel Plaza off of I-15. Fireworks, alcohol, tobacco, and gas. We hadn't stopped. Now, hiking up the ridge, I regretted not asking him to pull in so I could use the bathroom and buy some bottled water. It could have been enlightening to watch him interact with whoever worked there. I wondered what kind of reaction his presence provoked. Respect? Scorn? Fear? Or was he just another New Age snake oil salesman claiming Indian heritage? Would they even recognize him?

"This is the place," he said, punching the earth with his staff and sweeping his hand over the vast expanse of prismatic sandstone, frozen waves of geologic record lapping at an endless shore. "This is where we made our main camp for the vision quest." His manner and tone implied fulfillment of the job I'd hired him for. But no, we were far from done here.

"Do you still take kids on quests, with the fasting and staying up all night?"

He didn't answer. He traced a spiral in the dust with his staff, scrutinized me, and asked, "You think I'm responsible for what happened to your friend?"

"I don't know."

"His parents took on the risks. They signed a waiver. Yours did, too. Do you think the desert isn't dangerous? Do you think confronting it would *mean* anything if it wasn't?"

"I don't know what happened to Adam," I said. "But you do, I know you do. I didn't come all the way here to blame you. I just want to know what happened."

"Then you should have gone to his father."

"His father ate a gun a long time ago. And I don't know if his mother *ever* really knew what happened."

"You boys shouldn't have wandered off on your own."

I scanned the paths that branched off from the ridge. Some wound around sculpted rock formations that resembled faces in profile or the silhouettes of great spiny beasts. Others were lost among the sage and cacti. "This is where you showed us the stars," I said.

Wormbone nodded.

"All that snake-themed mumbo jumbo. Ironic, don't you think?"

His eyes narrowed.

"You pointed out Virgo, Hercules, and the Snake Handler near the horizon. You pointed out the bright star you called *the Heart of the Serpent*—"

"Unukalhai. That's the Arabic name. The double star in the serpent's throat."

"Yeah, you said *we* were like a double star, Adam and I. Connected by our own invisible gravity, like brothers."

"You were. Anyone could see that. But he burned brighter."

"His parents told everyone he died of a snakebite. But I was there when he killed the snake. It never bit him."

"He should have left it alone."

"So he deserved what happened to him?"

"You don't kill your avatar on a vision quest."

"We were delirious from deprivation and faced with a venomous snake. I think you set us up for that."

"Why would I do that?"

"The Curse of Yig."

Wormbone turned, grinding the end of his staff in the ground, and started back down the trail. "I brought you here, like you asked. You can hitch a ride back to the city from the truck stop, chum."

I drew the gun from under my shirt at the small of my back and cocked the hammer. He spun on me, nostrils flaring.

"I want my money's worth, medicine man. Take me to the arch where it happened."

■ ■ ■

Adam was contorted on the ground beside the severed snake when the men found us. Wormbone hung back while Lee and my dad knelt in the dust and tried to keep him from thrashing. When they finally overpowered him, my dad—pale, sweaty and wide-eyed—asked me what had happened, while Lee curled a finger into his son's mouth to keep him from choking on his own tongue.

Before I could answer, Wormbone asked, "Is he prone to seizures?"

"No," Lee said, never taking his eyes from Adam's bluing face.

"Allergic to bee stings?"

"What? No. Look, it was a snake. He was bitten by a snake."

"Was he?" Wormbone looked at me. He seemed so calm, like we were discussing the weather.

"No," I said. "It didn't bite him. It came after us but he killed it with the spade."

Lee cried out and yanked his finger from Adam's mouth. A ruby ribbon of blood ran down his hand. He stared at it in awe. "Bit me. *Jesus.*"

Adam shook his head in his father's lap, showing his teeth. I could swear they were fangs. We all jumped and shuffled back, all except for Wormbone who held his staff out in front of him, as if it would ward off the threat, and for a second I wondered if he was going to shove the stick in Adam's jaws to give him something to bite down on, like you might do to a dog.

Lee sucked the blood off his finger and dug through his pack, quickly losing patience and dumping the contents in the dirt. Adam hissed at him, and Lee scampered out of range, dragging his fingers through the scattered camping paraphernalia and seizing on a bright yellow plastic box. He popped the lid. A syringe and a set of suction cups spilled out, along with a few alcohol wipes. "Where did it bite him?" he yelled at me. I'd never seen an adult look so scared in my life.

"It *didn't* bite him," I said again, but Lee seemed unable to process the information and by then even I was wondering if I'd seen it wrong, missed something.

"It had to have," my father said. "Did it get him on the leg?"

"I don't know. I… I didn't see it bite him!"

Lee reached for Adam's exposed calf below his cargo shorts, but Adam kicked dirt at him and kept kicking until he gained some traction and was up on his feet, sprinting up the rise and through the sandstone arch.

The sun was sinking fast, the shadows of the rock formations stretching toward the horizon. My heart was flopping, a fish in a bucket. My eyes stung with sweat. Lee ran through the arch after Adam, and I went to follow, but my father stopped me with a palm to the hollow of my shoulder. "Wait here, Nathan. Just wait for us." He shot a glance at Wormbone and I could see all kinds of calculation in it: not trusting the man to help them restrain Adam, not trusting him to stay with me, and a suspicion that he wouldn't heed instructions anyway. The sound of Lee calling Adam's name echoed in the valley. My dad jogged through the arch, holding his hand out behind him in my direction, his fingers splayed. "Just… stay back," he said. "Let me go first."

But I followed him through the arch, leaving Wormbone staring at the severed body of the rattler in the blood-gummed sand.

Later there were dogs and a helicopter. The men called 911 from the Travel Plaza and the police came searching for Adam, ready to airlift him to Vegas for antivenom. But they never found him. Not all of him, anyway. What the dogs found tangled in the brush and cactus needles two days later was tatters of necrotic tissue, gossamer sheaths in the shapes of a boy's limbs, sloughed off and left behind.

■ ■ ■

It could have been yesterday when I'd last stood here with my father, Lee and Danny Wormbone, except that the season was different: cooler and with fewer yellow flowers in the creosote bushes. And now it was just the two of us. I followed my shadow through the arch. The sun had sunk below the cloud cover in the west, gilding the formations. I felt as if I were passing into a cathedral. The arch marked the pinnacle of the formation we had been climbing. On the other side it began its eastern descent through a series of interconnected open caves, each spilling into the next through terraced slopes of vermiculated red rock, illuminated at intervals where the dusty sunlight spilled through apertures in the sandstone. There were petroglyphs here as well, but they were different, less pictogram and more akin to cuneiform writing.

I worked my jaw and felt a pressure I hadn't been aware of open up in my inner ear. A sound like cicadas poured into my consciousness, an unnerving texture that made my stomach roil and churn.

Wormbone turned to me. I pointed the gun at his chest and jutted my chin toward the descending slopes. He shuffled down ahead of me, jabbing at strategic angles in the rock with his staff for balance. I followed in a crouch, using many of the same footholds, and taking it slower so as not to have need of changing the gun to my left hand. I had no doubt the old medicine man could be swift as a viper if I gave him an opportunity.

"What's that sound," I asked. "Rattlers?"

He paused in his descent and when he answered, his voice echoed in the stone vaults. "Those rattles are to a rattlesnake what a street fiddler is to a symphony, son."

It wasn't much of an answer, but before I could press him further, a new layer of sound emerged from the drone, weaving and winding through the percussive texture with a breathy, sinuous dissonance. A flute.

"Where is that music coming from?" I hoped my voice didn't sound panicked.

He was outpacing me now, passing into the lower bowels of the cave system. He didn't answer.

I asked again. "Who's making that music? Tell me."

His head swiveled toward me, his eyes radiating a jaundiced contempt in the fading light. "My tribe," he said. "Isn't that why you came? For the initiation you never had?"

I sat on the slope and slid down to him, landing in the dust just out of reach of his staff if he chose to swing it. I kept the gun on him all the while, and standing again, I aimed it at his face.

He took a step away.

"No," I said. "Wait." I cupped the heel of my right hand with my left and moved around him in a wide arc, keeping the sight blade aligned to his head, thinking of junkyard rats.

"When Adam got away from his father and passed through here… that wasn't the last time you saw him, was it?"

"No."

"Before, you said I should have gone to Adam's father. When the cops finished questioning us and let you go, that wasn't the last time you saw Lee, either. Was it?"

"No."

"I asked my mother about Adam's parents when I was home from college but she didn't want to talk about them. She said she and my father had a falling out with them because they'd found religion after losing their son. They'd become fanatical about it, maybe even a little crazy. Was it *your* religion they found? I always assumed Lee would kill you as soon as look at you again after what happened."

"He wanted to at first. But grief can take the fight out of a man. And I had a balm for that."

"A balm? What did you do? Con them into accepting your version of the afterlife? Tell them you could commune with the spirits of the dead? Take advantage of shattered, grieving parents with your mystic bullshit?"

"I didn't have to convince them I could commune with the dead. Their son *wasn't* dead. I helped them to commune with the living."

"That's a lie. They would have taken him home if he was alive."

"The desert was his home by then, the deep places of the earth for his body and the cold fathoms of the sky for his consciousness, a sine wave undulating in the dark reaches of the night."

"How long did it take you to suck them dry?"

"I asked for nothing. They paid tribute to the Father of Serpents with the carcasses of cats and dogs, which they fed their boy as well. It was a comfort to them… feeding him. They couldn't talk with him in any human tongue by then, but they knew it was him. They knew him by his eyes."

Something massive moved through a tunnel behind me, the sand crunching under its weight.

We had arrived at a level where the curved stone walls were honeycombed with openings. I scanned the arches in the murk and caught glimpses of silhouettes gliding past, the sounds of flute and rattles phasing in and out as they passed, sound merging with echo, substance with shadow.

A quick motion from Wormbone drew my attention back to him. He had raised his walking stick like a javelin and now dashed it at the rock at my feet where it clattered and bounced before the shape of the thing wavered in a scribble of gold light, emerging as a black snake. Wormbone's body dissolved in a twist of oily smoke trailing after it and vanishing up its nostrils.

I sidestepped the snake, slipped on the smooth rock and almost fell. The snake reared up in a coil and hissed. I fired a shot at it, felt the thunder of the gun punch my eardrums, and saw the spray of limestone chips where the bullet drilled into the rock. The snake slithered out of view behind an hourglass pillar as I fired again.

Sweating and trembling with adrenaline, I surveyed the cavernous space around me. Below, the terraced slopes continued their descent through cavities of eroded stone where shadows pulsed like pools of black water lapping against the sand. The chamber around me was relatively wide, with yawning apertures at intervals in the walls. Without pause for deliberation, I lunged through the nearest of these, hoping to find a more direct and open path to the valley floor and the trail back to the Jeep.

The chamber was round and high, the walls crawling with glistening sinuous shadows. Here and there ashen appendages reminiscent of human limbs emerged from the chaos of black motion, lit by the green phosphorescence of the central figure, which I first took to be a towering pillar of slime-covered stone. As my eyes adjusted to the darkness, the organic aspects of the form took precedence and I beheld the gently undulating form of the Father of Serpents.

A towering column of armored flesh, the pale ventral scales of the exposed underside bordered by a byzantine matrix of small dark scales that made the monster appear gem encrusted in its own light. It radiated billowing veils of energy behind which a pair of sinewy arms rose with the graceful fluidity of a conductor drawing an orchestra into the beat preceding a crash. They lashed forward revealing humanoid hands, beaded fingers splayed and tipped with keratin bulbs that rattled as the hands vibrated in a translucent blur. The sound overwhelmed my body and mind, lacerating my brainwaves with virulent interference, paralyzing me in the blazing topaz gaze of Yig.

The creature lowered its head and I felt the baleful scrutiny of those ancient eyes probing my mind from beneath the scaly spikes of an organic crown studded with dying stars. Its forked tongue flickered, a cloven flame, tasting my aura of fear and pheromone.

And then the scrying of my soul ceased and I was released.

I fell to my knees in the darkness, my fingers finding beads of my own sweat in the dust. I crawled backward to the sounds of grotesque motion from the braided perimeter and nearly wept with relief when my groping hand found bare rock to guide me back to the fissure I had entered through.

The light had leeched from the sky and I felt my way through the honeycombed rock on my belly letting gravity and an updraft of sage-scented air guide me down and down to the valley floor.

A spike of pain flared in the webbing of my left hand and I recoiled with a cry as the black king snake, the alter-shape of Wormbone, wound around my forearm and reared up in my face with a hiss. My reaction was reflexive. I shoved the pistol in its mouth, squeezed the trigger, and pissed myself when the roar of the shot decayed in a rain of bone and blood in the darkness.

Moaning, nearly blind and deaf, I rolled and scampered through the hollows until a chute of polished rock swallowed me down and shat me out under the desert stars.

■ ■ ■

When I was younger I wanted to be a writer someday. I never managed to get it together. Maybe I lacked confidence. Maybe I made excuses. I spent a lot of years drifting, anesthetizing myself, trying to forget what happened that summer. You thought I was trying to find myself, but I was trying to find my tribe.

I may have found them now. And this will be the only story I leave behind.

I'm sorry, Mom and Dad. You should talk to Renée about joining the congregation. It's the oldest religion on Earth.

I took the medicine man's Jeep down I-15 like the hordes of hell were on my trail, and I've holed up in a seedy motel on the outskirts of Vegas to set this down.

The skein of shed flesh that I've been depositing in the bathtub is almost the size of a man. Where the heel of my writing hand—my shooting hand—rubs against the paper, it's been worn through to black scales for a while already.

I probably shouldn't have left the valley. I don't know how I'll get back. I may have to travel beside the highway by night and hide in culverts when the sun is up.

I wonder if I will know Adam when I see him, smell him, read his heat signature in the dark. And I wonder if he will still burn brighter.

Yig

The serpent has always been regarded as the wisest of beasts. It is deathless because it renews its life each time it sheds its skin. For this reason the Greeks associated it with their god of healing, Asclepius. He carries the symbol of the serpent twined about his staff. Hermes, the Greek god of wisdom, bears a rod upon which two serpents are entwined.

In the creation myth of the Hebrews, which they adopted from the Babylonians, the knowledge of good and evil was a gift from the god of serpents, who in the Torah remains un-named. It is associated with evil, but that is a false teaching. For the race of man, the gift of wisdom from the serpent meant liberation from the slavery of ignorance.

Serpents are ancient creatures whose species crawled on the earth long before the first beginning of human beings. They existed in the same forms they have now when the world was infested by monstrous reptilian beings the size of houses, and they continued unchanged when those monsters perished.

The serpents worship a deathless old one as their god. He is a shape-changer who appears sometimes as a large snake, but other times as a manlike figure with the head of a serpent covered in scales. Always he has been feared by men, who have called him such names as the Evil Lizard and the Encircler of the World. Those who worship this god do so to turn away his wrath.

The Egyptians named this god Apophis and feared that he would one day devour the sun the way a snake swallows a hen's egg. They called him "he who is spat out" and believed he arose from the saliva of the goddess of the night sky. There is wisdom in this, for this god is whispered by deathless things that dwell in deep places to have fallen from the stars.

The black tribes of Africa sometimes call him Dhamballah, and dance the dance of serpents to summon him. It is his pleasure to possess those who dance well, and when they are possessed by his spirit, they lose the ability to speak, but fall on their bellies, hissing like snakes, and crawl upon the ground with a sinuous, twisting motion until he leaves them.

He has been given various names in different lands, but the most ancient of these is Yig. So he is called by the copper-skinned barbarian tribes that inhabit the most distant and least known wild places of this world, such as the great island that lies far to the west, beyond the Pillars of Hercules. They dance to appease his wrath. Any man of these tribes who slays a serpent is put to death, for there is no greater crime.

All serpents are the children of Yig. When men kill snakes out of malice or fear, the wrath of this ancient god is aroused against them. He visits them in the night and drives them insane, so that they see and hear snakes crawling everywhere, and mistake their fellow men for the scaly figure of this snake-headed god.

It is the pleasure of Yig to mate with women. Of this union are born deformed offspring with scaly skin who writhe on their bellies and hiss with their long forked tongues. Such monstrous births are known as the Curse of Yig, and seldom survive beyond their first year. Even when they live to maturity, they are idiots bereft of speech who cannot use their hands, but lie naked on the floor and try to bite the feet of those who pass them by.

It is rumored that Yig is worshipped with human sacrifices along with Cthulhu by the ancient race from the stars that dwells deep beneath the earth in a vast cavern known as K'n-yan. This alien race regard Yig as the vital principle in all living things. By the tail-beats of the great serpent they marked their days, and by the shedding of his skin their years.

In their cavern they represented Yig and Cthulhu together as a pair of crouching statues that glare at each other, as though from some deep enmity. They built shrines to these gods, who they may have believed were descended from the primal gods who are known as the twin blasphemies, Nug and Yeb.

It was perhaps from this original practice in K'n-yan of marking the passage of time with Yig, the deathless serpent, that our philosophers and alchemists began to represent eternity in the form of a serpent that bites its own tail, thereby suggesting a circle without a beginning or an end.

Much of our own reverence for the serpent may descend from the worship of Yig by the copper-skinned race of K'n-yan, who in the distant past dwelt upon the surface of the earth and held intercourse with man. To them we may also assign our deep-rooted fear of this creature, who more than any other living thing has been held in the highest esteem yet paradoxically also in the deepest revulsion by human beings.

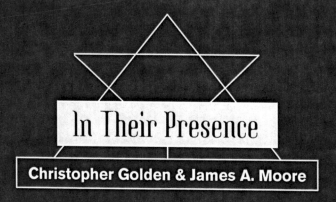

In Their Presence

Christopher Golden & James A. Moore

Harrington said it was Jacques Cousteau's fault.

Three years earlier the explorer had found a wrecked Greek ship and had pulled up treasures from the depths of the sea. Harrington blamed Cousteau like it was a joke, but Professor Jacoby wasn't convinced. He'd dealt with men like Harrington before—wealthy men who cultivated an air of sophistication in certain company but whose true goal was the acquisition of more wealth. Some of them, again like Harrington, also sought fame.

Jacoby cared little for money or fame unless they could be pressed into service as part of his own true goal, which was knowledge. The professor had made a life out of unraveling mysteries and mapping the unexplored fringes of history and folklore.

Thus, as little as they enjoyed each other's company, Jacoby and Harrington did enjoy a certain symbiosis, each feeding off the other's interests and pursuits. Even so, neither had imagined those pursuits would land them in the middle of the Arctic Ocean, aboard a small vessel called the *Burleson*, with a quiet, weathered, stiff-backed old whaler named John Wilson in the captain's chair, and a crew of New England sailors whose good humor had been swiftly bleeding out as the voyage went on and the nights grew longer and colder.

Professor Edgar Jacoby and Mr. Samuel Harrington agreed on very little, and on less with the passing days, but on this single thing they were in accord: neither gave a tinker's damn about the happiness of the crew. The boat belonged to Harrington, which meant every man from the captain on down was in his employ. They were being paid for their work and their time, and if the voyage bore fruit, they would reap a share of the rewards. Harrington, of course, would get the lion's share, but such it had always been and such would it forever be.

"Benson!" a voice shouted. "Gimme a hand here! The boys are up!"

Crewmen thundered across the deck. The shout had come from Doug Trumbull, the first mate, and Jacoby also rushed aft in response. The frigid Arctic wind lashed and stung what little of his skin was exposed, yet he felt flushed with the heat of anticipation.

The divers came up fast, dragged onto the deck, their suits rimed with ice. They emerged from the depths with chattering teeth and nearly uncontrollable shakes. The things men would do for the promise of riches were almost as fascinating as where they would go to find them. Jacoby rushed from man to man as they tore off their masks. When he identified the dive master, Toby Hobbs, he hovered.

"Mr. Hobbs!" he called, as the crew got the divers to their feet and started them toward the hatch that led belowdecks.

Toby gave Jacoby a nod, and the professor felt a fresh rush of exultation. He turned toward Benson and Trumbull.

"Raise the net, and be careful about it! Like your mother's life depends on it!"

Tired of being ordered about by a skinny, aging academic they rightly assumed hadn't done a day's real labor in his life, the men exchanged frustrated glances but set about to work. As they began hauling in the net, Harrington appeared on deck, aromatic smoke rising from his pipe and swirling away on the Arctic wind. His eyes gleamed, but they were the only sign of his excitement. He puffed his pipe and waited.

Jacoby had pored over the records relating to the sinking of the *Eleanor Lockley*. She'd been at the bottom of the sea more than eighty years, and for perhaps the first thirty of those years, men had sought her wreckage. Over time, as the hope of finding her waned, so did any interest in the unfortunate vessel. A violent and unexpected storm had driven her off course. Prior research into the storm and the ship's planned route had led to searches further south, but Jacoby had followed a unique line of inquiry, studying all records related to the captain of the *Eleanor Lockley*, a man named Elijah Fancher. Captain Fancher had spent four years as mate on board one of the ships seeking the fabled Northwest Passage, which meant he had great knowledge of and experience with Arctic waters. Most skippers, faced with a massive storm building on the horizon, would have sailed south in an effort to circumnavigate the deadly weather.

Professor Jacoby had theorized that Fancher had instead turned north, daring the treacherous Arctic waters.

From there, Jacoby could only count fate as his muse. He'd persuaded Harrington—who had reaped significant reward from financing several of Jacoby's earlier excursions—to supply the boat and crew. They'd only been searching the area Jacoby had pinpointed for six days when Toby's divers had discovered the wreck of the *Eleanor Lockley*.

The area where the ship had finally come to rest was isolated and according to the divers the vessel was mostly intact and only two hundred feet below them. There were several very large holes in the sides of the *Eleanor Lockley* and no indication as to what might have caused them.

But it wasn't the ship they were after. What they wanted was her cargo.

Endless rumors circulated, as was so often the case with lost ships. Some journalists writing in the era of the disappearance of the *Eleanor Lockley* had reported stories suggesting no storm had scuttled the ship, that she had instead fallen prey to pirates, thanks to her mysterious cargo. That no pirates sailed the extreme north seas meant nothing, of course. Always, there were those who insisted the improbable was the most likely solution. And pirates sold more newspapers than bad weather, shipwreck or no shipwreck.

Jacoby could not pretend that he was immune to the lure of whatever treasures might be found in the wreck of the *Eleanor Lockley.* But he wanted to know what had sunk her, what she had been carrying, and why there were so many odd rumors about how she'd gone down. If the ship had managed to escape the path of the storm, then what had caused her to sink?

His desire for answers did not overwhelm his good sense, however. Jacoby's inquiries were intellectual rather than physical. Harrington was paying his divers handsomely so neither of them had to do the job themselves. Ten minutes in the frigid Arctic waters would leave any man screaming in agony, his extremities cramping as the blood flowed to the center of his body in an effort to keep him alive a few more minutes. Heavily insulated diving suits were the only way to survive such conditions, and Jacoby hated confined spaces almost as much as he disliked the idea of freezing to death. Even being belowdecks on board the ship elicited a discomforting wave of claustrophobia. The notion of squeezing into one of the heavy rubber and canvas contraptions and a diver's helmet was unthinkable.

So Jacoby wouldn't dive. But when the divers had been brought into the ship's belly to get warm, while Benson and the others started pulling up the net loaded with crates from the wreckage below, he was right there waiting. Out of courtesy, no one touched the crates until the divers had changed clothes and had something warm to drink. Jacoby could barely resist, but Harrington had insisted. The crates were carried down into the hold and half the crew gathered there to help or simply to observe.

When the moment came, it was Harrington who did the honors, with Benson and Mackey assisting him. Harrington was footing the bill, so it was his prerogative, and it worked to Jacoby's advantage in any case, as he wouldn't have trusted any of the crew with his camera equipment.

He started snapping photos the moment Harrington inserted the crowbar under the lid of the first crate. When the top came free with a screech, the professor felt his heart flutter as he clicked the camera again. He caught a whiff of the stink wafting from the crate and heard several of the sailors reacting in disgust. Benson and Mackey backed away, but Jacoby stepped forward, camera in hand. He and Harrington gazed into a bed of organic rot. Whatever had been inside had decayed over the decades, despite the crates having been very well sealed.

Harrington shot Jacoby a murderous glare. "They'd better not all be like this, or we'll put the damn crates back in the water, and you'll be inside one of 'em."

Jacoby held his breath and took his pictures, fascinated by the remains, in spite of Harrington's disappointment. There were portions of shells and one claw that looked like it belonged to a lobster roughly the size of a bear. He snapped several photos and then agreed it was time to remove the remains from the ship as quickly as possible. They simply weren't equipped to preserve what was left.

A few crates held papers and maps that had not completely rotted away thanks to being pressed together. While there were a few snatches of discernable writing, the fragments meant nothing to them and the documents were otherwise a complete loss. The slightest touch reduced the works to sludge.

Just as the group was becoming disheartened—and Jacoby began to worry that Harrington would follow through on his threats—a true find was discovered amongst the remaining haul. Not a crate, but a passenger's steamer trunk. Within that waterlogged box was a small chest carved from what appeared to be ivory. The surface had been etched with strange runes, the likes of which Jacoby had never seen.

Harrington made to open the chest but Jacoby stopped him. "Not yet, my friend. Let me get proper photographic evidence. If we do this the right way we get as much exposure as Cousteau, and we'll have men lining up to finance our next voyage. You won't have to risk your own bankroll anymore."

Pipe clenched in his teeth, Harrington narrowed his eyes in displeasure. Then he seemed to examine the ivory box afresh and to consider the damage the crowbar might have caused. "Let's not waste time,

Professor. The weather's been cooperating, but this time of year is unpredictable and I don't want to be here in a serious gale."

Jacoby went through a kit of gentler instruments he had brought along, but in the end they settled on a simple, slender letter opener. Harrington worked it around beneath the lid of the ivory chest until he'd broken the latch. In those few minutes, Jacoby blew through two full rolls of film. He'd done a fair job of familiarizing himself with at least the appearance of most known hieroglyphs and archaic written languages and what he saw was not at all familiar to him. The chest's markings were unique and he wanted to be certain he had thoroughly documented them, in case Harrington's manhandling did permanent damage.

Contrary to its smallish size, the chest was heavy. Harrington had needed Benson's help to hoist it from the steamer trunk, and it took both men to remove the lid and set it aside. Jacoby had to rethink his initial assessment. It looked like ivory, but whatever the case was made of, it seemed far heavier. He made a mental note as the men reached inside and began extracting their newly found treasures.

Four stones, each roughly the size of a loaf of bread, each covered with endless tiny etchings similar to the markings on the not-ivory chest. Whoever had carved the stones had not contented themselves merely with those etchings, for each had also been carved into a likeness that seemed almost blasphemous. The first was a crouching winged figure, half aquatic nightmare and half bat. The second resembled a sinister, hooded man, followed by a third comprised of teeth and tongues and eyes in a swirling cloud. The last took the shape of a fusion of wings and pincered legs. Gazing upon the pieces hurt Jacoby's eyes, and glancing about, he realized he was not alone in this response.

Harrington strained to lift one of the pieces, his arms shaking, muscles standing out in hard cords. Finally, Benson had to help him place the object on the metal table.

"It's heavier than it should be," Harrington said. He looked defensive but no one in the room doubted his strength. The strain had been obvious on both of the men.

At that moment something slipped from the chest and fell across the table. Jacoby never even considered taking a photograph. The entire event happened too quickly, and even if he'd thought of it, the odd globule of light—he couldn't have described its color to save his life—seethed across the metal table, then simply evaporated like ice dropped on a hot griddle.

Aside from the stones and that strange, impossible light, the only thing inside the chest was a long, wide cylinder, perhaps twice the size of the four sculpted figures. Unlike the figures this was metallic, a dull gray with a few small indentations at the top and the base but otherwise unremarkable.

"What the hell is that supposed to be?" one crewman asked.

"Never mind that... is no one going to remark upon that light? It just—"

"Quiet," Harrington muttered. "Let the professor finish his work and then we'll start sorting out what it all means."

Jacoby nodded to him, then began to snap photos of the cylinder. He was about to ask Benson to turn it over, but he couldn't get the words out. A sudden wave of nausea swept through him. His stomach lurched and his mouth watered with vile, sour spittle. His heart thudded in his chest and he stepped away, dropping his camera from hands gone suddenly numb. The sound of it breaking caused him to cry out inside, but that despairing voice in his head seemed quite distant.

One hand over his mouth, fighting the urge, Jacoby saw that he was not the only one affected. All of the men around him were also overwhelmed.

The sickness hit hard and fast and then it lingered.

Several men vomited, including Jacoby, and after a while spent trying to stand and recover themselves, they cleaned their messes and made their way to their cabins.

It wasn't food poisoning.

Jacoby knew that as sure as he breathed. It was something else entirely and all he could think about was the odd, heavy essence he had seen dissolve into the table. At the time he had been overwhelmed by the pure strangeness of everything to do with that carved chest, but now whenever he thought of that glob of light, the queasy feeling in his gut returned. Whatever it had been, it had marked them all.

Sweating, feverish, shaking from the sheer strain of his now dry heaves, Jacoby fell onto his cot and curled into himself.

And dreamed.

In his dreams the void between the stars is filled with unknowable colors. The planets look vibrant and alive in ways he's never imagined and the vast gulf of deepest space echoes with impossible sounds. He tries to look away, to find a spot that isn't so overwhelming to his senses.

To his left a planet seethes with dark vitality and a swarm of nightmares lifts from the planet's surface, sweeping into the darkness between the worlds, searching, seeking. They move on wings made of the aether and they sing in a single, communal voice that fills his mind with angry screams.

A nightmare made solid rides the cosmic currents beside him, its body encased in layers of hard shell. Its many legs curl close to the carapace, thick, deadly pincers held tightly to the body. The head of the thing resembles a bee's skull, but covered with a cluster of flagella that wave and undulate, long tendrils that pulse and convulse like newborn maggots.

There are eyes within that nest. They study him with intense curiosity…

Professor Jacoby woke to the sound of men whimpering and moaning in their sleep, and rose weakly from his cot to explore the ship.

Though the waters were calm, the deck seemed to sway and buck beneath him. No one stood on watch. The entire crew lay in a stupor brought on by whatever had slid from the chest. Jacoby himself didn't think he'd be moving for long.

Still, he made it down into the hold and to the table where the stone figures lay. He rested in the closest chair, his eyes drawn to the odd markings. They called to him or seemed to and his hands wandered to the stone that he now saw was shaped a bit like his dream companion. In his dream the creature had extraordinary wings, great sails that were designed to traverse the cosmic winds. The statue's wings were nubs, and if not for the clear markings he'd surely have thought that time had

worn them down to almost nothing. His fingers touched the hard surface, softly tracing the markings.

With his head spinning and the room going along for the ride, Jacoby
took comfort from the solidity and reality of the stone. That very comfort
allowed him to lapse into another, deeper, rest.

Deeper dreams.

*They roam the spaces between the stars, soar in places astronomers only
dream of, and astrologers can never hope to imagine.*

The Mi-Go.

*Has he thought them hideous? No. Theirs is a different beauty, but it is
beauty all the same. In his dream he moves amongst the heavens. Planets alive
and dead are his companions, great clouds of energies never seen by mortal eyes
are his guiding lights. They call to him and the rest of his kin, draw them from
Yuggoth and their earlier homes, infinite nests in the darkest corners of the universe, where they learned secrets known to only a few before them. Gods walk
among the stars and hide in the folded darkness of reality and whisper their
intoxicating secrets to those who are courageous enough to listen.*

Jacoby awoke in a hard sweat. His breath came in cold gasps as he staggered out of the hold, climbing up to the deck, the ship heaving and
swaying around him. He expected to be adrift, the crew still moaning
sickly in their sleep. Instead, the men were topside, securing everything
as the ship rolled and pitched in a storm that churned the surrounding
ocean and sent wind and freezing rain slashing across the deck.

For a time it was all hands called to handle the storm. Later, when
the waters had calmed and the worst of the blow was done, the crew
gathered together in the mess and drank coffee, though not a one seemed
inclined to risk food.

Harrington sipped at his strong brew and looked at the captain.
"Wilson? You want to brief them, or shall I?"

"Your boat," Wilson replied.

"Fine." Harrington glanced around. "I managed a radio call. The
prop's been damaged but we've all been ill for two days, so no one's
been down to investigate as yet. If it can be repaired, all right, but in the

meantime it wouldn't hurt my feelings if a nearby vessel could come along and offer us aid."

"Two days?" Jacoby's voice broke as he said the words. It couldn't have been that long!

Harrington nodded. "Two days. Whatever made us sick, it kept us down a while. No one more than you, Professor."

Emerson, the closest they had to a real doctor on board, nodded agreement and then started setting out cups. "No one has an appetite, but we'll need to drink down some broth and water at the least."

There were grumbles and Jacoby's was among them. Still, he could feel how badly his body needed fluids. *You need to stay alive. You need to be patient*, his mind whispered to him. *They're coming.*

He said nothing but he frowned at the notion. Harrington had radioed for help, but Jacoby didn't think whoever might respond to that summons was the "*they*" he had in mind. He had no idea who his own "they" might be or why he felt so excited when he thought about it. The question haunted him.

The storm had done just enough damage. Though the boat was seaworthy, Toby had reluctantly wrestled on one of the dive suits and gone down into the icy water only to confirm that the props were indeed damaged. They had the tools to at least attempt repairs, but they'd all been ill, and the time it would take underwater to make those repairs meant multiple dives spaced out across days, with no guarantee of success. Even Toby wasn't willing to make the attempt until he stopped feeling like his guts were going to erupt at any given moment.

Harrington made additional calls on the radio but no answers came save for occasional bursts of static. The air was bitterly cold and the crew continued on, struggling with bouts of heavy nausea and a general apathy that had enveloped them all without explanation. This malaise struck each of them so profoundly that none seemed especially worried about their plight.

Jacoby felt compelled to write of his concerns in the journal he'd been keeping, but even that didn't go as well as he'd hoped. His handwriting was a nervous scrawl that lacked the energy to complete full sentences, sometimes full words.

The nightmares continued, worming their way into his deepest self, both conscious and unconscious. He woke wanting to flee, but had nowhere to run. The *Burleson* was crippled, waiting for a diver who was healthy enough to attempt lengthy underwater repairs or the appearance of another vessel.

Perhaps a week passed in this manner, but then, in the midst of static, a message came through from the *Ashleigh Michaels*. Help was on the way, though it would be several days before it arrived.

Most of that time was lost in nausea and dreams. The sole exception came in the form of a burial at sea for Thomas Benson, the man who'd helped Harrington move the heavy stones from the ivory chest. He had succumbed after ten days of dreadful illness that waxed and waned with no apparent rationale. When a crewman discovered him in his cabin, Benson's flesh was gray. His skin flaked away upon contact, revealing muscles and bones that crumbled like charred wood.

Others felt sick, but no one else died from the illness.

Though it had taken a great deal of effort Harrington and the captain had put their prized stone figures back into the chest and sealed it. The not-ivory box lay in a corner of the cargo hold and Jacoby spent most of his time down there with a light, studying the markings on the stones and on the box. He made his own guesses as to what the unsettling symbols meant, leaps of logic and intuition based on various symbols and runic writings he'd encountered in other cultures, but the entire matter was little more than a game of conjecture, until the *Ashleigh Michaels* pulled alongside the *Burleson* and its captain came on deck.

The *Burleson* was a working man's ship. It was old and sturdy, sturdy enough to survive a storm that would have completely scuttled a smaller vessel. The *Ashleigh Michaels* was a yacht that had no sane reason for being in the Arctic waters.

The captain was not a sailor. He was a tall, lean, and scholarly man with a receding hairline and the hands of an intellectual. He introduced himself as David Ivers, but Jacoby was less interested in his name than in the frantic glint in his dark eyes, a shimmer of desperation so evident that even his thick glasses could not hide it.

Most of the crew came onto the deck to see the newcomers. Aside from the captain there was a small crew on the yacht. They remained on the other boat, not a man among them showing the least interest in having anything to do with the *Burleson*.

Harrington and Captain Wilson introduced themselves to Ivers, the latter shaking the man's hand with almost tearful gratitude. Ivers studied him and then the rest of the crew.

"Gentlemen, I've read your messages," Ivers said. "I need only see what you've found."

Harrington frowned. "What are you talking about? We called for help—"

"And here I am," Ivers replied.

"To help us or to poach our discoveries?" Jacoby snapped, surprising himself with the ferocity of his accusation.

He'd been contemplating the rapid deterioration of his employer. Harrington had been a strong man, but the voyage—the long days since their discovery in particular—had taken a terrible toll on him. He muttered almost constantly beneath his breath and he'd developed a nervous tick under his left eye, which grew markedly worse at the announcement of Ivers's demand. In that moment, though, Jacoby understood that he himself was in no better condition. He felt that old nausea roiling in his gut, as familiar now as the blur of his failing vision. Spectacles could correct the latter, but the former had come to stay.

"It's a simple request," Ivers said. "On the radio, you said you'd brought something up from the wreck of the *Eleanor Lockley*. I merely want to see it. Feed my curiosity, sir. It's a small price to pay for whatever help we may offer."

Muttering, clearly reluctant, Harrington nevertheless complied. He led the way into the ship's hold with Jacoby, Trumbull, and several others in tow, and showed the not-ivory chest to the man who had come to their aid.

Harrington was reaching to open his prize when Ivers spoke to him.

"Step back from the chest, please, sir. It can only cause you more harm."

"What do you mean?" Harrington's angry voice held a tremor that had not been there even a day earlier.

"It might already be too late, but you have to abandon this ship and come aboard mine, and do it quickly. All of you. And you've got to leave anything you pulled up from that wreck behind."

"What are you talking about, man?" Jacoby demanded. "We can't just leave. The ship can be repaired. As for the chest—"

"Don't be a fool," Ivers said. "I can see it in you. The sheen of your skin, the widening of your eyes. You can feel the way those stone figures call out and your fragile flesh cannot endure it much longer. Even if you could survive more of that exposure, it wouldn't matter. They'll have heard the call. They'll be coming!"

"Who?" Harrington demanded. "Who are *they*?"

But he did not ask that question like a man who thought Ivers might be raving. He asked like a man who already knew something was coming. As Jacoby did. As Jacoby imagined they all did.

Ivers glanced in revulsion at the figures inside the carved chest. "The Mi-Go are coming for what you've found and they're likely already on their way."

Mi-Go. The word was like a slap across Jacoby's face and he staggered back at its utterance. He had dreamed of them, of course, had been dreaming of them since the trunk holding the chest and the rare prizes inside had been brought on board the *Burleson*. But to hear another speaking of them was deeply unsettling.

"Which of you is Professor Jacoby?" Ivers glanced around, nodding in greeting when Jacoby stepped forward. "I'm here because of you, Professor. You sent a query regarding the history of the *Eleanor Lockley* to my office at Miskatonic University. Somehow it went astray, misplaced. By the time it reached my hands and I attempted to contact you by telephone, you had already departed on this voyage. I began to retrace your steps, to recreate your research, and when I realized that you might actually find the damned ship, I knew my only choice was to pursue you, and hope that I could reach you before you managed to drag anything to the surface that rightly belongs on the ocean floor. When I received the distress call from Mr. Harrington, I knew I was too late."

Jacoby stared at him, that old sickness roiling in his gut. "Too late? What are you saying?"

Harrington sneered. "He's saying he hoped to beat us to the *Eleanor Lockley*, to claim her treasures for himself!"

Ivers—*Professor* Ivers, Jacoby now remembered—shook his head, throwing up his hands. "I'm too late to stop you doing the foolish thing you've done, but it may not be too late to save your lives. Scuttle this ship, gentlemen. Send her to the bottom with all that you've dredged up. Come across to my own boat and I'll see you home as safely as fate will allow."

"What kind of fools do you take us for?" Harrington demanded. "Scuttle the ship? Do you have any idea what that would cost me?"

"No matter how high the cost might be, it's still cheaper than paying the price of staying behind," Ivers replied. "You're in great danger, Harrington. Every minute on board this ship risks your health, your sanity and your very lives."

Sensing the rising hostility in both men, Jacoby intervened, suggesting they all move to the mess hall, the only place on the boat where everyone could settle together with relative ease, though settle was hardly the right word. The men gathered, they shifted and did their best to remain calm, but after nearly two weeks of feeling ill and dealing with the crisis on board few of them seemed capable of anything but agitation.

"All right," Harrington said, reluctantly. He glanced at Wilson. "Though the captain argued against it, Professor Jacoby has prevailed upon me to let you say your piece. Were I feeling any better, I'd have ignored him, but given the sweat on my brow and the bile I keep fighting down—and the fact that most of these boys don't look as if they feel much better—I'll listen. But be quick about it. Whatever we're going to do, I'd have it done as soon as possible."

Ivers gazed about the mess hall and then focused again on Harrington and Jacoby. He spoke clearly and calmly, but his words sounded like madness.

"Gentlemen, you have found something that should not exist. You have found the remains of a legend, artifacts that will doubtless prove deadly if you continue to remain in their presence."

A muttering went about the crew, but Ivers forged ahead.

"In eighteen hundred and seventy-three the *Eleanor Lockley* set out from Norway with a cargo that contained the fruit of an archaeological excavation involving two professors from Miskatonic University, where I am currently employed. Walter Emerson, the man in charge of the expedition, wrote that he believed they had uncovered real evidence of intelligent life on other planets.

"The rumors about the place had been growing for decades. Old journals, tales passed down from the Vikings, whispers of visions experienced by those who wandered the mountains as if drawn there by forces they could not understand. There were variations, but all spoke of strange, insectoid creatures called the Mi-Go by locals and Yuggothians by others. According to the markings found on the stones discovered during that archaeological dig, the creatures were believed to fly between worlds, without the use of ships, soaring the cosmos without fear of the eternal cold and without need to breathe anything we would think of as air."

"Pure fantasy," the first mate murmured, and others clearly agreed.

Ivers went on, undaunted. "The lore transcribed from the figures discovered in Norway—the figures I can only imagine rest in your ship's hold at this very moment—described the Mi-Go as capable of feats of science unimaginable in the era when those stones were carved. Hell, they're unimaginable now. They were said to be able to transfer the full intellect of a man long dead from one place to another. Even across the stars."

"Rubbish!" Harrington pounded his fist into the table where he sat, but winced afterward, his muscles and flesh made tender by the current situation.

"Let me finish, please. The translation of the stones was made easier, according to the men from Miskatonic, by the assistance of a man whose mind was held inside a metallic cylinder. One I can only assume you found alongside those carved figures, inside that chest."

Professor Jacoby held his breath. How could Ivers know about the cylinder... unless he was telling the truth? He once again had to fight for calm in the room but eventually the crew settled enough for Ivers to continue his tale.

"The men spoke with that mind through the use of technologies beyond their reckoning. According to that disembodied soul, the site they'd found was a waystation of sorts. The Mi-Go used the locale to convene in preparation for their journeys between worlds.

"There were other elements to the tale, of course. Several of the laborers the dig employed grew ill and wasted away. The notes became less rational over time, and there was talk of spectral shapes appearing at night, coming closer to the camp with each passing day. Some of the workers quit, but the men from Miskatonic doubled their pay and the others stayed, in spite of their mounting terror. What they never considered v.as that the Mi-Go might return.

"There are no notes from what happened then, only a claim from one of the locals that the Mi-Go had come and attacked the archaeologists at their camp. The good news was that the creatures were not prepared for resistance. At least one of those celestial nightmares was shot and killed, and Dr. Emerson was able to escape. He returned in the morning, gathered what he could of his findings, and departed on the earliest ship that would give him passage—the *Eleanor Lockley*. Emerson sent one final message at the time of his departure, a single sheet of paper noting that he was setting sail with the artifacts recovered from the dig... including the corpse of one of the Mi-Go, which he called 'a celestial devil.' You can imagine the excitement at the university."

Jacoby *could* imagine it. God help him, he could.

"As all of you know, the ship was lost at sea. Until now. I believe the Mi-Go themselves were responsible for the sinking of that ship, if only to keep the treasures you've discovered a secret from the world. In your hold is the detailed history of the Mi-Go's existence on our planet. And if they destroyed one ship to bury those secrets, they will surely destroy another."

Ivers stood up, looking around at the crew of the *Burleson*. "Please, gentlemen, for your own sake, abandon this ship and come with me before it is too late."

That was when the arguments began.

Tell a man that he is sick and should seek help and if he feels ill he will likely agree. Tell that same man that in order to save himself he must abandon his dreams of fame and fortune, and he will stand firm in his need to defend those dreams.

Ivers was adamant. They needed to abandon the ship.

The very thought made Jacoby feel sicker than ever.

"You're asking us to give up a fortune." Harrington summed up the thoughts of a lot of the men.

"I'm asking you to save yourselves. I can take you with me. I cannot take those cursed items."

"You're a man of science, Ivers. You can't possibly believe in curses."

"I'm a man of science, indeed, Mr. Harrington. That means I keep an open mind. We are well aware that there are elements in this world which can kill us but are invisible to the naked eye. Radiation from a nuclear blast can kill well after the explosion itself."

He gestured with his soft, scholarly hands. "Look at yourselves. Your hair is thinning, your skin is sallow, and you have little or no appetite. That's because of the very 'treasures' you brought up from the depths. Leave them, and you should recover. Stay with them and you'll continue to deteriorate until your only hope is that you die before the Mi-Go come for you. My crew has remained on the yacht because they refuse to be tainted by the presence of those stone figures, or whatever else was with them. I myself am uncomfortable with the idea of being here as long as I have."

Captain Wilson took a step forward. "What if we threw them overboard? Surely there's no need to scuttle the ship?"

"I think it's too late for that. The human body can mend, but I think the ship itself has been tainted." Ivers paused. "This boat is sick."

Ivers looked at his watch.

"Two hours, gentlemen. I need your decision then. I'm going back to the *Ashleigh Michaels*. Be on the deck in two hours if you wish to leave with us." The man looked around and then squinted through the port-hole at the sky outside. "The sun will set in no more than four hours and I intend to be well away from here before that happens."

"You're not seriously considering staying here?" Harrington asked.

Jacoby flinched at the question. The whites of Harrington's eyes had taken on a faint yellowish tint. He'd lost weight and, yes, his hair seemed thinner. It was a revelation. Until Ivers had mentioned it, Jacoby had barely noticed the change in the crew, or perhaps he had simply chosen not to see.

"I have to stay here, Samuel," Jacoby said. "I have to know. I have to see if there really are creatures from another world like the ones I've seen in my dreams."

Harrington flinched at that. "*Our* dreams. I've seen them too. They're hideous."

Jacoby felt a terrible yearning. "I think they're magnificent."

Harrington stared at the table between them. "It's almost time. Is there anything I can do to convince you to leave? If Ivers is right—"

"I'll die, yes." Jacoby took a deep breath. "But if he's wrong we're losing what is perhaps the most important discovery in human history." He knew exactly what to say to bring home his point. "And this way, if nothing happens, you can send someone back to tow the ship in."

Harrington pondered for a moment, drew a deep breath, and then departed. Jacoby never saw him again.

For two nights there was nothing. With the rest of the crew gone, Jacoby spent his time studying the stone figures and looking over his notes. He lamented the loss of all the translations that the archaeologists from Miskatonic had documented and the lack of whatever knowledge or equipment must be required to open or communicate with whatever consciousness resided within the cylinder.

One by one he lugged them up to the deck, wanting to breathe in the open. Wanting the signal to be clear.

When the Northern Lights shone, he found a new and wondrous gift. The cylinder was of a metal he could not identify and when he touched it his senses seemed sharper than before. Contact with that odd metal made his fingers tingle, but it also altered his perceptions. Colors were different. He could see an energy that moved through the ship, stirred by breezes he could not feel, but painting every surface in the boat itself. This, he suspected, was the "taint" of which Ivers had spoken. He could even see it within his own flesh, moving, seeping deeper and deeper into his very essence.

The chest, the stones, even the cylinder itself all looked different when the lights above and the metal he touched worked their influences together. The stone figures were so much larger than they first appeared. He studied them the longest, caressing their surfaces, tracing the carved lines, first while holding the cylinder in his free hand, and then without it. When seen with his special sight they were several times larger and they vibrated, humming and moving, much of their substance hidden from the world by a differing frequency. Colors that could not be seen by the naked eye or felt by the unsuspecting flesh were there to be explored, dazzling in their complexities.

When his hands left the cylinder the world was once more a bleak and dismal place. Whatever the metal of the cylinder, he found its influence extraordinary. Looking at the stars while touching it let him see the same magnificent spectrum of forms he knew in his dreams, though they were made faint and weakened by distance. The presence of the cylinder kept him warm, so that the Arctic wind could not harm him. He felt the cold, but his body felt heated from within.

When he slept, which was quite often, he dreamed of the creatures he'd seen before, their iridescent shells gleaming and their magnificent wings unfurling, spanning impossible space.

In one of his dreams a voice whispered softly, "Not all can fly between the stars. Those who are here seek out other ways to bring their brethren to them. There are places where tunnels have been carved through the fabric of the universe."

On that occasion he awoke to find that he had rested his head against the cylinder in his fitful sleep.

At the end of the third day, as the sun was setting, the storms came in and shook the *Burleson* the way a dog shakes a favored toy. Jacoby lay across the cylinder and the stones to make certain they would not be swept overboard. He held on to the base of a funnel and prayed he would not get sick again. What little he'd consumed, mostly broth and canned fruit, had stayed inside him for a change and he didn't know that he would survive another bout of nausea.

And he had to survive. He had to be here when they arrived.

As a young man he had been dedicated to his faith in Christ, and in the Christian god. The war had ended that for him, but now, oddly, he began to have a new hope, a new belief. Was it possible that men had misinterpreted what they had seen in the past? Was it possible that the angels he had heard so much about as a child might be something different? The creatures in his dreams did not look like the angels his parents and pastor had spoken of, but they came from the heavens and took a few fortunate souls with them from time to time.

Was it possible?

There was only one way to know.

The Mi-Go arrived with the quieting of the storm. As the wind died down, he detected a great humming noise, like a hornet buzzing past his ear, but so much greater in volume that he felt the sound in his chest and behind his eyes.

Was there fear in his heart at the sound? Yes, but also a thrill that ran through him, body and mind alike. Body and *soul*.

"Are you there?" he cried. "Are you real?"

He received no answer. Jacoby called out several times, searching the night-darkened deck before he finally saw movement.

They appeared to him in stages. Perhaps his mind would not allow more, perhaps they emerged from one of the tunnels in the cosmos that the voice had spoken of in his dreams. The shapes were larger than he expected, half hidden in the gloom of the dying storm and revealed best by the now-distant strobes of lightning, moving off.

The warmth surged inside of him, drying the freezing rain on his skin. The frost on the deck melted beneath his feet. He stood and gazed at them, enrapt, and he listened.

The sounds were closer, but softer now and Jacoby saw the closest of the

angels!

Mi-Go from behind as it looked down upon the chest that was not ivory, and upon the contents it had held, which were on display, there on the deck of the ship. One angel's limb became clear to his eyes. As it moved, other parts swam into focus, as if only certain facets of the thing existed in the world of his human senses at any one time. It shifted again and he saw that limb. The gray, multi-jointed appendage ended in three small claws, which held open the lid of the chest.

It shifted again, and his mind vaulted, trying to contain an inner scream of denial. Though the Mi-Go was real and present, it did not match the beauty of the beast he had seen in his dreams. This nightmare was malformed, with truncated wings that flapped softly as it compensated for the waves that still rocked the ship. The grace and beauty he had seen were gone, replaced by a loathsome shape, some kind of man-sized crustacean with thick, ungainly legs and a series of long, curving barbs that jutted from the sides of its abdomen. Six legs, each ending in a claw, save the two at the front that ended in heavy pincers capable of cutting a man in half.

It released the lid of the chest, turning to look again upon the treasures that had been drawn from it.

"No!" Jacoby cried, and he dove toward them.

Did he reach for that cylinder, desperate for a weapon, or simply to deprive this disappointing, faded angel of its prize? Jacoby did not know. But the moment he touched the cylinder, he realized his error. His senses opened up and he saw, once more, the iridescent glory he had seen in his dreams.

How could he have doubted?

Surely the eyes of mere mortals were not enough. With the cylinder's influence his vision was clearer. The carapace was more graceful when seen properly and the blunt wings that he'd seen fluttering were far greater, moving with soft ripples and causing an undulation in the unusual energies he only saw when he was in contact with his prize.

Jacoby saw them all, then. Touching the cylinder, he saw how many of the Mi-Go were with him. Though he should have been terrified, he rejoiced.

"I think I have waited all of my life to see you. To know you."

He spoke aloud, though barely aware of the fact.

The closest of the Mi-Go spoke back, perhaps only in his mind. It asked him to explain himself... his presence. The voice echoed within him, a symphony of noises made by the wings that only existed in the aether. He suspected that if he let go of his prize he would have heard only more of the horrific buzzing noises. He dared not let go, just in case the effect faded and was lost forever.

"I know you are leaving here. I know you came for the stones, for your history, and perhaps for this." He rubbed his hand over the surface of the cylinder. "But please, please take me with you. I need to know, you see. I need to understand the world out there, among the stars."

The Mi-Go nearest him—the first he had seen—turned to look at him more closely. The different antennae and slithering tendrils that covered its head shifted and studied him slowly, absorbing the details of him. The massive claws clicked and clattered softly as it observed him.

The voice was still distorted, but Jacoby listened through the unsettling reverberations and focused as intently as he ever had.

We cannot carry you easily, the voice said. *There is no way to know if you would survive without the protection of the cylinder. We are made to breathe between the stars and you are not.*

"It doesn't matter," he said. "I'm dying already. I can feel that. Please, take me with you. Let me see as you see, if only for a moment."

The Mi-Go made noises that he could not decipher and the others, the ones that had already gathered up the stone carvings and returned them to the chest, responded.

They agreed.

Jacoby exulted, his heart full of a joy he had never known possible.

The nightmares he'd seen would surely never have been able to fly with the malformed, stunted wings on their gray backs, but the Mi-Go, the vibrant, vital

angels

creatures before him with their vast wings moving through the aether and beyond, were a different story.

He closed his eyes and felt those iridescent claws latch onto him, surround and embrace him. The wings of the Mi-Go sang and the one who had spoken rose softly from the ship and took him with it, lifted him through the barriers of the mortal world.

The clouds were alive. They hummed with their own song and that sonata joined briefly with the rapturous sound of angel wings. Above him the Northern Lights painted the skies and the universe itself, stretching so much farther than he'd ever imagined. Those lights, those magnificent shifting colors so far beyond the human spectrum, extended into the depths of eternity.

Jacoby wept. The cold that he had thought he would never feel again returned and grew worse. The ice that formed on his skin should have had him screaming in agony but it didn't hurt, not really.

Nor would it ever.

He was in the presence of angels.

The Mi-Go

Countless ages ago, before mankind arose from the mire, an alien warrior race came from the most distant reaches of the stars to settle themselves on the outermost world of the planetary spheres. This world is so distant, it cannot be seen in the night sky, but it exists midway between the sphere of Saturn and the sphere of the fixed stars. For know this—there are other crystalline spheres beyond that of Saturn, but because of their vast remoteness, our eyes are not keen enough to perceive them.

In appearance these creatures are monstrous and bear scant resemblance to any living thing on this terrestrial globe, unless it be the lobster, for they possess great claws on their hands and feet that cause terrible injuries to those they attack, but also other pairs of limbs more subtle for holding and carrying objects. Their wings are small and droop like wilted leaves. Countless feelers cover the ringed segments of their oblong heads. A kind of gray fungus grows over the hard shells of their bodies and gives them a whitish appearance in the moonlight, for they never show themselves beneath the rays of the sun.

This warrior race flourished upon the world they chose to call Yuggoth long before the creation of man, and there it would probably have remained, but that frozen globe was deficient in a mineral necessary to their survival, so they flew on their wings through the cold and darkness between the planets to our earth, which has this mineral in abundance. Here, they began to dig their mines.

The Elder Things, who already inhabited this world, contested the presence of these warriors. After long ages of constant war, the Mi-Go were driven off and returned to their own world. But they left behind small groups of their scientists, who hid themselves where their mines were dug, in remote ranges of hills or mountains.

The race of mankind was shaped by the Elder Things as a cosmic joke and acquired its wisdom as the ages passed, and all the while the spies of this warrior race from Yuggoth watched and recorded our progress. They are still here, watching us and waiting for the return of their armies.

In the mountains that rise far to the east of Asia Minor they are sometimes seen as they cross the snows. The men of the mountains call these creatures the Mi-Go in their own language. Their misshapen shapes make them seem hulking and clumsy beings, but this is an illusion, for they can move with swiftness when required to do so. The footprints they leave behind in the snow are strangely elongated.

So alien are these beings to our region of the cosmos that when they die from some violent mishap such as a fall from a high place, their bodies quickly decompose and melt into the air like ice beneath the sun. It is for this reason that no corpses of these creatures have ever been displayed, and why their very existence is no more than a legend whispered in the remote wild regions of the world.

It is said that these creatures worship Yog-Sothoth, Shub-Niggurath, and Nyarlathotep as their gods, and they hold sacred certain signs that appear on the moon of Yuggoth as it is viewed from their world. In the sciences they are unmatched in wisdom, except by the Great Race of Yith that can span time and has access to all the knowledge of eternity. They are especially expert in surgery and in their manipulations of the bodies of living things.

One matter is agreed upon by the chroniclers who write of these beings—the Mi-Go are unsurpassed in the pursuit of war, and in the making of terrible weapons of destruction. Should the armies of the Mi-Go return to this earthly sphere, the puny armies of men could not stand against them, but would be swept away as a child sweeps away its toys when it is bored of play. Mankind would become the slaves of this race, for they regard us as no more than beasts of burden to be used for their benefit.

All down the ages, small enclaves of the Mi-Go have hidden among us and marked our progress in the arts and sciences. They are able to disguise themselves so that they can walk among us. They also make pacts with certain men, who supply them with what they need and act as their covert agents. In this way, nothing we do remains hidden from their scrutiny, and no man is beyond their reach should they decide he poses a threat to their concealment. Those they cannot subvert with gold, they assassinate. So it has been from the dawn of human history, and so it will remain until the armies of the Mi-Go return from Yuggoth to conquer our world.

Dream a Little Dream of Me
A Sam Hunter Adventure

Jonathan Maberry

-1-

Some people are weird and some are so weird they abuse the privilege.

This guy was a classic example.

Oliver Boots was the kind of person they invented the word 'geek' for. Nearly seven feet tall but I doubted he weighed two hundred pounds. With narrow shoulders and narrower hips that made him look like a regular-sized person who'd been pulled on until he was all stretched out. Long, lugubrious face, huge brown eyes, and a beaky nose. Nothing about him was balanced. His nostrils were too big and his eyes too wide-set. Swollen lower lip beneath an almost nonexistent upper one. Lots of gums, tiny teeth. Hair that did not seem to understand the logic of the whole combing process, mostly black but streaked with brown. His complexion was strange. I know a lot of black guys, and I've seen every shade of skin from pale like Larry Wilmore to a true African skin tone that's so dark brown it really does look black. This guy was blacker than that. Funny thing is, I wasn't at all convinced he was African or even of African descent. He looked painted or dyed. Like some old Vaudeville guy wearing blackface. Talk about off-putting. I almost dismissed him as one of those fruitcakes who wants to *be* black but isn't and goes about it the wrong way.

The more I looked at him, the less I thought that was the case.

I have a really good sense of smell. Better than yours unless you're like me. I can smell makeup and most of the time I can name the brand. Cover Girl doesn't, for example, smell anything like Maybelline. When a client comes in I let my senses tell me as much or sometimes more than the person says about themselves. But I couldn't smell makeup. I could smell skin and blood. And I could tell you that he used tea-tree oil shampoo and Camay soap and had just a hint of Polo Blue spritzed on. I could smell salmon almondine on his breath and the gin brand from his last martini. Boodles. Very nice. What I could not smell, however, was the dye he used to turn his skin black. Not dark brown. *Black.*

Like I said, this guy was rocking the weird thing way over to the edge.

Understand, I'm not the kind of social misfit who usually stares at people—unless they're Claire over at Nick's Taproom, because you *have* to stare at Claire. I mean, c'mon!—but it was hard as hell not to gawp at Mr. Boots.

Even that. *Boots.* What kind of last name is that? It's a noun.

When he came into my office he had to duck under the doorframe. And after I waved him to a chair he sat down in a way that reminded me of one of those wooden clothes hanger things that someone folded wrong.

Even without the fraudulent black skin, tell me you wouldn't stare.

So, yeah, I stared. A bit.

He gave me the kind of look that said he was used to it, accepted it as a matter of course, and was waiting for the point where we got past it so we could get down to business. He had a neat trick for refocusing my attention, too. He placed a brown leather briefcase on the corner of my desk, popped the locks, positioned it so that when he opened it I couldn't see what was inside, and removed a yellow interoffice mail envelope that was intriguingly thick. He then placed this on the blotter at an exact distance between us. It drew my gaze from his Black-Hole-of-Calcutta nostrils and brought me to point like a hunting dog.

"Ten thousand dollars," he said.

"Hello," I said.

"Twenties, fifties and hundreds."

"Three of my favorite flavors."

He reached out and nudged it one inch closer to me. "This is half. The balance on completion of the assignment."

Sure, I wanted to grab the envelope and bear it away for some private time with my stack of outstanding bills. There was also a Bettinardi Model 2 Matt Kuchar blade-style putter that I wanted almost more than I wanted a blowjob. But I left the envelope where it was and sat back in my chair.

"When you say 'assignment'," I said, "what exactly are we talking about?"

"Can we first agree that you'll work for me?"

"No, we can't. I want to know what I'm signing on for."

He cocked his head to one side, like an ostrich examining a bug he might eat. "Does it matter?"

"Sure it does."

He made a show of looking around my office. Drab furniture that was fourth- or fifth-hand when I bought it from a thrift store. Wallpaper that was probably pasted up when Jimmy Carter was president. Some house plants dying a slow and horrible death. Low lights that tried and failed to soften the edges of the squalor. And me. Short, skinny, semi-tidy, with too much stubble and thinning hair. His eyes drifted back and locked on me. He wore a thin, knowing smile.

"And you're in a position to be selective about the kind of jobs you accept, Mr. Hunter?"

"I am, Mr. Boots," I said.

"Even for twenty thousand dollars?"

"Even for twenty million dollars."

We both smiled. He thought I was joking. I knew I wasn't.

Mr. Boots took a handkerchief from his pocket and dabbed at his lips, then neatly folded the cloth and put it back.

"It is my understanding that private investigators often provide additional services."

"Depends on the investigator," I said. "And it depends on the service."

"I'm looking for someone to champion my cause."

"Yeah, that means nothing to me. You're beating around the bush, Mr. Boots. How about you stop doing that and actually tell me what you'd like me to do for that much money. You have to know that it's a tad above my normal rates."

"There are private investigators who would walk into hell for that much money."

That was true enough. I know some P.I.s who will beat up a nun for a lot less. Israel Bohunk comes to mind. A professional rival who is arguably the least humane human being I've ever met. He sometimes provides protection for a dog-fighting ring run out of South Philly. His office is every bit as seedy as mine, I'll admit, but we have different reputations if you look close enough. I don't think there's anything he wouldn't do for money. No joke. And although I do have my more extreme moments once in a while, which resulted in me burying a few bodies in a landfill or in a swamp over in the Jersey Pine Barrens, my motivation isn't the same as Bohunk's.

There are others, too. The worst were the skip tracers and bounty hunters. They all run under nicknames they think make them sound cool. Bugsy the Mummy, Abel Cain, Dr. Snatch. Like that. Maybe it's that nobody has either the heart or the courage to tell them that their nicknames are stupid as shit.

"What kind of job?" I repeated, saying it slow, spacing the words.

"We would like you to pick up something and deliver it safely."

"What kind of something? I don't courier drugs or stolen goods."

He smiled. "It's a religious artifact. We want it delivered very quietly and without incident."

"Is it stolen?"

"Yes," he said.

-2-

"No," I said.

"Don't you want to know who it was stolen *from* before you turn us down?"

"Not really."

His smile widened. "Are you sure?"

I sighed. "Okay. Impress me."

"Nazis," said Mr. Boots.

I blinked. "A religious artifact stolen from the Nazis? Now I'm thinking you have me confused with Indiana Jones."

"Hardly."

"Nazis?" I said, studying him.

"Nazis," he said.

I sighed. "Okay, tell me."

-3-

Mr. Boots said, "During the Second World War the Nazis, as you've no doubt heard, went to great lengths to, um, *appropriate* a great deal of art, and there are legal battles ongoing even now to settle claims of ownership. The same is true of a variety of holy relics and objects of importance from various cultures. The Spear of Longinus, believed to be the weapon that pierced the side of Jesus Christ is one such item. Others include clippings from the beard of Muhammad, a tooth from the Buddha, the bones of Orestes and Theseus, the Holy Belt of the Virgin Mary, the Grapevine Cross…"

"The Ark of the Covenant?" I suggested.

"Oh, no," he said and gave a casual flick of his hand, "that's in an Orthodox church in Axum, Ethiopia. The Thule cultists never took possession of it."

I stared at him, waiting for the punch line of the joke, but he appeared to be serious about that statement. Wild.

Boots said, "The Thule Society was behind much of the Nazi drive to possess sacred objects that they believed had true mystical or spiritual power. During the war many of these objects were, regrettably, lost. There was a Thule repository in Dresden that was utterly destroyed by the Allied firebombing. So many powerful things were incinerated to the enduring loss of all."

I said nothing.

"I represent a group of individuals," said Boots, "who have gone to great lengths to recover some of these objects and return them to their rightful owners. We are privately funded and we are determined to remain discreet, even clandestine."

"Okay," I said.

"Although the war ended more than seventy years ago and most of the original Thule Society members are either dead or in nursing homes, the society itself lives on. With any group of hateful extremists there is never a paucity of people willing to take up the standard and continue this ugly work."

I nodded. I knew that to be true enough. Not specifically with the Thule Society, which I'd heard of but only in books, but with other kinds of cults and secret societies. "World has more than its share of fucktards," I said.

"Fucktard." He repeated the word, enjoying it. "Eloquent."

"I'm nothing if not eloquent."

We smiled at each other like we were just a couple of guys.

"So," I said, "you're telling me you stole something from neo-Nazis and you want me to pick it up from somewhere and deliver it somewhere?"

"In a nutshell."

I made come-along motions with my fingers. "More. That's not enough information."

"Fair enough. The Thule Society is still active, though it is naturally covert."

"Oh, naturally."

"Alas they are also very, um, aggressive," said Mr. Boots. "They are covetous people, oh dear me yes. And they are vengeful."

"What is it you stole that's got them so pissed off?"

He cocked his head again. "By way of answering that question, Mr. Hunter, let me ask this. What do you know of the Dreamlands?"

"As in Little Nemo?"

"That's Slumberland. I refer to the Dreamlands described in the writings of Howard Phillips Lovecraft. Are you familiar with that writer's works?"

I shrugged. "Some, I guess. But I don't read a lot of monster stories."

He arched an eyebrow. "Oh? Considering your, ah, *reputation*, I would have figured you to be quite a fan of Lovecraftian stories."

Now I cocked my head at him. "And what exactly do you mean by my 'reputation'?"

I was pretty sure we both knew what he meant. It's just that there aren't a lot of people who know who and what I am. My family knows, of course, because the apple doesn't fall far from the tree in the Hunter clan. A few close friends know. Some trusted clients. Mind you, there are some bad folks who *knew* but they are past tense. That's an occasional side effect of me being what I am.

Boots fished for a way to say it without saying it. "I know," he said.

I shook my head. "Give me a keyword so I know you're not dicking me around."

Mr. Boots considered. "Wolfsbane?"

"Aconite," I corrected. "I put that on my salad. Try again."

"Full moon?" he ventured.

"Good for night fishing. But otherwise it don't really mean shit. It's Hollywood stuff. Keep trying."

"Do I need to say the word?"

I grinned. "Why not? Are you afraid of the big bad wolf?"

He shrugged. "If I was afraid of you, Mr. Hunter, I would not be here."

"Which makes me wonder why you are here. If your group was strong enough or clever enough to steal the item in question from these Thule asswipes, then why do you need me—or anyone—to deliver it somewhere? I mean… shit, hop in a cab."

"Ah, and so we get to it," he said, leaning forward to place his incredibly bony elbows on his knobby knees. "The other party in this matter has engaged the services of a skilled retrieval specialist. He is someone we do not care to run afoul of. He has a certain reputation that I have been led to believe is in no way exaggerated."

"They hired a bounty hunter?"

"In a word, yes. It is someone with whom you are, by all accounts, familiar."

I sighed. "And will you tell me this guy's name?"

"Bohunk," said Mr. Boots. "Israel Bohunk."

I drummed my fingers on the desktop and frowned at him, then down at the thick envelope of delicious tens, twenties and fifties, and then at Mr. Boots again.

He said, "While I understand that Mr. Bohunk has a reputation for always getting whatever he goes after, I was reliably informed that you were meet to this task. Was I misled?"

It was a fair question and I took a moment to consider how to answer it. I knew a lot about Bohunk but had never gone up against him. Actually, I've never been alone with him. I've seen him in crowds, in clubs, in bail bond offices, and even in court buildings, but that's it. We've probably said fewer than a hundred words to each other. Most of our exchanges have been the kind of gunslinger nods guys like us use when we don't want to give anything away but at the same time want to send a certain message. Or, messages, really. One message *I see you.* The other, *I need you to see me.* There's a shit-ton of subtext to each. With certain people a small look, a lift of an eyebrow, a tightening of the lips, a half smile—they speak volumes.

Bohunk's probably heard some wild stuff about me. Some of it's true, depending on who's doing the telling. And if even half of the stories I've heard about him were half true, then he was not the kind of person anyone ever wants to go up against. Mind you, there are people who say that about me. But Bohunk's different. He's come through situations that he shouldn't have, which means that he has something else going for him besides the obvious brutality and noticeable lack of human compassion. And you can add to that the fact that he looks like the Hulk's bigger brother. He also has a crew of thugs that he runs with who could probably overthrow the average midsized country.

Boots frowned very deeply. "Are you going to opt out, Mr. Hunter?"

"No," I said. "I'm in."

"If it is not inconvenient, I need you to actually say that you accept this assignment. In those words."

"Sure. Fine. Whatever. I hereby formally accept this job. And the money. I definitely accept the money."

He looked greatly relieved. "And we have found our champion."

"Let's not get too hasty," I said. "I still need some background and you got us off the subject. What does any of this have to do with H.P. frigging Lovecraft?"

Mr. Boots bent and straightened the leg of his pants, smoothing the expensive cloth over his stick-thin leg. "My colleagues and I are of the opinion that his stories may not be entirely the stuff of Mr. Lovecraft's lurid imagination. It is our belief, in fact, that Mr. Lovecraft was something of a savant who did not dream up his stories in the way 'dreams' are viewed by the average person, but in fact wrote stories based on actual visions."

"Hunh," I grunted.

"*Religious* visions," he said.

"Wow," I said. "So... you're all batshit crazy. Is that the takeaway from this conversation?"

"Hardly. Nor is this a cult thing," said Boots. "This is a legitimate religion believed by more people than you would imagine." He paused and gave me an enigmatic little smile. "Many more people than you would imagine."

I said nothing.

"And these beliefs predate many of this world's most highly regarded and, um, *popular* religions."

"Okay," I said. "So what? You say this like you're a deacon of the church of Cthulhu. I mean… that is what we're talking about, right? Big guy, mouthful of tentacles, tendency to drive his worshippers batshit crazy. That guy?"

If it is possible for someone with skin as black as pitch to go pale, then that's what happened to Mr. Boots. He turned the color of a charcoal briquette. A dusty black. He recovered quickly, though. I'd said what I'd said half to be a smartass—because I like being a smartass—and half to see if I could get a rise out of him. To see where he stood. And apparently Boots stood foursquare inside the church of the bugfuck weird. He also got a little upset with me. Fair enough. I was trying to be offensive. It's a great way to gauge how serious a person was on a given subject.

Mr. Boots was clearly very serious, and pretty soon he had me convinced that this was his actual religion. I know, that takes a lot of open-minded acceptance because… hey, Cthulhu, y'know?

But as Hamlet was so fond of saying, "There are more things in heaven and earth, Horatio, than are dreamt of in your philosophy." Or words to that effect.

He made me a believer. Not in his faith but in the fact that he believed.

"What's the actual job?" I asked. "You keep sidestepping that. What is the actual object? What kind of relic is it?"

"It is a small statue," said Boots. "It is carved to represent the mountain Ngranek, a holy place on the isle of Oriab in the southern part of the Dreamlands. There is a minute map etched onto the base of the statue, written in the language of the guardians of that place, and it includes a spell that will open a doorway that will allow the faithful to travel from this world into that one."

"Uh huh," I said.

"You must understand, Mr. Hunter, that this is an item of great importance and great power. This is a place where great magic exists and where great magic can be learned. It is a place of infinite possibility, a place where the waters of many realities and unrealities merge and blend."

"Uh huh," I said again.

"It would be a terrible thing should the Thule Society appropriate this map. Therefore, we want you to go to where it is being kept, remove it, and protect it."

"Protect it? I thought you wanted it delivered."

Boots smiled. "In a manner of speaking. We want you to safeguard it using your, um, *particular* skill set. There is a very crucial planetary alignment occurring tonight. Gateways between worlds will be fragile at best. We want you to take possession of the stone and keep it safe overnight."

"You mean keep it with me?"

"Yes. Keep it with you and do whatever is necessary to keep it safe. As I say, we have been hoping to enlist you as our champion."

"Just keep it overnight?"

"Yes."

"And then what?"

"Then return it to us in the morning," said Boots. "By then the alignment will be shifting and the gateways will firm up. It is doubtful the Thule Society will be able to manage to open the doorway to the Dreamlands after the sun has risen."

I sat there and studied him. He sat there and studied me. The clock on the wall ticked its way through a whole bunch of empty seconds.

"You realize that I think you're absolutely out of your fucking mind," I said. "I mean you *get* that, right?"

His smile was very small on his very black face. "Have you ever required that your clients function on the same level of subjective sanity as yourself?"

"No, I suppose not."

"Nor do we." Mr. Boots uncrossed and recrossed his legs. "Now let me tell you the details."

-4-

The setup seemed pretty straightforward. The object was in the wall safe of Mr. Boot's office on Walnut Street in Center City. He recited the combination and had me remember it. He said that he could not go and get it himself because Bohunk and his crew were watching the building and if they accosted him they might force him to open the safe. He didn't come out and say that he feared Bohunk might kill him to get the artifact, but it was clear that's what he meant.

So, my goal was to slip in as discretely as possible, make my way to the eighteenth-floor office, open the safe, hide the object on my person, and get the hell out of there without being spotted. Then maybe go get lost for a few hours. Drive to Cape May and watch the sunrise. Take the turnpike to the Poconos and hang out at a casino. Whatever. Basically get lost, get off the radar so Bohunk couldn't find me. It doesn't sound easy and I knew it wouldn't be easy. Not with Israel Bohunk guarding the place.

The timetable was tight, but not so tight that I didn't have some elbowroom to do research. After Oliver Boots gangled his bony ass out of my office I cruised the Net and made a few calls.

Private investigators spend most of their careers doing background searches. It's a lot of computer stuff. Back in the day it used to be actual paperwork, poring over ledgers and poking through public records. Now just about everything has been digitized. It makes the world less interesting in some ways, but it makes my job a hell of a lot easier. Instead of wearing out the soles of my shoes and sweating my ass off in the July heat I sat in my office eating Popeye's chicken out of a tub, drinking Fanta and listening to old Tom Waits songs on my iPad, all while searching the endless databases, records, and websites. There are services and utilities P.I.s can subscribe to for deeper access than Joe Public will ever get. If you like your privacy that should scare you. Given enough time I can find out your pin number, routing number, shoe size, which prescription medicines you take, which porn sites you hit, how much debt you have, which charities you donate to, how many parking violations you have, how much mortgage or rent you owe, what your credit rating is, what your politics are, who your real friends are on Facebook and Twitter, where you spend your disposable income and what TV shows you binge-watch on Netflix. There are ways to keep guys like me out, but most of them don't work all that well.

The good news is that I'm not a stalker or a creep. I don't judge people. If some schmo wants to watch Italian midget biracial porn with golden showers, then God love 'em. I don't give a shit. On the other hand, if that same guy is embezzling money from his employer or buying dirty pictures of little kids, then yeah, we may have a problem. Depends on who's hired me, and it depends on what pushes my buttons. If I'm hired to get the goods on a cheating spouse, I'll get those goods, hand them over to the client, cash the check and forget about it. No judgment. If I'm hired to find actionable evidence on, say, a group of pornographers who are making fuck films of tweens? I may become more directly involved than just turning in a report. I might pay a visit to the video team and have a meaningful discussion with them. I've done that in the past. Like I said, I have buttons.

This thing with Boots wasn't pushing any of those buttons, but it was giving me a bad itch between the shoulder blades. Israel Bohunk was a very, very bad man and I had no desire whatsoever in determining which of us was the baddest dude in Philadelphia.

So I did some research to determine just what in the twinkly chartreuse fuck I'd gotten myself into.

I researched Boots first. There wasn't a whole lot. No birth record, no school. His name began appearing in articles related to the rare art and antiquities world. He was quoted in a few pieces—never with accompanying photo—in several magazines like *Aesthetica, Parkett, Tate Etc., Art Business Today*. Like that. And *The Journal of Conservation and Museum Studies*. Plus a bunch of incomprehensible trade journals for universities, religious groups, and purveyors of *objet d'art*. So, professionally at least, he seemed legit. Odd that he had no background data. It suggested that he wasn't born as 'Oliver Boots'. I wish I'd thought to ask for a look at his driver's license. From that I could have backtracked to get his Social Security number and maybe found his birth name.

The one thing I did verify is that he belonged to a group called the Dreamland Conservancy. So maybe he really did believe in the stuff Lovecraft wrote about. Truth to tell, I kind of lean toward believing, too. As the saying goes, I've *seen* some stuff.

Weird, weird, stuff. Over the last few years I've seen things that have made me a whole lot less likely to dismiss the things that go bump in the night as figments of my—or anyone's—imagination. After all, look at who I am. At what I am. I'm one of the things that bump around in the dark. The fact that I happen to be a good guy—or, good-*ish*, at least—doesn't change things.

After I ran dry on Boots I switched to Bohunk.

There was a lot about him on the Net. Turns out his name is, no joke, Israel Bohunk. I'd always thought it was a South Philly nickname. Like Nickie Grapes and Harry the Spoon. Nope. Israel Stallo Bohunk is the name on his driver's license and Social Security card. And on the copy of his birth certificate I found a scan of. At fifty-three he was older than I thought. He looked midthirties. I found some photos of him on-line and studied them. He is conspicuously large, with bodybuilder biceps, a massive chest, and a head that looked like a beer keg dressed up in a Halloween mask. Lots of coarse dark hair on his head, face, chest and forearms. And his complexion was, in its own way, as strange as Boots's. Where the tall skinny guy was pitch black, Bohunk was the color of stone. Gray as slate.

His criminal record was cleaner than I expected. He was picked up twice for questioning but no charges ever filed. That did not mean he was innocent. My guess was he was careful and had good lawyers.

Bohunk spent eight years as a private military contractor, which is a sanitized euphemism for 'mercenary'. Bohunk worked for Blue Diamond Security, a company that made Blackwater look like the Campfire Girls. They had ties to all sorts of shady groups including the Jakoby family, Hugo Vox and others. Bohunk spent time in Iraq, Afghanistan and elsewhere. The 'elsewhere' part was buried under some 'need to know' seals and even nosy private dicks don't need to know some things. Didn't matter. What I did find confirmed what I suspected. Bohunk was smart, well-trained, dangerous and very experienced.

But something was wrong. When I looked up info on his office I saw that he was no longer in a seedy hole like mine. He was now operating in style. Real style. He now had a large suite of offices in a respectable building on Market Street near City Hall. Wow. I hacked his tax returns and found that he employed twenty people. Way more than I thought. Two secretaries, three computer research specialists, a receptionist, and the rest were listed as 'general support staff'. When I ran some of them I found that this was another euphemism. In this case 'general support staff' meant 'hired muscle'. Some of them had criminal records. All of them had military backgrounds. A few belonged to wacko militia groups who are preparing for the day when the American government invades itself. Or something. I've never been able to sort out that kind of conspiracy paranoid bullshit.

My sense of unease about this case deepened the more I studied Bohunk's organization. I mean… I'm pretty tough but he has actual trained soldiers with combat experience and lots of guns.

My last search before heading out was to find out about the Gogol Building, which was on Walnut Street and Fifth. It was a big, brown and tan monstrosity of a place that reminded me of Dana's apartment in the original *Ghostbusters* movie. An ugly, overly ornate thing left over from the excesses of the *art deco* era. Lots of unusual angles, pitches, arches, and gargoyles. Not the tallest building in Philly, but in the top ten. It was once the world headquarters of the Gogol Trust, a banking and investments corporation, but it had changed hands twenty times in the last century. The current owner was—surprise surprise—the Dreamlands Trust. Oliver Boots had a suite of offices one flight down from the top.

The good news was that there were half a dozen banks of elevators and twenty stairwells. Bohunk could not watch all of those. The trick would be to find out which routes were being watched and then take one of the others. I figured the elevators would all be watched because who in their right mind would want to run up fifty-six flights of stairs?

Who, I ask you?

Sigh.

I'm not as young as I once was, and my body is a prime example of the phrase 'it's not the years it's the mileage'. The odometer on my knees and lower back has been around the dial way too many times. Which means that to do this right it would have to be the wolf and not the middle-aged dumpy man who made that climb. That came with its own set of problems.

I got up from my desk and prowled my office, nervous and jumpy. I paced for a few minutes, thinking it through, imagining all of the ways this could go wrong. All the ways I could fail. All the ways I could get killed. It was a dishearteningly long list.

I locked the door, went into my phone booth of a bathroom, changed into one of the sets of clothes I keep on hand for jobs where I need to blend in. I chose a set of khaki shorts and shirt that bore the embroidered patch from one of the world's foremost delivery companies. I added rubber-soled shoes and a billed cap. I slipped a heavy blackjack into my right front pocket. No gun, no knife. If things got that complicated I had other weapons. The sap was for persuasion of the obstinate. Useful in certain circumstances and, in a way, a kindness. The alternative was less pleasant.

I futzed around the office until I realized that I was stalling. I didn't want to take this job. It felt weird. Wrong in some way I couldn't quite describe. But there was an envelope in my office safe with a lot of very nice money in it. Money I needed. I had bills. I had alimony. I wanted to buy myself that putter, god damn it.

"Get your ass in gear, dickhead," I said to my reflection in the mirror next to the door.

So, yeah, I got my ass in gear.

-5-

I drove to Center City and parked three blocks away, and walked toward the Gogol Building. I had pictures of most of Bohunk's people on my phone—lifted from their service records online—and I had a lot of data about them memorized. Pretty sure I'd know them on sight. Wish I had something from each so I could have memorized their smell. Even in normal form I have a killer sense of smell. My spider-sense, more or less.

It was a blistering hot day in Philadelphia. Temperature and humidity both locked at 96. I felt like I was melting into the sidewalk. It was the kind of day that makes your whole body feel heavy and slow and stupid. There was a cart selling Italian water ices and I bought a cherry snow cone and ate it while I cased the joint. It's hard to look threatening while eating a snow cone. Only way to look less threatening is to go out walking a golden Labrador puppy. The vibe I was projecting was delivery guy trying to find a slice of chill on a day when the furnace doors were all open.

It was pretty easy to find the first five of Bohunk's team. They were sitting in cars with the motors running, windows up, air conditioning blasting. Any one person like that and you think he's waiting for someone to come out of the building. But when you see five big guys who might as well be wearing THUG t-shirts sitting at precise positions near entrances, you start to see the pattern. I risked walking past a couple of the cars so I could take a sniff. Sweat, testosterone, cheap cologne, inadequate deodorant, Coca-Cola, some residual weed, gun oil, and…

Incense?

That was weird. Smelled like temple incense, the kind they use at yoga centers. And I smelled it on two different of Bohunk's men.

It was a weird enough thing to jolt me. Plans are made based on an analysis of information. Intel, they call it in the military. Most things in life are predictable, which allows you to draw a plan of action even in the absence of total knowledge. When you encounter an anomaly it tends to make you pause, step back, and reconsider. Sometimes the anomaly is nothing, a momentary and unrelated weirdness. Had the incense smell only been on one of the thugs, I'd have noted it but not thought much about it beyond that. Maybe the thug did yoga. Or, more likely, he was sleeping with a woman who did yoga. But on two of them, though?

So I risked it and cased the other three cars with close walk-bys.

Incense. On all of them.

Exactly the same kind, and it wasn't a faint trace, not like you'd get if you stepped inside a head shop or a store selling New Age stuff. This was a heavy hit of it on all of them. They'd been inside a room with a lot of incense in the air, and they'd been in that room for a considerable time. My guess was at least an hour. It was soaked into their clothes and hair.

Yeah, I can tell. I told you already.

I fell back and went into a Starbucks to reconsider my plan of attack. Under what circumstances would these guys be exposed to incense? Boots had said that Bohunk was employed by the Thule Society to obtain the artifact. The Thules were a semimystical organization, and that suggested rituals. Rituals and incense go together like Philly cheesesteaks and high cholesterol. Did that mean that Bohunk was *part* of the Thule Society? If so, was it possible these thugs were more than Bohunk's muscle? Maybe they were all part of that relic-grabbing Hitler-worshipping crew of scary ass-hats?

Sure, that's a jump based on smelling incense, but a private investigator without gut instincts should consider another line of work.

Did that change my plan?

No, not really. I was pretty sure I hadn't been made, which meant that my FedEx cover was probably still good. I stayed in the Starbucks—which was cool and had a nice view of the Gogol Building—until one o'clock. That's when all of the employees who had flooded the streets for lunch began to trudge back in. Crowds make great protective cover. I left the café, crossed the street without hurry, carrying the faux package I'd been toting around all morning. It's an empty box with a false spring-loaded bottom that I'd taken away from a shoplifter once upon a time. Very smart, and there was enough tension on the spring that you could handle it and not realize there was a false trapdoor in the bottom. High tech for a guy like me.

I heard the crowd utter a collective sigh as they moved from the furnace heat of the streets to the mortuary cool of the lobby. They swarmed into the elevators and I went with them, looking nonchalant, but keeping alert. I saw two more of Bohunk's men in the lobby and there was one on the elevator with me. More incense smell. I left the elevator on the fifteenth floor because there were still plenty of office workers in the crowded car. I didn't want to wind up as the last person sharing the car with the Thule lackey.

The fifteenth floor was shared by a dozen small firms. Patent attorneys, accountants, and an actuary. I walked with purpose toward whatever office was at the end of the hall, conscious of being visible to the people on the elevator. When I heard the doors close, I turned around and ran back to the entrance of the fire stairs, which were on one end of a T-junction close to the elevator bank. No guards. No alarms on the doors. I eased the door open and spent ten seconds letting my nose do my reconnaissance for me. I had to shift a bit to maximize that. Half human, half wolf. I'd have gone all the way but I would have had to strip out of the clothes, or tear them. Didn't want to do either.

The stairwell was clear, but not all the way to the top.

There was a man up there. I could smell the meat of him. And the incense.

Bohunk was smart. He'd positioned a guard near the top floor. Not sure why he didn't just kick his way into Boots's office and crack the safe. Even with modern alarm systems there are ways. I know a couple of safecrackers who could probably steal Donald Trump's toupee collection without rousing Donald from his dreams of avarice. Boots said that there were alarms, and had given me the code, but he hadn't said they were anything special.

That had been niggling at the back of my mind all along.

What was keeping Bohunk's team *outside* of the office? What was making this so hard for them?

I seriously considered bagging this whole thing, going home, calling Boots for more information and trying it again tomorrow.

But...

Fuck it, I was already here.

I began climbing the steps from floor fifteen to floor forty-five.

-6-

First rule, cardio?

I know, I know. Go fuck yourself.

-7-

I went slowly. Partly to save my breath and avoid a coronary and partly to keep Bohunk's minion from hearing me. Even in human form I know how to move without making noise. Actually honed that skill set back when I was a cop in the Twin Cities. Noisy, clumsy cops get shot a lot more often than stealthy, careful ones.

I stopped on the fortieth floor to catch my breath and reassess. The thug was up there on forty-three, pacing in the narrow confines of the landing. He must have had an earbud in, listening to AC-DC. My ears are good enough to catch the spill from one of the earbuds, so I figured he had one in and the other bud dangling. He probably thought that was a smart move because it didn't totally block his hearing. It's not a smart move. The placement of one creates a confusion for human hearing. It reduces perception of what is being heard, especially if you're bored and if you like what you have on your iPod.

Stupid mistake.

He never heard me coming.

Not until I whipped the heavy lead blackjack across his ankle tendons. I was four steps down and he was looking at the closed fire door and not down the stairs. I caught him as he was pivoting for a turn in his pacing cadence. The blackjack is one of the old-school cop varieties—a heavy wafer of lead sewn between two paddle-shaped pieces of thick leather. Heavy and brutal, and apart from the crushing weight of the lead there is a stiff edge running around the business end of the weapon. Hold it one way and you have very precise blunt force trauma; but held at an angle you can rip an ugly trench through skin.

I gave him a little of both.

You don't man it out when you get clipped by a blackjack in the hands of an expert. You go right fucking down, and you go down hard and you go down hurt.

I caught him as he fell and helped him fall harder by jerking him face-forward toward the concrete landing. Things broke. Chin, cheek, teeth.

The thug never had a chance to make any sound louder than a grunt before he was out. He'd need some reconstructive work on the face. Maybe later I'd try to dredge up a little regret about that. Maybe, but probably not. Bohunk was a scumbag and I doubt he hired saints. This guy was one of the faces I memorized. A former soldier who had been thrown out of the army for messing with underage Afghani village girls. Hired by Blue Diamond because they only hired assholes like him.

So… sweet dreams, lumpy.

The smell of his blood, fresh and hot and reeking like freshly sheared copper, hit me hard. If I focus my senses on it I can get high, like someone getting second-hand stoned by being in a room where someone's smoking a blunt. I had to force my mind to focus as I patted him down.

He was armed to the teeth. A Sig Sauer with two extra magazines, and a small-frame .32 pistol in an ankle holster. A Buck lock-knife with a four-inch blade in his right front pants pocket. I sniffed it and smelled blood on that, too. Four, five days old. Female. Young. The wolf beneath my skin wanted to take a bite out of this shithead. His throat looked yummy. But now was not the time.

He wore a stone on a silver chain around his neck and I tore it off and held it up. At first I thought it was just a chunky lump of unshaped turquoise, but when I bent to study it I saw that it was a figure of what looked like Neptune. Or some similar kind of burly sea god. Heavy bearded face, fish tail, trident and attitude.

That was interesting as hell. I placed it on the landing next to him. Then I pocketed the .32, checked to make sure the goon was still breathing, and crept up the final flight of stairs.

The fire door was not locked. Useful. I opened it an inch and peered outside. There was a long, carpeted hallway, soft indirect lighting, some framed art. No people. No alarms, either. I left the stairwell and moved quickly and silently along the hall. There was only one door at the end and it was a very heavy slab of oak that Boots had told me had a steel core. The walls were also reinforced. No one was kicking that door in or using a sledgehammer to punch through the walls. A brass plate was affixed to the door at eye level.

THE DREAMLAND CONSERVANCY.

I bent close to the door and sniffed. Smelled wood, smelled metal, smelled the oil they used on the hinges. Not much else. So I dropped to a push-up position and sniffed at the bottom, but I struck out. The door had a rubber gasket along the frame that formed a tight seal, and the petroleum rubber blocked out anything from inside.

I got to my feet. There was a keypad mounted to the left of the door. Oliver Boots had provided the code but I sniffed the keys before I punched them.

Which is when I smelled something weird.

Incense.

Temple incense. Same kind. Fairly fresh.

I stepped back from the door and considered the possibilities. One was that one of Bohunk's men had tried to fudge his way past the combination. Another was that they *had* the combination and had already gotten inside. Maybe they were waiting for me in there. Other options suggested themselves, but I dismissed them as absurd.

The door remained shut and unhelpful. The guy I'd decked was still bleeding in the fire tower. Someone was going to find him eventually.

What was it Boots said? *We have found our champion.*

"Fuck it," I said.

And punched in the code.

The little red light on the keypad flicked over from red to green and the door lock clicked. No alarms rang. I pushed the door open and then faded to one side in case someone was in there prepared to shoot.

I waited.

No shots.

I went inside very quickly, moving left and ducking down behind a heavy armchair in the reception area. There was no one behind the desk, so I crossed to the glass door that led inside. Opened it. Expected to find cubicles or a set of offices with maybe a shared hall or common waiting area. That's not what I stepped into. It was a huge room with a high ceiling and tall, arched windows. No desks, no office equipment. The floor was made of rare polished marble that seemed to swirl with smoky grays, pale pinks, deep purples and inky blacks. Rich tapestries hung from the wall between each of the windows, and the embroidery was alive with representations of monsters and gods. There was something that looked like a stone altar, inlaid with turquoise, carnelian and lapis lazuli, and trimmed with filigrees of gold and silver. Set into the stone wall so that it bisected the stone altar was a heavy wall safe.

I was alone in the room and everything was still.

But everything was wrong.

-8-

The first thing I smelled was incense.

Yeah, *that* kind of incense.

And we're not talking trace amounts left behind by Bohunk or one of his goons. Sticks of it stood fuming in brass holders that had been placed on marble pedestals. There were maybe a dozen of them positioned around the room. The curling smoke filled the air like writhing snakes. Instead of electric lights there were braziers—actually goddamn braziers—filled with burning coals.

I looked around and said, very clearly and distinctly, "What the fuck?"

My words echoed strangely in the empty hall and lunged back at me in odd and meaningless shapes.

Nothing was currently making sense. Once again I nearly turned around and left. Bohunk and his thugs could *have* whatever this was. Oliver Boots had freaked me out pretty well when he was in my office, but now that I was standing in *his* office I was lost. I mean… what was this place? Definitely not an office.

Was it a temple? A church?

The creatures depicted on the tapestries were strange. A goat-headed monster who rose like a giant above a mass of worshippers whose bodies were torn and broken. A fish-god rising from the deeps as if in answer to the prayers of the people in a crooked church perched on the craggy lip of a sea cliff, yet the very arrival of the invoked god brought with it a tsunami that was poised to destroy the entire coastline. Another was a gray blob of a thing that looked like it was covered with festering sores. There was a giant spider with a human face, and something that looked like a pterosaur standing on a field of ice. One of them looked like a zombie but had webbed feet and eyes that burned with coal; there was a monstrous black goat around whose twisted legs clung hundreds of its deformed spawn. And there was something that looked like a gelatinous creature with innumerable humanlike eyes and mouths within its black mass. Others were less clearly defined—glowing orbs of light or darkness, or creatures that were shown to have one shape in half of the tapestry, but as they passed through a wall or dimensional veil, they changed into something else equally horrific.

A few of those images tickled a memory in the back of my mind. I hoped—even prayed—that it was a memory of some book I'd read or a monster movie I'd seen. But it didn't feel like that. It felt more like a much older memory. Something conjured from the primitive fears of the lizard brain. And even though the tapestries were cloth and metal wire and silk thread, they repelled me. I did not want to draw any closer to examine the images. No sir, not one step.

Instead I turned and ran over to the altar. I wanted to get that relic and get the hell out of this weird-ass version of Dodge.

The stone altar was split to allow the safe to be built into the wall. Each side of the altar was ten feet long, with a flat top. There were thick iron rings set in the four corners of each side.

The safe was massive, one of those huge old-style bank-vault doors that stood eight feet high. It had a big spoked wheel and a smaller combination dial. As I inched closer I saw there were designs carved onto the face of the altar, and those designs continued onto the metal surface of the vault. It was a very subtle but highly detailed landscape that showed a series of mountains rising in steps, each larger than the other. Waves crashed against the steep walls on one side, but between the mountains on the other side was a lush valley filled with strange trees bearing no resemblance to anything I recognized. A burning sun hung in the sky, but also representations of several moons and of distant worlds, some with rings like Saturn.

I knew what I was seeing was an artist's interpretation of the Dreamlands, that strange dimension created by H. P. Lovecraft for his story cycles. This whole room—this church, I suppose—was dedicated to a genuine belief in such a place, as well as in its strange gods and other creatures whose celestial designation I couldn't label.

A voice in my head told me to hurry. The rational part of my brain insisted that I make tracks because someone was going to find the guard I'd suckered. But that lizard brain whispered the truth. This room *scared* me.

Yeah, even a guy like me.

I reached for the combination dial and began turning. The code was simple. Eight to the left, fifty-one to the right, eleven to the left. But the second I touched it I snatched my hand back and stared at my fingers as bright red blood welled from a thin cut. There was blood on the dial, too, and I had to shift to allow the firelight to sparkle on the razor-sharp edge of a splinter that had been gouged from the dial.

"Fuck," I snarled, sucking the blood from my index finger.

Careful not to cut myself again, I entered the code. The tumblers clicked.

Click.

Click.

Click.

And I heard a sound deep within the mechanism. Not a click this time. It was different. Weirder. Almost organic.

Like a sigh.

Sweat broke out on my face and ran in lines down my cheeks.

I grasped the big wheel and, as instructed, spun it counterclockwise one full turn.

Another of those deep sighs.

And then the door shifted. Moved, almost as if pushed. Even so it took a lot of effort to pull that door open. It must have weighed three tons. The hinges squealed as if they were in pain and as the whole thing opened, trapped air inside blew out. It felt strangely moist and warm. Like breath.

Jesus Christ. Just like breath.

It smelled of rotting fish and salt.

I gagged and turned away for a moment. Sweat stung like tears in my eyes.

Hurry, screamed the voice in my head.

It took real effort to turn back, to pull the safe open the rest of the way, to step inside.

There wasn't much within the vault. A polished block four feet square that looked to be made from volcanic rock. On top of that was an envelope. Nothing else.

I burned five seconds just staring at the envelope. My name had been written across the front in flowing script.

"Oh, shit," I said aloud.

I picked up the envelope. It was heavy and expensive stock, unsealed. I removed the card from inside, leaving behind a bloody fingerprint. The card had a note written in the same elegant hand.

> *Thank you for being our champion.*
> *Your courage and sacrifice are appreciated.*

It was right about then that I heard the laughter from outside.

-9-

I dropped the card and whirled around, rushed to the vault doorway and gaped at what I saw.

The chamber outside was no longer empty. Several of the tapestries had been pushed aside to allow concealed doors to open. Figures emerged from the shadows. At least a dozen of them. Men and women. All very tall. All with intensely black skin. All wearing white silk robes. All of them smiling big smiles that showed lots of white, white teeth.

And directly in the center of the room, thick arms folded across a massive chest, stood Israel Bohunk.

He was laughing.

Everyone was laughing.

Except me.

-10-

"Sam motherfucking Hunter," said Bohunk as I stepped out of the vault.

I said nothing.

Every single one of the black-skinned people looked like Oliver Boots. Even the women. They were all the same height, same build.

"Feeling stupid yet?" asked Bohunk.

"Pretty stupid," I agreed.

Bohunk was really huge. His skin was that weird gray and he looked like you could break baseball bats off of him without raising a welt. His forearms were as big around as my biceps, and his biceps were insane. I've dated women with narrower waists. I bet his chest, fully expanded, was six feet around if it was an inch. Guy was a fucking brute. And he had that big, ugly bucket of a head.

He also had a Glock in a clamshell shoulder holster.

"I heard you had at least half a brain, Hunter," he said, "so I'm kind of surprised you didn't figure this out."

"Must be one of my slow days," I said. A line of cold sweat was running down my spine and pooling inside my tighty-whities.

"Have you figured it out yet? You know what's going on?"

"I know I've been fucked."

"*Are being* fucked," he corrected. "Present tense. This isn't the happy moment where we let you in on the gag and we all have a good laugh."

"Yeah, I'm getting that," I said. "But I didn't get the CliffsNotes on this, so help a brother out. What in the chartreuse fuck is going on?"

"Trap," he said.

"Yeah, pretty much figured the whole 'trap' part. What's eluding me is the 'why'? If you're in on this, then why hire me to sneak in here and get the relic?"

One of the tall weirdos detached himself from the crowd and walked up to stand next to Bohunk.

"Boots?" I asked.

"Good afternoon, Mr. Hunter," said Oliver Boots. "We are so very delighted that you could join us."

"First," I said, "let me just say—and I mean this in the nicest possible way—go fuck yourself."

Everyone had a good laugh about that. The crowd of weirdos laughed like crows. It was an ugly thing to hear. Bohunk had a deep bass rumble when he spoke but his laugh was a donkey bray, and he bent over and slapped his thighs.

Boots wiped a tear from the corner of his eye. "I deserved that, I suppose."

"You did," I said. "Care to tell me why I'm here? If it's not to protect the relic from ass-face here—" I pointed at Bohunk "—then what's the what?"

"I told you. It was all about protecting access to the Dreamlands."

"You said there was a relic..."

"Well, there is, but I may have misled you as to its size."

"You said it was carved to represent the mountain Ngranek on the isle of Oriab in the southern part of the Dreamlands and..." My words slowed and stopped. I turned and looked at the altar and the vault door.

"Ah," I said, "shit."

"Exactly. This altar is the relic and the map which describes the access is one of our greatest treasures."

I shook my head. "But you already *have* it."

"We have the doorway," said Boots, "and we know the way. Our problem is that the doorway is open and we want it shut. That is what we live for, protecting our world from those who would cross over from *your* world and bring with them their diseases and pollution."

"You lost me around the last bend. Why not just shut the freaking door?"

"They can't," said Bohunk.

"Why not?"

"Because the Thule Society wedged it open."

I looked from Bohunk to Boots and back again. "Huh?"

"Long story short," said Bohunk. "There really is a Thule Society and they really are a bunch of assholes who try to steal anything with even the stink of magic on it. All sorts of shit. You wouldn't believe what they've stolen over the last eighty-odd years. Can't keep their lily-white hands off of other people's shit."

"Uh huh. And you are an upstanding defender of the righteous."

Bohunk shrugged. "I never broke any laws that matter."

"Mr. Bohunk has been a cherished employee for many years now," said Boots. "He is a most efficient field operative. This entire operation was his idea."

"You're going to make me blush," said Bohunk.

"If the Thule Society wedged open the doorway, why hire me to steal the map for how to…" I stopped again, shaking my head. "No, none of this makes any sense. If the altar is the map and the door's already wedged open, then why the hell am I even here? Why is any of this happening? Are you fucktards planning on sacrificing me on that altar or some shit?"

"There's that delicious word again," said Boots. "Fucktard. So descriptive and useful."

The others of his kind tittered.

Bohunk took a step toward me and I backed up. A nervous reaction, sure, but it was also the wolf inside of me wanting to make sure lines of escape were clear. Bohunk held up his hands, palms out in a calm-down gesture.

"First off, sport," he said, "all this Lovecraft-Cthulhu-Dreamlands stuff? Crazy as it sounds, it's real. I mean it's *all* real. R'lyeh, the Mountains of Madness, the Necronomicon, Nyarlathotep, all of it. Real. Names were changed, sure, but otherwise this is all going on. Elder Gods, Outer Gods, Great Old Ones. Dude, the universe is a shit-ton bigger than you think it is. Worlds within worlds, worlds next to worlds. It can make your head spin. I mean... I used to have to drop acid to even *think* about this stuff, and my people buy into the whole 'larger world' thing anyway."

"Your people?" I echoed.

"Sure." He rapped his knuckles against his forehead. It sounded like stone banging on stone. "You think I got to look like this because of—what? Inbreeding? Having a crack-addict mother? A birth defect? Shit. You're not the only supernatural motherfucker trotting around and cashing in on the more lucrative aspects of his nature. No sir."

I licked my lips. "Which makes you... what? A golem?"

"Do I look Jewish?"

"Um...?"

"Ogre," he said, smiling with pride. "My whole family line is descended from Orcus, the Etruscan man-eating god. And, yes, before you ask, I do eat the occasional person. Only guys who fuck with me, though. And I cook them, because uncooked people are disgusting. I like a good rub to tenderize and bring out the—"

"Mr. Bohunk," said Boots, interrupting gently. Bohunk blinked.

"Oh, yeah, sorry. Caught up in the moment." He smiled at me. "Your people go back to Etruscan times, too. The *Benandanti*, the good wolves, am I right? What'd they call you during the Inquisition? The Hounds of God? Goody two-shoes werewolves? Kind of cool, I guess. Not as cool as Ogres or Nightgaunts and—"

"The hell's a Nightgaunt?" I asked.

"Oh," said Mr. Boots, "that would be us."

His brilliant white smile broadened as he reached up and took hold of something on the back of his head. Then with a sudden jerk of his arm he tore off his face, his skin and his clothes. I heard a ripping sound that was suspiciously like Velcro, and then Boots flung aside his disguise.

Beneath it all he was still as black as polished coal.

But he had no face at all.

None.

Behind him and around us the others tore away their skins, flinging them to the floor to stand revealed as the monsters they were. These things, these Nightgaunts, had skin that was slick and rubbery. It looked more fake than their false disguises had. They had no mouths, no eyes, no noses. The only feature on their heads was a pair of horns that curled around so the tips pointed toward their otherwise featureless foreheads. They had long fingers that ended in very sharp claws, and thin wings that fluttered from their shoulders. Long barbed tails whipped back and forth behind them.

I said, "Oh shit."

They laughed like carrion birds.

"So," said Bohunk, "what you are, is totally and completely fucked."

-11-

"But why?" I demanded, taking two more backward steps. I was almost hard up against the altar. Not the place I'd prefer to be, but the Nightgaunts had spread out to form a wide ring around me. "What do you *want*?"

"Here's the thing about being part of the supernatural side of the universe," said Bohunk. "Rituals. There's all these goddamn rituals. Everything has to be complicated. Cthulhu, Nodens and all of those gods, man oh man do they have a hard-on for rituals. And, hey, it's not like the Jews and Catholics and Scientologists and everyone else doesn't get into the act, too. Everyone likes to make things complicated. No one can just *believe* and let it go. My people, the ogres? We got our thing, too. We can't eat anyone who's not an enemy. It's stupid, but if we do it's like having irritable bowel syndrome. I shit razor blades for a week."

I said nothing because, really, what do you say to an ogre who's complaining about problems with his colon?

"So, to understand the nature of the ritual you're tied up in," he continued, "you got to understand who the Nightgaunts are and what they do. Their whole shtick is protecting that mountain, Ngranek, on the isle of Oriab. Travelers from all kinds of worlds, including some unlucky cocksuckers from *our* world, keep trying to go there. Don't ask why. Something to do with the living heart of their god and the sixteen sacred toadstools or some such shit. I don't know. Every time they try to explain it, I just tune them out."

"Mr. Bohunk, please," said Boots. And that was weird because he no longer had a mouth. But I'd already given up trying to make sense of today. That ship sailed, caught fire, hit an iceberg and sank.

"Okay, okay," said Bohunk. "Long story short, it's important for there to *be* a doorway—something about the energetic lifeblood of the universe—but it's supposed to be shut except under certain circumstances."

"Like the planetary convergence?" I suggested.

"Like that. Only Bootsie lied to you. It's during that convergence that the doorway *can* be shut. Or, shut properly, I guess."

Boots nodded his confirmation of this.

"The Thule dickheads managed to get it open," continued Bohunk. "Me and my boys were around and we fucked them up but good. They were delicious, too. We had a pig roast and my boy Denny made this barbecue sauce that—"

"Mr. Bohunk!" snapped Boots, his patience wearing thin.

"Right, right. Anyway, as far as the doorway, it was damage done. Fucking thing's stuck open. And all sorts of things getting into the Dreamlands."

I frowned and turned to look at the vault. "I don't—"

"No, the doorway is—whaddya call it, Bootsie?"

"Pan-dimensional," supplied the Nightgaunt. "Once open on this plane it opens on all planes. We have not been able to break the Thule spells. They used very powerful black magic. And that has forced us to use a dangerous and ancient spell. One that requires the willing sacrifice of a great champion of pure heart and great courage."

"Which," said Bohunk, giving me a big stage wink, "brings us to you."

I said, "Um... willing? Sacrifice? Champion?"

"Yeah," said Bohunk. "Bootsie tells me you took the job. Guess that's obvious 'cause you're here."

"Pure heart?"

"Well, there's always wiggle room," said Bohunk, and the Nightgaunts tittered.

"No, let's go back to the willing part. I agreed to a job, I never agreed to sacrifice anything."

"You did," said Boots. "You gave your word and you sealed the bargain with your own blood. There is no greater bond in this or any world. It is a blood bargain."

"Bullshit. You guys can take your bargain and your bag of tricks and shove them up your asses. Provided you have asses."

"They don't, actually," said Bohunk. "Weird, I know. And kind of disgusting. My point is that you are screwed, Hunter. Your blood is on the vault door, and the door is the relic. So... sucks to be you."

"And I'm just supposed to stretch out on the altar and let you cut my throat?"

Boots said, "No, Mr. Hunter, we expected you to fight us. You are, after all, a champion. And because you have a certain reputation for ferocity. Because you are a lycanthrope your blood and your soul energy will help us seal the doorway across all of the infinite worlds. You have a magnificent soul and it shines like a sun for those who can see it. All of that energy, that purity of purpose, that honesty and integrity, the *ferocity* that has earned you the reputation for being a true champion for the helpless, for the innocent... my oh my, that is a degree of spiritual force greater than anything we have used in ten thousand millennia. It is an honor to accept your sacrifice. You humble us."

"You," I said, "can go fuck yourself. I quit."

"You can't," he said, sounding almost sorry. "You gave your word."

"My word doesn't mean shit," I lied.

"You shed your blood to seal the deal."

"I cut my finger on a splinter. Which, by the way, was a cheap shot and a sneaky piece of bullshit."

"Nevertheless, a deal is a deal, and any deal made here on the altar is sealed across all of time and space."

"Save the Doctor Who bullcrap for someone who gives a rat's hairy balls."

"Ah, I'm so sorry you feel this way," said Boots. "But it is to be expected. It is a rare thing indeed for a person's soul force to be in alignment with their outer personality. But, no matter, we will help you live up to your agreement. We have asked Mr. Bohunk to assist us in completing the final part of the ritual."

"He can try."

"Oh, it's a done deal," Bohunk assured me, and all the Nightgaunts nodded. Their wings fluttered and creaked like leather. "And, for the record, sport, it's more than just you getting your throat cut. Nah. We got to cut your eyes out, cut your balls off. The more pain you're in, the more you suffer, the more noble your sacrifice is. That's bigger energy. Sucks for you but great for what Bootsie and his crew need. Great for the universe, I suppose."

"You're going to cut me up?" I said, feeling the blood drain from my face.

"Sure. There's a whole lot of cutting on today's program, and because you're a werewolf you'll actually live through almost all of it. Sucks, but there it is. We got silver chains, though, so…" He let it hang.

I glanced at the iron rings on the altar.

It was all there. Twelve Nightgaunts and one ogre. And me. Medium-sized guy who could become a medium-sized wolf.

As odds go, mine blew.

-12-

"You're going to have to earn it," I said, putting a little bit of the wolf's growl in my voice.

Israel Bohunk contrived not to faint from terror. "Yeah," he said, "that's why I'm here. You know, ogre and all."

"Never fought an ogre," I said, putting my hands in my pockets and trying to look like I was calm, cool and collected. "Didn't even believe in them until five minutes ago."

"Life's full of surprises," he said.

"Yes it is. You ever fight a werewolf before?" I asked.

"Nope, but I heard you guys taste great."

He laughed, I smiled. My heart was racing.

I asked, "You're not afraid I might cut *your* balls off?"

"Not really. My skin's as hard as granite. You'd break your little doggy nails. Sorry, sport, but this is how it ends."

"I didn't know ogres were that tough. Claw proof? Knife proof, too?"

"Sure. Bullets, too. They just bounce off. Not that it matters to you," he said. "From what I heard you don't even carry a gun."

"I'm thinking of taking it up," I told him.

And I drew the stolen .32 and shot him in his left eye.

-13-

Here's the thing…

I don't care how tough you are or how strong you are. I don't care if your skin is made of rocks or you're wearing a suit of armor. That's all well and good but I've found that a bullet in the brainpan will do 'er for just about everyone.

And eyes? Go on and tell me what kind of creature, natural or supernatural, has bulletproof eyes. You want to know how many?

Not one.

Not one fucking thing on earth or in any dimension you care to name.

The bullet punched through Bohunk's eye but it couldn't break through whatever the hell his skull was made of. So, instead, it bounced all over inside his skull and turned his brain to Swiss cheese.

Boo-fucking-hoo.

Bohunk fell backward against one of the Nightgaunts and dragged him down. The rest of them, including Oliver Boots, stood there and stared at their hired muscle. Blood leaked like tears from the burst eye-ball.

Then Boots looked at me. Or… turned his face to me. Without his disguise he didn't have eyes. Or a mouth. Or anything.

I shot him in the face. Three times.

As it turns out, Nightgaunts aren't bulletproof at all. Not even a little bit.

The bullets blew out the back of his skull and splattered the creatures behind him. One of the bullets clipped the top of another Nightgaunt's head and blew a quarter pound of brains across the floor.

By then the others were beginning to shake off their shock.

They came at me, tearing the air with their claws, their barbed tails whipping, wings lifting them so they could dive-bomb me.

I emptied the .32 and then let it drop because the hand holding it was no longer shaped for that sort of thing. No proper trigger finger, no op-posable thumb. Just claws and fur.

Distantly, as if off to one side of my mind, I could hear my clothes rip as my body changed. There was pain and there was blood. There always is. But there was also a lot of rage.

No. Let's call it by the right word.

There was hate.

Pure animal hate.

They came at me and tried to kill Sam Hunter the man. They tried to complete their sacrifice. To tear me apart. To use me, body and soul, to close the door. They tried to rip me apart and use me. They tried to destroy the man who had accepted the role of their champion.

But that man was gone.

Now it was only the wolf.

And, my oh my, the wolf was pissed.

-14-

As it turns out, Nightgaunts taste pretty good.
Like chicken.

Nightgaunts

The land of dreams is no less essential to us than our wak-ing landscape. We wander through both worlds confused, un-certain, fearful, distracted by glittering prizes, allured by false hopes, led astray by vanity and arrogance. In dreams we see, hear, touch, smell, taste, speak and remember, just as we do while awake. One third of our lives is given over to sleep, and much of that time is spent in dreams. How could something that occupies so much of our thought and emotion be unimportant?

The creatures of dreams are as real to us as the beasts in the field, the birds in the trees, the fish in the sea. They give us joy. They cause us sorrow. And if they choose, they end our lives. For those who die in dreams also die in the flesh. Just as there are no beauties so fine as the beauties of a dream, there are no horrors so keen as those that inhabit our nightmares.

One such species of horror is known as the nightgaunt due to its extreme thinness. It is so thin that it appears to be cut from a length of black cloth that gives back no reflection. The body of the nightgaunt shows itself only as a winged outline of shadow with inward-curved horns, a forked tail, clawed fingers, and blank faces that have no features.

The creatures do not speak or make any sound. They de-light in causing fear and come to those who slumber in large flocks on their leathern wings, chiefly to young children or even infants soon after they fall asleep. Night after night they come to terrify the young child, and thereby reap the greatest bounty of terror, for the anticipation of the coming fear magnifies its force

Some sages assert that they are nourished by blood, but how can this be when they have no mouths? No, the nightgaunts are sustained by the emotion of fear, which is the strongest and purest of human emotions. The children so afflicted abhor sleep and do their best to stay awake, but it is the nature of the very young to sleep in spite of themselves, and when their heavy eyelids close at last, the nightgaunts come.

Their thinness allows them to slip through the smallest crack at the window frame or beneath a door. They enter the chamber of the sleeping child in their numbers, as many as two score of them at a time, and snatch the child from his bed, stifling his screams with their paws. They grab him by the flesh of the belly, and their fingers produce a strange sensation that subdues the child's resistance. It is both a tickling and a crawling, as though worms squirmed in the child's flesh.

The black skins of the nightgaunts have a revolting smooth texture to the touch that is like the slickness on the belly of a frog. With their long clawed fingers they lift the child high above their heads and carry him out the opened window and into the starry night air, bearing the child high into the heavens on their silent, bat-like black wings. These abductions they accomplish with such skill and stealth that the mothers never wake.

Far above the distant mountains in the land of Thok they carry him. To magnify the terror of the child, that is both their joy and nourishment, the nightgaunts toss him back and forth between them through the whistling, star-shot darkness. They pretend to drop him and then catch him up at the last instant. Around and around the flying flock, from one to the next they throw the screaming child, who is too high above the ground for any below to hear his cries.

At last, after they have extracted the full amount of his terror, and the child is exhausted, they let him fall from their grasp

For miles he tumbles down through the starry blackness, the sharp peaks of the mountains below looming ever nearer. The child knows with certainty that should he fail to wake before he strikes those peaks, he will surely die, and usually he is able to wake himself in time.

It is not the purpose of the nightgaunts to kill, but to terrify. They know that most children will wake before they strike the ground. But sometimes it happens that a child does not wake up, and then he is found in his bed in the morning by his mother, cold and still and dead. Such inexplicable deaths of young children in their beds are not uncommon, but the cause of death is seldom guessed.

It is said that the nightgaunts worship hoary Nodens, an ancient god about whom little is known. It may be that this god rules over dreamless sleep. Nodens is titled Lord of the Abyss and it is whispered of this primal being that he defies the power of the old ones, even that of Nyarlathotep.

The nightgaunts dwell in the Dreamlands, and make their dens in caves near the mountain Ngranek. They can only intrude on the waking world at the margin between sleep and wakefulness, when we lie half in one world and half in the other. At these times they may sometimes be glimpsed in the gloom with our open eyes.

The fear they inspire at these moments is intense, for that is the fundamental aspect of their nature. No man, regardless of his courage, can look upon them unmoved by fear. They exist to terrify. They embody nightmare. They are the tormentors of our childhood, and they are always with us even when we cease to be aware of them in our dreams.

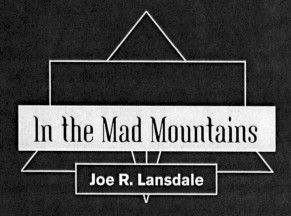

In the Mad Mountains

Joe R. Lansdale

Slept, awoke, slept, awoke, miserable life.
   —Franz Kafka

Reality is that which, when you stop believing in it, doesn't go away.
   —Philip K. Dick

The oldest and strongest emotion of mankind is fear. And the oldest and strongest kind of fear is fear of the unknown.
   —H.P. Lovecraft

The moon was bright. The sea was black. The waves rolled and the bodies rolled with it. The dead ones and the live ones, screaming and dying, begging and pleading, praying and crying to the unconcerned sea.

Behind them the great ship tipped up as if to give a final display of its former magnificence, its bow parting the night-waters like a knife through chocolate, pointing its stern to the sky, slipping slowly beneath the cold waves, breaking in half as it rode down into the bottomless sea.

Boilers hissed, and the steam coughed up a great white cloud. The cloud pinned itself against the moon-bright sky, then faded like a fleeting dream.

The lifeboats bobbed and the survivors in the water swam for them, called to them. One of the boats, Number Three, stuffed full of human misery and taking on water, tried to rescue more survivors, and when it did it tipped, ejected two of its riders, then righted itself again. A man in nightclothes, and a woman wearing a fur coat, fell out. The coat took on water, grew heavy, and dragged her down. A shark rose up close to the boat with its mouth wide open, its teeth gleaming as if polished by rags. Its eyes rolled back in ecstasy, and then the man was in its jaws. The shark's teeth snapped together and blood blew wide and into the boat, along with a soft bed slipper. The shark took half of the man down under, the other half of him bobbed, and then another shark drove up from below and bit the other half, carried it down and away into Davy Jones' Locker.

Those that had swam for it, those remaining near Lifeboat Number Three, were taken by the sharks. The water grew thick with fins and an oily film of blood, the sounds of cries cut short. Then a wave caught Lifeboat Number Three and those still in it, pushed it forward, leaving the other lifeboats and the struggling swimmers near them far behind, bobbing like fishing corks.

There was a great strike of lightning in the distance, splitting what had been a clear sky with an electric crack of fire. When it flashed, those in Lifeboat Number Three saw a great iceberg, a cold but beaconing mass; something solid, waiting in the distance, lying jagged and white against the tumbling sea. Far beyond was an irregular rise of what appeared to be mountains. Out of the formerly clear night sky came a dark cloud, wide and thick as all creation. It sacked the moon. For the occupants in Lifeboat Number Three there was a sensation of being wrapped in black cotton.

The lightning flashed again and everything was bright, and then it was gone, and all was dark and empty again. They rode like that on the waves in the darkness, lighted now and then by bolts of lightning, cold rain driving down from the churning sky. They cupped the water that collected in the bottom of the boat with their hands and drank from it, parched. There was water all about them, water full of salt that would make them choke, sicken, and die, but this water was fresh, and their bodies called for it.

They went through an eternity of jumping sea, darkness, and lightning-torn sky, and then they bumped against the iceberg, and then the boat was pushed back out to sea. Then eternity ended and there was light and the storm passed and the sun peeked shyly over the waters and showed the survivors that there were still fins visible in its wide expanse. The sharks were waiting.

An iceberg was in sight, perhaps the one they had glimpsed before and bounced off of, possibly another, perhaps even the one their great ship had struck. Certainly it was a different view of the ice because to their surprise they could see great ships of times long past pushed onto and into the berg, sometimes completely housed by it, like flies trapped and visible in blue-white amber. Attached to the berg, and somewhat in the distance, they could again see a flat expanse of ice, and that became their destination.

There were six oars in the boat and twelve survivors, eight men and four women. One of the men, a young fellow named Gavin, took charge without asking, called out for rowers, and soon six men held the six oars and cranked them, shoving Lifeboat Number Three toward an icy shore. One of the men, an older gent, collapsed at the oar and a young woman took it and began to row.

A gap in the flat ice was their destination, and they were able to row the boat to that spot and land it as if it were a beach. They climbed out of the boat—except the man who had collapsed—and onto the ice, and with fingers and feet aching from the cold, were able to pull the lifeboat out of the water, at least far enough for everyone to disembark.

The man who remained in the boat couldn't be roused. By the time they were able to lift him out and onto the ice, he was dead. Ice had formed where his nose had ran, and around the corners of his mouth and eyes. They stretched him out and pulled his arms across his chest.

Gavin said, "We have to leave him here, for now."

Another man, English, about Gavin's age, said, "Seems less than appropriate."

"You can carry him on your back if you like," said another of the men, middle-aged, an American.

"I suppose not," said the Englishman. "The women must be our first concern."

"Looks to me like we've come to a state of every man and woman for himself," said the younger American.

The young woman who had rowed said, "Seems to me it would be wiser if we all stuck together, helped one another. I think, as a woman, I can help the others as much as you."

"All of you do what you like," said the younger American. "I'm not bound to anyone."

Gavin said, "Very well then. Let's see who wants to stick together."

A quick poll was taken. Only the young American was not in agreement. "Very well," the young man said. "I'll strike out on my own."

"To where?" said Gavin. "Seems to me that we'll all end up in the same places."

"Could be," said the young American, "but I prefer to bear responsibility for me and no one else."

"Good luck to you then," Gavin said. "What's your name in case we have to say a few words over you, lower you into the water and such?"

"If that's the case, leave me where I fall," said the man, "but just for the record, the name is Hardin."

"First or last?" the woman asked.

"It'll do for both," said Hardin, and he started out walking across the ice in the direction of one of the great, frozen ships not encased in an iceberg, but instead pushed up on the ice.

The others watched Hardin for a while. He passed the ship and kept walking. The Englishman who had spoken before said, "He isn't much of a team player, is he. Very American."

"I'm American," Gavin said.

"So you are," the Englishman said. "No offense. James Carruthers is my name."

"I'm Amelia Brand," said the woman who had rowed and suggested they stay together. "Also American."

An older woman, English, said, "They call me Duchess, but we can introduce ourselves later. Seems to me it would be wise to search out some sort of shelter, and one of the ships appear to be our only possibilities."

No one else seemed even the least bit interested in talking, or giving their names. They looked defeated and ready to collapse.

"True enough," Gavin said, and looked out across the ice at the ice-captured ship. Hardin was still visible, but far away. Considering the ice, he was making good time.

Gavin started out. Amelia walked beside him. The others fell in line behind them. Glancing back, Gavin saw the wild water had lifted Lifeboat Number Three off the ice and carried it back out to sea.

They kept walking, and came to the first ship.

After a bit, Amelia said, pointing, "Right there. At the stern. I think we can board it the easiest. We'll just have to go easy."

It was a large and ancient ship of dark wood. It looked surprisingly sturdy, and the back end, with its rise of ice against it, appeared to be their way in.

"Might as well," said Duchess. "In an hour it's likely we'll all be dead, and if I can find a way to become only slightly warmer, I'd prefer to die that way."

The side of the ship was high and there were tatters of sails partly encased in ice like damaged butterfly wings. They made their way up the slope that led to the stern, but it was slick beyond the ability of all but Gavin, Amelia, and the Englishman, Carruthers.

The three of them worked up the slope, finding pocks in the ice they could use to climb. When they made the summit and boarded the ship, they cautiously made for the wheelhouse. The view glass in the wheelhouse was frosted over and the door was jammed with ice, but the three of them leaned up against it and nudged it loose, knocking it back with an explosion of shattering ice and a surprising feeling of warmth, if for no other reason than the wind was blocked by the walls and the glass.

It was short-lived comfort, for in the next moment they saw a body hung up in the wheel. It was a man in a thick coat. His face was not visible, and for a moment it appeared he had been hung there with his back against the wheel, but within an instant they saw that this was not the case. It was the face that was misplaced. His neck was long and twisted, and his head had been wrenched about to face the opposite direction. His legs had collapsed beneath him, but his arms, caught up in the wheel, held him in place. There was a large gap in the top of his head, crusted with frozen blood.

Gavin stood where he could see the man's face. His mouth was wide open and so were his eyes, and they were glazed with ice; the eyeballs looked like two marbles in the bottom of a glass of water, his top lip was curled back from his teeth, and the teeth looked like stalactites, cracked and broken as they were.

"My god," said Carruthers.

"How could this happen?" said Amelia. "What could have done this?"

"Let's consider later," said Gavin. "It might be best to see if we can get the others up."

Gavin unfastened the latches on the cabinets and looked inside. Eventually he found a thick coil of rope.

"This should do for starters," he said.

They pulled the others up. It took some time, and the old woman, Duchess, had the hardest bout with it, but they got her on board with only a slight sprain to her ankle and some problems with her breathing. She heaved the cold air in and out like a bellows. After everyone was aboard the ship they removed the dead body at the wheel, took it out on deck and slipped it over the far side. It was a sad thing to do to what had once been a living human being, but Gavin and the others could see nothing else for it. Leaving it there was demoralizing.

The body was stiff as a hammer and went sliding over the rise of ice like a kid on holiday, making a kind of scratching sound as it glided along. Finally it drifted off the rise and shot out onto the ice and lay there like a sunning seal. Gavin said that later he'd try to get the body out to sea, which seemed more fitting than just leaving it on the cold ice, but he knew as the others did, that it was a lie. He figured, as they all did, that they would soon be dead. Already their wet clothing had turned icy.

In the galley section they found a door had been knocked down, and with enough force to shatter it into several pieces. Not far beyond that they found a man's body with a large hole in its head, the blood around the wound frozen over so it looked like someone had scooped a chunk out of a ripe tomato with a spoon. The revolver that had killed him was still clutched in his right hand. Obviously the scoop in his head had been made after he had shot himself, but by whom and why?

His body had to go over the side too, but it was becoming so cold, one of their number, a little middle-aged man they later learned was named Cyril, tried to get the gun out of the man's hand to use on himself, but the weapon was frozen in the dead man's fist, firm as if it were part of his fingers.

Gavin and Carruthers wrestled Cyril away from the gun that he was trying frantically to tug from the dead man's hand. They wrestled him to the floor, pulling the dead man along with them, yanking on the gun and taking two of the dead man's fingers with it, snapping them free like frozen asparagus sprouts.

"Kill me, but get off of me," Cyril said. "The cold, it's too much."

That ended the fight, and when it was done, Gavin and Carruthers were too weak to care anymore. Together, all of the survivors wandered off across the galley and down the steps into the hold below the upper deck. They found blankets there, and clothes, jackets, gloves, scarves, and wool hats. A veritable stockpile of items. They each peeled off and redressed. The women rid themselves of their wet clothes and dried on the blankets and wrapped themselves in them so that they might dress beneath them, though anything to be seen had been seen. Amelia was the only one that didn't follow that path. She boldly removed her clothes and dried in full view, and then dressed, in full sight of the men who had thrown modestly completely out the window.

Gavin took note of Amelia. What he saw he liked, though beyond that note of admiration, he was too cold for biological consideration, too eager to dress in dry and warmer clothes.

A few minutes later, with all of them dressed in dry clothes and wearing thick, hooded coats taken from the larder, fat gloves on their hands, blankets draped over their shoulders, the world seemed slightly brighter, even if lit up only by a crack of fading sunlight through a split in the roof of the ship. Cyril, who moments before had been ready to shoot himself in the head, seemed happier and more secure. A bit of warmth had lifted everyone's spirits.

When they were dressed, they went back up the steps and found a storage room off the main section of the galley, and in there they found a man hanging from one of the meat hooks on the wall. A short piece of rope was tied about his neck and he had his hands stuck down through his belt. His head had been broken open like the others, again, most likely after death. He hung like smoked meat. Actual smoked meat dangled on either side of him, and like the man with the gun in his hand, they left him there, but took one of the smoked hogs down and carried it back below where it was warmer. They made it warmer yet by tying ropes across the length of the hold, finding plenty of them about, and from the ropes they dangled thick blankets and made a series of crude tents.

It was much warmer that way, and when Amelia found a small grate stove, they moved it to the side of the ship where there was a crack in the wall, and busted up some odds and ends they found, crates and an old chair, and built a fire. There were plenty of working matches that had been wrapped securely in waxed paper and then stuffed into leather bags, and there was tinder to get a fire started. When it was lit and burning, the smoke rose up through the split in the ceiling, drifted out through the wheelhouse and away. They cut strips of the hanging meat with Gavin's pocketknife. It was as fresh as the day it had been frozen. They warmed it at the fire and ate like starving wolves. Even with all that had happened to them at sea, the sharks, the cold rain, the dark toss on the waves, the dead bodies, for a moment they were hopeful.

Later, Gavin and Amelia and Carruthers went and dropped the other bodies down the slide of ice and out onto the flat of it. Finished with that disconcerting chore, they returned to the hold and ate more meat.

Amelia, after eating, said to Gavin, "How old do you think this ship is?"

"1800s, I guess. I don't really know, but that seems right. An old sailing ship that went latitude when it should have went longitude. That's me trying to be cute. I don't know one from the other."

"Nor do I."

"I suppose it tried to enter an opening in the ice, tried to survive here, but things went wrong."

"What do you think happened here, besides things went wrong?"

Gavin shook his head. "I don't know. Someone on board must have gone crazy and killed the men we found. As for the other sailors, no idea."

Gavin and Amelia moved to the far side of the hold and gathered up between two barrels, sitting close together for warmth. They could see the others nearby, in the tents or just outside of them.

"What do you think of our chances?" she said.

"Grim."

"I think you're right, but believe it or not, I'm optimistic."

"Are you now?"

"I am now. We have warmth and food, and maybe we'll be found. And if not that, maybe we can find a way to leave."

"That would be a neat trick," he said. "I have no idea where we are, and I have a feeling that our ship didn't either. It all looks wrong out there."

"Wrong?" Amelia said.

"Yeah. I don't know exactly. Stars and moon, even the sea and the sky. Even in the daylight, it all looks odd."

"Have you been at sea in a lifeboat before?"

"No," Gavin said. "I admit I haven't, and could have gone my whole life without it."

"Maybe everything looks different when you're in a small boat at sea."

"I suppose," he said. "But it all seems so odd. The ship was lost before we hit the berg. I overheard a crew member say something about being lost, that the stars weren't right."

"You think he meant the constellations?"

"I guess."

"But what about the navigational equipment? You don't need stars to guide anymore."

"Sailors still depend on them, though. I think the equipment went south, and then they tried the stars, and the stars were wrong."

"Or the sailors were out of practice."

"Maybe. But even the air tastes funny."

"When it's cold, and you're in an old ship, I think the air would taste funny."

"You're right, of course, but it seems so odd."

Amelia was thinking the same, but unlike Gavin, she wasn't yet ready to admit it.

They watched as the crack of light in the ship grew darker, then was relighted as the moon rose.

"Sitting and waiting to run out of food doesn't appeal to me."

"There's a lot of food. I saw canned goods as well. The cold has probably preserved them. Water we can manage by melting ice."

"Still, there's an end to it. It's best to find a way to leave, a boat we can manage."

"It won't be this one. It's got splits in the sides. And it's too damn big."

"I don't know how we leave," Amelia said. "Only that in time, we have to, by boat or by discovery, or by death."

They slept, and when the morning light came, Amelia awoke. Gavin was gone. Bundled in her navy coat and with a blanket draped over her shoulders, she went exploring and discovered upstairs that the others had heated up the galley stove. It was a big stove, and they were roasting the hanging meat in it. There was a tremendous amount of warmth from the stove. It felt good. The fuel for the fire had been made from coal in a bin in the galley. There was still quite a bit of coal left. That alone was reassuring.

Gavin was supervising the cooking. As it turned out he had been a chef in a large hotel in New York City. He told them about it while the meat cooked. He told them his mother was an heiress, his father was in oil and gas and loved airplanes. No one else volunteered their history, not even Amelia.

When the meat was done, they ate. There was a lot of meat, and it was determined then that they needed to stretch it out as far as possible until another plan could be hatched. Cyril suggested they eat as much as they wanted and then go out and lay down on the ice and wait for death, who would most likely show up wearing a heavy coat and carrying an ice cutter.

"Don't be silly," Amelia said. "We need to see if we can find fishing equipment for more food. The other ships can provide wood for fuel when the coal runs out."

"And when the wood runs out. What then?" Duchess said, her old skin having grown tight in the cool air.

"Perhaps we'll be rescued," Amelia said. "Perhaps we can rescue ourselves. Perhaps if this is the edge of a continent, or even some icy island, there will be someone living here. Somewhere."

"Like Eskimos?" Duchess said.

"Like anyone," Amelia said.

"Aren't you the hopeful one," Carruthers said.

"I am at that, and I'm more hopeful if we do what we can to survive for as long as we can, have a purpose. I saw lifeboats on the deck, and we might cast to sea in one of those."

"I've told you how I feel about that," Gavin said.

"We had a lifeboat," Cyril said. "We were glad to get out of it."

"If we provision, take warm clothes, and perhaps prepare a sail, we might have a chance," Amelia said.

"Are you a sailor?" Cyril said.

"No, but I prefer to try something other than giving up."

"Die here in this ship, out on the ice, or at sea, makes no difference," Cyril said. "We're going to die. Have you forgotten the dead sailors? Someone killed them."

Gavin laughed. "Yeah, but not yesterday, not fifty years ago, but well over a hundred years ago. I doubt the murderer is alive and waiting on the ice, ready to sneak back on the ship and chop holes in our heads."

"Maybe it was some kind of animal," Cyril said. "Could be that. Like a polar bear. Another one could be around."

"Bears bite and claw," Duchess said. "They don't hit you in the head with some kind of weapon, an axe perhaps."

"One thing that would be helpful in your case, Cyril," Gavin said, "is if you're going to die, and constantly talk about it, go ahead and get it over with. That leaves more food for us. That gun probably wouldn't have worked anyway. Who knows? But you can always strip and lie on the ice like you suggested. That was your idea, wasn't it? Die on the ice? I've come to think that's not a bad idea for you at all. Anything to shut your negativity up. I mean, hell, I know things are bad, and I may not want to go to sea, but I'm not ready to throw in the towel just yet, even if I'm not sure we have a towel to toss."

The others, none of which had much to say before, and hadn't even given their names, chimed in with agreement. "Yeah, shut up about dying all the time," one of the older men said. "Go out and die, but shut up."

Cyril, now that he was warm, and in spite of his words, seemed a little less inclined to follow his own suggestion. He said, "Well, I'm just saying, things aren't looking too good."

"You think you're the only one that's made that observation?" Amelia said. "What we need to do is first decide how much food is to be provided to each of us, how far we can stretch it. No midnight snacks."

She looked around at the others. They nodded in agreement.

"Then," she said, "we need to find fishing equipment and put some sort of fishing crew together. After that, we can think about the boat, the sail, and for those who want to stay, they can. For those who would like to leave, we can try. The boats, I saw two. That way we can have two crews."

"Some crews we'll be," Carruthers said.

"I saw nautical books on board," Gavin said. "I'm good at learning things from books, maybe I can figure something out."

"Somehow," Cyril said, "I doubt there will be among those nautical books one about basic sailing."

"We can find out," Gavin said.

Amelia and Gavin discovered the sick bay on a search of the ship, and found that the table used for patients was folded out from the wall and covered in blood. Something had happened on board besides being marooned. The dead sailors were proof of that. Their wounds didn't seem to fit any type of available weapon. Duchess was right. Bears and other animals seemed unlikely. Did they turn on one another in claustrophobic fury? Cannibalism? There was food, so why resort to such? And here in the sick bay, had someone been wounded due to fighting? Had someone tried to help them, and if so, where were the rest of the bodies? Why weren't they frozen on board?

The general consensus among the group was that there had been some kind of mutiny, perhaps after the ship was marooned, and a blood bath incurred. Where the survivors, if any, had ended up was unknown, but certainly the ship had sailed a crew larger than the dead men they found. Perhaps they had struck out to find what they could discover, or escape whoever, or whatever, was killing them in that head-smashing fashion.

In another part of the ship, fishing tackle was located and fishing expeditions were sent out to cast heavy lines in the cold water, using small pieces of meat for bait, and in time, the intestines from landed fish, or smaller fish, were hooked and put back in the water as bait. Fish near the ice seemed ravenous, and they successfully pulled large catches from the icy waters, cut them up, and cooked them in the great galley stove. With a reasonable supply of renewable food somewhat assured, the spirits of all involved increased.

This went on for a few days, the meals alternating between the meat in the galley and the fish from the sea, and then Amelia said she wanted to explore, see if there were other things they could use from the ice-locked ships, and so after a night of high wind and blowing snow, she and Gavin started out on an expedition. The daylight sky seemed as odd as the night sky had been, though the storm had long blown out. The sunlight was somewhat green on the horizon and cool yellow above them, like a light doughy crust on the sky.

Another point of contention, which had first been addressed by Carruthers, was the fact that there was day and night. It seemed logical, considering the ice, that they might well be at a point on the globe where night reigned for long periods before giving way to daylight for equally long stretches. But that wasn't the case here. Day came with its strange green and yellow tints and an anemic red-hazed sun that soon turned egg-yolk yellow. Day gave it up within hours to thick, blue-black darkness with a greasy moon that appeared to wobble when not being observed directly. The stars moved in great swirls, as if the earth and all the darkness and pulsing orbs were slowly traveling toward an exit by cosmic drain. None of this fit the fact that they had been crossing a calm and warm ocean the night before, but another weird factor was no one could remember ever having boarded the ship, and they could only remember vagaries of the trip, some events on board, drinks and dancing. Trying to discuss this led to a lot of quiet moments. No one remembered where they were going, or why they had chosen to be at sea, or for that matter, none could even remember if they were crossing the Atlantic or the Pacific. Atlantic seemed more likely to lead them to ice, still no one knew for sure. It was a distressing fact that could only be discussed briefly. It was like trying to remember what had happened in the womb.

Gavin carried the pistol with him, though he wasn't sure it worked. He didn't see any reason to need it, but it made him feel better somehow.

They looked where they had dropped the body of their comrade over the side of the ship with the long-dead sailors, but no bodies were there. Something had taken them away. Polar bears? So far nothing of the sort had been seen. There were no tracks and no drag marks, but considering the constantly blowing wind and renewing ice, as well as blankets of snow, there was nothing unusual about that.

After walking for a time, they began to feel certain they were not on an iceberg at all, but a large mass of ice that stretched far to the horizon. There were ships locked into it here and there, and some of the ships were more modern. Dog sleds were found, buried in the ice, and finally they came upon a prop airplane, blood red in color. It seemed to have landed smoothly and sat there as if ready for takeoff. The exception being the wheels, which were sunk into the ice. Its nose was lifted upward, the tail was resting on the ice. In the far background, mountains, tinged puke green by the light, rose up high and misty. As they stared at them, they appeared to move, ever so slightly.

"How can that be?" Amelia said. "Moving mountains?"

"A mirage," Gavin said. "The movement part, anyway."

"Sure looked like it moved. It was subtle, but I saw it."

"Me too, but mountains don't move. Has to be a trick of the light… But the plane, it's here. It's an Electra. Late thirties or forties, I'm reasonably sure. My father owned one. Or one very similar. No expert, but I'm a little knowledgeable on recognizing a few of them. My dad also had models of a lot of other kinds of planes. So I was aware of certain things about them without really being highly knowledgeable."

"Can you fly?"

"Well, unlikely it could fly. Probably froze up. I only have a general idea how it's done. You know, from listening to my dad. And it would only comfortably carry two. Of course, those two could be us. Even so, I'd probably manage, at best, to run it into the sea, or take it up and have it come down too fast and on the nose."

Amelia let the thought of flying away with Gavin run around in her head. She owed the others nothing. Still, it seemed like a rotten thing to contemplate.

She examined the plane, saw that the hatch door was flung open. It had steps leading from the door to the ground. She walked up them and stuck her head inside.

"Jesus," she said. "It's warm in here. How could that be?"

Gavin climbed the steps and looked in. He stepped inside beside her. "It's more than warm, it's been flown. The motor has only been off a short time, that's why it's warm in here, even with the door open. Engine heat."

"That means someone just left it," Amelia said.

They went outside and looked around. No sign of anyone. They prowled the outside of the plane, gently touched its underbelly. No doubt. Gavin was right. The engine was warm.

"How can that be?" Amelia said, moving her hand away from the plane.

"Just because it's from another era doesn't mean it hasn't been kept in good condition, even flown recently by some plane enthusiast. But how anyone would end up way out here in a small plane like that is hard to guess."

"Where's the pilot?" Amelia said.

"They may have force landed here, fuel or weather reasons. A number of possibilities. Engine trouble, perhaps. They went outside to look about, trying to figure things out, same as us, or deciding to pee, when the storm hit. Remember how fast that storm came? I was looking at that crack in the ship. The sky was clear. I could see the moon. And then there was a moan of storm and a blow of snow, and the sky went white. It happened in the time it takes to blink. The pilot could have been trapped outside and unable to make it back to the plane. They might have been covered by snow, iced over. Hell, we could be standing on them. Or they stumbled off blind, walked into a snowbank or the sea. It would be easy to become lost in a storm like that."

"Could be," Amelia said. "Think about how we ended up here. We were fine on our ship one minute, and the next, we weren't."

"Warm, clear seas, and then some place full of ice," Gavin said.

"Exactly. And we don't even know why we were on the ship, how we got there."

"I thought it would come back to me. Thought we were all in shock. Now, I'm not so sure. What I am sure of is things aren't right here, Amelia. All these ships and planes. It's as if they all went through some hole and ended up here. Maybe a hundred years ago, maybe five minutes ago."

The wind swirled particles of snow. It seemed chill enough to freeze an open flame.

Amelia tugged her scarf tight over her mouth and the tip of her nose. "Why are we standing here? Let's get inside the plane for a while."

They stepped inside, closed the door against the wind and the cold. Already the warmth was dying.

Prowling the front of the plane, in a pocket by the controls, Amelia found a small revolver. It was loaded with five rounds.

"Now we're both armed, in case we're attacked by a seabird," Amelia said.

"I think there's a lot more than seabirds to fear out here," Gavin said. "At first I didn't think so, but now I wonder. More I think about it, the more worried I am. Maybe those ships haven't been here as long as it seems."

"The hole in time idea?"

"Something like that."

"Right now I'm not ruling anything out," Amelia said.

They looked about. There were a few clothes in the plane and a small mattress. They searched for anything usable, but found nothing other than the gun, and a sweater that Amelia took with her as they left, slipping it on and then putting her coat back on over it. It gave her a bulky appearance, but the sweater was flexible beneath the coat, and she was warmer. They found a flight manual, a couple of hardback books, but nothing else. They left it all.

At the view glass, they looked out at the sky. It had turned azure and there were strange strips of yellow and gold leaking into it, and even as they watched those gave way to blue then black. Amelia said, "The sky's colors are always changing."

"Nothing seems right here," Gavin said.

The moon appeared like a blister, high and full, ready to pop. The stars were plentiful, but it was as if a hand had stirred them into new formations. They were of varying sizes, like coins and pinheads tacked to the heavens. There were large numbers of jetting streaks, shooting stars, red, blue, and green, and variations of those colors. Amelia was reminded of schools of bright darting fish in an inky pond.

They decided it was best to return. The night was bright, and in time the plane would grow cold. So out they went, carefully stepping onto the moon-glared ice.

Using ships and sleds they had passed before as their guides, they made their way back to the ship where their companions waited. The wind kicked up, and the already intense cold became nearly unbearable. Tugging the collars of their coats tight around their necks, wrapping their scarves around their heads like bandages, leaving only their eyes visible, they continued. Snow was as thick as exploded goose down blown loose from a pillow.

They stumbled forward, trying their best to keep an eyeline back to their ship. Now and then there was a gap in the blowing snow, and it gave them an occasional glimpse of a recognizable ice formation, but those kinds of things could change quickly, reshaped by snow and wind.

Amelia tripped over one of the dog sleds they had encountered earlier. As she was rising, the wind and blowing snow shifted, and she saw moving in the brief gap of white, a naked man wearing a strange and oversized headdress. The head gear was flapping and blowing in the wind with the frantic movements of a bird with its feet tied to the ground. It was visible for an instant, then gone.

"Did you see that?" Amelia said.

"Hardin," Gavin said. "It was Hardin."

"Naked? Wandering through snow? How could that be?"

"How could it be anyone?"

They tried to see Hardin again, but the snow had wrapped him up and hidden him away.

"What was he wearing on his head?" she asked.

"No idea."

"Should we try and find him?"

Gavin shook his head. "We are lost ourselves. And remember, he didn't want to be found. Maybe he stripped down to die quicker."

"But he's been out here for days now."

"Perhaps he holed up somewhere for a while before he made his final move."

"So he hung out, then today stripped naked, put on a weird head-dress, and wandered out in the snow?"

"Hell. I don't know, Amelia. I know what you know."

They found themselves, without discussing it, moving away from where Hardin had been seen, heading away from the direction he had taken. Trudging on for some distance, they ran up against the wall of a ship. They immediately knew it was not their ship. Its wood was black and tarred where there had been repairs. They found it too high to access by normal means, but near the bow they discovered there was a crude ladder, and though it was slippery, they managed it, and climbed on board.

The interior of the ship was a brief respite from the blowing wind and snow.

They combed the ship. No food supplies or frozen bodies were found. The crew had obviously abandoned the sailing rig, taking whatever was edible with them, as well as stripping it of furniture and the like. Most likely to make sleds to drag their goods, or to provide firewood. The vessel seemed to be from a similar era as the ship where their group had ended up. The lifeboats had been removed, and Amelia wondered if they had made it to somewhere safe by sea, or were they dead on the ice, preserved like frozen sardines with the tops of their heads torn open? And how long ago did this ship arrive here?

"You know what's odd," Amelia said. "In the back of my mind I feel like I know the answer to this, or a piece of it, but I just can't get that answer to surface."

"I know exactly what you mean," Gavin said.

In the back of the ship's hold they found a mass of blankets, and they covered themselves in them, pulling them over their heads, and then they laid on others, and listened to the snow blast about outside. Cold air came through cracks in the ship and licked at them, but the stack of blankets warmed them, and they lay there reveling in the warmth.

Snuggled close together, and without suggestion, they touched noses. They lay in silence for a while, and then Amelia reached out and touched Gavin, and then Gavin touched her, and then their lips pressed together. They pulled at one another's clothes, and for a time they were all right beneath the mass of blankets, wriggling into each other, as if trying to be absorbed by the other's warmth.

When they were finished they lay panting beneath the blankets, as snug and comfortable as they had been since landing in the wet ocean, and then on the ice.

"Guess we needed that," Amelia said.

"Needed and wanted," Gavin said.

Amelia nestled into Gavin's arms. He was strong. She could feel the muscles in his arm beneath her neck.

"The wind has stopped," Amelia said.

"Now we're back to living in the real world. Or the unreal world. Whatever the hell kind of world we are in. Look. I think the smartest thing would be, when the storm calms, we go back to our ship, bring rope, use one of the dog sleds to drag lumber back for firewood. You know, chop it out of this one with the axe. We can mount expeditions that can take us farther, the way you suggested. Figure out some way to make tents, devise heating vessels to take with us. Go as far as we can, using our ship as base."

"We will need to make snowshoes to travel long distances," Amelia said. "I think we can figure out how to do that. There's a lot of odds and ends on board our ship. And to go back to my theme, seeing what's out there is better than waiting to freeze, or eventually starving."

"I've come to agree," Gavin said. "Especially now that I have another reason to live."

Amelia touched his face and kissed him. "You mean me, right?"

Gavin laughed. "Of course. But listen, girl. I'm willing to try and see what we can find, but to be honest, I don't expect that within a few miles we will come to green grass and cows grazing in a pasture."

"We could try my other plan, use one of the lifeboats, rig a sail of some sort. Try and find land. Land that isn't freezing. Land where someone lives and things make sense. I know. I've suggested it before, and no one has been keen on the idea, but it's still something to consider."

"I'd rather die on the ice than in some boat on a black-ass sea."

"I'd rather not die," Amelia said. "Period."

"A fine sentiment," Gavin said. "But for the time being we have food at the ship, and we can carry some of these blankets with us to add to our store there. Later we can come back for more, bring some of the others so we can tote more supplies."

"Provided we can get them to leave the ship to do anything but fish."

"Food from the sea has proven reasonably certain," Gavin said. "What's out here beyond the ships, toward the mountains, there's nothing certain about that."

The snow quit swirling and the wind ceased to howl. Moonlight speared through the cracks in the ship. They dressed and climbed off the ship and started walking again. The night was clear and bright, so bright it was as if they were walking under a giant streetlamp. The wind had left snow piled on the ice. As they walked, they came across footprints—bare footprints.

Amelia said, "Hardin?"

"Possibly."

They went surely in the direction of their ship, able to see landmarks now—ships and sleds and juts of ice they recognized that were close to their destination. Before long they came to a broad snowbank, and lying in it was Hardin.

He was facedown and there was blood on the snow, it had crystallized like ruby jewels and smears of strawberry jam.

Amelia bent down and looked close at Hardin. Finally, with help from Gavin, she rolled him over. It was difficult, and Hardin made a ripping sound as the ice tore away from his flesh. His mouth was open, his eyes were wide. He had died with his nostrils flared, like a horse blowing air. High on his forehead was a tear in his skull, wide and deep.

"He looks terrified," Gavin said.

"Yes, and look here."

There were drag marks in the blood. There were places in the snow that gave the impression of an octopus wriggling, and then the places grew larger, and finally there was a great shape in the snow. It was a cylindrical shape with a large star at the top. There were thrash marks in the snow all around it. They could see marks where it had crawled off across the snow, its size swelling.

"Whatever it was," Amelia said. "It grows rapidly."

"And it came out of Hardin's head."

"Or attached itself to him. What in hell does that?"

"I don't know, but here's another thing," Gavin said. "He walked."

"Perhaps not on his own power," she said.

"That's insane."

"You saw what was on his head. Some kind of parasite. He may have been dead for days, moving around, but not truly alive, being fed on and articulated like a puppet by that monster."

"All right, but the question has to be, what does this parasite feed on normally if humans aren't in supply?"

"Seals. Sea life. Maybe it's sea life itself, comes on shore from time to time, but exists in the waters as well. Maybe it eats what it eats because it's there to eat, not because it needs it for sustenance. Something left that imprint, and whatever it is, is certainly not human."

They traveled on, tingling with unease. They felt as if they were being watched, but when they looked, nothing was there. Just mounds of snow, a few juts of ice in the peculiar moon and starlight. Still, the persistent feeling of being observed moved with them, and with it came a strange feeling of nausea, as if they were breathing air that had been disgorged by something foul, a primitive perception that something primal and dangerous was nearby.

"Suddenly I'm hoping this pistol works," Gavin said, pulled it from his pocket and held it in his gloved hand.

Amelia followed suit with the pistol she had found in the plane.

They trudged along with their pistols, and walking near the waterline, they saw a lifeboat banging up against the ice.

"It's Lifeboat Number Three," Amelia said. "It washed up here."

"Well, I never want to be in it again," Gavin said. "I hate water."

"And you took a trip on a ship?"

"Thought I might meet women."

Amelia laughed. "That part worked."

As they watched, the dark waters caught up the boat and moved it out into the night. The moonlight coated the lifeboat in silver paint, and they watched until it bobbed up and down and out of sight, as if hiding behind the waves.

They continued until their ship was in sight, then tucked their guns away. When they climbed the ice at the stern and stepped on board, they found a sheet of dark ice running from the bridge to the stairs that led to the hold. The ship was as quiet as a snail's progress.

"That looks like blood," Amelia said, pushing back her jacket hood, unwinding the scarf over her face. Gavin pushed his own hood back, pulled down his scarf.

They pulled their pistols again, followed the dark trail, crept down the stairs, trying not to slip on the ice. At the bottom of the stairs they encountered cold, though not freezing cold. There were remnants of warmth from human bodies and a near-dead fire in the small stove below. The coals glowed weakly through ash and semi-devoured chunks of wood formerly belonging to what might have been a chifferobe.

There was a clank toward the back of the hold, in the shadows, and Amelia and Gavin hesitated, then eased in that direction, pistols at the ready.

Movement.

Something running in the dark.

Gavin said, "Hey folks. It's us."

A flash of shadows, something whirling in the dark, catching moonbeams from a crack in the hold. A flutter of rubbery movement atop something, and then it was gone.

Amelia turned to the right where she heard a faint sound, saw nothing, then turned completely around.

That's when a shadow broke loose and darted into the moonlight, came for Amelia with a shriek and a flash of tentacles.

It was Duchess, or what she had been. Her head was broken open and a great mass of writhing tentacles flapped from her skull. A bladder shape dangled out of a wide crack in her forehead, and the bladder almost covered her eyes. She was stripped of clothing. Her saggy breasts flapped like something skinned. Her hands were reaching, her mouth was screeching.

Just as Duchess reached her, Amelia lifted the pistol and shot her in the face, right above the bridge of the nose, right below the wide crack in her skull. Duchess's hands brushed Amelia's shoulders and a black mess came from the bladder inside her skull, squished out and into the moonlight in one long squirt. The beast in Duchess's head tore loose from its cranial house, flipped through the air, smashed against the deck, began to puff and swell like a bagpipe.

Duchess's lifeless body collapsed in a heap at Amelia's feet. The thing on the floor hissed, then squeaked, and then revealed an extended torso that slid slickly out of the bladder like a fat rat from a greased pipe. Its body was tubular and long with a star-fish head. It swelled as it slithered. Sucker-covered tentacles extended from the cylindrical portion of its body, slapped at the floor and waved in the fat slit of moonlight as if trying to grab the moon's attention.

Amelia stepped close and shot the star-head. Tentacles snapped out, smacked the top of her hand, nearly knocking the gun loose, leaving a circular welt, red and inflamed, just above her thumb. It made a gaseous sound and slid greasily across the floor as if pulled on a rope, collapsed, tentacles falling and flailing like electrified noodles.

Amelia heard Gavin's gun snap without firing, snap again. Amelia turned and shot at what was charging across the floor at them, Cyril, his head broken open, giving ride to one of the tentacle-bearing bladders. She shot directly for the bladder this time, and when she did, the black goo went up and out, darker than the shadows around it. Cyril stumbled as if he had stepped into a hole, fell facedown, his naked ass humping up in the air once, then collapsing, his pelvis slamming against the floor. The creature detached from Cyril, scuttled away. Amelia was about to shoot again, but Gavin stopped her.

"Save the shot," he said. He tossed his useless pistol aside. There was an axe near the stove, one they had used to shatter wood for burning. Gavin grabbed it, swung it into the creature, chopping the star-head loose, causing a dark mess to gush across the floor.

"Jesus," Amelia said. "What are those things?"

Gavin trembled. "I'm going to guess nothing known to science."

Gavin made his way to the stove, picked up the matches that lay on the floor nearby, scooped out a partly lit stick of wood from the stove, waved it about in the cold air until it flamed slightly. Amelia, all the while, was turning with her pistol, watching. She had one shell left, as the revolver had only housed five loads. Gavin's gun was useless, packed as it was with ineffectual loads.

Gavin wagged the small torch about. In the shadows they saw a heap of nude bodies. The remains of their lifeboat companions. Cautiously, Amelia and Gavin moved nearer. All of the heads were broken open, but none contained their former passengers. Carruthers lay on top. All of them were nude. Either their clothes had been ripped from them by the creatures, or they had torn them loose themselves, as if the things made their bodies boil.

Something clattered in the dark.

They turned. Gavin lifted the small torch. Creatures fluttered in the light and hustled away. Nothing was seen distinctly.

"They're all over the place," Gavin said.

"We have to go," Amelia said. "Right now."

Gavin dropped the torch, and carrying the axe at a battle-ready position, he and Amelia rushed up the steps, onto the deck, and over the side where the ice was high. They scrambled so quickly they fell into one another and slid down the ice in a tumble. At the bottom of their fall, they looked up. There, on the deck, were the things, tentacles waving about like drunks saying howdy. The creatures pushed together. At first Amelia thought it was for warmth, and then she thought: No, they live here. They endure here.

As they watched, the things came together, tighter. There was a great slurping sound, and then they hooked together and twisted and writhed and became one large, bulbous shape with a multitude of heads and an array of tentacles. It started to edge over the side of the ship.

Amelia and Gavin began to run.

They ran along the snow-flecked ice, falling from time to time, and when they looked back, they saw the thing dropping off the side of the ship, falling a goodly distance, striking the ice heavily, and then rolling and gliding after them.

The snow began to flurry again. It blew down from the sky in a white funnel. It spread wide and wet against them, pushed them like a cold, damp hand. They wound their scarves around their mouths as they ran, pulled their hoods down tight, only looked back when they feared it might be at their very heels, but soon it was lost to them, disappearing within a swirling surge of blinding snow.

Winded, they began to trudge, having no idea where they were heading. Without snowshoes, it was a hard trek. Eventually they came to the plane, its bright red skin flaring up between the swirling flakes of snow. They stood and stared at it.

"I'm so cold I don't care if that thing catches up with me," Gavin said. "I've got to get warm. If only for a little while."

Amelia nodded. "Yeah. That thing can have me, but only if I get a bit warm first."

They slipped inside, having to really tug the door free this time, the whole machine having been touched with frost. They closed the door and locked it. They moved to the cockpit and looked out. There was nothing to see. Just snow. It had ceased to flurry as violently as before, but it was still blowing.

After a brief rest, Amelia looked around the plane, more carefully this time, found a few rounds of overlooked ammunition, enough to fill her pistol. There was a flare gun they had not found in their initial search, and there were four flares in a box beneath the cockpit. Gavin took the flare gun and loaded a flare in it. It wasn't a perfect weapon, but it was something. Gavin stuck the remaining flares in his coat pocket. Finally, exhausted, they laid down on the mattress together, and without meaning to, fell asleep.

At some point, much later, Amelia thought she heard a kind of coughing, and then a loud growl. She tried to awake, but exhaustion held her. If the things were on her, then they could have her. She was warm and exhausted by fear. She couldn't move a muscle.

Shortly the growling ceased, and Amelia drifted back down into deep sleep. Down in that dark well of exhaustion she sensed a darkness even more complete. Things moved in the dark, bounded about inside her head. Images struck her like bullets, but then they were gone, unidentified. It was a sensation of some terrible intelligence, a feeling of having a hole in the fabric of reality through which all manner of things could slip. She slept deep down in that crawling dark, but yet, it was still a deep sleep and in time even the horrors down there in her dreams let her be.

When Amelia awoke, Gavin was missing.

Or so she thought. She sat up. He was sitting in the pilot chair in the cockpit. It was daylight. She went to join him, sat in the co-pilot chair. Gavin had a manual in his lap and was reading.

"No monsters yet?" she said.

"I think we lost them, confused them, or they're taking a nap. I don't know. You know what? I can fly this. Theoretically, anyway."

"Will it fly?"

"The engine was warm not that long ago. It hasn't been ruined by the cold yet. While you slept, I tried it. After a few false starts it fired. "

Amelia realized this was what she had heard while sleeping. Not the roar of some monster, but the roar of a machine.

"I think it hasn't been in the cold so long the engine is ruined, frozen up. It's cold, though. I think the pilot was driven down by a sudden storm. Nothing in the sky one moment, the next a storm. They probably flew here through some dimensional gap, the way we sailed here in the ship. Slipped right through, like a child's toy through a crack in the floor."

"Then why haven't you flown us out, if you're so sure you can do it."

"I'm not all that sure, actually. Like I said, theoretically, I can fly us out. I cut the engine because I could tell it was stuttering. I wanted it to warm a bit more, or rather I have plans to warm it, and running it before it's warmer would just use up gas, and I couldn't see to fly anyway. I couldn't see six inches in front of me. I got started, though. While you slept I used a board and dug around the wheels, freed them. Wore me out. I'm going to build a fire out front of the plane to warm it more. It might ruin things, catch the damn plane on fire, or it might improve things. I don't know. But if the storm passes, as the daylight comes, the sun will warm the engine and then I'll warm it with a bit of fire."

"A bit of fire might be too much fire. Why not just let the sun warm it?"

"It will be warmer, but it won't be warm," Gavin said. "The sun will need some help."

"That would be the fire," Amelia said.

Gavin nodded. "If it's warm, then we might fly out. For all I know I won't be able to fly it at all. Or I'll manage to get it up, only to have it come right back down. Or say I get it up and we fly away. Where are we flying too? How much fuel do we have? Still, what else is there? You with me?"

"Get us up, and fly us out," Amelia said. "You can do it. Any place is better than here."

It seemed like a long time, sitting in the cockpit waiting for daylight. Sitting there expecting the monsters to arrive and break through the plane and knock holes in their heads, cause them to tear off their clothes and turn them into naked staggering corpses. They sat back and waited for light, but it was a nervous wait.

The wind died down, the snow blew out, and the daylight finally came. The sun looked at first like a gooey hot-pink lozenge. It turned slowly from pink to orange, spread light like a hot infection across the horizon.

Amelia and Gavin dragged the mattress outside, under the front of the plane, cut it open with the axe. The cotton stuffing inside sprang up through the splits. They piled debris from inside the plane on top of that. They tore pages from the books they had discovered, and used them for tinder. Gavin used the matches he had taken from the ship to light the pages. Gradually the flames caught, sputtered, began to eat the tinder and the pages. They watched the pile burn, and watched for any tentacle-bearing visitors that might show.

When the fire was licking at the bottom of the plane, they went inside and waited. Gavin said, "Here's to no unfortunate explosions."

"I agree," Amelia said.

They touched their fists as if they held drinks in their hands.

They watched as the flames grew and licked up around the nose, saw the paint start to bubble and flake.

"I think it's time," Gavin said.

Gavin tried turning the engine over.

It did nothing at first. And then it coughed, and then it died, and then Gavin tried again. It coughed again, started to die, but clung to life, blurted and chugged, and then began to roar. Eventually, it began to hum.

Gavin took another look at the manual, which he had again placed in his lap, said, "Let me see now."

"That does not inspire confidence," Amelia said.

"All right. I got this. Mostly."

Gavin touched the controls, managed to move the plane, rock it along on its wheels, veer it to the right, away from the direction of the fire and the sea. Then he gunned it. It rolled and slid on the ice. As they rattled forward on the slick surface, it seemed as if the plane might come apart.

But there were worse things happening. They saw it coming across the ice, the star-heads united into one fat star-head, a hunk of dark meat coated in sun-glimmered slime with pulsing bladders and thrashing tentacles. Somehow it had found them, heard them perhaps, seen the fire. It was directly in their path.

"Ah hell," Gavin said.

He worked the controls, turned the plane a little, moving to the left of the creature.

Now Gavin turned again, placing the creature at the rear of the plane. The plane slipped and wobbled, but continued to rush over the ice.

"I forget how to lift," Gavin said.

"What?"

"I forget how to lift off. Damn. I just read it."

Amelia grabbed the manual. "All right, let me see... No that's how to land."

"The ice ends."

"What?"

Amelia looked up. The ice sheet had a drop off, and the drop off was jagged and deep.

"Turn," she said. "Turn the goddamn plane."

Gavin turned to his left, the wheels managing to stay on the ice, but not without sliding. They could see the creature again from this position, out the side window. It was rising up and smashing down on the ice, throwing up crushed sparkles like fragments of shattered glass, then it inched forward with the flexibility of a caterpillar, rising up again, smashing down, repeating the method, traveling at surprising speed. The plane was moving away from it, though, gaining speed and gaining space.

"Okay. The throttle," Amelia said. "Listen to me, now. Do what I say."

Slowly and loudly she read out the instruction booklet. Gavin following them as well as he understood them, the machine lifting up, then coming down on the wheels, bouncing, slipping, yet moving forward. Not too distantly in front of them were large snowbanks.

"It's now or never," Gavin said.

Amelia read from the manual, and Gavin, listening intently, did as he was told, trying to be careful about it, trying to cause the plane to rise.

The plane jumped up into the frosty air like a flame-red moth, into the richly dripping sunlight. Below, the white face of the earth shimmered and the montage monster hastened across it, lifted its great starred head toward the vanishing plane, its shadow falling down behind it to lie dark on the ice. It cried out loud enough to be heard even inside the speeding plane, then the beast fell apart. The creatures from which it had been constructed came unstuck and collapsed against the ice, their multitude of shadows falling with them.

The plane sailed on.

For a time, Amelia and Gavin coasted in the sun-rich sky, over the ice, toward a green haze drifting above jagged mountain peaks.

Gavin tipped the wheel, the nose lifted, and the plane sailed up. When he was as high as he felt he could comfortably go, he leveled out. The mist, white and foamy as mad-dog froth, parted gently. Below them were wet mountaintops, and straight before them were higher mountains tipped by clouds. To the right of those peaks was a V-shaped gap.

"There," Amelia said, pointing at the gap. "Go there."

"You know I don't really know how to fly, right?"

"You know enough," Amelia said. "You learned more from your dad than you thought, and that manual. We're up here, aren't we? Go there."

Gavin tilted the plane to the right, then settled it, set a nose-aligned course for the gap in the mountains. Shortly, they were in the center of the gap, mountains on either side of them. When they came to the other side there was a valley of ice and snow, and far to the left there was the darkness of the great waters. Directly before them were more mountains, and above those a green mist shimmered with sunlight. They saw something on the ice directly below them that took their breath away.

There were spires, golden and silver, and what could have been thick glass or ice, great structural rises of wicked geometry. Littered before the structures, in a kind of avenue, were what looked to be white humps of stones.

"My god," Gavin said. "A city. The place is enormous."

"How could those things build this?"

"Most likely they didn't," Gavin said. "But whoever built it, built it while drunk."

And on and on the city stretched, toward the blue-black mountains tipped by what looked like a green fungus.

As they neared them, Amelia felt as if a great presence was moving behind the sky and sliding down and into her thoughts. It was the same as during her sleep in the plane, but more intense. In fact, it was painful, even nauseating. She felt stuffed with thought and information she couldn't define.

They flew above the irregular city, watching with awe. When they finally passed over it and the rocky avenue, Gavin turned the plane for a return pass, and when he did, the plane coughed, sputtered, and started going down.

"Out of fuel," Gavin said.

"Priceless," Amelia said.

"I'll try and glide it."

There was a stretch of ice beyond the avenue, and as the plane began to spit and sputter and hurry down, Gavin leveled it, cruised over the avenue toward the ice. It was not a perfect plan, but they were less likely to catch the wheels in the rocks and flip.

Gavin said, "I'm pretty sure I can land it." His hands trembled at the controls.

"No doubt, one way or another you will," Amelia said.

The plane's engines sputtered and died.

Gavin did his best to glide it down and smooth it out for a landing, but the plane was moving fast and he was uncertain what to do. Amelia read frantically aloud from the instruction manual. She was reading it when they came within twenty feet of the ice. She stopped reading then. There was nothing else left to say, and no time to say it.

The plane came down on the ice and the wheels touched. The plane bounced, way up, then back down, went into a sideways skid, and then Gavin lost control and the nose dipped and hit the ice, and the plane spun and started coming apart.

The cold brought Amelia around. She could see the sky. It was odd, that sky. She thought she was seeing reflections off the ice, but instead she was looking as through a transparent wall. She could see people walking, riding horses, clattering about in wagons, cars of all eras driving, boats sailing and planes flying. There was depth to her view. People stacked on top of one another as they walked, drove, flew, or sailed. People floated by, sleeping in their beds, and there were the star-head things, and monstrous, unidentifiable visions, and all the images collided and passed through one another like ghosts. She was flooded with the soul-crushing realization that she was less than a speck of dust in the cosmos. The knowledge of her insignificance in the chaotic universe overwhelmed her with sadness and self-pity. Whatever was out there not only had a physical presence, it had a powerful presence in her unconscious, a place where it revealed itself more and more.

She awoke with something warm and wet running down her face. She lifted her hand and opened her eyes. She saw blood was on her gloved fingers. There were tears in her eyes. She touched the wound on her head. Not bad she determined, a scrape.

The sensation passed. She tried to sit up, only to realize she was in the plane seat, and it was lying with its back on the ice, and she was lying in it. It had come free of the plane and she was sliding along the ice with it.

She rolled out of the chair, put her gloved hands on the ice, got her knees under her and stood up. She wobbled. There was wreckage strewn across the ice. There was a vast churn of rising black smoke. Gavin came walking out of the smoke and into the clear carrying the axe he had taken from the ship, and now recovered from the wreckage of the plane. His face was bloody and blackened from smoke, he had a limp, but he was alive.

As they came together and embraced, Gavin said, "Told you I could land it."

They both laughed. It was a hearty laugh, a bit insane really.

"What now?" Amelia said.

"I think we have no other choice than the city. Out here we'll freeze. The wind is picking up, and it's damp, so if nothing else we have to get out of the wind."

"It's chancy."

"So is being out here. No shelter. No food. No plane."

They looked toward one of the buildings, a scrambled design of spires and humps, silver and gold, or so it had seemed from the sky. Now they could see that the light had played on it in a peculiar way, giving it a sheen of colors it did not entirely possess.

"Very well, then," Amelia said, and holding hands they started toward the structures.

They came to the rocky, white road, discovered the lumps were not stones, but skulls and bones, all of the skeletal parts pushed into the ice by time. There were animal skulls and bones amidst human bones and skulls, long and narrow skulls, wide and flat skulls, vertebrae of all manner were in the bone piles, many impossible to identify, some huge and dinosaur-like.

Amelia glanced at the city buildings, which stretched to one side as far as the eye could see, and to the other until they reached the sea. She stared at the building before them, saw it was connected to others by random design. It was hard to figure a pattern.

The wind whistled and hit them like a scythe of ice.

"You're right," she said. "We have to go inside."

They made their way inside the city.

■ ■ ■

It was warmer inside. No wind, and there seemed to be a source of heat. They didn't notice that until they were well inside and found the path beneath the structure divided and twisted into a multitude of narrow avenues, like a maze. The floor was smooth, but not slick, and the walls were the same.

Gavin marked the walls with the axe as they went, forming a Hansel and Gretel escape path. Soon they unwound their scarves and let them hang, they removed their gloves and stuffed them in coat pockets and loosed the top buttons on their shirts. It was comfortably warm.

They were eventually overtaken by exhaustion. Amelia said, "We should rest while we have the opportunity. I think I may be more banged-up than I first realized."

"We don't know what's inside this place," Gavin said.

"We know that right this minute we are okay. There is nothing more we can know in this place, and I don't know about you, but being in the cold, flying in an airplane with an untrained pilot, crash landing on the ice, has tuckered me a little."

Gavin chuckled. "Yeah. I'm pretty worn."

They stopped and leaned against the wall, stuck their feet out. The warmth inside the structure was pleasurable. It was like a nice down blanket, though there was a faint foul smell.

"I had this vision, of sorts," Amelia said. "Or maybe I actually saw something."

"Vision? Worlds and animals and people and things stacked on one another, flowing through one another. A feeling of… miasma."

"You too?"

"Yeah. I don't know what I was seeing exactly, but when I awoke it was in my head. I feel better awake than asleep, like out here I can see what is happening, but inside of my dreams I can feel what is happening, and it's worse."

"Like a truth was trying to be revealed?"

"Yeah," Gavin said. "Like that, and it was like my primitive brain understood it, but my logical brain couldn't wrap itself around it. Like the answer was in sight, but on a shelf too high for my mind to reach."

"Oh, I think I know. I think you know. Our minds know what's there on that shelf now, they just don't want to reach up and take hold of it. Don't want to know that truth. You see, Gavin, I think we saw a glimpse of the in-betweens."

"In-betweens?" he said, but she could tell it was mostly a rhetorical question. He knew exactly what she was talking about. She could see it in his eyes.

"Talking out loud," she said, "it's like finding a footstool and being able to reach that high shelf. What if there's a crack in our subconscious that allows us, from time to time, to slip from what we perceive as our own life, into a nightmare of sorts. One that's real. Not dream logic altogether, but a real place that we perceive as a nightmare, but sometimes it's more than that. A dimensional hole, like you suggested. We sometimes pass through it, like the people and things you saw in your dream. Not by choice, but by chance. The hole is there, and the right dream and the right time, well, we fall through. Or we're pulled through."

"Yeah," Gavin said, picking up where she left off, really feeling it now. "We get pulled in. Our world, the one where we're lying in bed, is now the dream, and we can't get back. The hole closes, or we just can't find it. Maybe on our old world, we're one of those who unexpectedly dies in their sleep. But what is us now, the us in this dimension, we stay here and experience whatever it is we find here, and our other self truly dies. We have left the building back home, so to speak."

"Exactly," Amelia said. "The things that people see in nightmares, monsters. Perhaps they really see them. At a distance sometimes. See them, and then the dreamer slides back to where they belong. Sometimes they don't. And perhaps, sometimes it works the other way. What's on the other side seeps into our world like a kind of cosmic sewage."

Gavin interrupted her before she could speak another word.

"And us, and all the people on the ship, the others who came here, the pilot of the plane, we all fell through the same hole. We were having different dreams, but we all fell through, and then we were all having a similar dream. Some of us dreamed of a ship, and we all were on board, and the dream ship slipped through. Same for the plane, the other ships, and dog sleds. Say someone was traveling over the ice, an explorer for example, pulled by sled dogs, and that night he makes his tent and he dreams. Dreams himself into another dimension, this dimension, and the dogs go with him. Imagination becomes flesh and blood because he and his dream have passed through that dimensional hole. We've collectively dreamed ourselves into another reality. We've fallen into our subconscious and we can't get out. We have all found the same pit on the other side of the hole."

Amelia was silent for a long time before she spoke.

"As much as it can be explained, that's it. I feel it in my bones. Whatever is here in this horrid world is not just those star-heads, but something else of greater intelligence. Something that stands here waiting at the hole in our dreams, waiting for something or someone to slip through."

"To what purpose?"

Amelia reflected a moment, then, "It's like we're experiencing some eternal truth, and the horrid thing about it is, it's nothing wonderful. It's merely a place where we go and suffer. A sort of hell inside the mind that becomes solid. The Christian hell may not be Christian, but it may not be myth. And in our case, it's not fire on the other side, but ice."

"Maybe we can dream ourselves out," Gavin said.

"Do you feel that you can?"

Gavin shook his head. "No. I feel the gap to the other side has winked closed, and dreaming doesn't open it. Dreaming just makes you susceptible when the gap is open, is my guess. Dreaming here you just get tapped into by this intelligence, as you called it. It wants us, for whatever reason, but the reason isn't reasonable."

Amelia laughed. "That makes no sense."

"Because it isn't within our concept of logic. It wants what we can't understand. Things that would make no sense whatsoever to us. It feels hopeless."

"It's giving us the knowledge it wants us to have," Amelia said. "And only because it's a knowledge that fills us with defeat. And here's another thing, who says that knowledge is real? That may be part of its powers. It effects the mind, lets you imagine what it wants you to imagine. You can control it to a certain extent, but the closer you are to it, and we must be right on top of it, the stronger that power is. We have to decide not to let it defeat us with negative thoughts and uncomfortable revelations, because they may all be projection, and not reality."

"All right," Gavin said. "All right. We won't let it win."

They rested a while, and without meaning to, they slept. It came over them as if they had been drugged. They fought it but it won, and they dreamed. A dream of great darkness rising up to overwhelm them, swallow them down and take them away, chewing up flesh and sucking out souls, their little sparks of life force being sucked away into some horrid eternity even worse than where they were.

When they awoke, they saw no remedy to their problem other than to explore, plotting together to see if they could find and kill this thing that was wiggling in their brains. That was the plan. They would kill it. They had a gun and an axe, and Gavin still had the flare gun and flares in his coat pocket. They had something to fight with, and that meant they had a chance.

There was an array of irregular pathways that twisted and turned, and there were spears of light coming in through gaps in the structure, and the sunlight lit the halls and walls with enough intermittent illumination they could see clearly. They chose one of the pathways and followed it. It became narrow and low, and to exit it, they had to crawl on their hands and knees for some distance before it opened into a larger chamber. A smell like all the death and rot that had ever occurred wafted toward them in a hot, sticky stench. Gavin was overwhelmed by it, and threw up against the wall.

"Might want to step around that," he said, wiping his mouth.

"May have some to add to it," Amelia said.

They pulled their scarves around their noses and mouths and kept going. The chamber went wide, and then it went small. The stink intensified. They came to narrow halls again, and they kept going, not searching for anything in particular, but searching.

They arrived at a great drop off, wide and deep and full of stink, lit by cracks of light from above. Hanging over the pit, fastened there by a scarf to what looked like a dry hose running above her, was a woman. She was wearing khaki pants and a leather jacket. She wore pilot gear, goggles pushed up on her head, and tight on her skull was a leather cap with ear flaps. Her skin was yellow, and her neck was long. The meat was beginning to rot, speeded up by the hot stink rising from the pit beneath her. Her feet dangled over the great and stinking pit, and one boot was slipping free of her rotting flesh, soon to fall into the pit below.

"The pilot," Gavin said. "Has to be. She ended up here somehow, and it must have been too much for her. The things we felt she must have felt, that damn presence, force, whatever. She didn't have anyone to bolster her and give her strength. She was on her own, so she just quit."

Amelia nodded, looked down into the pit.

"What is that?"

There was very little light now, just a split of gold through a crack here and there, so Gavin put a flare in his gun, fired it downwards. It glowed bright, and then it hit something below and sputtered with a reddish glare. The pit was full of blackened meat and rotting guts and all manner of offal.

Slowly Amelia's face paled.

"What?" Gavin said, staring at her face in the rising glow of the flare.

"I've got it figured, Gavin, and it's worse than we thought. This isn't a building. This place isn't a city. Above, those aren't hoses. They're veins, or arteries. Down below, that's afterbirth. We're inside a corpse, a drying one. Like a huge mollusk. Don't you see, Gavin? Down below, that's a womb. The star-shaped things. They were born here. Look around. There aren't any corridors. Those are artery paths that we've walked through, chambers for organs. Not humanlike organs, but organ housings just the same. And this is the birth canal, and down below, the womb. The bones we saw outside, they're from this thing's digestive system, crapped out and onto the ground where they were dried by time and cold wind. Bones of humans and all manner of creatures that have ended up here. Those star-heads, they link up and grow, become solid at some point, don't separate anymore, and then they give birth and die, leaving these shells."

"You're sensing this?" Gavin asked.

"No. I'm speculating this, or you'd feel the same thing. Perhaps they're hermaphrodite. Once birth is completed, the host for the children dies. The replacements feed on what they can find. Maybe even their mother, or whatever this thing can be called. And then they feed on whatever comes through the dream hole. These aren't buildings in a city. These are the remains of dead creatures, and they have given birth and left their remains, and the cycle continues."

Gavin looked about. "Maybe," he said.

"I can't be absolutely sure I'm right, but close enough, I think. What I am certain of, is I don't think being here is a good idea. We are too close to whatever that primal power is, the thing we sense, the thing that pulls us in from our dreams, it's nearby. And that can't be good. We have to find food, drinkable water. And most important, I can't stand this stink anymore."

They went back the way they had come, following the axe scratches, seeking the exit, fearing the arrival of the star-heads.

The cold was almost welcome.

They moved along the bone walk, toward the mountains, choosing a central range that looked dark with dirt and green with foliage, but no sooner had they started out, then the central mountain range trembled. The stretch of the horizon trembled. The green mist that floated above the mountains was sucked back toward the peaks, as if inhaled, and then the mist was blown back out in a great whirling wad, as if by a sleeping drunk.

And then they understood.

There were no cities, and there were no mountains. Only giant, ir-regular-shaped shells of creatures. Old ones that had given birth. Some larger than others.

Some as big as mountain ranges that still lived and were most likely stuffed tight with new life being baked inside a womb, and in this case, a womb much larger than any of those that had made up the false city. For before them was a beast. Not a mountain, but an impossible slug. The flesh had yet to harden. It trembled like jello and it was vast.

The mountain trembled again, and then moved. Ever so slowly, but it moved. It was easy to outrun, of course. It inched its way along. It would take days for it to reach where they now ran. But they soon came up against the coal-black sea, stood on the shore with nowhere to go. Waves crashed in against the ice, flowing up to the toes of their boots. Gavin began to cry.

"It's all insane," he said. "That pilot was right after all."

Amelia touched his shoulder.

There was a banging to their left. It made them both jump. It was their old friend, Lifeboat Number Three. It had drifted away and back again, sailing crewless along the stretch of icy shore.

"Fate doesn't hate us after all," Amelia said.

Gavin laughed. He turned and looked back toward the mountain. It was difficult to tell it had moved. It seemed in the same place, but he knew it had. Tentacles, the size and length of four-lane highways, lifted off of the beast and snapped at the sky. They had appeared like rows of rock and dirt, but now they were revealed for what they were. The ice screeched with the monster's glacial progress.

Amelia ran to the boat, slipped on the ice, struggled to her feet and grabbed at it. The back end of it swung around, banging against the hard ice. Another few minutes and they would never have known it was there. It would have washed out to sea again.

Amelia held the boat and looked at Gavin.

"The oars are still in it."

Gavin hurried to join her. He smiled at her. She smiled back. And then the smile dropped off her face.

Coming much closer than the mountain were the star-heads that they had outdistanced. They were as one again, larger than before, but smaller by far than the mountainous monster. They moved much faster than their creator, slurping over the ice, tentacles flaring, mouths open, showing multitudinous teeth, licking at the air with a plethora of what might have been tongues.

"This can't be real," Gavin said. "It's a mad house. One mad thing and then another. I have to wake up."

"I'd rather not stay here and find out if it's a dream, Gavin. Come on. We have to go. Now."

They pushed the boat into the water and climbed aboard, pushed at the ice with the oars, shoved out into the dark and raging waters. They began to row savagely.

The star-head thing moved to the edge of the water and broke apart and its many bodies spilled into the waves.

Amelia and Gavin rowed wildly. The star-heads swam fast, cruising through the water, tentacles tucked. On they came, and soon Amelia and Gavin knew there was no chance of outdistancing them. Amelia pulled her pistol and waited. The star-heads loomed out of the sea, tentacles flashing, attempting to clutch. Amelia fired, time after time, wounded some, possibly killing others. The waters were slick with blood. Gavin swung the axe until it hung up in one of the creatures and was pulled from his grasp, taken away from him and carried into the sea.

For a moment the attack subsided. The pistol was empty. The spare loads she had found in the plane had been used. The axe was gone. There was only the flare gun. Gavin pulled it from his coat and laid it in the bottom of the boat. They clutched their oars as weapons, and waited. They were sitting at different ends of the boat, and they positioned themselves on their knees, ready to fight.

The star-heads came again, came in swarms of speeding bodies and whip-snapping tentacles. Amelia and Gavin swung the oars, slamming down on star-heads as they peeked up over the rim of the boat. Tentacles slapped about like limbs whipped by a violent storm. Amelia felt them brush her, burning her with their sucker mouths, but they failed to manage a solid grip. She frantically wiggled free and swung the oar, knocking them aside.

"Oh god," she heard Gavin say. She glanced back. One of the star-heads had risen up beside the boat and whip-snapped its tentacles around Gavin and his oar, causing it to lie against his chest; the paddle part of the oar pointed up as if in swordlike salute. The star-head dropped completely back into the water, its tentacles stretched out, and lifted Gavin up like a mother holding a young child on display.

Gavin stared down at Amelia as he was hoisted out of the boat and dangled above the water. Amelia leaned out and swung the oar, struck the tentacles with it, but they were too strong, their grip too tight. They continued to cling to Gavin.

Gavin's face was as bland and white as the ice. He ceased to struggle, dangled in the monster's grip. The tentacles coiled him close and pulled him away, took him down under with little more than a delicate splash.

Amelia began to scream at the beasts, as if bad language might frighten them. She continued to struggle, whipping the oar through the air, contacting other star-heads. They came in a horde now. Tentacles flicked everywhere, popped at her legs, snapped against her arms. The black water turned greasy with blood. Star-heads were grabbing at the boat from all sides, shaking it with their tentacles, trying to tear it apart or pull it down under. Gavin's head, minus his body, surfaced, rolled, and then was taken by a star-head's wide open mouth. As the thing started to jerk Gavin's head below, fins broke the surface of the water.

Sharks. A mass of them.

A great white leaped out of the waves, rolled its black eyes up inside its head as it snapped at the star-head's tentacles, pulled it and the remains of Gavin down with it. Sharks began to jump from the waves as easy as flying fish. They grabbed the star-heads in their toothy mouths, crunched them like dry toast, then pulled the remains of their squirming meals into the deeps.

More sharks came and went, like a pack of wolves, cutting through the blood-slick waters, snapping at the star-heads quickly, darting away and under, only to rise and circle back and strike again.

And then the battle ceased. The sharks had won. Both sharks and star-heads were gone. One to eat, one to be eaten.

The night rolled in and a ragged moon floated up out of the sea, found a place to hang against the sky. The waters churned and the boat jumped. Exhausted, Amelia lay down in the boat and was eased into sleep by exhaustion. The dark things moved inside her head.

When Amelia awoke the next morning it was still dark, but light was bleeding in with squirts of red, and in short time the sun trembled up and turned bright gold. She thought of Gavin, almost expecting to see him when she had the strength to rise from the bottom of the boat, but his fate was soon sharp in her memory. All she could think about was how he had been taken away by different monsters of the sea. Yet, the sharks had been her saviors. She picked up the flare gun. Gavin had never loaded it. It was useless. She dropped it in the boat.

After a long time, the sun warmed the boat and the sea, and she found a dead shark floating on its back in the water, the bottom half of its tail eaten off in what had probably been a continued and cannibalistic shark frenzy from the night before. She paddled up beside it and saw that its belly was ripped open, and strings of innards hung out of it. A meal abandoned for whatever reason. She reached down and pulled the creature's insides loose, tugged them into the boat, snapping them off, tossing them on the floor of the craft like enormous tomato-sauced noodles. The guts were filled with offal. She shook that out as best she could, washed it clean with the waters of the sea, then ate it raw. It tasted good at first, but then when she was past her savage hunger, it made her stomach churn. Still, she scooped more out of the shark and tossed it in the bottom of the boat for later.

She had no idea what to do. Perhaps the only choice was to try and see if she could find a place farther down on the slate of ice where the mountainous monster and the star-heads didn't dwell. If such a place existed.

It was surprisingly warm, considering the ice. From way out she could see the mountainous creature. It took up all her eyeline when she looked to the shore. It had moved ever closer, changing the landscape in an amazing way, slipping along on a monstrous trail of slime that oozed out from under it and greased its way toward the sea.

It was massive. She would have to sail for days to get around it, if that was even possible.

Amelia ate some more of the shark, but the guts had gone bad in the sunlight. She vomited over the side.

Amelia counted four days at sea, and then she lost count. She had been lucky. A fairly large fish had leaped into the boat, and she had bashed its head with an oar. She ate its brains where the oar had broken its skull, ripped it open with her bare hands and used her teeth on the soft belly, biting off chunks, wolfing it down. It was far more palatable than the shark had been, and when she finished, she was refreshed. It was all she would have that day, and by next day she was hungry again, but no prize fish presented itself. She did manage to nab a few floating chunks of ice and suck on those for water.

She sailed hungry through a day and night. She wasn't sleeping. It was too dark down there in her dreams, so she tried to stay awake. Inside her thoughts the creature continued to come to her. It didn't speak to her, but it communicated with her nonetheless. It was a terrible communication that made her dreams scream and her skin crawl.

Her hunger helped keep her awake.

Another fish might present itself, and that was something to think about instead of the monster that stretched for as far as she could see. Earlier in the day she had seen a seal, or something quite like one, swimming near the boat, not too far underwater, quite visible when the sun hit the waves just right. She hoped she might come across another, one more foolish, willing to rise up and present its head to be banged with an oar.

By midday the boat had actually caught an underwater current of some sort, and it drifted out and away from the shoreline. But then an odd thing happened. It was discernable, but only a little, and near impossible to assimilate mentally. The mountain had reached beyond the shoreline. It was about to enter the water. And that's what happened. The entire icy shoreline cracked with an ear-piercing sound, and the great mountain dropped straight into the water, part of it disappearing like the fabled continent of Atlantis. Monstrous tentacles writhed from it.

It was so insane Amelia began to gulp air, like a fish that had been docked.

As the mountain slipped into the water, the sea rose up and the boat rose with it. The weight of the mountainous monster, a small continent of sorts, swelled the sea level. The impossible creature kept drifting down into the waters, and then abruptly it ceased to drift. It had hit bottom, but still the peaks of it rose out of the sea and the tentacles, as big as redwood trees, thrashed at the air and smacked the water like an angry child. The broken ice popped up before it and along its impossible length in iceberg chunks, bobbing like ice cubes in a glass.

The boat was borne toward the shoreline, which was entirely taken up by the behemoth. And then, all along the visible part of the beast, there was a horizontal fissure. The fissure spread wide with a cracking sound so loud Amelia covered her ears. The fissure spread for miles. There were jagged rows of teeth inside it, each the size of mountaintops, and there was spittle on the teeth, running in great wet beads, as if it was tumbling snow from an avalanche, and rising out of the great mouth was a sudsy foam, like white lava from a volcano. The teeth snapped together with an explosion so loud it deafened Amelia. When the impossible mouth opened again, it became wider yet; the bottom of it touched the sea. The water flowed into it with the briskness of a tsunami, and in the drag of it, the lifeboat jetted toward the mouth.

Amelia grabbed the oars and tried to use them, but it was useless. The rush of the water toward the open mouth of the creature was too strong and too swift; it could not be denied.

She saw the great fissure of a mouth tremble, and then the boat came closer, flowing now with even greater speed.

"Why?" she yelled to the wind and water. "I am nothing. I'm not even an appetizer."

Amelia began to laugh, loud and hysterical. She could hear herself, and it frightened her to hear it, but she couldn't stop.

And then the little fly-speck of a boat, with its smaller laughing speck inside, entered into the trembling, foam-flecked mouth that was a length beyond full view of the eye, and tumbled as if over a vast waterfall. The boat banged against one of the jagged teeth like a gnat hitting a skyscraper, came apart, and it and Amelia, who gave one last great laugh, were churned beneath the water and carried into the monster's gullet, along with creatures of the sea.

Elder Things

Before there was any life on the barren rocks of this terrestrial globe, but only living things in the oceans, a race of intelligent beings descended from the heavens. They came flying down on their wings through the cosmic jelly that fills the spaces between the stars after a journey that had spanned half the cosmos and taken aeons to complete.

Theon, the blind Greek sculptor, glimpsed them in a dream and described their form to his disciple, Philip the Wise. He writes that in appearance, they were like short, stout trees that walked on five rustling fronds sprouting from their bases. Five broad ridges ran up and down their trunks like the staves of a barrel. From each ridge extended a branching appendage the creatures used as we use our hands. From between these ridges unfolded five wings shaped like fans, which they used to fly through the air or swim beneath the water with astonishing swiftness. They had flat heads of a kind that resembled a multi-colored starfish. On each of the five points was an eye, and between the points were stalks with mouths on their ends. These were also five in number.

These beings, who are sometimes called the Elder Things because they were the first race from the stars to colonize our world, were at home on the dry land or beneath the waves of the sea, for they could breathe water or air with equal ease, and could move through the water with great swiftness on their beating wings. They chose to live in the oceans because, at that early period in our world's history, the land was completely lifeless.

In the depths they built their cities from stone blocks so massive, it would be impossible for men to move them, but they were easily lifted into place by a race of slaves bred by these wise Elder Things for this purpose. These slaves were called shoggoths, and they are said to be the strongest living beings that ever existed.

In appearance like amorphous sacks of dirty translucent fluid, the shoggoths possess the remarkable ability to extend at will hands or legs or organs of perception. They lifted the great stones by flowing beneath them and expanding their bodies. In this way they could shift and raise weights that appeared impossible to move. When angered they could throw down the stones of a wall as easily as they had raised them.

For long ages the Elder Things ruled this world beneath the waves. When living creatures crawled from the oceans to the land, and lush forests covered the hills and valleys, the Elder Things moved from the sea to the land and built more cities in the open air.

They had the minds of sages and were wise beyond our reckoning. They made and molded the flesh of living things the way a potter makes pots of different shapes. It is whispered that one of their creations was the human species, but why they created us is unknown. Some say we were made to be a food animal, as we ourselves might breed a sheep or a goat, for the Elder Things were flesh eaters. Others say that we were created for their amusement, as grotesque and comical monsters to be stared at and mocked.

As the aeons continued to pass, other alien races descended from the stars to our world and began to make war against the Elder Things for mastery of the earth. The Elder Things fought against Cthulhu and his spawn, the Mi-Go, and the Great Race of Yith. The devastation wrought by these battles rendered much of the surface of the world unable to support habitation. The Elder Things were gradually driven from the surface of the land by these wars, back to their original cities deep beneath the sea, and their numbers diminished.

The most terrible of their wars was the uprising of their own slaves, the shoggoths, who over the ages became intelligent and threw off the mind control of the Elder Things. They sought to kill their masters so that they would be free. The Elder Things defeated the army of shoggoths using terrible weapons, but the destruction these weapons caused to the earth was tremendous. They retreated to their last great land city far to the south, and abided there in peace until the coming of the age of endless winter, when their city was covered by a creeping sheet of ice.

It is rumored that the last remnants of the Elder Things may have fled their frozen city and retreated into caverns deep beneath the mountains, where perchance they still dwell. Their cities are all destroyed, and no Elder Thing has been seen by the eyes of men, although blind Theon and others have glimpsed them in dreams. If relics of their vanished civilization survive, it can only be in the waste places of this world, where no man dares to travel, or in the frozen desolation at the poles, where there is only snow and ice.

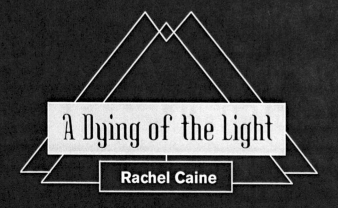

A Dying of the Light

Rachel Caine

You can adjust to all kinds of things, no matter how depressing they may be. Working in a facility that deals with Alzheimer's patients, for instance; sure, it might be distressing at first, how they grab onto you with wild, panicked desperation and stare, unable to articulate the howling darkness inside their minds. How they beg you to save them from being sucked down into it.

But you get used to it. Sad fact. You can get used to anything.

At the time I met the newest resident of Shady Grove, I'd just become a Licensed Elder Care Technician—that's what my paystub said, anyway, and it earned me a sweet twenty bucks an hour. I was relatively new at the whole Elder Care game, but most of the time, it wasn't so bad. I mean, you had to have a strong stomach; there's a whole lot of waste spillage involved, if you know what I mean, but I've never been squeamish about bodily fluids. Shit, blood, urine, vomit… it never made me sympathy puke, though some of my coworkers just couldn't deal. I was the one who got emergency mop-and-bucket duty for the most part, and I was fine with it. My colleagues usually bumped me some extra cookies or something at breaks to make up for it.

What was harder for me were the faces of our patients—excuse me, *residents*. The blank, slack, yet still somehow *living* faces, continually struggling to climb out of whatever pit they'd fallen into inside their skulls. The human body is tough, and a lot of the time it just doesn't know how to quit, even when the fight's long lost. I was always as gentle as I could be with them, even the ones who hit the skids and took a wrenching left turn into screaming, spitting, biting, punching, you name it. My facility didn't get those as much. There were—air quote—*special facilities* for those cases. I'd only been slapped or hit a couple of times, once by a tiny little lady who just the day before had been the sweetest, most fragile thing.

They changed, you see. They all changed, eventually. And there was never any going back, just a long, slow march down into the dark.

I was in my seventh month of the job when destiny moved in. Well, *moved in* wasn't quite right; she was wheeled in from St. Gregory Hospital one rainy afternoon, and as I watched them roll her down the hall and into room 422, I thought, *she'll take some work.* The old lady who passed me was bedridden, and worse, she had the thousand-yard, dead stare of an end-stager… if anybody was still home in that graying head, she sat in the dark, silent and alone. Better than combative, but not by much. Special care would need to be taken to ensure she didn't develop bedsores, and she was probably on a boatload of meds, too.

Not my wing, thank God, I thought, right before Chris, the nursing supervisor, stuck his head out of his office and beckoned me over. He was sorting out boxes of medications, logging them in on charts, and labeling them with room numbers, and while he worked he jerked his pointed chin in the direction that the gurney had taken, toward 422.

"She's yours," he said. Chris—Christophe, really—had a rich, soft Jamaican accent that always reminded me of some sun-drenched shore far from our dim old Arkham, Massachusetts, nursing facility. "They asked for you special."

This part of the state always seemed gloomy, overcast, raining, or managed to be dour and played out even on sunny days; a little Jamaican beach fantasy wasn't a bad thing. Christophe was also tall, broad-shouldered, and had the most perfect, poreless skin I'd ever seen on a man. He had a white-ink tattoo on his shoulder that rumor said was a *voudon* symbol, but I figured it was probably just picked out of a design book somewhere in Boston, and neither Chris nor the tattooist had the vaguest idea what it really was.

Still, for all his charm and warmth and handsome features, many of the staff, especially those with Caribbean backgrounds, minded their manners around Christophe.

"Wait, what?" His words finally registered on me like the brassy clang of a bell. "I—what? That's not my wing!"

"Special request," he said again, and gave me a broad, amused smile. "Your fame is spreading, Rose."

"That is *not* my fault." Somehow, when I'd done my job and nothing but, an enterprising blogger had twisted me into an ALZ whisperer who could charm difficult patients into miracle recoveries. For one thing, that poor old man hadn't even been properly demented, just neglected and lonely. For another, half of what that damn post had said was nonsense anyway. "Please don't make me some bullshit plastic dashboard saint."

"We can charge extra if we sell action figures."

"You asshole."

He shrugged. "She's your patient. Saint Rose."

I flipped him off, and he crossed himself, and we parted friends, I hoped. I wasn't really upset. The new patient—*resident*—wouldn't be too much trouble. If I could persuade Christophe to let me spend more time with her, I might be able to cut down on some of the emergency shit detail I usually inherited. A little more quality time with a person, even a nearly dead one, was much better.

And I did like being able to make their dark days a little brighter, even if they could only see it in glimpses and shadows. Wasn't really cool to say that around the others, who all complained about the work and the lousy pay and the heavy lifting, but I didn't mind all that, mainly because I'd done worse. Ever clean out portable toilets? This beat that by miles.

I stopped by the main office and picked up a Welcome Pack, which was kind of a joke because most of our residents were too far gone to understand what we were giving them, and anyway it was just soap, tissues, a lap blanket, things like that. Things their families, if they had any, forgot to provide. It came in a cheery yellow wicker basket with some sugar-free candies and Depends. I carried it over to room 422, where the ambulance attendants who'd brought her were just finishing up transferring her from the gurney to the small medical-grade bed where she'd finish up her life. One of them handed me the paperwork, and I looked it over. "Acanthus Porter," I said. "Huh. Sounds familiar. Should I know her?"

The younger one shrugged, but the older, about thirty, said, "Yeah, she was some kind of movie star back when dirt was new. Couldn't tell now, huh?"

"Don't get cocky," I said. "You won't be the handsome specimen you are now at her age, either."

He laughed. I read the rest over quickly—the usual stuff, statements about her condition, meds, a do not resuscitate order, contact info for her next of kin, which included a daughter and son who hadn't bothered to show up to see her moved into what was almost certainly her last residence. Both local. I signed the transfer and handed it back, and got a bag of stuff that was all Acanthus Porter had now in terms of worldly possessions: mostly nightgowns and robes. No valuables, thank God; those had to be locked up in the office safe. I could never understand why people put Grandma's jewel collection in her room, when Grandma was dotty enough to flush it down the toilet.

The ambulance guys left, and shut the door, and I put Acanthus Porter's things into the small chest by her bed. Her belongings only took up two of the four drawers. Sad. I put the Depends in the bottom drawer and the candy arranged in a nice little bowl by her bed, and tried to spread the rest of it around so it looked less like a cell and more like a home.

As I was spreading the cheery plaid lap blanket over her, I looked up into Mrs. Porter's face. She was as wrinkled as a raisin, pale and bloodless, and her blue eyes—which had probably been a stunning cornflower blue in her prime—stared blankly, faded and dull. No sign of life in her, though the pulse at her throat still beat, and her frail little chest rose and fell. I took her hand. It was chill and slack, and the skin was thin enough to see through, like something half-formed and unborn. I could see the shadows of bones, feel the ridges of thickened joints.

Her hand tightened on mine with sudden, shocking strength. It didn't surprise me; Alzheimer's patients were capable of that kind of thing. Their minds were wasting away, but the body was slower to follow. And the body was afraid.

Her grip hurt, but I didn't wince. "It's all right," I said, and gently eased some of the gray hair off her forehead. She was sweating a little. "Acanthus, it's all right. You're safe here. My name is Rose. I'm going to take care of you."

I kept my tone gentle. The words really didn't matter; I could have recited the phone book to the same effect, because at her stage, patients lost the ability to keep up with the meaning of sentences. They responded to touch, and to tone, and sure enough, gradually the grip around my hand slackened and fell away. I felt the sting of cuts and looked down. She'd dug in with her nails and left little red crescents in two spots. *I should have nails that good*, I thought, and almost laughed. I'd cut them short later.

"I'll bet you're hungry," I told her, in the same warm, soothing voice. "I have to warn you, the food's pretty crap, but I'll get you something tasty, all right? Something soft and warm. And some pudding. You like pudding, I'll bet."

I got up to go, and when I did, something… happened. I don't believe in ghosts, or demons. I'd always believed in what I could see and feel, and I believed that everything had a reason. Everything.

So all I can say about it is that I felt a wind out of nowhere blow up from beneath us, from the damn *floor*, and it felt hot and yet somehow *clammy*, like the skin of something dead a long time. It was so strong it felt as if it would tear the skin off my bones, and then it was gone, and I realized—though believe me, I know it doesn't make sense—that the shocking blast hadn't so much as ruffled the cheery green curtains on the window. I experienced a terrible stillness in that room, a *presence* like something awful smothering me with a wet, hot mouth, and I covered my face and, as strong-stomached as I am, I almost vomited into my hands.

Then it was gone. Just… gone.

I turned back to the bed, and the frail little woman dying on it, and another inexplicable feeling swept over me. A hot flash of utter horror, as if I was staring at something that *should not be,* then I blinked and it was over, except for the incredibly fast pulse of my heart and the sickening taste at the back of my throat.

Acanthus Porter sat up in bed and looked at me with cold, shining blue eyes. There was something wrong in the tilt of her head, the set of her shoulders, as if she'd put on the wrong skin.

I bit back the urge to scream and managed to say, fairly calmly, "Acanthus? Can you hear me?" Maybe, I told myself, there's nothing really wrong at all. Alzheimer's patients didn't react well to changes in environment; routines were everything to them. Maybe she'd just frozen out during the transfer and was starting to come back a little. Weird, but not unprecedented.

That fragile, desperate hope shattered when Acanthus opened her wrinkled little mouth and out poured a sound that was so wrong, so chilling, it sounded more like metal shrieking under pressure than a voice. *Loud,* so loud I had to clap my hands over my ears. It physically hurt, and when it finally died away I heard myself screaming in protest.

Acanthus dropped back to the pillows as if a puppeteer had cut her strings, with dead-but-alive eyes staring up at the ceiling, just as Christophe banged open the door to the room and charged in. He skidded to a halt, staring at me and breathing fast.

"What the hell are you screaming about?" he demanded. I slowly took my hands away from my ears, still watching Acanthus the way I might a poisonous spider on my pillow. "My God, Rose, you could have raised the dead! I'll have half the hall agitated the rest of the day after that!"

It slowly penetrated to me that he hadn't heard Acanthus's awful, metallic shriek *at all*. He'd only heard me, screaming for no apparent reason.

Acanthus lay limp on the bed, breathing evenly, a fragile old lady without much of a mind left, and I knew I couldn't tell him what I'd seen. Not if I wanted to keep my job.

I made up some story about seeing a rat and left him to hunt it down while I ran to the bathroom to throw up. My body needed to expel *something*, and if it couldn't get rid of the image of Acanthus upright in that bed, her eyes bright and dead inside, that *voice*...

Breakfast would have to do.

■ □ ■

So, yeah, I thought about leaving—just quitting, walking off the job, never coming back. Problem is that, at least in Arkham, there are a limited number of jobs for someone like me, and I *liked* what I did. I couldn't afford a bad reference out of Shady Groves, or Christophe spreading the word I was unstable. I just had to find a way to never be alone with Acanthus again.

Easier said than done, but I managed for a while; I kept the door open to her room and engaged other caregivers in conversations while changing her clothes and sheets and bathing her and turning her and feeding her. She was a warm, malleable doll in my hands, though from time to time I saw that flash of cold intelligence in her eyes and was glad I had someone else to chat with, someone to offer me protection. Somehow, I knew it wouldn't happen when there were other witnesses.

That didn't last, of course. I was dressing Acanthus in her nightgown after her bath when my friend Marisela was called away to tend to someone who'd had a fall, and the instant Marisela was gone the old lady's faded eyes flicked over to fix on mine. Utterly *present*. Utterly terrifying.

I let go of her. She should have fallen back to the pillows, but instead she stayed where she was, half-reclined, floating on the air... and then she sat up.

She swung her stick-thin legs over the edge of the bed and *stood*.

I'd moved back by then, well back, out of grabbing range. I didn't know what was coming. There was that damp heat in the room again, with a strange edge of chill underneath, and something wrong, *very wrong*, in the way Acanthus stood on her two feet. Stroke patients sometimes relearned how to sit, stand, walk, talk… but even then, they looked *human* in their bodies. Just uncertain and clumsy.

Acanthus looked wrong. And not at all uncertain.

"Jesus," I breathed. She was staring at me with those greedy, wet eyes—observing every little tic and breath and muscle. I had the odd, creepy idea that she was *learning*. She suddenly cocked her head to an angle that just *had* to hurt, too far over, too sudden, and then slowly straightened it again. Took a slow, shuffling step toward me. "Oh Jesus Christ—" The dread had taken hold of me hard, but I couldn't let it paralyze me. *She's just a frail old lady, what the hell are you afraid of?*

It made me feel physically ill to push through the dread, but I moved *to* her, not away, and took her arm. Thin, velvety skin slid loose over muscles that, though wasted, felt cable-strong beneath.

"Acanthus?" My voice sounded high and strange, and there was a tremble in it, just as there was in my grip on her forearm. "Dear, you should sit down. I don't think you should be standing up."

She obligingly sat on the edge of the bed. I felt her body shifting, trying to find a balance that, even in an Alzheimer's patient, should have had some instinct to it… but it felt like she'd never done this before. I held her in place until she was steady, then let go. I rubbed my palm down the fabric of my uniform pants, trying to scrub off the feel of her flesh, but I somehow managed to smile. "That's good, Mrs. Porter. Very good."

She opened her mouth, and I winced and flinched, waiting for that metallic screech. Instead, breath whistled out. Not words, just air. She was trying to talk, I thought, but didn't know how. There was a dim kind of surprise in her eyes now. *Harder than she thought*, I realized. She would have to learn things.

Things most humans took for granted.

It isn't her, some part of me insisted, still repulsed. Violently afraid. *That thing isn't Acanthus Porter. It's some... stranger.*

Like I said, I'm a practical girl. Unimaginative. Solid.

So I pushed that aside and went to get Christophe, and togeth-er we marveled at the miracle of Acanthus Porter, a vegetative-state Alzheimer's patient who was learning to walk and talk and move again.

■ ■ ■

It took months of slow progress, and I began to believe that I'd had some kind of strange episode. She was just a little old lady who'd some-how woken up again from her ALZ slumber, a miracle case that doc-tors studied and shook their heads and said scientific things that boiled down to utter ignorance. She became something of a media darling, though we forbade cameras inside the facility; I had to answer questions once in front of a battery of reporters, and that was awful. Meanwhile, Acanthus learned to walk, though she used assistance at first; she learned to do simple tasks that kindergarteners learned, like matching shapes and colors. She began to understand letters and numbers. It was as if she'd never had any of that knowledge, but it didn't take long for her to master that part of her education, and soon she was reading with speed. Too much speed. I caught her a few times leafing through books with sure, avid movements, her light, bulging eyes drinking in words faster than I ever could. When she noticed me, she slowed to a more... normal pace, tracing her skeletal finger along the pages and mouthing them si-lently to herself.

She learned to speak, of course. It never sounded quite natural, more like someone to whom it was a second language with all the wrong vowels. Natural enough, I told myself. It was amazing she spoke at all, or walked, or breathed, or lived. Based on the condition I'd seen her in when she'd rolled in the doors of Shady Grove, I'd have given her six months, tops.

For an entire year, she rehabilitated herself into something that was almost normal, but never quite... human.

That was never clearer than when her children finally came to see her around Christmas, halfway through her rehab. The daughter was a portly fortyish woman with a pursed-up mouth and stress lines around her eyes; she looked mousy and unhappy to be there. The son was one of those high-powered executive types, with a cell phone constantly at his ear and buzzing with texts, and a bespoke suit and silk tie and a haircut that cost more than my paycheck.

They both had the exact same reaction to their mother: not relief and joy at seeing her improving again, but revulsion.

It happened almost immediately as they walked into the common room, where Acanthus sat by herself in the corner. They moved in about halfway to her, and then, in unison, both her children just stopped and stared.

The daughter said, "That's not Mom." There was horror in her voice. "Ken, that's *not*."

"No," her brother agreed. He'd been texting as he walked, but now he just put the phone in his pocket, forgotten, and stared. "What are you people playing at? That's not our mother!"

"Acanthus Porter? And you're Ken and Darlene? Her children?"

"Yes, but—" Darlene kept staring with a kind of shaking dread I knew all too well. I still felt it, though I'd gotten used to the sensation. "It *looks* like her, but it's—not *her*."

Christophe's soothing, strong presence came up behind us, and he said, "Is there a problem, Rose?"

"I think Acanthus's children are just a little shocked," I said. "She's suffered some damage due to strokes and the Alzheimer's, and she might not be quite what you remember—"

"No," Ken cut me off. He actually took a step back, and I couldn't imagine this soul-crushing businessman had ever done that before. He wasn't a retreat kind of guy. "No, it's not right. This isn't right. I can't do this!"

His mother, I saw, had looked up to watch us with those soulless, yet avid, eyes. She had loose sheets of paper in front of her, and she was writing on them, but she never looked down at her hands or the page as the pen moved. It was an eerie sight.

While Ken turned on his heel and stalked away at a walk so fast it might as well have been a run, Darlene managed to stay put. Daughters always felt more obligated, I'd found, even when their instincts told them there was nothing they could do.

"Just say hello to her," I said to the Darlene. "You'll feel better. Just a quick hello, and you can go."

She nodded jerkily, and her eyes—cornflower blue, as Acanthus's must have been in her younger days—were wet with something that wasn't tears, but was more purely horror, as though I was a bully forcing her to touch something dead and rotten. But she went with me. Heavy, slow steps. She halted about five feet away while I walked over to perch on a chair next to Acanthus. Being so close to her was a strange sensation, still; she felt warm and solid and real, but there was an energy coming off her that jangled my nerves, like being too close to a power line. She'd just had a bath, but there was a smell that never quite went away, something like a hot, fetid swamp.

She was writing very quickly. Her pen moved over the paper right to left, the opposite of how English would be written, but she wasn't writing English. I wasn't certain what it was. It had some strange loops to it, and too many vowels, and though it looked like English letters there were subtle signs it wasn't at all. Her writing was neat and precise, and very fast. In one corner, she'd sketched some kind of plant, but no kind I'd ever seen before; it had an unsettling look to it, with an organic geometry that seemed monstrous even as a flower, and a sinuous stem that writhed and curled into roots like claws.

She finished the page abruptly and dropped her pen. It rolled off on the floor, but she didn't seem to notice. She stared at her daughter with wide, strange eyes, and her daughter stared back in mortal terror with tears streaming down her face, and when she said "Mama?" it was in a little-girl voice that spoke of nightmares and monsters under the bed.

Acanthus Porter smiled and said, "Darlene, how good to see you. How are the children?"

It sounded normal, although there were strange lilts to the words, odd accents. Darlene's reaction was out of proportion. She stumbled backwards, ran into a table that held an abandoned game of checkers, and overturned that as she pushed through. Red and black plastic chips rattled over the floor, and Marisela, feeding gelatin to an elderly man in a wheelchair, glared and got up to clean the mess.

Darlene bolted from the room. *Ran.* The door slammed behind her.

"Goodbye," Acanthus said, in the same flat, uninvolved voice, and looked at me. "Will you get my pen, dear?"

There was no warmth in the endearment. I bent over and retrieved the pen. "What are you writing?"

She smiled. It was a strange kind of expression—secretive, cynical, delighted all at once. "A history," she said.

"What language is that?"

She said nothing. Just kept smiling. On impulse, I took out my cell phone and snapped a pic, and when I did, that smile vanished. What was left didn't look… happy. "What are you doing?" Her voice had taken on a metallic undertone, and I remembered the unnatural, piercing shriek of her first day at Shady Groves—worse, I *heard* it, like it was happening all over again. There was something in it that wouldn't go away. I managed to hold my reaction to a flinch.

"I just wanted to see if I could find out what language it is," I said. "It's beautiful. You must have learned it somewhere."

Acanthus said nothing to that, but watched me for another long moment, then picked up her pen and began another page. Line after line flowed, seamless and utterly unknown.

I got on Google and did a reverse image search, and *boom.* There it was. Page after page of the exact same looping, upright, foreign script, only in an ancient faded ink. Some pages in the scans were decorated with those same eerie, unnatural plant illustrations, and no two were the same. There were other pages, even more unsettling, with miniature women swollen with pregnancy, feet in a tub of liquid, arms thrust into strange tubes. Prisoners. The eerie menace of it vibrated off the screen at me.

The Voynich manuscript, the results told me. *Written in the fifteenth or sixteenth century. Author unknown. Language unknown. Illustrations of plants unknown to science.* It existed in the Beinecke Rare Book and Manuscript Library at Yale in their private collection.

How was that possible? How would *Acanthus Porter* have come in contact with that manuscript, which had only recently even become available to public view, in such detail that she could reproduce entire pages line by line?

The whole thing gave me the shivers and an intensely bad feeling in the pit of my stomach.

I took Acanthus to the lunchroom and escaped. She had a table all to herself, since every attempt to sit another patient with her, even the most quiet and oblivious ones, had resulted in agitation (one docile old lady had cried hopelessly for days after), and I left her to manage the meatloaf and pudding on her own while I got some alone time. My duties had narrowed down to just caring for Acanthus; she was a star pupil for Shady Groves, and I was the only caregiver she'd accept. I now slept there, which sucked, but at least I had my own private room and bath, and my salary had more than doubled. Acanthus didn't require any help during the night, thank God, because even as armored to her as I was now, I couldn't imagine having to deal with her in the dark. The thought terrified me.

Reading about the Voynich manuscript led me to other strange anomalies. Living in Arkham had always had a dark side; there were rumors all my life of cults, evil books, monsters lurking just beyond our senses. Somehow, things that would seem ridiculous in New York City or Seattle seemed utterly possible here, and it didn't surprise me to find out that there were people who claimed to know about the Voynich manuscript. One of them was an old professor named Peaslee—Wingate Peaslee II—who was somehow still clinging to an endowed chair at Miskatonic University. He'd written a few papers positing that the Voynich book was a phenomenon related to his grandfather's case, Professor Nathaniel Peaslee. I couldn't find much online about that; it seemed like the papers he was talking about were kept under lock and key at Miskatonic, and I'd have to talk to Peaslee to gain access.

Was it really that important?

I didn't know.

I turned off the light, shut off the computer, and dreamed, very strangely, of cities under the wrong stars, soaring towers winking with odd lights, and shadows moving that did not look in the least human.

And of a black, slender tower, featureless, without windows or doors, like a monster's clawed finger poking out of the ground. On dreaming of that building, I woke up shaking and cold and clammy, and it took me the rest of the night to shake the feeling that, as I'd been observing the tower, something inside it had watched me with a long, slow, cold regard.

And it would not forget.

■ ■ ■

I took a rare day off and went to see Professor Peaslee. To my surprise, he was an elegant old man, compact and dapper, with silver-fox hair and dark eyes that glowed with intelligence and interest. His office in the dour old Psychology Building of Miskatonic University was near the back, without much of a view, and it was small and packed with books and papers that definitely weren't there for show.

"Welcome, welcome," he told me, and shuffled a stack of books off a dusty old armchair, which he pulled across the threadbare Persian carpet to sit across from his desk. As I sat, I noticed row after row of skulls on top of the bookcases—animal skulls, mostly, some I recognized and a few I couldn't. Perched across from me, directly above Professor Peaslee's head, sat a human skull, gleaming in the soft morning light.

"Friend of yours?" I asked, nodding at the skull. He turned and looked, then turned back to me. Still had his smile on, but it had gone brittle at the edges.

"My grandfather's," he said. "He insisted on a thorough examination of his body, followed by a donation to science. He had certain...

experiences… that he thought might have resulted in abnormalities. We didn't find anything."

"And you keep that *here*?"

Peaslee shrugged. "This was his office. I thought he'd feel most at home here, with his books. Now, Miss Hartman, how can I be of help?"

"I understand you think your grandfather's papers are somehow related to the Voynich manuscript. I'd like to take a look, if you don't mind."

His white eyebrows rose high, and wrinkles folded his forehead, but somehow he didn't seem all that surprised. "That's an unusual request. Few these days have any interest in my grandfather. The Voynich book still attracts curiosity seekers, of course, and puzzle addicts. Are you certain you want to investigate this?"

"Why? It's just a book, isn't it?"

He sat back, staring at me for a long moment, and then said, "If you don't mind me saying, Miss Hartman, you have a certain… look to you. It's subtle, a tension around your eyes, the way you hold yourself. I've seen it before. It runs in my family, to anyone who ever encountered my grandfather after his… collapse, in 1908. I saw that in my own father, who was the only member of the family to stick by Nathaniel's side in that difficult time. I only met my grandfather once, near the end of his days, but I still vividly remember the… the *feeling* of being in his presence. It leaves a mark. And I see the same mark on you."

I wanted to tell him the whole story of Acanthus Porter, but I couldn't. Didn't dare. I just shrugged and stayed quiet, and he kept observing me for another long moment before he said, "Have you started to dream yet?"

That shocked me into a flinch. "What?"

"The ancient city. The black tower. Trap doors. Shadows moving between the lights."

He'd just described *exactly* what I'd dreamed, except for trap doors, and I had the sense that might be the worst thing of all. I wondered how long it had taken him to have the dream, and how often it came back. It scared me to think I'd never be rid of it.

"I'd like to see the papers," I said again, and with a sigh Wingate Peaslee II stood up and walked to a painting of a particularly unpleasant stretch of Arkham coastline showing a strange iridescence in the water. I couldn't shake the feeling there was something hiding in those foaming waves, massive and horrifying. Peaslee slid it aside to reveal a quite modern safe. He punched in a code and retrieved a sheaf of yellowing paper from inside.

"Are you sure?" he asked me. "Because once you've read these things, you can't go back. For your safety, Miss Hartman, please. Reconsider."

I had to *know* what was wrong with Mrs. Porter. I could never sleep again until I understood. Until I knew what my dream had been about, and how what she did was related to this long-dead professor with his skull staring down on me.

I reached out, took the papers, and began reading the horrible, chilling ramblings of Nathanial Wingate Peaslee. There was no sound in the office other than the turning of the pages. I couldn't stop. I devoured the cramped, handwritten sentences, speeding faster and faster, and with every page came another shock of recognition.

It was clear that I had no remembrance of my identity and my past, though for some reason I seemed anxious to conceal this lack of knowledge. My eyes glazed strangely at the persons around me, and the flections of my facial muscles were altogether unfamiliar.

Something in my aspect and speech seemed to excite vague fears and aversions in every one I met, as if I were a being infinitely removed from all that is normal and healthful... My own family formed no exception. From the moment of my strange waking my wife had regarded me with extreme horror and loathing, vowing that I was some utter alien usurping the body of her husband.

I remembered Ken and Darlene Porter abandoning their mother, Ken immediately, Darlene in a horrified rush. I remembered my own reaction to Acanthus, the one that pulsed deep inside me still.

It was the same. Exactly the same.

Peaslee's story was incredible and obviously the work of someone in the grip of serious delusions—after all, he seriously believed that he'd been possessed by an alien intelligence from across space and time, who'd come to learn of humanity. Who could visit, and had visited, countless species through the universe and the fabric of time, seeking new ones into which they could shift their bodies (granted, a pretty cost-effective form of space travel). Even so, it was the dreams that resonated most strongly with me. The idea that the great city that I'd dreamed in such horrifying detail had been in his mind, too. And with his son, and his grandson.

As if it actually existed. Or had, sometime in the distant past.

The last part of the story, of his discoveries, seemed more impossible than the beginning. I finished, and sat back, thinking. Peaslee watched me with bright eyes that, for an unsettling flash of a moment, reminded me of the way that Acanthus watched me.

"Well?" he asked, with barely concealed eagerness. "Does it shed any light?"

"I still don't know how it relates to the Voynich manuscript," I said. In answer, he took one last piece of paper—one he'd held back—and put it on the desk, facing me.

There, on a cream-colored page, marched neat, perfect lines of the exact same script that I'd seen flowing from Acanthus's pen that morning. And inked in strange, sinuous lines, a drawing of an otherworldly plant that reminded me unsettlingly of a mouth, teeth, and legs that would jitter and scurry to carry it along.

"My grandfather drew many pages like this toward the end of his life," Peaslee said. "He claimed he couldn't get the images out of his head, and he hoped that by putting them to paper he'd find relief. I don't think it worked. When I heard of the Voynich manuscript, imagine my shock to see that some poor unfortunate *four hundred years ago* suffered from the same obsession... the same window locked open in his mind onto madness. My grandfather, an educated and kind man, ended his days raving in Arkham Sanitarium for the Criminally Insane. Toward the end, he was shrieking in a language no one could identify. It was a ghastly affair that scarred my poor father deeply, and I am convinced it cut his own life short."

He waited for me to tell my story, to blurt out the tale of Acanthus Porter, but I didn't. I thanked him in barely audible whispers, grabbed my bag, and got the hell out. The Miskatonic halls seemed drenched in shadows so thick I could feel them drag on my skin as I hurried away, toward the dim, cloudy light outside. A breeze blew in from the sea, and I shuddered. It felt damp and clammy and wrong and held a dark, swampy odor I recognized.

I drove back to Acanthus Porter, simply because I didn't know where else to turn.

◼ ◼ ◼

The next few days brought an unexpected flurry of events. First, Mrs. Porter got a visitor—a buttoned-up, sharply dressed lawyer, who had her fill out paperwork without any involvement from me. She dealt with him as sharply as any rational person, and speed-read the documents he put in front of her, legalese and all, before signing with bold slashes of her pen on the last page. I asked what it was about, but she didn't answer. She asked for more paper, and I watched her draw more unsettling illustrations, and write more obscure, unknown lines of text. When I asked what she was doing, I got a one-word answer.

"Waiting."

She didn't have to wait long. Two days later, Ken and Darlene made another appearance. They were shaken and angry, and Ken was clutching a piece of official-looking paper in one hand. He stormed in and found his mother writing, as usual, in the corner of the common room. Like Darlene before him, he came to a sudden halt five feet away, well out of touching distance, and brandished the paper in front of him. "What's the meaning of this, Mother?"

Acanthus didn't look up. I suppose Ken didn't know to be grateful for that. She was carefully inking in details of an illustration of what looked like an astrological symbol, but nothing I recognized. "It's self-evident," she said. "Isn't it?"

"It withdraws our power of attorney for you!"

"It does," she agreed. "I feel it is time for me to take over my own affairs again."

"But—"

She looked up then, and whatever Ken would have said, it died in his throat, rotted, and turned to dust. There was something wild and alien in Acanthus's look, something awful I couldn't even comprehend. "I will require money," she said. "For what I need to do. So I will take it."

Darlene, who'd been hiding behind Ken, stepped out and, keeping her gaze averted from her mother, said, "Mama, maybe you should let us handle your finances—"

"You have the papers," Acanthus said. "Now go away. I don't need you."

Darlene flinched, and Ken actually growled somewhere deep in his throat, like a dog hopelessly facing a bear, and then backed away. I realized he didn't want to turn his back on his mother. Darlene didn't have such qualms; she turned and hurried out as fast as she could without running.

Acanthus laughed. Or, at least, I think it was a laugh. It didn't sound amused, or human, but there was a rhythm to it that approximated laughter. The short hairs on the back of my neck stood on end.

The laugh cut off abruptly, and her head turned toward me. I didn't look. I stared hard at the lines of text on the page in front of her, the half-inked drawing.

"You," she said. "I'll need you to come with me."

I swallowed hard and shook my head. "I have a job here. I'm not going anywhere."

"A million dollars," she told me. "A million dollars to accompany me. Surely that will be better than *this*." She indicated the room of Alzheimer's patients with a contemptuous jerk of one hand, as if slapping them away. "I need you. Rose."

It was, I thought, an attempt to sound warm. Human. It failed. But *a million dollars...* I stared at her doubtfully. To someone at my wage rate, a million bucks sounded like miracle money. Life-changing money. *If she has it,* I thought. I cleared my throat. "I'd have to know you're serious," I said. "I have to see the money."

She gave that awful laugh again, took another piece of paper, and wrote something down—not in the strange, alien script this time. In English. Perfect cursive, old school rounded letters and numbers, like a calligrapher. It gave the phone number of someone named Elliott Lange. "Ask him," she said. "He will show you."

I took out my phone and dialed and got an immediate, crisp voice on the other end saying, "Law Offices of Elliott Lange, how many I direct your call?"

"Mr. Lange, please," I said, and swallowed hard.

"Who may I say is calling?"

"Rose Hartman. I'm the… attendant to Mrs. Porter."

While waiting, I switched to the Internet and looked up Elliott Lange. He was a high-powered Arkham lawyer specializing in estates and wills, and I recognized his picture. He'd been the man bringing papers to Acanthus to sign.

The one who'd cut her children clean out of the process.

"Lange," said a clipped, businesslike voice on the other end of the line. "Miss Hartman? Any problems with Mrs. Porter?"

"No, I just—"

Acanthus's withered hand snatched the phone away from me and put it to her ear. "Tell her how much money I have," she said, and handed the phone back.

Lange was silent on the other end, then said, "I see. This is irregular."

"Tell me about it," I said. "She offered me a million dollars. Does she, ah, actually have it?"

"You can safely assume that. She could offer you ten times that without any problem. You'll forgive me for not being more specific."

"Of course," I said. "Look, I don't want this to look like I'm taking advantage…"

"Put Mrs. Porter on the phone and I'll verify." I handed it to the old lady and walked away. She talked for a while, then put the phone down and gestured for me to come back. I picked up and found Lange still on the line. "It's settled. I'm drawing up papers for her to sign. You're fire-walled from any undue influence charges."

"No offense, Mr. Lange, but I've met her kids."

"So have I. She's leaving them everything else, an estate in the hundreds of millions. They're not going to care. She just wants a million for you, and a million for herself."

"A million for *her*? What for?"

"Travel," he said. "I'll wire your cash to you tomorrow. Give my assistant your bank information. And Miss Hartman?"

"Yes?"

He hesitated. Up to that point, it had been a brusque, just-the-facts conversation. But his tone was entirely different when he said, "This may be a breach of protocol, but... I wouldn't go with her. Not for any amount of money. You understand?"

I did. I said, "How much cash do *you* have in the bank? Because if it's more than five hundred bucks, I don't think we're operating from the same starting point on that one. Besides, I know her. I'm with her every day."

"Point taken. I hope—I hope to hear from you soon."

That was it. Next thing, his assistant was asking for my bank info, and I gave it, and when I hung up the call, Acanthus Porter was watching me.

She said, "Pack."

■ ■ ■

It was a long flight. Arkham to Boston, Boston to New York, New York to Melbourne. I worried Mrs. Porter wouldn't be able to cope with the rapid changes, the rush, the security, but I shouldn't have; she seemed vital, healthy, full of sharp energy. We flew first class, and oddly, the passengers in the row behind and ahead of us requested new accommodations in business class instead of being nearby. Bad dreams, I guessed; my head had been full of them every time I tried to close my eyes. I saw the city, the towers. I saw strange, half-seen creatures floating in the dark skies. I saw huge, bolted trap doors that seemed to strain and bend with pressure from below. I felt the whispering touch of an ancient, utterly incomprehensible darkness that bubbled around me like black oil.

We arrived in Melbourne, and I staggered off the plane sick and weak from proximity to Acanthus Porter. I seriously considered abandoning the old woman and fleeing back to safety, but she didn't give me the chance; we marched directly to a waiting chauffeur and black car, and from there we were whisked off to another airport, and another smaller, claustrophobic plane. This new plane only held the two of us, plus a silent crew who avoided even looking in our direction. They were *so* quiet, in fact, that I wondered who they were. One of them made a gesture to Acanthus at one point that was very like a bow.

Strange.

I don't know how long we traveled, or how far. It became a blur. I lost the will to eat, to sleep, to even try to find a way out and away from her; it was as if she'd somehow *harnessed* me, and I felt energy draining out of me just from standing in her shadow. I couldn't think. I couldn't imagine my old life before her, the other sweet old people I'd cared for, Christophe, Marisela, all my other friends who'd just... disappeared. I had a family, somewhere, who must have been thinking of me—a mother, a father, two sisters. Hadn't talked to them in a year, now.

I couldn't remember their faces. All I could see was shadows, and all I could feel was that awful, soul-sucking wind that had brought Acanthus Porter—or what walked inside her—into this world.

I wondered if it had taken part of me away at the same time.

We finally arrived at our destination. By that time, we were traveling in a sturdy, large desert vehicle, something almost military in size, and when we exited we were in the sandy wastes of Western Australia, away from the coast and into the Outback. To call it desolate would be an understatement; it was one of the harshest places on earth, and my Arkham-adapted skin cooked in the first moments of being under that staring, hostile sun. Even the hat some kind soldier-type gave me didn't help. I felt dazed from the jet lag and lack of food and sleep. I didn't know why I was here.

Acanthus Porter knew.

I struggled along with her, a caregiver for someone who needed no help at all, and the million dollars I'd traded for my soul seemed far, far away. Useless. Lost. There was nothing here, and whatever was coming next would be worse. No amount of money was worth this, because I realized with a dreadful certainty I was never, ever going back.

It was night when we finally staggered to a halt in a place that seemed no different from the others—windswept and empty—until I realized that what I'd taken for a boulder was actually wind-eroded stone block. It still had some kind of script incised into it, something that looked almost notational, like the strange symbols they use for higher mathematics. I wanted to touch it, but I was afraid to. There was energy in that stone, and I was so horribly, mortally weary.

I was staring at the stone, and realizing there were more stones, *many* more, scattered around us, when several people came out of the swirling sand and darkness to gather with us in the middle. A young man of around twenty who seemed of South American ancestry. A middle-aged Chinese woman with a younger man in tow. An older African man who had the muscular, wiry build of a runner.

Those four, and the two of us.

"You didn't bring what you promised," Acanthus said, and pointed to the South American and the African men. "Why not?"

"I lost them," the South American said, and shrugged. "They saw."

"When?"

"Years back. They saw the glory to come, but they could not understand *when*. The instructions were imprecise, I did not understand the time of this place. I lost them fifty years ago. They sacrificed too early, and too far away."

Acanthus looked at the African. "And you?"

"Mine is gone as well," he said. "But longer ago. He did not understand what was meant by *Taman Shud*. At least he was here on these lands, where he could be heard. He echoes."

"He echoes," said the others, in unison, except for the poor Chinese man, as frightened and out of place as me. *Echoes*. This place did echo, horribly, as if it existed all around me, these fallen stones rising into solid structures, and the shadows of black towers piercing even higher toward the stars. *Echoes.* This place vibrated with a horrible dark energy, and I remembered the scream from Acanthus's mouth, the rending metal shriek, the trap door bulging in the depths under pressure, the shadows on the stars.

Shadows licking over my skin.

I felt sick, thirsty, hungry, disoriented. *Taman Shud.* I knew those words. I saw them. I saw... I saw...

I saw two men on a hillside far, far from here, in thick trench coats buttoned tight in the blazing sun, fitting lead masks over their eyes. They were reading instructions in a language I couldn't understand, yet I knew what it meant... *"16:30 be at the specified location. 18:30 ingest capsules, after the effect protect metals await signal mask."*

It made no sense. I saw them check watches. Take some strange capsules with the air of ceremony. Lift their faces to the blazing sky.

Fall to the ground and stretch themselves out as if they slept.

I watched them die.

And then I was somewhere else, in a nauseating spiral of movement, on a beach, with a man in an old-fashioned suit who took a capsule from a pocket, raised his face to the night sky, and swallowed the medication down. He stood with his neck craned at a completely unnatural angle, and he changed words and numbers under his breath, and then suddenly said, "Taman Shud," and sat down against the seawall, as if he'd become tired. He looked at rest there, legs crossed, arms at his sides.

He died staring at the sky.

None of it made sense. None of it.

I realized, with a jolt, that the Chinese man was trying to run away now. He fell over a hidden stone block, and in a strange burst of moonlight I saw the stone was black, *black*, and I knew without being told that it had fallen from that eerie, awful black tower that had stood here hundreds of thousands of years ago, that stood here *now*, in shadows, in whispers, and he screamed as if he was being consumed, and he was, he was, I saw it eat him. But not his body.

I saw it eat his soul. I saw the oily blackness slide over his eyes, and then he was dead.

The other four nodded in unison: young, old, from four corners of the earth. All somehow *not themselves.*

And then they all turned to me.

No. No, I had a million dollars. I was going to go home. I was going to change my life. I was going to be... I was going to be...

I fell through a black hole, into Hell, and my last sight was of the four of them lifting up their hands, but they weren't hands, the shadows behind them were different, awful, *wrong,* and Acanthus smiled, and I saw nothing there but darkness.

I grabbed for a handhold in the black, and felt rock slip through my fingers. I tried again as I plummeted down, and down, and finally my fingers caught something. It broke free, but my fall slowed, and the next grip I caught and held. I hung there, suspended, gasping, desperate. There was light here, but... a *dark* kind of light, like the glow from some-thing rotting in a grave. The stench was overwhelming: that swampy odor I'd sensed constantly from Acanthus. I felt that wind again, pushing at me, sucking at me, hot and cold at once, and clammy as the skin of a corpse.

Taman Shud, it whispered, and I saw the strange, reaching tendrils of the plants from the Voynich manuscript, and the ones that had grown obscenely from the tip of Acanthus's pen.

Something touched my legs. Slithered around them.

Pulled.

I fell, screaming, and when I landed, I hit hard on a rocky floor that was strangely flat. *Blocks.* I felt around and touched carvings that burned my skin, leached into me like poison, and I screamed and crawled away toward a half-seen light. The only light I knew.

Rose, something whispered down there. *You are Rose.* But that wasn't me saying it. Something else.

The time is here. It is time.

I lurched to my feet and ran before it could touch me again. Whatever Acanthus was, she was better than what dwelled down here. I needed to go *up*.

I burst into a room, and the light hit me like a fist, driving me to my knees. It blazed up in a column of cold blue, and lit up tilted spires and columns, broken arches like the fantastic skull of an ancient beast. It was *massive*, on a scale like nothing I understood, and yet there were shelves, shelves with metal boxes. Each shelf was as tall as I, each box almost half my size. One had fallen at my feet, and when I reached down to move it I found it was light, wrongly light. There were knobs on it, and my hands moved without any direction of my own, turning, pushing, pulling in a complex code until the box's top folded back. Inside were pages coated in some strange oily substance.

Voynich pages, but new and vital, the colors bursting from the paper.

I could read them now. It was the history of a world, a long-lost world vanished into dust. A people gone into shadows, who had never been people at all, but something else. They'd observed us. Manipulated us.

Invaded us.

They were gone now, and only a few left. Only a few surviving.

Only four.

I held the pages and listened to the dark around me as it whispered my name. Four of them lived, up on the surface, and four of them held the darkness down here, by giving it sacrifices. Souls to taste and chew until there was nothing left.

There was a darkness at the heart of our world, and it wanted to eat us all.

You are chosen, I heard Acanthus whisper in my ear. *It is the last act we can perform, we four of the Great Race of Yith. We survived so long, traveling through bodies. Through time. Here we prisoned the darkness. Here we built our cities. Now you must save your race, Rose.*

You must close the door.

There should have been more of us, I realized. The two men dead on a hillside in Brazil in 1966. A man dead in Australia, on a beach, in 1948. The terrified Chinese man who'd died just moments ago.

Four to close the door.

Now, just me. Rose Hartman of Arkham, Massachusetts. I knew this place. I'd read Wingate Peaslee's horrible account of falling here, of the Great Lost Library of Pnakotus, of the trap doors hiding the end of the world.

They were open.

He'd opened them. He hadn't meant to do it, but from the moment that Peaslee walked these stones, he'd doomed us all.

I stood up, still holding the Voynich pages, and staggered on. The blue flame followed me, lighting my way, holding shadows back. It flickered and whipped in the wind that tore at me and ripped my clothes, yanked hair from my head, scoured away skin. I kept going.

There was no choice. They'd given me none.

The yawning, gaping hole into chaos lay down a spiral of stone, and I half ran, half rolled down toward it, gasping what air I could and clawing my way the last three feet. The trap door was open. It was a massive thing, a dozen feet across and thick as a battleship's armor plate. There was no way I could push it shut. It had been blown back on its massive hinges and lay flush to the floor. Even if I'd had a lever, I didn't have the strength. Four of us together couldn't have done it.

I threw back my head and screamed, "What do you want me to do?" It was a shout to Acanthus Porter. To *God.* To the cold and uncaring stars and the moon hovering over the sand, and to anyone, anything who would listen.

They came out of the shadows, then. Shapes, from the corner of my eye—giant conical things, ten feet high, clicking and scraping with strange, chitinous claws but gliding like something from a nightmare. I felt them pouring into me, screaming in a language I could not understand, could not *bear.* The Great Race, the last memory of them, lost in the shadows of time.

And here. With me.

For the first time, I understood. Acanthus was not the evil; she was the light, a feeble and dying light, trying to talk to a world that could not hear. Did not see the danger beneath.

Would not believe. They'd found the darkness here, on Earth, when they'd come hundreds of thousands of years ago, and they'd locked it away.

I understand. I believe. Like Wingate Peaslee, I had no choice.

The Great Race knew that eventually the trap door would open, and all would be lost. The Great Race—Acanthus's race—controlled *time.* And that, suddenly, made a mad kind of sense to me.

And I knew what they wanted. What I had to do. My feeble human strength could never move that trap door and close it. What was open would be open.

Take me to a time when it was still closed, I told them. *Take me to the past.*

And in a rush, I was falling through a vast, cold space, into the same cavern I stood in a hundred years later, but not the same. The journey made me sick, weak, horribly *stretched,* but I knew I was right.

The trap door was shut. Bolted, bulging from beneath, but still sealed. I could hear scraping from the opposite side.

It wanted out, that horrible evil.

There was a massive archway towering above me, something like the exposed rib of a dinosaur the size of a city; millions of blocks, each the weight of a car. It had stood all this time, standing watch.

But it was fragile. In my time, a hundred years hence, parts of it had fallen.

Not much time, the Great Race whispered to me. *You are fading into history. Your world is fading. We can help you no more.*

Every arch has a keystone, a point of weakness. This one was far up, above my head, but I'd always been a good climber, with a practical girl's knack for heights. I found handholds. Footholds.

Climbed.

The keystone was already crumbling under the weight of millennia. I braced my back against the wall and put my feet against it and pushed, pushed, cried out and pushed again.

It slid. Just a little.

I realized that if I continued to push, the arch would crush me as it fell.

No. Not after all this. Don't make me do this.

But something told me the Great Race had seen this. Knew this. Knew *me.*

Acanthus's metallic voice whispered in my ear. *Everything dies,* she said. *Even time. Even us. We can flee no more. We die here too.*

I remembered the light going out in the eyes of my patients back in Shady Grove, the slow and bitter slide into the dark. Maybe dying for this was better.

It was damn sure faster.

"I'm dying a millionaire," I said out loud, in a place that had never heard human speech, and I laughed. It sounded pure. It sounded right.

And I pushed the last crucial inch, and the keystone shattered.

I had time to see the millions of blocks break and fall, clanging and burying the trap door beneath a mountain of inscribed stone, and it was the last block, the very last one, that hurtled down toward me in a killing arc.

The light died, and I died in the dark.

◼ ◻ ◼

I awoke.

My limbs felt frail and unfamiliar. My eyes saw colors that made no sense. Sounds blared at me in a confusing, awful spiral.

Some alien creature touched me and chittered, and I thought, *no no no,* and then I understood. I hadn't died. This was Acanthus's last, horrible gift... the gift of life. She'd pushed me forward, through time, into another body.

I looked down at myself, and screamed. My body was a vast chitinous mass of sharp joined legs and the thorax of an insect, armor as black and iridescent as spilled, dirty oil. I saw in brilliant opal fragments from a hundred eyes just how monstrous I really was.

And as I screamed, I knew where I was—in a place of care, with strange, chitinous creatures who stroked me with insectile palps and tried to comfort me as I struggled for control of an alien body. A nursing home of monsters.

My new world.

The Great Race was gone. I was the last. And one day, I would write a manuscript of Earth, of plants long dead, of a people lost to dust. I had saved them, but even rescue doesn't last. Time destroys all things. And even time dies.

This was the end of my world, the inheritors of the human race. I could see the sun on the horizon through an opening in the burrow where I lay on my back, and the sun burned old and red and feeble.

I was here, at the dying of the light.

And I laughed.

AUTHOR'S NOTE:

The Voynich manuscript actually does exist in the Beinecke Rare Book and Manuscript Library at Yale. You can view the book and pages here: *http://beinecke.library.yale.edu/collections/highlights/voynich-manuscript*

The "Taman Shud" case in Australia is one of the most famous in that country and is still unsolved as of this writing. More here: *http://coolinterestingstuff.com/the-very-strange-case-of-taman-shud*

The "Lead Masks" case occurred in Brazil in 1966 and is still extremely odd and puzzling as well: *https://en.wikipedia.org/wiki/Lead_Masks_Case*

My mother has Alzheimer's disease. Immediately, upon reading "The Shadow Out of Time," the story upon which this is based, I realized that end-stage Alzheimer's patients would be a modern, eerie twist on the story of Professor Peaslee. I've incorporated many elements of his story, including the Lost Library City of Pnakotus, into what I hope is a worthy Lovecraftian effort.

Great Race of Yith

The beings who referred to themselves as the Great Race fled from their own world of Yith when their scientists predicted its imminent destruction due to a cataclysm within its depths. They could not save their world in spite of the advanced state of their sciences, so flight was the only course open to them. Their exodus was through time as well as through space, for it is a curious peculiarity of this race that it has the ability to span the ages. This it cannot do in the flesh, but only in the mind.

When the Great Race came for refuge to our world, long before the creation of humankind by the Elder Things, they were forced to select a form of life already flourishing here that was suitable to contain their bodiless intellects. The species selected by them is unknown to our sages, nor does any trace of their existence remain, but inhuman beings long of life that dwell beneath the ground say they were large cone-shaped beings that moved across the ground on a single foot like a snail. They had branching limbs and well-developed eyes, two things essential to the Great Race if they were to continue to pursue their sciences, which were their primary occupations.

As their world of Yith crumbled and burned, they cast their minds across the fathomless gulfs of space and time, and into these conical creatures. The minds of the creatures were displaced by this invasion, but having no vessels into which they could enter, and no knowledge of the transference of minds from one body to another, they perished.

The Great Race had chosen well. Their new bodies were resistant to disease and injury, and long of life. Their branching limbs enabled them to build a great civilization on the surface of our planet unmolested, for at this time in the history of our world the Elder Things were still living in the oceans and had no use for the land.

For millions of years they prospered on our world. During that span they were forced to fight many wars with the other alien races that contested for dominance of the earth, but their advanced science always enabled them to prevail. All of the knowledge of the entire future was available to them to draw upon, for they could send their minds into the future temporarily to inhabit a creature of a future age for the purpose of acquiring future sciences. This made them virtually unbeatable in war.

At length, however, there came a new wave of invaders from between the stars that the Great Race realized it could not defeat. To escape subjugation at the hands of this coming invasion, the Great Race determined to leave their conical bodies and leap into the far future of our world, to a time long after the passing away of humanity. In the future it is said that they displaced the minds of a race of giant golden insects, the ruling race of that distant time. There they remain, or rather, there they will remain, safe from their enemies in the past.

Although the Great Race had no interaction with humanity, it is claimed that remnants of their cities yet remain beneath the sands of the desert places of the world. The sands preserve what they conceal. In some future period, the capricious winds may begin to blow in a new direction, and uncover these cities to wondering eyes. Those who speak about such things caution listeners to stay far away from these cities, for the creatures from which the Great Race fled in terror still remain there, haunting the buried ruins. And if the Great Race feared them so much that it felt compelled to escape from them into the future, how much more reason does frail humanity have to avoid them?

Down, Deep Down, Below the Waves

Seanan McGuire

Jeremy plucked the white mouse from its tank as easily as he would pick an apple from a tree, grabbing the squirming, indignant rodent without hesitation or concern. The mouse squeaked once in furious indignation, no doubt calling upon whatever small, unheeded gods were responsible for the protection of laboratory animals. Jeremy ignored the sound, holding the mouse steady as he moved his syringe into position.

"I'm not saying that you have to run right out and jump into bed with somebody, okay?" he said, continuing our earlier conversation as if he weren't holding a struggling research specimen in his left hand. Jeremy was like that. He had a lot of compassion for living things, but his ability to compartmentalize was impressive, even to me. He was the sort of man who, under the right leadership, could probably have been talked into some remarkable human rights violations. But he knew that about himself. No one in our lab policed their actions more tightly than Jeremy.

"That's a good thing, because I'm not planning to," I said, folding my arms and leaning back against the counter. "Were you planning to scare that mouse to death before you injected the serum? I ask out of scientific curiosity, and not because it will fuck up our results. Even though, spoiler alert, it will fuck up our results."

"What? Oh!" Jeremy turned and frowned at the struggling mouse like he was seeing it for the first time—which maybe, in a way, he was. It had been background noise before. Now it was real. "Sorry, Mr. Mouse. Let me just give you your daily dose of carcinogens, and we can put you back in your box."

The needle slid into the mouse's belly with venomous smoothness, the fang of the great serpent called "Science," which had more worshippers than most gods could ever dream of. The mouse squeaked once more and then was silent, consumed by the tremors wracking its body. Jeremy placed the rodent gently back in its enclosure, treating it with more care now than he'd shown when it seemed healthy.

"Six more days of this and the tumors should start to become visible under the skin, if this specimen follows the path charted by the last twenty," he said. "We'll have concrete results by the end of the week."

"Causing cancer in lab mice isn't 'concrete results,'" I said. "These things have been inbred and twisted until *sneezing* gives them cancer. We should be trying to induce tumors in something that hasn't been primed for twenty generations. You want to make the headlines? Induce tumors in bees."

"You hate bees."

"Yes."

"I'm not going to figure out a way to cause cancer in bees just because you don't like them. They have enough problems."

"Colony collapse disorder is sort of like bee cancer, if you treat each bee in a hive as functionally serving the same role as a cell in a larger body."

For a moment—one beautiful moment—Jeremy looked like he was seriously considering it. I smiled winsomely, hoping to keep him distracted with the thought of cancerous bees, dancing and dying through fields of flowers. Maybe it was a little cruel to the bees, but it wasn't like I was actually killing them by offering a thought experiment, and if

Jeremy was focusing on science, he wasn't focusing on my lack of a social life.

Alas, good things never last. I learned that when I was just a little girl. Jeremy shook himself back into the present and frowned at me. "That was a mean trick."

"Yes," I agreed. It was best not to argue when he was right. That would spark more argument, and could take up the entire day.

"You *need* to get out more. It's not healthy for you to spend all your time in the lab."

"Uh, hello?" I held up a hand, counting off my fingers as I said, "First, pot, meet kettle. Second, grad students are *supposed* to spend all our time in the lab. Third, if we don't get results by the end of the month, they're going to give our lab to Terry and her weird plant project. Four, my grants all run out at the end of the semester, and I promised my family I would come home. So this is sort of my last hurrah. Dating can wait until I've got my doctorate."

Jeremy crossed his arms and scowled at me. I recognized that face. "About that. What is this crap about you giving up everything to go home to your weird hick family? They don't deserve you."

"You can call them all the names you want. They'll still be my family, and that will still be where I belong."

"You're really going to give it up?" Jeremy shook his head. "I don't understand you. I mean, I *really* don't understand you. You're brilliant. You're beautiful. And you're going to give up everything to go back to what, a bed and breakfast with a nice view of the Atlantic? Come on, Violet. I know you want more than that. You have to."

"Oh, believe me, I do." And I did. I wanted the sea, the blue-black sea, the great wide expanse of endless water. I wanted the benthic and the abyssal and the clear, shallow water that looked like glass in the sunlight. I wanted it all. And the first step was, as Jeremy so charmingly put it, a bed and breakfast with a nice view of the Atlantic, where a private room had been waiting for me since the day that I was born.

All I had to do was get there and show that I was worthy. All I had to do was get results. I pushed away from the counter. "I'm hungry. Are you hungry?"

"I could eat."

"Great. Let's go."

■ □ ■

There's nothing quite like Harvard in the fall. New students in their carefully chosen outfits, wandering like lost lambs in need of a shepherd; returning students, half of them in pajamas, the other half dressed for the job interviews they have scheduled after class. The specter of student loans hanging over all but the very rich and the very careful, crushing mountains of debt and madness primed to come crashing down as soon as the stars were right.

My family *is* very rich, and very careful. I've managed to swing enough grants to make my standard of living believable, keeping me connected to my peer group and capable of sympathizing with their concerns, but the bulk of my expenses have always been covered. It's important for the family to have a few like me in every generation, bold explorers who will go out into the world and come home with pockets full of treasure more precious than pearls—knowledge, understanding, and the scientific methods to spread that understanding further.

Jeremy strode across the campus like a young demigod, his back straight and his hair ruffled by the breeze. Some of the passing undergrads looked after him with lust in their eyes. Most were science majors and had seen him walking in the faculty halls, putting him far enough above them to be desirable, but far enough below the professors to be safe. Humans are an innately aspirational species, always wanting the next rung on the ladder, but always afraid to reach too far, lest their grip fail them, and they fall. That odd combination of courage and cowardice has served them remarkably well, all things considered, keeping them striving without allowing them to wipe themselves out.

I trailed along in Jeremy's wake, largely unnoticed by the student body. I didn't teach; I barely graded. I stuck to the lab, to the needles and the mice and the endless march of charts and graphs and information. Jeremy would have been lost without me. Everyone in our department knew it. And he repaid me by drawing the focus of the people who might otherwise have kept me from my work. It was a symbiotic relationship, like the clownfish and the anemone, and every time I thought too hard about it, I realized anew that I was going to miss it when it ended.

The off-campus pizza joint that we had claimed as our own during the first year of our program was packed, as always, with bodies both collegiate and civilian. Jeremy cut a path through them, making space for me to slide through the crowd unnoticed, until we came to the round table at the very back. Several of our classmates were already there— Terry of the weird plant project, Christine of the epigenetic data analysis, and Michael of the I wasn't really sure but it involved a lot of maggots project. Jeremy dropped into an open chair. I did the same, with slightly more grace.

A shaker of parmesan was near my side of the table. I palmed it while Jeremy exchanged enthusiastic greetings with our supposed "friends." We were all in constant competition for lab space, funding, and publication credits. Even though our fields were dissimilar enough that I would have expected us all to have the freedom to work as we liked, it seemed like we were forever stepping on one another's toes. Only the fact that Jeremy and I were running a combined experiment—his tumors, my documentation of social changes in mice that had been infected—kept us from being at each other's throats like everyone else.

To be fair, it helped that I didn't actually *care* about any of this. My classmates were counting on long careers in their chosen fields. I was only ever counting on the sea.

Christine flashed a quick, expensive smile at me, showing the result of decades of orthodontia. "Hey, Violet," she said. "How's every little thing?" Her accent was landlocked and syrupy sweet, Minnesota perfect. When we'd first met, I hadn't been able to understand a damn thing she said. Coastal accents were something I'd grown up with. Speech defects were no problem at all. But vowels that stretched like storm warnings and snapped like sails? That was something I hadn't been prepared for.

"Every little thing is fine," I said. "How's every little thing with you?"

Michael groaned. "You did it," he said, in an accusing tone. "You asked her. You asked her *with your face*. Do you hate us all? Is this how you show your hatred?"

"I was being polite," I said. That was all I had time for before Christine launched into a long, detailed description of her day. Terry put her hands over her face. Michael dropped his head to the table. I smiled, looking attentive and like I actually gave a damn, all the while unscrewing the container of parmesan and tipping cheese out onto the floor.

Getting the test tube out of my pocket and transferring its contents to the cheese container was more difficult, since I couldn't risk anyone noticing my moving hands. There were some things that my fellow grad students accepted unquestioningly, such as when Michael had spent an entire week wearing the same Hawaiian shirt, "for luck," or when Terry gave up all fruits and vegetables that hadn't been harvested according to Jainist standards. Replacing their favorite powdery cheese-based condiment with a mixture of my own creation was not on that list. There would be questions.

No one would like my answers.

Christine was still talking when I finished doctoring the cheese. I cocked my head to the side and waited for her to take a breath. Then, quick as a striking eel, I asked, "Did we want to order a pizza?"

Everyone started talking at once. Jeremy pulled out his phone and began taking notes, trying to work out how much pizza we would actually need, and what the optimum mix of toppings would be. I demanded mushrooms, as always, and took advantage of the chaos to slip the cheese back onto the table. No one noticed. No one ever did. I had been pulling this trick on this group of people for three years, and not once had I been caught, which spoke more to their remarkable self-centeredness than it did to my incredible skills at sleight of hand and misdirection.

When the pizza arrived, everyone dumped parmesan on it like the stuff was about to be outlawed. So as not to stand out, I did the same. I just used a shaker I had swiped from another table, combining it with the excuse that I didn't want to wait for Terry to be done. She liked cheese so much that sometimes she ate it directly out of her palm. Monitoring her dosage had been a nightmare, and now that we were moving into the final stage, I had given up. Let her have as much as she wanted. I had my data.

The pizza tasted like tomato sauce and garlic and charcoal, the bottom burnt black by the speed with which this particular parlor pumped out their pies. I ate enough to be sociable, then put down my half-consumed slice and smiled winsomely at my classmates, my comrades, the people who'd defined my grad school experience. We weren't friends. We could never have been friends. But out of everyone in the world, these were the people who understood what my life had been since I'd arrived at Harvard, a shy biology student from U.C. Santa Cruz, whose academic career had taken her first very far, and then very close to home.

"I wanted to ask you all for a favor," I said. They went still, curiosity and suspicion in their eyes. I never asked for favors. That wasn't my role in the social group. I *performed* favors, giving selflessly of my time, my intellect, and my snack drawer, when Terry inevitably forgot that she was a mammal and couldn't photosynthesize like her beloved plants.

"What do you need?" asked Jeremy. Then, brightening: "Did you want us to vet a potential date?"

"What? No. Ew. I told you already, I'm not interested in dating." I was interested in marriage, but there were specific ways for that to be arranged, very particular forms to be observed. My parents would have forgiven me for a sticky, ill-considered tryst while I was away at school. I would never have forgiven myself. "You all know my grants run out at the end of the semester…"

As I had expected, they all began talking at once again, trying to offer solutions, some practical, some ridiculous. I said nothing. It was best if I let them run themselves down, talking themselves into the inevitable silence.

When they quieted, I said, "I'm going to miss you too, but this is for the best, honestly. The experience always mattered more to me than the degree. Now I want to give you something in return. My parents want me to come home for spring break, and they've invited me to bring you all along. There's plenty of room at the inn, so to speak."

The silence remained intact. It was well known that my parents operated a bed and breakfast in the sleepy little seaside town where I'd been born. Miles from anywhere, sheltered by natural cliff walls, surrounded by the sea, it was the perfect place to raise a family. We didn't get many tourists, but the ones who came for a season always went home raving about our hospitality, our food, and the incredible clarity of the air. Why, sometimes, it seemed like the air was so clean that the stars didn't even glimmer. It was the perfect place, as long as you were prepared for its little... eccentricities.

I had never been shy about where I came from, but I had also never extended an invitation home before. Certainly not for the entire group at once. I could see the calculations in their eyes, the war between curiosity and caution playing out all over again. I picked up my pizza and gnawed idly at the crust, feeling the crunchy dough press up against my gums and ease the ache there a bit. I was running out of time. If my friends didn't agree to my proposal, I would need to find a way to convince them.

The idea was not appealing. Some experiments only work if the rat enters the maze willingly, and I have never been a fan of using physical force when a temptingly waved piece of cheese will do.

"I hate to ask, because I'm sure it makes me sound cheap, but... would your folks be expecting us to pay for rooms?" Christine's cheeks colored red. "I know, I know. It's just that most of my cash is already spoken for, and I really can't afford a seaside getaway. No matter how nice it sounds."

"All expenses paid," I said soothingly. "My parents aren't rich—" lying had gotten so much easier in the time I'd been at Harvard "—but they own the bed and breakfast free and clear, and if they have to cook anyway, it doesn't really cost them anything to feed my friends. You'll have to bring your own beer. That's the one thing they won't be providing. They just want to thank you for being such good friends to me, and meet you all at least once before we're not all together." I let my voice break, just a little.

That was all it took. "Oh, Violet," said Terry, her eyes suddenly bright with tears. "Of course we'll come. We'd love to meet your family."

"Yeah," said Jeremy. "It'll be fun."

"Thank you," I said. "Thank you all."

It might not be fun. But it was sure going to be something.

■ □ ■

The mice ripened in their enclosures, tumors swelling and bursting under the skin. Terry's fruits ripened on the vine, and she fed them to us, a rainbow of sweet flesh and seeds like jewels, and twice as precious in the eyes of the woman who had nurtured them. She grew black tomatoes and beans the color of bruises, and I stole what I could for the gardens back at home. Mama would love watching the black fruits grow and darken, like the water before the storm, and we always needed something new for the table. There wasn't much variety for the landlocked, who tired of fish yet still wanted to stay close to home, where they could be helpful if the need arose.

Presumably Christine and Michael had their own means of marking the passage of time, something involving genetic drift and maggot pupation, but I didn't care, and so I didn't ask. What I cared about was that they continued to meet us at the pizza parlor twice a month, and kept pouring powdery cheese over their already cheesy meals. Christine had started licking it off her fingers, a quick, compulsive gesture that she didn't seem to realize was happening until it was over. Michael wasn't so obvious, but I couldn't remember the last time I'd seen him blink. According to my notes, it had been over a month.

Dutifully, I wrote down the results of the mouse studies I was conducting with Jeremy in one notebook, and the results of the studies I was conducting on my classmates in another. My handwriting was better in the first, and filled with excited ink blotches and misspelled words in the second. It was hard to dredge up much enthusiasm for mice, considering how close my *real* work was to coming to an end.

It would have been easy to charter a bus to take us home, but that would have meant leaving all the cars on campus. Terry didn't drive, but Michael, Christine, and Jeremy did. That many abandoned vehicles would point far too quickly to us having left as a group, and might raise questions when classes resumed and half the life sciences grad students didn't reappear. No. Better to give everyone a gas card and say that my parents wanted my friends to have the freedom to explore the coast at will. Better to lie a little now, and make the big lies easier down the line.

Jeremy watched as I lugged my things out to his car. His expression was torn between amusement and dismay, finally tipping over the edge when I came out with my third suitcase.

"You're coming back at the end of the break, right?" he asked. "I know your funding extends to the end of the semester. You've told us that often enough. We might still have a breakthrough that could pay for the rest of your education."

"I'm not giving up, Jeremy," I said, shoving the suitcase into the backseat. "I want to finish my project as much as anybody. But I also want to be realistic. If that means offloading a few things I don't need to have regular access to, in order to make moving out easier, I'm going to do it. I'm sorry."

"It's okay," he said, sounding distinctly uncomfortable. "I just… I really want you to finish your research, that's all. You've got a brilliant scientific mind. You shouldn't wind up rotting away in some little seaside town just because your family didn't have the money to keep you where you belonged."

I had long since learned to see the digs people made at my family as pitiful attempts at complimenting me. I wasn't "like" the other girls who came from small coastal backgrounds. I wasn't the hick my background told my peers to expect, and so they heaped praise upon me for overcoming my early limitations. It was insulting. It was wrongheaded and cruel and for a long time, it had been enough to keep my feelings from getting in the way of my work. But they meant it—all of it—in the nicest, least offensive way possible.

We're so proud of you for being better than the people who bore you, raised you, and loved you enough to send you out into the world when they could easily have kept you home for your own good.

We're so impressed that you were able to grow up with a focused intellect and the ability to tie your own shoes, considering the obstacles you had to overcome.

We're so amazed that you can speak properly and dress yourself, since you should have been a babbling, half-naked cavegirl.

I smiled at Jeremy, showing him my natural, slightly uneven teeth. They had been slanting subtly for weeks now; I was pushing them back into their sockets every morning before I went outside. The signs were all there, for people who knew how to look for them; people who hadn't privately filed the marks as folk nonsense and fairy tales, better left forgotten. Better left to seaside hicks.

"I promise you, no matter where I wind up, I won't rot away," I said. "Are you all packed and ready to go?"

"I've just been waiting for you."

"Then let's go. I want to get there before the others; the last thing we need is for them to wander off into town because they get tired of waiting."

Jeremy laughed. Actually laughed, like this was the funniest thing I'd ever said. Hatred kindled in my chest, surprisingly bright given how much time I spent finding ways to bank it back, to tamp it down. "Oh, like there's that much town for them to wander into," he said.

I shrugged, feeling the fluid shift of muscles under my skin. I was running out of time. Soon, I would have all the time in the world. It wasn't a contradiction. It just looked like one when viewed from the outside.

I wouldn't be viewing it from the outside for much longer.

"You'd be surprised," I said. "Innsmouth has a way of sneaking up on you."

■ □ ■

There was a time when Innsmouth was isolated, unfamiliar, even for-bidden, blocked off from the ceaselessly searching hands and eyes of men by the shape of the land, which curled around our coves and cav-erns like the hand of a nurturing parent, protecting and concealing us. But the cities spread, and the roads reached out in fungal waves, see-king the points of greatest weakness. They grew across the body of Massachusetts, poisoning it even as they connected it to the rest of the continent. My parents liked to talk about the days when it was a long voyage from "civilization" to our doorstep.

It took Jeremy ninety minutes. It would have taken an hour, but there was traffic. There was always traffic getting out of Boston, which attracted cars like spilled jam attracted ants.

"This is why you never go to see your family, isn't it?" he asked, after the fifth time we were cut off by an asshole in a Lexus.

"One of the reasons," I said, trying to sound like I wasn't entertain-ing pleasant fantasies of murder. The asshole in the Lexus would have opened like a flower after the correct sequence of cuts, blossoming into something beautiful. Best of all, the beautiful thing he could have be-come would never have cut anyone else off on the highway. Beautiful things had better ways to spend their time than behind the wheel.

Then we came around the final curve in the road, and the Atlantic was spread out before us like a gleaming sapphire sheet, and I stopped thinking about murder. I stopped thinking about anything but the sea, and how it was already a beautiful thing, no knives or bloodshed re-quired.

"Wow," breathed Jeremy, and for the first time I was in total agree-ment with him about something that didn't involve the poisonous kiss of the great god Science.

We drove down the winding road that led into Innsmouth, playing peekaboo with the shoreline all the way. Trees blocked our view about half the time, keeping us from seeing the waves break against the rocks. My ancestors had planted many of those trees, designing this stretch of road as carefully as Jeremy and I had designed the mazes we used to keep the mice distracted and happy. Men were happy when they could see the sea, as long as they never saw too much. When they saw too much, they began to understand, and when they understood...

There were realities the human mind was never meant to withstand, pressures that it was never meant to survive. Knowledge was like the sea. Go too deep, and the crushing weight of it could kill you.

"Wow," said Jeremy again, when the road leveled off and we cruised into town, past the old-fashioned houses and the wrought-iron streetlights that graced every corner. It was like driving into the past, into an age a hundred years dead and buried. He was gaping openly, twisting in his seat to get a better look at the shop windows and the elegant curves of architecture. "Are you sure people *live* here? This isn't, like, Disneyland for tourists?"

"Welcome to Innsmouth," I said. "Founded in 1612 by settlers who wanted a place where they could live peacefully and raise their families according to their own traditions, without worrying about outside interference. Unlike most of the coastal towns around here, there was never a refounding. We've been living on and working this shore for four hundred years."

Jeremy took his eyes off the town long enough to give me a questioning, sidelong look. "Boston was founded in 1620," he said. "Your town can't be older than Boston."

"No one's ever told the town that," I said. "You can find our land deeds and our articles of incorporation at Town Hall, if you're really curious."

"I guess that explains your accent."

I blinked. "I beg your pardon?"

"It's just..." Jeremy took a hand off the wheel and waved it vaguely, encompassing everything around us. "You've always said that you were from Massachusetts, but you don't have any accent I've ever heard before. I figured you might have had speech therapy when you were a kid, or something. If this town is really older than Boston, though, it makes sense that you would have grown up with a different regional accent. This is, like, someone's graduate project, right here. I bet you have linguistic tics that are so population specific that no one even hears them anymore."

Oh, we heard them. We heard them, and we spent the bulk of our time trying to beat them out of ourselves if we were ever intending to cross the town line, because people gravitated toward strangeness, so we were only allowed to leave during the brief time when we were *normal*. Such a pretty, petty, pointless word.

I said none of that. I only pointed to the turnoff that would take us from the main road to my family's home and said, "This way."

Jeremy obligingly turned, looking slightly dismayed as Innsmouth dropped away behind us. "I thought we were staying in town."

"Technically, we are. The town limits encompass six miles of shoreline. If we ever wanted to sell, everyone who lives here would walk away a millionaire."

Human families living in our homes; human children playing on our beaches, unaware of what slumbered, peacefully dreaming, only a few fathoms away. It was a charmingly terrible thought, the sort of world that could never be allowed to exist. The consequences of a few brightly-colored shovels and pails would be too terrible for words.

I leaned back in my seat, still smiling, still speaking. "There are three bed and breakfasts in town. My parents are generally believed to operate the nicest one. We certainly have the best view. But you'll see for yourself soon enough. Keep driving. We're almost there now. We're almost home."

Jeremy said nothing, sensing, on some deep, primate level, that there was nothing for him to say. The road twisted beneath us like the body of a great eel, like a tentacle reaching out to take what it wanted from the world, until we came around the final curve, and there it was, standing beautiful and bleak against the skyline. My home.

Relaxation came all at once, so profound that I could feel my muscles soften all the way down to where they brushed against the bone. I was back. Finally, after years of care packages and quiet refusals, I was back where I belonged.

"Holy shit," said Jeremy. "Does Dracula live with you?"

"Only on summer vacation, and he tips well," I said blithely.

"Holy *shit*."

Normally, I would have called him on his failure to come up with something better. He was a scientist: he prided himself on always knowing the right words to describe a situation. But I had to admit that it was nice to have him so impressed with my childhood home, which I hadn't seen in so many, many years. We had all known that if I came back, I wouldn't leave again. The longing for the sea would have been too great.

It already was. "Carver's Landing," I said, swallowing the sudden thickness of my voice and hoping he wouldn't notice. "Built in 1625, after the original house burned down in an unfortunate candle incident. My ancestors wanted to make a statement about how we didn't die in fire; we only died in water, and we refused to fear it."

Jeremy didn't say anything. He didn't even tease me about having a house with a name. He really *was* in shock.

Most New England bed and breakfasts were quaint things, suitable for the cover of little pamphlets intended to be distributed at local bus stations and airports. Not so Carver's Landing. Our family home was a glorious four-story monstrosity, built right up on the edge of the cliff, so that any shift in the tectonic plates would send us tumbling down, down, down below the waves, where anyone who saw us fall would presume we had gone to a watery grave. The wood was white, weathered by wind and coated in salt; the architecture was Colonial, with striking Victorian influences. It was the sort of house that should have been the topic of thesis papers written by wide-eyed history students. It had grown organically under the hands and hammers of generations; it had seen a nation rise. And we rented rooms for fifty dollars a night to tourists lucky or foolish enough to make a wrong turn and find themselves in Innsmouth for the night.

Jeremy drove slowly down the shallow hillside separating us from the house. A small paved lot cupped the left side of Carver's Landing. Three cars were already there, all more than twenty years old, their sides pitted and rusted by saltwater and wind. I wrinkled my nose at the sight of them. It was time to open the garage and pull out something a little newer. Caution was important, sure, but so was having a car that would actually run. So was not attracting attention for driving a junker.

Jeremy pulled his shining silver hybrid into a space a safe distance from the other cars, like a gray shark sliding past whales, and I realized dimly that I was ashamed of my family's choices. I was ashamed of the rust and the salt and the decay, of things I'd viewed as natural and right when I was a child, growing up eternally in sight of the sea. I had been out in the world too long. It had been necessary for my work, and I didn't regret doing as was required of me—I could never regret doing as was required of me, not when the world was so wide, and the landlocked parts of it so dangerous and wild—but I had still been out in the world too long. It was time, and past time, for me to have come home.

"You unload the trunk," I said. "I'll go get us a luggage cart." I didn't give him time to answer or object before I was shoving my door open with my foot and running for the kitchen door. The curtains were drawn, but I knew that someone was watching us. Someone was always watching at Carver's Landing. Someone had always been watching at school, too, but there they tried to pretend that they weren't, that privacy was a thing that could exist on land, even though anyone with any sense would know it was a lie.

The door was unlocked. I flung myself through, and there was my older sister, still taller than me, still straight-backed and flat-faced—*poor thing, to be so long grown, and still here*—and when she stepped aside, there was my mother, short and hunched and smiling her sea-changed smile, and I threw myself into her arms, and I was finally, finally home.

■ ■ ■

By the time I finished greeting my family, two more cars had arrived in the parking lot. I collected my sister and a luggage cart and went out to meet them.

Christine was uncurling herself from the driver's seat of her car, a long, foreign flower trying to decide whether she could flourish in unfamiliar soil. She offered a polite Midwestern smile as my sister and I approached. "Violet," she said. "I was afraid you'd run off and deserted us. Who's this?"

"I'm Violet's mother," said my sister, and my heart burned for her, and for the world we had to live beside. She smiled charmingly as she stepped toward Christine, holding out her hand. "You must be Christine. I've heard so much about you, but I must admit, Violet never told us how lovely you were."

"Oh," said Christine brightly, smiling as she tossed her hair. "It's lovely to meet you, Ms. Carver. Your home is… wow. It's really something."

"Wait until you see the inside," said my sister, and laughed, and kept laughing as the rest of my classmates got out of their cars and began loading their bags onto the luggage cart. They would all be distracted by the sound, I knew, by the bright simplicity of it. They wouldn't be looking at her cold, calculating eyes, or at the curtains behind her, which twitched as our parents and siblings stole glances at us.

The door opened. Two of our brothers, both my age, emerged to help with the bags. Chattering, excited, and unaware, the other students followed me inside, ready to begin their seaside escape. Get away from your problems, get away from your woes, get away from the real world—get away from everything except for the sea, which cannot be run from once the waves have noticed your presence. Once the sea has become aware, it can only be survived, and not many can manage that much.

Despite the fact that spring was often our "busy" season, my parents had accepted no bookings for the month, and every room was open. Christine and Jeremy were settled with seaside views, while Terry and Michael had to content themselves with the sweeping cliffs behind the town. None of them complained, at least not in my hearing, and I was grateful. All of them would be able to hear the sea, to smell it in the air, but the last part of my study involved denying two of them the sight of it.

"Oh, Violet, it's beautiful," said Terry, gazing rapturously out her window at the tree-covered hills. Most of it was virgin forest. We had little interest in cutting down the trees that protected us from prying eyes, and when we were alone at home, we kept our houses cool, verging into cold. Leave the tropics for those who were not predestined to go down into the unrelenting deeps. Heat was a luxury of the land, and it was better not to get too accustomed to something that could never stay.

"I never really thought about it," I said. My own window faced the water, of course. No one I knew who lived in Innsmouth voluntarily faced away from the waves. Still, she looked so happy... I stepped closer, pointing to a distant rocky outcropping. "There used to be a house there, a long time ago. It burned down in a thunderstorm. The fire never spread to the trees, and since the family who owned the place owned all the surrounding woodlands, no one else has ever tried to develop there."

"It's like traveling backward through time." Terry shook her head. "How are you not crawling in conservationists?"

"Most of them are out at Devil's Reef, doing marine impact studies."

Terry turned to me, eyes wide. "We're near Devil's Reef?"

I nodded. The government's "accidental" bombing of Devil's Reef back in 1928 was still taught in wildlife conservation classes, which pointed to the destruction of both the habitat and several potentially undiscovered species—a lot of the fish caught in that area were unique, unknown to science—as a clear example of why we needed more protected areas. Devil's Reef had been locked down for decades. Human ships patrolled the waters; human scientists cataloged and studied the fish, excited by each new find, all blissfully unaware of what they would find if they dove too deep.

Sometimes one of them did. And then it was all very sad, and their colleagues were reminded to respect the sea.

"We can't take a boat out to the reef itself, of course, but we can get pretty close," I said. "Maybe we could go sailing in a few days, and let you see the rocks that break the surface."

Terry smiled brightly. "I would like that."

"Then I'll see what we can do," I said. "Dinner's in an hour. Fish chowder. I hope you're hungry."

"Starving," she said.

I felt a little guilty as I let myself out of the room and started down the hall. None of my friends had volunteered for this. They thought they were having a nice vacation that would end when they returned to their lives with suntans and new stories. They didn't understand.

But then, the mice hadn't volunteered either. And none of my friends, when pressed, had hesitated a moment before picking up the needle.

■ ■ ■

Mother might have been offended by being relegated to the kitchen while Pansy pretended to be her, but she still knew her role; the stew was thick and rich with cream, and the smell of the sedatives rolling off the bowls belonging to my friends was strong enough that it was a miracle none of them noticed. One by one, they filled their mouths, only to swallow, look puzzled, and lose consciousness. Christine was the first to pass out, followed in short order by Michael, and then by Terry, who slumped gently forward, already snoring.

Jeremy was the last. He stopped, spoon halfway back to his bowl, and gave me a deeply befuddled, deeply betrayed look. "Violet," he said, and his tongue twisted; it didn't want to do as he said. His befuddlement deepened. "Wha' did you do?" he asked, words slurring at the end.

I said nothing. I just looked at him solemnly, and waited until his head struck the table next to his bowl. The spoon skittered from his hand, coming to a stop when it hit the base of the soup tureen. Those of us who had joined my friends for dinner—my brothers, my sister Pansy, a few selected folks from town who were supposed to make the gathering seem realistic—sat in silence for several seconds. Finally, I pulled out my phone and checked the stopwatch app that had been running since the soup was served.

"Thirty-seven seconds," I said. "They should be out cold for at least an hour. Are the rooms ready for them?"

"They are," said my mother, from behind me. Her voice was thick with undercurrents and dark with tidal flows. I turned to her. She was standing in the doorway, her thinning hair slicked down wet against her flattening skull, and she was so hideous that men would have screamed to see her, and so beautiful that she took my breath away. "Everything is as you asked. Now I have to ask you a question, my arrogant, risk-taking girl. Are you sure? Do you really think this will work?"

I nodded solemnly. "I do." Her voice was distorted, like she was speaking through thick mud. The Innsmouth accent had claimed her speech almost entirely. Underwater, her new voice would sound like the ringing of a bell, clean and clear and so perfect that it could never have existed in the open, impure air. She had nearly completed the change.

She was looking at me dubiously. All my family was. Undaunted, I pressed on. "When I started this experiment, I told you what it would entail, and you agreed. Dagon—"

"Not this again," grumbled my eldest brother. Half his teeth were needled fishhooks, designed to catch and keep the creatures of the abyssal zone. It was almost a race between him and my mother, whose blood had never been as pure as my father's. He had been gone before I left for Harvard, slipping silently down to the city beneath Devil's Reef while I was at Santa Cruz. And that right there—the difference between my mother and my brother, and my poor, still almost-human sister—was the reason that they needed me so badly.

I looked at my brother, and I didn't flinch. "Dagon chose me for a reason. I'll make Him proud. I'll make you all proud."

"And if you don't?" There was a challenge in his voice, naked to the world.

"Then I'll have failed, and I'll answer to Him when I go down below the waves," I said. "Letting me try cost us nothing but time, and if we can't afford a little time, who can?"

My classmates were still sleeping. Christine was drooling. I looked at them, studying them, *memorizing* them as they were now. All this would change soon.

"Besides," I said. "If this doesn't work, they'll taste like anybody else. Now help me get them upstairs."

■ ■ ■

Christine and Michael woke alone. One more control on an already complicated experiment. Jeremy was still out, thanks to an additional dose of sedatives slipped between his cheek and gums. I was sitting by Terry's bedside, making notes in my journal, when she jerked on the cuffs that held her to the bed. It was a small motion, but enough to cause the chain to clink against the bedframe. I lifted my head in time to see her open her eyes and blink groggily in my direction.

"Violet?" she asked, voice thick with sleep. "Did I doze off?"

She tried to sit up. The cuffs held her fast. Panic flashed through her eyes, taking the last of the drowsiness with it.

"Violet?" There was a shrill note to my name this time. She still hadn't fully processed what was happening to her. This time, she strained against the cuffs hard enough to shift the bedframe slightly, and to yank at the IV line connected to the inside of her left elbow. She stopped, and stared at the needle like she had never seen anything like it.

"There's an excellent chance your great-great-grandmother was from Innsmouth," I said calmly, looking back to my journal. "Did you know? I suppose not, since you didn't seem to recognize the name of the town. She had two children before she died. Your great-great-grandfather remarried, and had three more children by his second wife, who always presented the entire brood as her own. I guess remarriage wasn't as commonplace back then, which seems odd, given the overall mortality rate. It's hard to be absolutely certain who descended from which woman, but I'm ninety percent sure at this point that you descended from your great-great-grandfather's first wife. We'll know soon, I guess."

"Violet, this isn't funny."

I glanced up. "It's not supposed to be. I'm telling you why you're here."

Terry stared at me. *"What?"*

"You're here because there's a very good chance that you're descended from your great-great-grandfather's first wife," I said. "She was weak. She hadn't even started to show the Innsmouth look when she died. I suppose that's why her children never showed it—or if they did, we can't find any record. At least one of them reached adulthood. That's simple math. Your great-great-grandfather had five children by two wives, and four of them lived to have children of their own. If you are, in fact, descended from an Innsmouth woman, we'll know in a few days."

Genuine fear flashed across her face. "A few... a few *days?* Violet, I have to get back to the school. You can't just keep me here. The others will notice if I disappear."

"The others aren't noticing anything right now, except for their own predicaments," I said. "Christine has been screaming nonstop for the last two hours. Michael won't stop laughing."

"You're insane." Her voice dropped to a whisper. "Where's Jeremy?"

"Still asleep. I'll go to wake him soon." I tried to sound reassuring. "I wouldn't worry about it, honestly. We'll keep you comfortable. We put the catheter in while you were asleep, so you won't have to go through that messy ordeal, and in a few days, we'll know everything we need to."

"You can't..."

"I'm a scientist," I said. "This is exactly what I *can* do."

She was screaming at me as I got up and left the room, closing the door neatly behind myself and cutting off her shouts at the same time. Soundproofing had so many excellent uses. Checking my journal one last time to be sure I had all the notes I needed, I started down the hall toward Jeremy's room, steeling my expression as I went. He would never know how easy he'd had it, working with mice. Mice couldn't talk back, or ask why you were doing this to them... or figure out that they were in the control group.

All four members of my little "social group" had been consuming a powder made from my extracted, purified plasma, mixed with various biogenic chemicals, for the past year and a half. I had monitored dosages, dates, everything, and watched them all for signs of transformation. Two of them had confirmed Innsmouth heritage, the bloodlines too thin and attenuated to allow them to hear Dagon calling without outside aid. The other two were human, as ordinary and temporary as anyone else. All of them would be told that they were Innsmouth-born. All of them would be encouraged to listen for Dagon's voice whispering to them through my blood, which was even now dripping, one pure, perfect drop at a time, through their IV lines.

Two could see the sea; two could see the land. One of each group had Innsmouth blood; one did not. For however long it took, they would eat the same, drink the same, experience all the same physical stimuli, and then…

Then we would see what we would see.

Quietly, I let myself into Jeremy's room and sat down, reopening my journal and resuming my documentation of the day. It was easy to lose myself in my notes, letting the simple facts of the experiment take priority over everything around me. It was harder to keep going. Harder than I'd ever thought it would be when I had first sat down at the table and explained to my parents what I wanted to do, how I wanted to go among the outsiders and look for the missing cousins, the ones we had always known existed, so far from the singing of the sea. I had come to them with Dagon's voice in my heart and the great god Science in my hands, and when they had let me go, I had promised them that the world of men wouldn't change me, could *never* change me. I was a daughter of Innsmouth, beloved of Dagon, destined for the sea. Nothing as small or simple as the company of humans could change that.

I had been young then. I had been a fool, unaware of the way rational scientists could sometimes fall in love with their laboratory animals, disrupting experiments and risking years of work for the sake of saving something with a lifespan no longer than a sneeze. I had believed my morality to be absolute and unassailable, and I certainly hadn't expected to find myself feeling sorry for them.

There was no room for pity here. Two of them would almost certainly die. My control group. I would have been happier if I'd been able to find more than four experimental subjects, but I had also wanted a fifty-fifty split, and even finding two of the lost cousins in a place where I could gain their trust had been a trial. I had followed hundreds of genealogies and family records to wind up back at Harvard, discarding schools with only one Innsmouth descendant, or whose resident cousins were too young, or too old, or too involved in fields where I would have no excuse for access. Harvard had been the only choice, and years of effort had been required to woo the four of them.

Unless my treatments were more effective than they had any right to be, the two with no Innsmouth blood would leave me very soon. But the two who had an ancestral claim to these shores…

They might still have a chance.

Jeremy made a small, confused sound. I looked up, and smiled.

◼ ◼ ◼

"Violet? What's wrong?" My sister stood, frowning at me as I leaned, white-faced and shaking, in the kitchen doorway. Silently, I held out my hand, showing her the contents of my palm. Two human incisors, both intact down to the root, blood-tipped and pearly.

Her eyes widened.

"Are your teeth falling out?" she asked, looking at my face, my hair, searching for some sign that my transition had accelerated.

I shook my head. "My teeth have been loose for weeks, but I think it's because of the immune response triggered when I harvested my plasma. They stopped weakening when I started spreading the harvests out among the family." The words came easily, devoid of emotional response. If only everything were that easy. "They belong to Terry. The girl in the room that looks out over the forest."

How she had screamed when the teeth started dropping out of her head, when the hair started wisping from her scalp. How she had fought, how she had kicked, how she had done her best to deny what was happening to her. It would have been impressive, if it hadn't been so frightening. She could hurt herself, and until we knew where she was in her transition, I didn't want to risk it. Sedating her would be a solution. It might be the only solution. It was still something to be avoided for as long as possible.

"Does this mean the process is working?" My sister made no effort to conceal the excitement in her voice. If this worked—if I could activate the sleeping seeds of Dagon that waited, eternally patient, in each of us—

then she might be able to follow our father to the city below Devil's Reef decades sooner than her thinning blood would have otherwise allowed.

I couldn't blame her for her excitement. I couldn't join her in it, either. Not with Christine's death so fresh in my mind. She'd lost all her teeth, too, and her fingers had twisted as the bones struggled to reshape themselves, following biological imperatives that were alien to her too-human flesh. She had still *tasted* human when we disposed of her body according to the best and most traditional methods available to us. I'd fed her, one spoonful at a time, to her surviving classmates. They would never know, unless they lived. And if they lived, the life of one human woman would no longer seem so important.

"I don't know," I said quietly. "They're all changing. They're all... becoming something more. But none of them is transforming with any real speed. Michael stopped breathing this morning. I had to give him CPR." And his bones had been soft under my hands, almost like cartilage, bending and yielding until I'd been afraid of crushing his sternum. "They may survive. They may all die."

Terry's teeth were falling out. Jeremy was completely bald, and his eyes had developed nictitating membranes that slid closed a second before he blinked. Michael's skeleton was going soft, and his irises had taken on a flat, coppery cast that looked more like metal than flesh. They were all changing. They had all changed.

We were so far past the point of no return that it couldn't even be seen on a clear day.

The authorities had come to the house weeks ago. I had hidden upstairs while they spoke to my sister in the kitchen, asking whether she had noticed anything wrong with the car when my friends and I had left to drive back to Boston. She had shaken her head and wept almost believable tears, asking again and again whether they thought that I was dead or simply missing. Then she had mentioned, as if offhandedly, that we had been planning to drive down the coast before heading back to school.

The footage of our cars being pulled out of the Atlantic had been shown on all the news programs two days later. There had been no bodies, of course, but there had been blood, and the windows had been broken. It wasn't hard to go from the images on the screen to the thought that we'd been pulled from the vehicle by the current, and would never be seen again.

At least part of that was true. None of my test subjects were ever going to be seen in the world of men again, and as for me... I had done my time outside of Innsmouth. I would stay here until my own returning was upon me, and then I would go, gladly, to the depths and the abyssopelagic dark below Devil's Reef, where I could drift, and dream with Dagon, and allow my false idols and service to Science to fall away from me, no longer needed, no longer required.

My sister regarded me gravely. "Do you think this is going to work?"

"I don't know." I looked down at the teeth in my hand. "I honestly don't."

■ ■ ■

They had been locked in their rooms for almost a month when Jeremy surprised me. I unlocked the door, pushed it open, and found his bed empty, the window standing ajar. For a moment, I froze, trying to understand what I was seeing. The bowl containing his breakfast fell from my suddenly nerveless fingers.

"Jeremy?" I whispered. Then I bolted for the bed, jerking back the covers like he might be hiding there, somehow sandwiched between the blanket and the sheet. "Jeremy!"

I never heard him moving behind me. I was completely oblivious when the chair slammed into my back, knocking me forward. He hit me a second time, harder, before he turned and ran, fleeing down the hall.

Humans are hardy, resilient—mortal. Even unfinished and larval as I effectively was, I was still a daughter of Innsmouth. I shrugged off the blow and turned to run after him, my feet slipping in the spilled soup on the floor near the door. The stairs were steep, and his damp footprints— the soup again—told me I was on the right track, at least until I reached the ground floor. He had enough of a head start that I only knew which way he had gone when I heard the back door slam behind him.

There wasn't time to inform my siblings, not if I wanted to stop him before he could reach the street and go looking for a payphone. I ran after him, out into the bright outside world, where the sea slammed against the shore like the beating of a vast, immortal heart. Then I stopped.

Jeremy was some twenty yards ahead of me, standing motionless on the place where the soil gave way to sand. The sun glinted off the polished dome of his skull, catching odd, iridescent highlights from his skin. I hadn't seen him in the sunlight before, not since his changes had truly begun. He was glorious. He was beautiful.

I walked to join him. He glanced my way, flat copper irises shielded from the sun by his half-deployed nictitating membranes, and he did not run.

"What did you do?" he asked. His words were mushy, soft. All his teeth had fallen out the week before, and while I could see the needles of his new teeth pressing against his gums, they hadn't broken through yet. He'd develop the Innsmouth lisp soon, assuming the transformations continued, that his body was able to endure the strain. "What did you do to us? *Why?*"

"Why did you give cancer to all those mice?" I shrugged. "I needed to know if it was possible. I was telling you the truth when I said you had Innsmouth blood." A runaway girl, a local boy, a relationship cut short when her parents had followed her trail to the Massachusetts coastline. It was an old story, and one that had played out in every coastal town like ours. But in the case of Jeremy's long-buried ancestor, there had been things about her suitor that she hadn't been aware of. She had carried his Innsmouth blood back to Iowa, where it had run through the generations like a poisonous silver line, finally pooling, dilute and deadly, in the veins of a man who wanted to change the world.

Jeremy turned to give me a shocked, even hurt look. The newly inhuman lines of his face didn't quite suit the expression. Deep Ones are many things. We're very rarely shocked. "This is nothing like the mice.

We're *human beings,* and you took us captive and… *did* things to us. It's not the same at all."

"You were human beings who experimented on lower life forms to see what would happen to them, and because you thought you had the right," I said. "I read your Bible, you know. Years ago, when I first started at U.C. Santa Cruz. I wanted to… understand, I suppose. I wanted to *know.* And it said that God had given you dominion over all the plants and animals of the world, which meant that turning mice into explosive tumor machines was just fine. You were doing what God told you to do."

Jeremy didn't say anything. He just turned, slowly, to look back at the sea. I think that was the moment when he understood. The moment he stopped fighting.

"My God told me things, too, although I think He spoke to me a bit more directly than yours spoke to you. He said that some of His children had lost their way and needed someone to guide them home. He said that if I could figure out the way to do that, I could even help the faithful here in Innsmouth." A world where we could *choose* to return to the sea, to swim with Mother Hydra, to be glorious and smooth and darting through the depths like falling stars. To live forever, and not worry about the fragile human skins of our tadpole state.

"That didn't give you the right."

"If your God gave you the right to put the needle to the mouse, then my God gave me the right to put the needle to the man." I offered him my hand. "Come on. I need to get you back to the house."

"The sea doesn't let me sleep."

I dropped my hand.

"I can hear it, always. I think it's trying to talk to me. I've started hearing words when the surf hits the shore."

"What does it say?"

Jeremy turned to me, expression bleak. He was so beautiful, with his skin gleaming iridescent, and his sunken eyes. I would never have believed he could be so beautiful. "It's saying 'come home to me.'"

"You're not hearing the sea," I said, and offered him my hand again. This time, he took it. His skin was cooler than mine. He would dive below Devil's Reef before I did; he would see the abyssopelagic, and understand. I would have been envious, if I hadn't been so relieved. "You're hearing the voice of Dagon. He's welcoming you. He's welcoming you home."

Terry would need to be moved to a room that faced the sea; she deserved the chance to hear Him too, especially when she was doing so much better than Michael. Especially if hearing Dagon might mean that she would live. It would invalidate the experimental controls, but those didn't matter anymore; the human rules of scientific inquiry had only ever been a formality. I was bringing the lost children of Dagon home.

So much needed to be done. So much needed to be accomplished. My sister would be my first willing volunteer, and my heart swelled to think of her, finally beautiful, finally going home. But that was in the future. For now, I stood hand in hand with my first success, and turned to the sea, and listened to the distant voice of Dagon calling us to come down, deep down, below the waves.

The Deep Ones

The race of sea-dwelling creatures called the Deep Ones are the offshoots of the god Dagon and his union with the female monster known as the Hydra by the Greeks. In appearance, Dagon is said to be an enormous being shaped somewhat like a man, but with the head of a fish, long scaly arms, and short powerful legs. The appearance of Hydra is unknown, but it may be that the Greek legend of the monster known as the Hydra contains some suggestion of her true form. The Greeks say this monster is of vast size, serpentine, with numerous heads that respawn if they are cut off.

The details of how the engendering of offspring between Dagon and Hydra was accomplished or what it entailed are not know, but it is a curious fact that the Deep Ones, being like humans in their size and general appearance, have the ability to interbreed with men and women. This they are always eager to do, for the blood of the Deep Ones is weak from countless generations of inbreeding, and they require the vigor of human hybrids to restore vitality and fertility to their race. This caused the Greek philosopher Philolaus to speculate that humans and Deep Ones are at root the same species.

It was sightings of the Deep Ones by mariners that gave rise to the wondrous tales of mermaids and mermen that are told wherever men dwell near the sea. The Deep Ones make their many-pillared cities in trenches beneath the ocean, and have no need to ever walk upon the land, but their curiosity concerning the doings of humanity causes them to sometimes approach fishing villages or trading ports. They hold conversations with any man or woman they chance to encounter on the sands, for they have the power of speech and are ever willing to enter into trade with our kind.

The males of the species covet some of the tools and machines fashioned by men from steel, and their females are delighted by our finer silks. In return for these goods, they give gold, for it is said that they have gold in abundance due to the countless thousands of treasure ships that have foundered in storms or struck reefs and sunk beneath the waves over the millennia of human history. The Deep Ones know where all these ships lie.

They have great skill in the making of jewelry out of gold and gems, and on occasion will exchange these adornments for human goods, but their bodies are so strangely distorted that this jewelry fits humans poorly.

The heads of the Deep Ones resemble those of some bottom-dwelling fishes, being broad and high, hairless, and lacking ears, and their faces are wide like that of a frog. They have flat noses and mouths like great slits. Bulbous eyes project from the sides of their heads. Necks they have none, but in the sides of their heads are rows of flaps that serve them like gills to breathe beneath the water. These allow the Deep Ones to stay submerged indefinitely, although they also have lungs to breathe air when they walk upon the dry land.

Their bodies are thick, their skin gray and slick to the touch, like that of a frog or a fish. A spiny ridge runs down the center of their hunched backs. Between their elongated fingers and toes are webs of skin they use as aids in swimming. Their arms are long and powerful, but their legs stunted, so that when they move on the land, they do so with the aid of sticks held in their hands to prop themselves upright, or they hop like frogs.

They are immune to disease or old age, but can only die from violence. Dagon himself, the father of their race, may be no more than a Deep One of immemorial years, who over time has grown in size, as some undersea creatures are said to never stop growing for the entire span of their lives. If true, it seems this growth is immensely slow, or does not begin until these creatures are ancient, for apart from Dagon they are not much larger than human stature.

For the purpose of trading and breeding with human beings, they have made many pacts with islanders in remote lands, who agree to keep their existence secret. Scarcely any coastal human habitation is distant from one or more of the undersea cities where they dwell. In matters of business they keep their word, and trade with honor. The human women they take for breeding they make their wives, and honor with marriage ceremonies enacted on the beach by their priests.

The offspring of male Deep Ones and their human wives are wholly human in appearance when they are born, but as they mature they develop physical traits that cause them to more and more resemble their fathers. At a certain mature age, they are able to breathe wholly through their neck gills, and then they leave their lives upon the surface and go to live in the cities of the Deep Ones, returning from time to time to visit their human family—for know you that the Deep Ones prize the ties of family above all things.

These beings are advanced in the arts of warfare, and in their countless millions it would be an easy matter for them to overwhelm the surface of the world, conquer and enslave our race, or if they wished, destroy it utterly. However, they do not covet the dry land, and prefer to trade and breed with us in secret, as it suits their needs.

There is a sign inscribed on certain small stones that the Deep Ones respect in a religious way and will not cross over. Those islanders who wish to terminate their trade and inter-marriage with the Deep Ones scatter these stones along their beaches to express aversion. In doing so they risk a terrible wrath, for the Deep Ones do not like to be spurned and will exact vengeance when the chance presents itself. No vessel, large or small, may pass across the waves without their sufferance.

It may be that the signs engraved upon these small stones are linked to an enormous white obelisk carved all over its surface with alien letters and signs that resemble sea creatures. This obelisk great Dagon himself is said to cherish and adore deep beneath the sea, but of its origin, whether on this world or a world among the distant stars, nothing is known.

BRETT J. TALLEY

THAT WHICH SHOULD NOT BE

1st Place
Winner

J ✦ S

Horror Fiction
20⬦⬦ 11

HE WHO WALKS IN SHADOW

BRETT J. TALLEY

RED EQUINOX

DOUGLAS WYNNE

CPSIA information can be obtained at www.ICGtesting.com
Printed in the USA
LVOW11s1528280116

472714LV00008B/1015/P